MW00647101
REINA

# THE MYSTERIES
# OF
# POMPEY HOLLOW

**Postwar Historical Fiction**

**JEROME MARK ANTIL**

ISBN: 978-1-7332091-9-9
Library of Congress Control Number: 2020913552

TIME: POST WAR 1948-1949

Historical references offered by:
Judy Clancy Conway; Marty Bays; Dale Barber; Don Chubb; New Woodstock Historical Society; Charles Shea; Cincinnatus NY Historical Society; Pompey NY Historical Society; Cortland NY Historical Society; Cazenovia Public Library; Carthage NY Historical Society; Binghamton NY Historical Society.



Inspired by my wife and muse, Pamela. Some characters are made from actual childhood friends. Some are combinations of my brothers and sisters: James Joseph, Paul Robert, Richard Francis, Frederick Holman, Michael Charles Jr., Dorothy Louise, and Mary Margaret. My mom and dad are real.

JMA

## TABLE OF CONTENTS

FOREWORD
I: Labor Day, 1948
2: Have No Fears, Adventure Nears
3: A Lifetime Adventure Pass!
4: Cemetery Secrets
5: Bunny Magnate
6: It's the Numbers
7: Idle Summer, Hands
8: Under Attack
9: Sheriff Todd Hood
10: Back to School
11: The Plan
12: In the Soup
13: The Thanksgiving Chicken Coup!
14: Running Amuck!
15: Image Problems
16: A Peek at Death
17: A New Plan
18: Happy Thanksgiving
19: Christmas
20: So Many to Think About
21: A Big Oops!
22: Skating Party
23: O Holy Night!
EPILOGUE: Some of 1951 and Most of 1952

TO MY DAUGHTER

## FOREWORD

If you're of a mind to wonder who Aunt Kate is in this book, you'd appreciate the legend. It came to light after the war, the year following our move to Delphi Falls, when my dad took me aside and told me the family secret about Aunt Kate's name—in secret.

I was seven, maybe closer to eight, when a close friend of mine, a nice old man, died. My tears for the loss of my old friend jarred my dad. It's been my thought that it was then when my dad came to realize that children born just before the Pearl Harbor attack, like his boy Jerry—that's me—already had childhoods of too many lost someones throughout the war we grew up in. It dawned on my dad that our young eyes had witnessed a frightening, cruel world at war for more than five years. A war that killed 80 million people.

"Seven, eight, and nine-year-old boys and girls today," he concluded, "have already lived through a horrendous war, and are sadly much older and wiser than their years for it."

I remember my dad kneeling on one knee and looking me straight in the eye. "You've earned the right to deserve the truth, son, Aunt Kate is not your aunt."

"What do you mean she isn't my aunt, Dad?"

"She never was."

"I don't understand."

"She's your grandmother, son."

"Aunt Kate is my grandmother?"

"Her name is Catherine Bell."

"My aunt—Aunt Kate is my grandmother? I don't understand."

"It's Christmastime, son. I thought you'd like to know the truth."

As the story goes, in 1902, my real grandmother gave birth to a daughter, who would become my mom in 1941. When my mother was just a four-year-old little girl, in 1906, her mother's (Aunt

Kate's) husband (my real grandfather) ran off like the rotten-tomato lowlife scumbag bastard he turned out to be, abandoning them both—my mom and her mom, my grandmother. (My words—my dad never uttered a curse word in his life.)

Turned out 'Aunt Kate's' sister and her loving husband loved the little girl who would grow up to be my mother so much they legally adopted her (making the girl's real mother legally my aunt–but she was still my real grandmother). This was done in those days so people wouldn't be saying things about a single mother with a child in 1906. It was frowned on in those days. Growing up in the 1940s we were led to believe the lady who was my mom's real mother was my aunt, Aunt Kate. After Dad told me the secret, anytime Aunt Kate visited the house and would read to me and tuck me in with a good-night kiss, I'd be certain to reach up and put my hand gently to the sweet old lady's velvety soft, wrinkled cheek, and whisper the secret.

"Night, Grammy, I love you."

That would help her sleep warmer on those evenings, I was certain.

Learning the truth about my grandmother changed my life. It surely did. It taught me it was never too early to say hello to someone—the war us kids lived through had already taught me and my friends it might be too late to say goodbye, so don't ever be afraid to say what's on your mind.

This story is about me, in my own words, the year I learned the family secret.

JMA

**Thanks, Dad**

My dad, Big Mike, at the falls.

## DELPHI FALLS PARK, N.Y.

## CHAPTER ONE
## LABOR DAY, 1949

My dad was the tallest man we knew anywhere at six feet, six inches–even taller in his dress hat. Many called him "Big Mike." No matter when you saw him, he always wore suspenders, nice ties and a really happy smile and was ready with a wink of the eye to sit down to hear any stories about our great adventures, the taller, the better.

He found me staring out my window in a trance, sitting on the edge of my bed. His head narrowly missed the top of the door frame as he carried in two large bread boxes he had borrowed from the bakery in Cortland, and that Mom had packed with clothes.

"Whatcha doin', Jerry me boy?"

He put both boxes on the bed opposite me. My name was scribbled in large crayon letters on the side of the one he picked up from the stack and placed on my bed next to me. He pulled up the flaps to show me that it was my clothes that were to be put away.

"Why'd we move way out here, Dad?"

"The war's over, son, now we can get the materials we need and fix the place up and make it into a nice home."

"But we're out in the woods, Dad."

"Think of it, Jerry me boy—eighty-four acres, with our own two waterfalls. Your mom and I used to picnic out here on our Sunday drives. You weren't even born. I bought it before the war, son, during the Great Depression."

"Dad, I've been sitting here watching the road down by the front gate for exactly twenty-two minutes and there hasn't been one car drive by yet. That's pretty depressing. Where are we, in Africa?"

Dad sat down on the other bed.

"You'll like the country, son, even more than Cortland. Here you can get out of the house, go exploring, without asking.

Not like the city."

"We're in the woods."

"You'll have so many more adventures here, son."

"Did you see how tall the cliffs are, Dad? They're jahoomus."

"Out here you'll meet a whole new set of friends, I promise."

"But—"

"Just be patient, son. Give it time."

I interrupted—pointed out at the road.

"Twenty-three minutes, seventeen seconds—a junky old beat-up truck."

"Jerry, look at your first day in a different school tomorrow as a big adventure. Make every day a new adventure. It'll be fun. We each have to write our own books in this life, son. No one will write them for us."

"The only people I met all week were carpenters from Cortland. We're, like, lost in the wilderness."

Dad reflected a moment and met my challenge head on.

"You met Charlie Pitts."

"Yes."

"Well, Mr. Pitts to you."

"I know."

"You like him?"

"Yes."

"Mr. Pitts has a small farm about a mile away with a horse and buggy. It's just down to the corner and right, about halfway up the hill."

"He has a real horse and buggy?"

"He does, and he's going to take care of chickens for us, so we can have eggs."

"Real chickens, like live chickens, Dad?"

"Real chickens, son, and I think it would be a good adventure for you to walk to his farm every week and pick up the eggs. Would you like to do that? See his horse and buggy?"

"Sure."

"Good! That's your chore starting this week. Picking up our eggs. Ask your mother what day."

I turned from the window and looked in my box,

recognizing my P.F. Flyer sneakers on top of the pile. Dad palmed his shirtsleeve back and looked at his wristwatch. Seeing the time, he stood, gazed out my window.

"Son, that's Mr. Parker across the way."

I stood up to look.

"Where?"

Dad pointed out the window.

"Farmer Parker and Mrs. Parker live in that house—over there across the way—he's walking toward the side of the road now."

"Where's he going, Dad?"

"He's about to call his cows in."

"What do you mean call his cows?"

"For their night milking. The cows have to be milked twice a day."

"And he just calls them and they come?"

"You've never seen that done before, Jerry. Why don't you run over there, fast as you can, and watch how he does it?"

I sat back on the bed and looked at my boxes again.

"Now?"

"You can put your things away later."

"I can?"

"Don't forget to introduce yourself like I taught you. Offer your hand. Shake his hand."

"I will."

"Now go! Run!"

I jumped up.

"Dad, will you reset my alarm clock?"

"Hand it here, son. Did it unwind?"

"I don't have a stopwatch, so I set all the hands at twelve when I started to watch the road so I could count the minutes and seconds easier."

Dad grinned.

"Run!"

I ran out of the house, down the eighty or ninety yards to the front gate for the first time, turned left up the short, steep, curving hill on Cardner Road to where Mr. Parker was standing.

I introduced myself and shook his hand.

Farmer Parker in overalls, blue work shirt, and train

engineer hat smiled and handed me his hoe to hold for him like he needed my help while he held both opened hands by his mouth like a megaphone and yodeled up to the steep pasture hill on the other side of the road from his house and barn. Watching him cow calling began to give me a new look on the different world I was in now. He wasn't embarrassed to sing out.

"Caho bossies! Caho bossies!"—meaning, "Come home, bossies!"

It was almost like I was in the audience at a stage play, and he was on stage performing like he was an actor in a Saturday morning picture show at the movie house. He stood there and yodeled as if no one was watching him, until we saw the cow's heads moving and they started walking down the path on the hill. I cautiously stood behind him, being as I'd never seen a cow up close before. At least I hadn't seen one that wasn't behind a barbed wire fence. I wasn't about to take any chances. Twenty cows came down off the hill and through the gate, slowly crossing the road, passing gently by and down his drive toward the back of the barn.

Farmer Parker turned to me, took the hoe from my hand and shook my hand again.

"Nice to meet you, Jerry. You come back anytime. Right now, I've got some cows to feed and milk."

He adjusted his train engineer hat, turned on his heel and started down the slope of a gravel driveway toward the barn.

Mrs. Parker stepped out from behind a screen door onto their gray back porch, emptied a white porcelain bowl of dishwater on her rose bush, and waved hello just as she was walking back into the house. I waved hello and walked home.

When I got to my room there was a book on my pillow. My copy of the Hardy Boys' *Secret of the Old Mill,* which I must have left in the car. I pulled open the drawers on my side of the closet, stuffed my clothes in, butted them closed, and stepped into the hall. Mom and Dad's bedroom had a door on either side. I took the shortcut through their room to the dining room and kitchen. The cupboards were opened—on top, over the counters, and the bottom, near the floor. Mom and Dad were emptying boxes of dishes, the toaster, waffle iron, pots, pans, bowls, soup cans, and cereal boxes, putting them away.

My oldest brother, Mike, was standing in the dining room with a pencil over his ear. He was wearing a new white chef's apron he had asked for as one of his graduation presents. Dad got it at the bakery.

"What cha doing?" I asked.

"I'm taking inventory," Mike said.

"What's that mean, inventory?"

"Don't bother me, I'm busy."

On the table in front of him were two shoe boxes filled with an assortment of strange, smelly foods, spices, relishes, muddy mustards, and smushed olives. Everything in little tin cans with printing on them and small glass jars with lids and labels. My brother collected junky food no normal person would give a whit about. Stuff so bad they'd never put it in big cans or pint bottles. He saved up for it and an old Chevy he paid thirty dollars for, working all summer. He was wrapping the cans and bottles in the shoe boxes to take with him to college in a couple of weeks. A new electric hot plate was on the table, sitting on top of its box. Probably another graduation present, I guessed, so he could stink up his dorm room with this stuff, cooking. I stepped closer to check it out. He pointed a bunch of garlic in my direction.

"Don't even think about it."

"Huh!?"

"Don't touch a thing."

I couldn't stand the smells. He acted as if I'd even go near this stuff.

I had to be patient. Mike hadn't been the same since his face cleared up, that's for sure, and now he had his driver's license. Mike had always been a snob. He thought hot dogs were disgusting and that most table food, except for maybe corn-on-the-cob and watermelon, were scraps for common people. Not for him. He said he had good taste. He graduated high school in June with what Mom called "honors." Dad called them "delusions."

Something about him just wasn't normal anymore. Even Mom couldn't put a finger on it, saying, "It's a stage."

Dad said, "Well, I hope he gets on one"—that is, a stagecoach— "and it leaves before he makes us all nuts."

I was just a kid, what would I know, but I'd read enough

of the Hardy Boys detective mysteries to understand what clues were and my suspicion was that Mike was becoming a gourmet, which, for all I knew, could be a strange disease with considerable inclinations.

I stood there and stared at my own brother taking his inventory. He'd hold up jars and tiny cans like a chemist in a scary movie laboratory, reading the labels. His lips mouthed the French or Italian words on them. Mike always talked about being a surgeon after college, so he could discover cures, live a life of importance and elegance, not live like us—as commoners. At least that's what he said the time he caught Dick drinking milk straight out of the milk bottle and admonished, "One doesn't have *to be* a disgusting pig, if one chooses not *to be* one."

Dick looked him in the eye, tilted the half-empty bottle up, took a last swig from it, and handed it to Mike, saying, "To BE or not to BE." Then he belched and walked away.

Even though he'd grown as tall as Dad, and they both had the same first name, Mike, there was no way he was ready to go off to college alone with a hot plate. I had my reasons for believing this. From the car on Sunday, I overheard Mom standing on the sidewalk talking to Father Lynch in front of our new church in Manlius. They were going on about Mike and his heading off to Lemoyne College. I could swear the "gourmet" word came up, causing me to sit up straight and press my ear to an opening in the car window. Father Lynch sure enough leaned close to Mom and asked, "You don't suppose Mike has capers, do you, Mary?"

I knew it, I thought. I knew Mike had something. I quietly rolled the window down further, not drawing any attention, and not wanting to miss a word.

"I'm almost certain he does, Father," Mom confessed. "He's had them for some time now."

"Oh my," Father Lynch said. "Capers are so rare, so rare indeed, ever since the war—most difficult to get. Wish the lad luck in college for me, Mary. My prayers are with him."

I had no idea what a caper was, but that was all the proof I needed. I knew it was enough to suspect this gourmet thing was serious, maybe even rare and "incommunicable," like those diseases I heard about on Army Radio all during the war.

I wasn't putting it past Mike to eat ants or grasshoppers,

maybe even frogs and lizards, just like in the pictures in the *National Geographic* magazine he kept in his room. This sort of thing was an addiction. Why, he could open the lid of one of those little glass jars filled with something disgusting—take a big whiff of it just as easily as he could warm up for his "at bat" in a Sunday baseball game over at the stone quarry. It just wasn't normal.

Dad saw me staring at Mike's mess on the table, and probably didn't want me to get infected.

"Son, the radio was delivered today. Go plug it in and listen to your shows."

"Where's Dick?" I asked.

"Mr. Rowe went back to Cortland in a bakery truck to bring the last load of boxes," Dad said. "Dick rode with him to say goodbye to his friends in our old neighborhood. They'll both be here any minute. They'll be along."

"Did you put your clothes away?" Mom asked.

"Yes ma'am."

"I heard NBC is rebroadcasting Superman and Sergeant Preston radio programs as a Labor Day treat because school starts tomorrow," Dad said.

"They are?"

"You missed them last night. Go tune them in, son."

"Okay."

I leaned my back against the dining room wall and slid along, edging around Mike, making sure nothing he was touching got on me. I made my way into the living room. Walking over to the radio I could see out the front window, and the bakery truck was coming through the front gate down by the road. Dick would be here any minute. I plugged it in. I got down on the floor in front of the Zenith and turned its familiar old knob to "on."

While I waited for the radio to warm up, it dawned on me how much Superman and I had in common. Superman came from Planet Krypton. He crash-landed in a field in the country when he was a kid, and he grew up on a farm. I came from Cortland, a city, where last year I could walk to school. Now I was out in the country, in the middle of nowhere. I was surrounded by woods and waterfalls and had a farm with lots of cows right across the road. Superman rode a school bus to school—now I had to take a school bus to school.

Any Superman radio fan my age knew that, like him, we were all *faster than a speeding bullet—more powerful than a locomotive.* He could leap tall buildings, though, in a single bound. *Look!—up in the sky. It's a bird, it's a plane—it's Superman!*

I sat and waited, watching the comforting, glowing dial on the Zenith I had relied on all through the war. Its golden hands pointing to radio station numbers shaped like streaks of lightning. During the war we would sit on the floor at night and listen to war news from London, Africa, or the South Pacific. We'd hear about the bombings and killings—of planes being shot down and ships being torpedoed and sunk. We could hear the ship-to-shore Morse Code messages.

The only relief kids had throughout the war was sitting on the floor and listening to Superman or some other radio program to help keep our minds off the atrocity of it all. If their parents could afford it, some kids got the new comic, *Captain America.* His comic book came out a month before I was born in 1941. Although my life may have been turned upside down all summer not knowing we were going to move into the wilderness at the Delphi Falls, at least I still had my favorite floor model Zenith radio, and I had my friend Superman on Sunday and Wednesday nights.

Maybe I could survive.

As the radio tubes warmed and brightened, their soft glow reflected off the wall behind, the scratchy hissing sounds coming through the speakers evolved to whistles and then to a clear voice of a radio announcer.

Just then Dick appeared. First his head, poking cautiously in through the front hall doorway. He peeked around, casing the joint, to see who was in the living room with me and if the coast was clear. Seeing I was alone, he scooted toward me and, with a quick slide on the rug, sat down next to me on the floor. With Dick I always had a sense something was up when he made an entrance like that. I was usually right.

"Where've you been?" I asked.

"Cortland, with Mr. Rowe."

"Did you go to our house?"

"It's not our house anymore, but yes, we picked up some boxes there." "You mean Dad sold our house?"

"Somebody's already moving in."

"I'm ruined."

"How?"

"We're stuck here in the woods forever. Now my whole life is ruined."

Dick didn't respond.

"See anybody in the neighborhood?"

Dick sat up and lifted his head and gave me a sheepish grin. He was sporting the prettiest, brand-new black eye, a sort of raspberry jam, blue-grape-purple-colored shiner.

"Yeah, I saw Patty Kelly washing her dog."

"Holy Cobako!" I gasped.

I had only seen one other black eye like it before—in a Saturday morning picture show. I was impressed. His shiner couldn't have been two hours old, still puffy around the eyelid. The white of his eyeball was a beet red. He stared at me as if he was trying to read in my expression how he looked—or just how much trouble he might be in for having a black eye.

"What happened to you?" I asked.

The sound of my voice jolted his stare.

"Huh?"

He turned his good eye and looked at the Zenith radio dial. He was stalling to buy time—maybe so he could come up with an answer Mom would buy. Believable lies didn't come easy. He had to think of one fast. He turned again, looked at me, and tested one in a loud, whispered threat, using his best machinegun gangster Jimmy Cagney murder mystery movie voice.

"Okay—listen up, pal. You'd better hear me good or you're done for. You threw a baseball at me when I wasn't lookin', see? Yeah, that's it—you threw a baseball, and it was a wild pitch and the ball went wild and it cold-cocked me in the eye—yeah, that's it—that's what happened. It cold-cocked me when I wasn't lookin', you got it, punk? That's the way it was, ya little squirt. Squeal on me and I'll pulverize ya."

Dick knew I'd help him, but he also knew he wouldn't pulverize me if I didn't. He just had an image to keep up.

"What happened?"

"I kissed Patty Kelly and got slugged."

Now this I believed. Dick had a reputation for liking girls and thinking they all liked him. I imagined Patty's brothers, cousins, or even her father and mother catching Dick kissing Patty and taking him behind our garage in Cortland and whupping up on him. Mom wouldn't have minded Mrs. Kelly pounding him—Patty was Dick's age but only half his size and really shy.

"Patty's boyfriend caught you, right?"

Dick didn't say a word.

"Did Bobby Grumman see you kiss her?"

No response.

"He told, right?"

No response.

"It was Patty's dad, wasn't it?"

No response.

"C'mon, what happened?" I begged.

Dick tightened his lips and edged them over to the side of his face with the good eye, in a devilish smirk.

"Patty slugged me."

I stopped breathing. My imagination whirred. I fell sideways, tipping like a falling tree to the floor with a thud, giggling, holding my sides, gasping for air.

Dick was twelve, the smartest kid in the whole family—with a genius IQ. His problems started when someone told him how smart he was when he was little and ever since he'd managed to do something really stupid, with regularity, to get into some scrape or trouble constantly. Seems ever since they told him his actual IQ and what it meant, he'd either think everything he did was okay, because he was so smart (his brain could never be wrong), or he couldn't help himself because his brain was faster than he was and his body couldn't keep up. Here I was, my first day in the wilderness, and I already had to lie for him, again, or else. I spent more time in the church confessional confessing my lies about Dick's sins than I did confessing my own sins.

The Superman music began, so we both sat up to listen.

"Why'd we move from Cortland here to Delphi Falls?" I asked during a commercial.

"I guess because we have more people than we had rooms in the house in Cortland," Dick said.

"That doesn't make sense," I said.

"Mom and Dad wanted us to grow up in the country. I don't know—lots of reasons."

He mumbled something intelligent about the war being over, about the Iron Curtain in Russia, the atomic bomb and air raids.

I thought—why?

"We moved right in front of two seventy or eighty-foot waterfalls."

"Sixty-foot," Dick said.

"It's like we're in the woods," I said.

The falls bothered me because I never imagined water could make so much noise.

"I think I'm going to hate the country," I said under my breath.

"Shut up," Dick said.

"I miss my friends," I said.

"I got it worse than you," Dick mumbled.

"How?"

"I'm twelve—what are you? Seven? Eight? Nine?"

"Huh?"

"I'm older."

"What's that supposed to mean?"

"Being older I knew my friends longer than you knew any of your friends."

Dick was making absolutely no sense whatsoever, again.

"Shut up," I said.

Just then a radio announcer told about the runaway train coming down around the side of the mountain, and of Superman, seeing this from two hundred miles away, flying in and lifting the car that was stuck at the railway crossing up over his head. He got it off the railroad track just in the nick of time and saved the family and their dog. Listening to Superman was always the good part of my week.

Later that night, I lay in bed looking back over my head out the window of my new room with a rattling window frame and no curtains. I stared past the glare of the front porch light at the stars in the distance and I thought about farmer Parker's yodeling and the cows and how gentle they seemed, crossing the road and walking by. My window frame rattled from the sounds of the water crashing over the falls in the back yard.

"Will somebody close the door, please?" I shouted in the dark.

"It's been closed two hours. Shut up and go to sleep," Dick growled from his room.

"Don't say *shut up,* dear," Mom warned from their bedroom.

The next morning, I had to get on a school bus, which I'd never done before—ride to a school I'd never seen before and meet a teacher I didn't even know. That was all my brain remembered thinking about before I fell asleep.

Walking behind Dick down our long dirt driveway, I repeated to myself with every step I took to the front gate—

"This is an adventure. This is an adventure. This is an adventure."

Mr. Skelton, the school bus driver of the big yellow #21 school bus, wore a newsboy hat like Babe Ruth wore in the book we had about the Great Bambino—just like the hat I wore in Cortland when I had to wear my knickers, knee socks, and newsboy cap to school.

Mr. Skelton said, "Hello," when the bus door opened. He seemed nice enough but gave the impression that part of his job was not smiling— especially after he saw Dick's shiner. He'd squint his eyes tight, curling his forehead up, wrinkling bushy eyebrows as he looked up through the mirror and back at the kids to make sure nobody was getting into trouble on the bus. His eyes followed Dick through his mirror all the way to the back of the bus, as if he wanted to remember exactly where he sat down.

I sat in the first empty seat behind Mr. Skelton.

I looked attentively out the bus window at sights as we would drive by. Nearly everything I saw was new to me. Big red barns with tall silos, cows grazing on hillsides and in green pastures. Some were brown but most had black and white spots on them like farmer Parker's cows. At one stop, Dale Barber got on and made me his instant friend with a big grin. He sat down next to me. Dale Barber had big locks of wavy brown hair, in need of a trim but wet and neatly combed. He had freckles on his nose and smiley eyes. He liked to talk and tell jokes. I soon learned he was in my grade. Dale would point and tell me who lived in every house we passed by—if there were kids who lived there, what grades they were in; how many cows were in each barn—how many heifers they had— if their bull had a ring through its nose or not.

"You ought a walk over and meet the Parkers. It's just across the way from your house," Dale said. "He's a nice man."

"I already met them."

"You did? When?"

"Last night," I said.

"His dog's called Buddy and he don't bite," Dale said.

"I know, I petted Buddy."

"Well there ya go," Dale said, pleased with my spirit of adventure.

A line of kids got on the bus in the center of the Delphi hamlet. Dale told me everybody's name as they passed our seat. One boy stepped on with a baseball glove on his hand. Dale called him *Bases* and said he was in our grade. Dale invited Bases to sit with us through my tour of the countryside ride to school, scrunching me to the window for better lookout vantage.

Dale's tour continued. He would point at things as we passed by.

"That's where the Cooks live—back around behind those trees near that barn. There's a ton of Cooks, every one of them good at sports."

The bus slowly began its climb up a steep hill.

"This hill we're going up would be good sledding in the winter if we were allowed," Dale said.

"We ain't allowed," Bases said.

"I've never been on a sled," I said.

"You've never been on a sled?" Dale barked in disbelief.

"No," I said.

"Shut up!" Bases growled.

"Where you from, anyway, Mars?" Dale asked.

"Cortland."

"Are you American?" Bases asked.

"Yes."

"What's your name?"

"Jerry, but my mother calls me Jerome in front of

people."

"That's American," Dale said.

"Are you poor? No sled, you must be poor," Bases said.

"No hills on Helen Avenue in Cortland. We just don't have a sled," I said.

"We have a toboggan and a sled," Dale said.

The bus climbed over the top of the long hill and leveled off, picking up speed.

"You sure could go fast sledding on that hill, I'll bet," I said.

"Too many milk and farm trucks use that hill," Dale said. "Best sledding is at the Pidgeon place. One of 'em— Bobby Pidgeon—is in our grade."

Dale pointed a finger. "See that barn over there, in the middle?"

"I see it."

"That's the Dwyer farm."

"Okay."

"They're big farmers, came with the pilgrims, I think."

"They're pilgrims?" I asked.

"See that boy behind us back there with the red baseball cap?" Bases asked.

I turned around to look.

"That's Ray Randall. He's a good baseball pitcher," Bases said. "I watch them play at the stone quarry."

"What's a stone quarry?" I asked.

"The stone quarry—everybody knows the stone quarry," Bases said.

"Not everybody," Dale said.

"Well everybody I—" Bases started.

"He's been here one day, how's he s'pose to know what a stone quarry is?" Dale asked.

"Oh, right," Bases said.

There was no talking for about half a mile.

"On Sundays the older guys pay me a dime each to fetch foul balls outta the creek," Bases said. "The creek behind the quarry."

"That farm on the corner we're going to turn at up ahead is where Conway lives. Lots of land, lots of cows and corn. Big farm."

Dale went on and on.

He had a way about him. He could find the best in everyone and everything. He said his nickname at home was "Bub," but I could call him Barber. From that moment on, Barber it was.

I couldn't help looking over at Linda Oats with her curly red hair, freckles, and blue eyes. She sat on the seat across the aisle. She was very pretty. She was older and probably a Presbyterian, with my luck. The rest of the kids getting on the bus were bigger, like high school older, and sat in the back.

By the time we were pulling past Shea's store near the school, Barber had me pretty well convinced he knew just about everything important there was to know about the country. When we arrived at school, I didn't know where to go, so I followed Barber.

Turning a corner in one hallway Barber stopped short, causing me to bump into him.

"Oh, jeez." Barber said.

"What?" I asked.

"I forgot which way we're supposed to go."

We ended up in the principal's office, asking directions. Mr. Mobley had golden hair and was smiling as we walked into his office. First thought that came to my mind was school principal was a post for which it was strange for me to see a man.

At my old school, St. Mary's Catholic in Cortland, where I had just moved from, all the teachers and old people who walked the halls looking important were nuns. We called them "Sisters." They were religious ladies who prayed a lot and never married. They wore long, black veils over their heads, white starched hoods around their faces, black dresses that went to the floor, and oversize rosary beads tied around their waists.

"What's your name, son?" Mr. Mobley asked.

"Jerome Mark Antil," I said above all the noise.

"Come along boys, let's find your classroom."

Mr. Mobley walked us through the busy first-day-of-school halls to our classroom just a few doors from his office. When he opened the door to the back of the room, I knew this was it, do or die. We were late and every kid in there was about to spend most of the next decade with me.

"Mrs. Heffernan," he announced while holding the door open, "here's a special delivery for you on this first day of school."

Thirty-nine kids turned around in their seats and stared.

"I believe you know this lad, Mr. Barber. I would like to introduce you to Mr. Antil. Young Jeremiah Mark here is our new pupil. His family moved to the Delphi Falls from Cortland."

"Huh?!" I grunted at his mispronunciation of my name.

Mrs. Heffernan wore wire-rimmed spectacles. Her hair rolled around the top of her head like the snakes we make from clay we got at Christmas. Two pencils stuck out on the side of her hair like tenpenny nails.

"Everyone, say good morning to Jeremiah Mark," Mrs. Heffernan said.

"Good morning, Jeremiah Mark," the kids shouted.

I didn't say anything.

She raised her head almost backward, looking under the bottoms of her spectacles as she walked over and placed her hand on the back of my neck gently steering me to an empty desk.

"This will be your desk until we get settled, Jeremiah."

I lost sight of Barber somewhere in the crowded room. I wasn't anywhere near his desk. My hand could feel the initials carved in my desktop as I sat down behind a boy who turned around and grinned at me with two missing teeth. It was almost as if he knew that he would grow up to be mayor or something and was counting on my vote. He had enough curly hair for several people but seemed an agreeable sort.

Now at home we always called the bathroom a "bathroom." Sometimes Gourmet Mike called it a "John," and my aunts, Mary and Dorothy, referred to a bathroom as the "potty," but, all in all, it pretty much was a bathroom. That was clear. But for some strange reason, probably known only to a board of education and people in too many meetings, different upstate New York schools in the 1940s chose to call their bathrooms different names.

At St. Mary's Catholic in Cortland, a bathroom was called a *lavatory*—and the time I had the accident and peed while sitting in the sandbox in kindergarten, that was called a sandbox, not a lavatory.

Maybe it was a Catholic school thing. Lavatories didn't have bathtubs in them, so perhaps it would be a lie to call them bathrooms.

Wouldn't you know? I was in Mrs. Heffernan's grade precisely two minutes when I had to go. Not being certain of the procedure in this new environment, I cautiously raised my arm and held it tall in the air, just as I would have at St. Mary's, to see if that would work.

"Yes, Jeremiah?"

Except for the mispronunciation of my name, so far, so good.

"Sister, may I go to the lavatory, please?"

With what appeared to be downright impudence, my blurt of an old school habit, "Sister," and the sound of that other word, *lavatory*, caused all motion and noise in the room to stop. Every kid turned their heads in my direction, frozen with mouths opened, wondering what language I was speaking. The mayor, in the desk in front of me, raised his arm, and without waiting to be called on, shouted, "Can I move to another desk, Mrs. Heffernan?"

I could hear Bases whisper, "I don't think he's American."

After the stunned silence obviously caused by me, an alien from another planet's language and the audacity of my calling Mrs. Heffernan "Sister," everyone began laughing while rumbling among themselves various secret messages, like, "Hurry to the cafeteria at lunch hour—fill a table so he can't sit with us."

Stirrings from the same group who, just minutes before, had yelled, "Good Morning, Jeremiah," like they meant it, was taking on a whole "Stations-of-the-Cross" crucifixion tone. I could feel the crowd turning on me.

Mrs. Heffernan gave me an understanding smile.

"You may be excused, Jeremiah."

"For what?" I asked.

"You may go."

"Oh, thank you, teacher," I said.

"You may go to the basement," she said.

"Huh? Where?"

"Jeremiah, go to the basement."

I got up from my desk, went out into the hall, leaving the snickering behind and started looking for stairs to the basement. While I looked, I remembered being told about my grandmother in Minnesota having a toilet outdoors behind their house they called an outhouse. Even Barber was kind enough to point out a few outhouses on the bus ride to school, but I never heard of a bathroom in the basement. I went down the only stairs I could find and saw three big doors at the bottom. One door opened to a dark, empty gymnasium, so I knew that wasn't it. The next was to a room filled with musical instruments, so that wasn't it, but I did like the looks of the big horn in the back of the room that I found out later was a tuba. I opened the last door and looked in to see a big furnace. I could see the warm light glowing from the side of it, so I assumed it had coal burning in it. City kids would know these things. For sure this was the basement because furnaces were in basements.

A man in coveralls with a push broom in his hand turned my way.

"Son, why aren't you in class?"

"Mister, I'm looking for the lavatory in the basement because I have to go to the bathroom, and Mrs. Heffernan told me to go to the basement."

Another man was with him. I have no idea what they said to each other, but the man in coveralls shook his head, and I had a sense he was laughing at me or the lavatory word again. My patience was pushed to the limit.

"Son, we call bathrooms 'basement' here.

"Huh?"

"People with outhouses—"

"What's an outhouse?" I asked.

"You never heard of no outhouse, son?"

"No."

"It's where a body goes when they ain't no plumbing in the house."

"Why do they go there?" I asked.

"To take care of business, just like you've got to now."

"Oh," I said. "when they go to the bathroom?"

"Yes."

"So why do they call an outhouse a basement?" I asked.

"Folks with outhouses have potty chairs in their cellars or basements, son."

"Why?"

"That's so they can use them in lightning storms or in winter blizzards when they can't get to 'em out back."

"Oh."

"Least I guess that's why we call bathrooms 'basements' here."

I still had to pee.

"Who's your teacher, son?"

I thought, *where am I, in Poland?*

It was the only foreign country that came to mind.

I repeated "Mrs. Heffernan," and he told me, pausing in midsentence, and turning to his coworker and articulating in a stage-aside mocking of King's English, "There's a *bawtharrrrooom* next door to Mr. Mobley's office." Then he asked if I knew where that was.

I went back up the stairs, down the long empty hall and made it to the "basement" just in a nick of time. Returning to my classroom, I paused outside the door and gave some thought as to how far it might be if I were to leave now and walk home—made my getaway—and I wondered if I could ever find my house in the woods, if I did. I pushed the door open. As I expected, heads turned and followed me around to my desk. I sat down. The mayor was still in front of me but cowering up against his desktop.

Mrs. Heffernan stopped reading to the class.

"Jeremiah, come here a moment, please."

For some strange reason, I almost felt like my always-in-trouble brother Dick—certain I was about to go on trial and must stand in the corner or be expelled from school. My mind raced—maybe I was in trouble for taking too long. I got up slowly and walked to the front of the room and stood by Mrs. Heffernan's desk.

I would have easily settled for any of that—a trial, standing in the corner, being expelled from school—for it was worse than anything. My new teacher, Mrs. Heffernan had noticed, under her glasses, that my pants' fly was unbuttoned. All throughout the war pants never came with zippers, they all came with buttoned flies. America needed the metal that made zippers so we could build tanks and jeeps and airplanes and bullets. Mom told me that. Forgetting to button my fly was what I did regularly, it seemed. After putting the pencil back into her hair nest and looking away, she proceeded to point at my unbuttoned fly.

"I think you forgot something, Jeremiah."

"My name is Jerome, Mrs. Heffernan, not Jeremiah."

"I see, dear."

"It's Jerome," I mumbled as I groped each button in turn.

"Jerome it is," she said.

She continued to point while looking up at the ceiling, waiting for me to fasten each, with my back to the whole class. All the boys got buggy-eyed glad it wasn't them standing up here on display for this humiliation. The girls mostly put their hands over their mouths and giggled.

"Leave him alone, you guys!" a girl in the front row barked.

Her words did seem to break the ice—made me look almost human. On the way back to my seat I got a couple of invites to sit at tables at lunch hour. I glanced over at the girl in front who had spoken up for me. She sat at her desk with her hands clasped. Catching my eye, she pushed out her lower lip and puffed away a curl hanging over her eye and smiled.

When the lunch bell rang, the class was excused for lunch and we headed to the cafeteria. I found myself walking down the hall with a kid from the next desk row over. He wore big, thick glasses and had a pocket comb sticking out from his back pocket. He was Bobby Holbrook. I couldn't help watching his eyes when he lifted his paper lunch sack up close to his face, opened it and peeked in. He then twisted the top closed tight again.

"What's your name?" I asked.

"Holbrook," Holbrook said.

"I'm Jerry," I said.

"I thought you told Mrs. Heffernan it was Jerome?"

"Call me Jerry."

The sack Holbrook carried looked wrinkled and worn, oil-stained —many trips from home to school and back. He looked hungry, and I could sense his disappointment after peering in the sack.

"How many kids you got at your house?" Holbrook asked.

"Tons of aunts and uncles and cousins at holidays," I said. "But me and my brother Dick mostly."

"Only three, eh?" he asked.

"My brother Mike is going to college next week, so he doesn't count, I guess."

"We got eleven," Holbrook said.

"Eleven? Wow," I said.

"Plus there's Mom and Dad and two cousins living with us who lost their parents in the war. In France, I think."

"Your mom pack you lunch every day?" I asked.

"Yep."

"What'd she make ya today?"

"What do you mean?" Holbrook asked.

"What's in your sack?"

Holbrook stalled answering and kept walking.

"What'd she make?" I repeated.

"Oh, a sandwich and an apple," he said.

"Sandwich and apple?" I asked.

"I never get all that hungry at lunch."

I knew better. Any kid who lived through the war anywhere in the world would know better. The rumpled lunch sack and his having to peek in it and his big family were giveaways. My guess was Holbrook hadn't even had breakfast. Either that or the eleven or so kids at his house took turns eating a good lunch. American kids born in the late thirties and early 1940s could tell when other kids were rehearsed on what they would say to keep from being embarrassed or sad. We had keen sensitivity about these things. Like those not having enough to eat, or those losing a brother or a parent in the war. We pretty much all had one thing in common—we knew what it was like to live most of our lives with an entire world at war. We knew how to look after each other when the grownups couldn't always be around. That sense of responsibility plus five years of scrimping and sacrifice, of food rationing and sharing with other—we just knew.

"Sandwich? What kind of sandwich?" I asked. "I like

sandwiches better than almost anything."

Holbrook shifted his eyes around, hoping no one in the hall could hear him. "Ketchup," he said, under his breath.

I knew there was no such thing as a ketchup sandwich for a real lunch. Kids whose families on hard times sometimes got ketchup or honey or sugar sandwiches—just so they could hold a sandwich—to make them feel like everyone else. Dad told me poor kids in the south sometimes got molasses sandwiches to take to school.

"Ketchup, my favorite," I mumbled.

While we were walking, I dug into my right pocket, pulled out my lunch quarter—reached around under my left arm and poked it to the side of his ribs.

"Wanna trade?"

Holbrook looked down at the quarter and then over at me.

"What's your name?"

"Already told ya—Jerry."

Holbrook looked at the quarter again.

"For real," I said, looking straight into his eyes. "Trade."

He stared at me as we walked.

"I love ketchup," I said.

He gave me a kind of look that let me know he knew he could trust me. We made the trade—as we would do every day forward through all our school years together. He would have done the same for me.

It was then when Holbrook and I bonded and started laughing and talking like we were old friends. He told me his dad was a part-time brakeman for the railroad, and they lived on Berry Road. He said his dad was buying the house from a farmer for seven hundred dollars and they had no hot water, but they did have three small waterfalls and a creek behind it that their land touched. We found ourselves walking behind Barber down the hall to the cafeteria.

"Who's the girl who spoke up in class?" I asked. "The one in the front row."

"Mary Crane. She lives near me."

He pointed down the hall.

"That's her by the cafeteria door, looking at the bulletin

board. Maybe we can sit with her."

Mary caught Holbrook's eye and waited for us.

"Hi Jerome," Mary said.

"Call him Jerry," Holbrook said.

"I already know Holbrook," Mary said. "We ride on the same bus. You guys want to sit together?"

Barber joined us, and he flagged Bases and we found a table and talked all through lunch. Holbrook was enjoying his hot meal so much I could tell he hadn't had breakfast. While I was opening the paper sack I traded my lunch quarter for, Mary came up from behind, reached around me, and slid a small bottle of milk near my lunch sack for me to drink. She cupped her hand over her mouth and whispered in my ear, "I saw what you did."

Mary lived not too far from the Holbrooks, and she knew how many kids they had and how hard their father worked to put food on the table.

She walked around, sat down and smiled through some loose strands of her hair.

We all talked like we had known each other for the longest time, while most of the other kids had run out to the playground after eating. My new set of friends assured me that I would grow to like the country, in time.

Mary agreed.

"We moved here this summer from Manlius," Mary said.

"You like it now?" I asked.

"You'll get used to it soon enough," Mary said.

"Where'd you live during the war?" I asked.

"I had to live with my grandmother, in Syracuse, after Dad went off to war when I was three."

"Is Syracuse nice?" I asked.

"The city was scary."

"Was it?"

"When my daddy came back home wearing a uniform after the war, I cried and hid under the bed."

"Why'd you cry?"

"I didn't even recognize him. He was gone three years."

"Oh."

"Now I deliver newspapers early in the morning to earn extra money."

"Where?"

"On my road."

"You're not afraid anymore?"

"No way. My dad drives me around my whole route before he goes to work. He loves driving his new Ford. He'll drive me anywhere I need to go."

"Money for college?" I asked.

"Just money," Mary said. "For things we may need. Maybe for college, too."

"What's your dad do?" I asked.

"He's a blacksmith."

"That's neat—a blacksmith for horses?"

"He works on cars mostly. He worked on army tanks in the war."

"Big army tanks like General Patton tanks?"

"I guess. He can fix almost anything that needs fixing. What's your dad do?"

"He works in a bakery."

Barber added, "Jerry, there's a boy, Randy, whose dad can't tell him what he did in the war because of the secrets—"

"For real?" I asked.

"You can ride with him on his milk truck, if you want."

"Milk truck? He's like a milk man?"

"No, this is a big milk truck. His dad hauls milk cans from farms to the dairy. Randy rides with him on Saturdays and Sundays if you ever want to go—let me know."

Lunch in the cafeteria this day made it a good day.

Finally, the bell rang and school let out. For the whole first week our class had to line up and walk to the buses together. Mr. Skelton was still sitting on the bus. This was all so new to me. I wondered if he sat there all day, waiting for us, or if he got to go home or go for a walk during the day.

The ride home was entertaining, because I got to sit with Barber again and learn about everything on the other side of the road. I saw that he lived on a big farm with barns with silos and good stuff like animals and tractors and trucks and machines. I saw Linda Oats get off the bus on the corner of our road. What could have been better than having the prettiest girl on the bus live on the very same road I lived on?

The bus stopped at our house, and Dick and I got off. We stood a
minute, looked around, taking it all in. This was our first walk from a school bus up our long dirt driveway to the house. We studied everything around us in both fear and wonderment.

"Look at that up there," Dick said.

"Up where?" I asked.

"That big rock, it's sticking out from that cliff up there near the top. It's huge for a rock."

"It's white," I said. "I've never seen a white rock before."

"The white rock," Dick said as we walked toward the house.

The tall trees that towered in the woods on the top of shale and rock cliffs, the creek trickling down next to the cliff behind the small barn and barn garage that stood side by side. The house that once was an old public park—Delphi Falls Park—and square dance pavilion was now our house. It was all still new to us, and still intimidating.

"I'm going to check out the barn and see if that old popsicle cart is

worth fixing," Dick said.

He saw a popsicle tricycle-cart at the used bicycle shop in Cortland. It had been backed into by a milk delivery truck and smashed against a brick wall. He traded his Log Cabin Syrup coin bank can filled with Indian Head pennies for it and talked Mr. Rowe into hauling it up with the moving boxes.

"Popsicle cart? You mean you got a pedal cart to sell popsicles with?" "Yeah—dented-up pretty bad, though."

The minute I heard him say he wondered if it could be fixed, I had an idea, but I didn't say anything. The girl at school, Mary—her dad was a blacksmith. I was about to figure a way to give Dick's popsicle cart to Mary for her dad to fix so she could make extra money selling popsicles. I thought about her buying me milk at lunch with her own money. I knew she was going to be a friend. Dick owed me for the black eye I fibbed about for him. I just had to figure how to make his popsicle cart disappear and show up at Mary's without Dick having a brain hemorrhage, but I had no time to think about it. I was still recounting in my mind the Superman radio episode from the night before, when he flew two hundred miles in two seconds and saved the family from the high-speed, bone-crushing oncoming train. Today, after a first day at a new school, me, disguised as Superman, was going to go swimming out back under the monster falls, where my dad said there was a good swimming hole. I was getting undressed when I saw Dick through my window walking from the swings to the barn garage. I knew Dad was at work, and I knew Mom wasn't at home, so I thought—why not?

Thinking was something I would always try to do regardless of how much trouble I seemed to get into. A boy would think as a precaution, in case someone asked, "What were you thinking?"

But right then I had more important things on my mind. Superman, disguised as me, Jerry, was going to check out the waterfalls for the first time, and—I thought—if I was going to the falls as Superman, I was faster than a speeding bullet, and if I was faster than a speeding bullet, no one could see me—and if no one could see me—and nobody was home anyway, I didn't have to wear anything at all. No swimsuit. Nada. Nothing. Naked as a jaybird.

It all made perfectly good sense to me.

Out through the living room's back door I ran—like a flash—truly faster than a speeding bullet. I was a sonic streaking blur, all the way from my room, through the house and the entire distance to the waterfall. It was so cool—my Superman speed—my feet barely touching the ground.

Under the waterfalls I could hardly hear myself think, with the water crashing down more than seventy feet into a swimming hole below. On the tall shale cliff by the creek, I found stone fossils from prehistoric times. In the creek, I could see minnows and tiny crawfish going under rocks. I would watch the water start at the top of the falls and keep an eye on it all the way down until it splashed in the water below.

When it was time to go back to the house, I waded across the creek—very carefully, so as not to slip or stub my toes on rocks—and as I got to the other side, I knew my Superman powers would take over again, so I could get back to my bedroom unseen.

Off I shot, like a rocket—the house instantly appearing

closer and closer—and I saw with my x-ray vision that the back door to the living room was wide open.

Funny, I didn't remember leaving that door opened.

Oh well, not to worry. I was a bullet speeding through the air, and I got closer and the closer I got, the more I convinced myself I could make
the living room with one big single leap, no steps, and off I went—up, up, and away!

I sailed through the air, through the open doorway and landed on both bare feet perfectly, coming to a sudden stop, balancing myself upright just a few feet inside the door, on the living room rug.

"Why hello, Jerome," Mrs. Heffernan said, looking over her spectacles this time.

"Huh?!"

"Your mother was nice enough to invite me over for a visit and a cup of tea."

I stood there frozen—stark butt-naked, looking stupid.

"Aren't you chilly, dear?" Mom asked.

Her tea was spilling from her cup, onto the coffee table.

Mrs. Heffernan handed her a napkin.

I didn't say a word. I actually think I went blind for a moment. I turned around and walked through the living room, down the hall, and into my room, where I collapsed forward on my bed.

This was only my first day at school, in the country.

I covered my head with my pillow, my mind going a complete blank, again.

Lesson one—it's a basement, not a lavatory. Lesson two—button my fly. Lesson three—Mrs. Heffernan is a Mrs.—not Sister. Lesson four—Superman wears swim trunks, and nobody told me.

How was a boy to know that, listening to him on the radio?

## CHAPTER TWO
## HAVE NO FEARS, ADVENTURE NEARS

I was telling my dad about Holbrook's ketchup sandwich; how big and poor his family was and how it reminded me of the war again just as though it was still going on. I told him how Mary Crane cried and hid under her bed when her dad came home from the war in uniform and how he now drove her early in the morning before he went to work so she could deliver newspapers on their road to earn extra money. I told him about the boy, Randy, whose dad couldn't talk about the war because of the top-secret things he worked on. With the dashboard lights reflecting on his eyes I could tell Dad understood everything I was feeling.

That evening, as I knelt on new linoleum, leaned on my new (to me) bed, it seemed fitting to make my reflections the only way I knew how—my bedtime prayers. The family seemed settled into a new routine, a new culture, but my memories of Cortland kept churning up for some reason. The painful part was I wasn't sure why.

"Now I lay me down to sleep, I pray the Lord my soul to keep. If I should die before I wake, I pray the Lord my soul to take."

I had become used to the war, witnessing its five-year entirety from the year of my birth. I still wasn't used to the "country" I knew little about; the edge of a steep hill next to a house I'd never seen before late this summer; the dark woods that had sixty-foot trees at the bottom of it that looked like three- hundred-foot trees at the top of the hill; the seventy-foot waterfall behind our house thundering constantly, like it was alive and wanted to bust free from the rock and boulders it plummeted over all day and night, and the creek by the cliff on the other side of a one-story dance pavilion that was converted into a house I still could get lost in.

I liked the kids I was meeting—Holbrook and the others, Barber, Mary, and Bases. I liked Mr. Pitts's farm, where I went and got eggs every week, and farmer Parker's, where I'd watch the cows come home, but my thoughts were clouded with a "homesickness" that would come over me from time to time, thinking I was missing a part of me because of our move. I missed the Cortland part of me that saw the beginning, middle, and end of the war that affected every family, every neighbor—and brought us all together. I still had nightmares about the time I was out in the back yard and the sky darkened with low-flying bombers, bush hopping their way to England so they could bomb Hitler. I could remember watching Mom weep while we listened to President Roosevelt's funeral on the Zenith radio. I was confused by the new empty, detached feeling I had from time to time.

Suddenly, in the dark—a hand touched my shoulder.

"Pssssst—Jerry—pssssst!"

"Huh?"

"Want to go fishing, son?"

It was my dad, waking me up to go fishing with him. He'd never taken me fishing alone when we lived in the city. The whole family would go together to Little York Lake on Sundays to picnic and fish, and we'd listen to Walter Winchell's radio broadcast or to the "Stop the Music" radio show on the way home. None of the lights were on in the house, and no one was awake, so I knew this would mean I'd get to ride with Dad in the car, which was great, because he knew how to have one big adventure after another. He had his work suit and tie on, which I didn't understand. I sat right up, got dressed, and walked through the dark to the car. So we wouldn't wake anyone, he started the car with the lights off, backed around, and drove down the driveway toward the gate. He turned them on when we were on the road.

See what I mean? How many people could have done that without backing into the swings or swiping the side of the barn garage or dumping the car into the creek? Just my dad! That alone was an adventure, and we weren't even out of our driveway yet.

"Where're we going, Dad?"

I only asked because of his dress clothes, and wasn't sure if it was night or morning, but it was fun to be up this late or this early—whichever it was—with my dad, and knowing inside every house we drove by, everyone was asleep and missing out on everything.

"How's school, son?"

"It's okay."

"How were your first few days?"

"Mr. Mobley thinks my name is Jeremiah Mark."

Dad smiled. "I'm impressed. Not even a week and you already have two names, just like Superman and Clark Kent."

I sat up a little taller.

"We're going to Little York Lake and catch some sunfish or perch—but first, we'll go to Bucky's Diner in Cortland and get some breakfast. Later I have to make some stops at grocery stores in Auburn, Seneca Falls, and Fayetteville before we go home. I thought you'd like the ride."

Holy cow! I loved Bucky's Diner because it was open all night and Dad and Bucky were good friends. Bucky always had a big white apron wrapped around him that almost reached the floor like a dress, and a white string tied around his waist to hold it up. He wore a paper hat that looked like an army hat, and it said "New York State Fair" on it.

Dad worked at his and Mr. Durkee's bakery in Homer, which was right next to Cortland where we used to live, and he'd always stop at grocery stores to see if the bread was straight on the shelves, for the customers to see it—and wait just a minute—

"Cortland?" I asked.

It dawned on me what he just said. I hadn't been in Cortland since we moved to the country. I had forgotten how far we drove to Delphi Falls before that Labor Day. It seemed like hours.

"Is Cortland far away?"

"Thirty-five, maybe forty minutes, son."

"Is that all, Dad? For real?"

"Just about as long as it takes to listen to your Superman radio program, Jerry me boy. I had a feeling you'd like to see Cortland again."

"I thought we moved to China, like a million miles away, and it was close by all the time?"

It wasn't long before we were driving past Shea's corner store, the school, and heading out through the other side of the village.

"Where's this road go, Dad?"

"It goes to Tully, and then we'll go south to Homer on 11. Pretend you're on a steamship freighter, Jerry me boy, sailing from one port adventure to the next. You are exploring the world, protecting it from evildoers and enemies of mankind."

"Like Hitler and Mussolini," I mumbled.

Dad grinned.

Dad was great. While he was encouraging me to become the Superman we both suspected was inside me, I saw in the distance a country road sign leaning to the left. I kept my eyes on it, trying to make it out.

When I could read it I shouted, "Berry Road. Dad, that's Berry Road. That's where Holbrook lives."

Slowing the car down, Dad said, "Well, let's go have a look."

"For real, Dad?"

"It can't be that long of a road. We'll drive it up and back. What clues do you have about his house, Jerry?"

I was amazed. Dad turned on Berry Road just as easy as he made it around the swings and the barn at home. He didn't even have to think about it. He was great!

"His house is next to a creek. That's all I know."

"That's a good clue, son, maybe all we need. Where there's a creek, there should be a bridge. Keep a look out for a small bridge, just like the one by our house."

A couple of miles up, we drove over a bluff where there was a curve in the road.

"There's a bridge, Dad. There's a bridge."

It was a short concrete bridge, two or three feet high, the width of the creek on both sides of the road.

"That white house there by the maple tree could be Holbrook's," Dad said. "We'll turn around up here and head to Cortland, but maybe now you know. Ask him on Monday. Ask him if they have a white, two-story house with blue shingles."

We could see a car up ahead with its interior lights on, driving slowly, near the side of the road, almost like it had a flat tire. I could see someone in the back seat. Then I saw an arm flip out the rear window and a rolled-up newspaper flew high before landing on a lawn.

"Up ahead, is that a Ford?" I asked.

"It is a Ford, why?"

"Can we get close? I wanna see who that is. They are delivering newspapers. It might be Mary and her dad."

Another rolled-up newspaper burst from the arm leaning out the open rear window, higher than the last one, and it landed in the middle of another lawn.

"If that's Mary, she has a good arm," Dad said. "She'd be a dandy outfielder."

Dad pulled next to the Ford. I rolled down my window.

"That's her. That's Mary. That's her for sure in the back seat, delivering newspapers."

Dad tooted the horn a short friendly toot and waved at Mr. Crane, who smiled and waved back. I waved at Mary. She caught my eye and waved with a grin as Dad slowed down, pulled into a driveway, and backed around so we could get on our way again.

"Her dad drives her every morning."

"I remember you telling me. Nice girl."

What an adventure we were having, and it wasn't even daylight.

In Cortland, we drove to the side of Bucky's Diner and parked. I felt like I had traveled around the world. I would have never dreamed I would see it again since we moved.

When we walked in, I sat on my favorite counter stool like I always had when we went there before. I made my compulsory two or three spins around on it, pushing off from the counter every time I circled around. Bucky was in his apron and hat, just as I remembered him. Then, like always when we went to Bucky's, Dad took a shiny quarter out of his pocket and with his thumb flipped it way up in the air, so it blurred it spun so fast through the air, high enough nearly to touch the ceiling.

"Call it, Bucky!" he shouted, not taking his eyes off the flying quarter on its descent.

The game they played was if Bucky called heads or tails, and if the coin landed the way Bucky called it, Dad would give him the quarter for his coffee. Win or lose, Bucky would put both his hands on the counter, jump his legs up sideways, and click his heels together in the air. If Bucky didn't call it right, Dad's coffee was free. It was fun, and everyone in the diner would gather around and watch. I knew coffee was a dime, and one time I asked Dad if he felt bad losing a quarter if he lost. He said no, he did it so that if Bucky lost, he could make up for the free coffee the next time by winning a quarter. Dad was nice like that.

"We need two egg and bacon sandwiches on white, wrapped in wax paper, if you can, Bucky," Dad said.

"Sounds like you're going fishing," Bucky said.

"Jerry and I plan to go empty the sunfish and perch out of Little York Lake before the sun comes up. We want to catch them napping."

"How 'bout I wrap a piece of fresh apple pie to keep the boy awake?" Bucky asked.

Dad winked at him like that would be nice, and after he took the last sip from his coffee, Bucky handed him a paper sack and we went out to the car. It was still dark outside.

I was getting pretty good about putting a worm on a hook so it would stay, in the daylight, but it was way too dark, and way too early in the morning to see what I was doing. I would take a worm out of the coffee tin and hand it to Dad. He hooked the worms for me. We sat on the end of the wooden dock with our legs hanging over for about an hour. I caught three sunfish. Dad caught one bullhead.

Dad lifted the stringer out of the water with four fish dangling on it.

"What do you say we put these fish back in the lake to grow a bit more?" he asked. "We know just where they live, so we will catch them again when they're bigger and can make a nice meal."

Made perfect sense to me and after all, just going fishing alone with my dad was great! Before we ate our sandwiches, he held me by my legs and the back of my belt so I could reach down into the lake and rinse the worm smell off my hands good. He rinsed his, too, to get the worm guts and smell off.

We took the poles and everything back to the car just as the sun was starting to come out. Dad drove into Homer and around the back of the bakery, where everyone was working and hurrying about, walking up and down the stairs, and bakery delivery trucks parked everywhere were being loaded up with cartons of warm bread before the drivers took them out. It was then I learned why Dad wore his work suit and tie all the time—because bakers had to deliver bread all over, and since they wanted to deliver it fresh to the stores, the bakery had to run twenty-four hours a day. Everyone in the bakery would ask which boy I was (they could never keep us straight), and they would pat me on the head and tell me how much I had grown. It was nice to see nobody had forgotten us just because we'd moved. Dad went inside the bakery office, poured a cup of coffee for himself, and made a hot chocolate to go with my piece of apple pie.

"Let me do some business," he said, "and then we'll go."

I needed time to eat my pie, so I was okay with that—and besides, the sun was barely just coming out and I had had three adventures with my dad already.

After his business, we went down the back stairs to the car. He told me to crawl into the back seat and get some sleep because he was going to drive to Auburn and then to Seneca Falls to look at grocery stores before we went home. I could lie down in the back seat and fit perfectly. Dad turned the radio on, and I heard the music or the talking as he turned the dial for the best reception from town to town.

When I woke the sun was bright, and the car wasn't moving. I sat up, rubbed my eyes, trying to remember what I was doing in the back seat of the car, and saw we were parked in front of a grocery store somewhere in the country. There were no houses or farms anywhere around. I opened the door, got out, and went inside. I walked around one aisle by the vegetables but didn't see my dad. I turned a corner in the store by a pile of acorn squash—and still no dad. A comic book stand and a Superman comic caught my eye. I hadn't seen it before, so I paged through it a little while.

After I was done, I set the comic book back on the rack,

walked around the store, looking for Dad, and when I couldn't find him, I decided to go back to the car and wait there. He was probably doing business. I found the front door and walked outside.

The car was gone.

This can't be good, I thought, as I seemed to think more and more in those days since our move to the country.

I rushed back into the store and to the front counter. The man behind the counter was putting cartons of cigarettes on a shelf behind him and he had his glasses pushed up over his forehead, on the top of his head.

"Where's my dad?"

"Who are you, son?"

"I'm Jerry. Where's my daddy—Mike?"

The man smiled, told me right off he knew Big Mike, and started to talk to me. I told him I'd been asleep in the back seat and had come into the store to find him, and when I went back out, he was gone.

"Don't worry, little guy," the man chuckled. "Your dad will see he lost his boy as soon as he looks in the back seat, and he will turn that car around on a dime and come back right away, in a big hurry—I promise."

Well, this made me feel better, but I did think about crying.

What if he forgot he brought me this morning to the middle of nowhere, and just drove to all those places he was going to and never remembered me, and then I was here forever? It was a regular occurrence when either Mom or Dad, sitting at the supper table, looking at one of us, straight in the eye, would pause, in midsentence, and have to gather their thoughts—to recollect what our names were. One time Dad looked at me as if he was thinking, "I know your name. I remember driving you home from the hospital." I would have nightmares about being left in a store and my parents not remembering my name until a letter came, addressed to me, from the Army draft board.

The man came outside with me, handed me an orange popsicle, sat on the stoop, and pulled his glasses down so he could help me take the frozen wrapper off.

"I'll wait here with you, Jerry, because I just know your

dad will be along any minute now."

It took a lot to keep from crying, but the popsicle helped, and the man sitting there with me helped, too. I didn't feel all alone.

I'd have been okay being dumped in Cortland where I knew things, but this was the wilderness.

Off in the distance we could begin to see dust billowing up in the air from the road.

"Well, lookee at what we have here," the man said with a smile. "It sure 'nuff looks like Big Mike heading our way."

I could see a tiny light-green car coming this way from down the road.

"Dad's Oldsmobile is light green," I said.

"Please, God, let that be my dad," I said to myself. "I'll clean my room and do all the things I'm always supposed to do."

The light-green car got bigger and soon a long arm stretched out its window, straight up in the air, and waved at us as the car got closer, slowed down, and turned into the store's parking area. It sure was my dad—and that's when I started to cry. Not because I was sad or scared, but because I was happy. Happy to see that Dad didn't forget me.

He got out of the car, walked around and rubbed my head, laughing a big laugh.

"Thank Mr. Morgan for watching you, Jerry me boy. I discovered you weren't in the back seat when I wanted you to wake up and sing a song with me. "*Put another nickel in … in the nickelodeon … all I want is loving you and music—music—music—*"

That was one of my dad's favorite songs, which Theresa Brewer sang on the radio. We sang it together loud so we could hear it because we had the car windows open.

This time I sat in the front seat, wondering what the next Jeremiah Mark adventure would be.

## CHAPTER THREE
## A LIFETIME ADVENTURE PASS!

My thirst for adventure started at sunup this Saturday. I snuck into Gourmet Mike's room and was negotiating with my half-asleep brother on the advantages of his getting out of bed and driving me to the Saturday morning picture show movie house I discovered up in Cazenovia. He was leaving for college the next day.

John Wayne was in a movie showing there. Not only would they have a regular Superman serial and morning cartoons, but at noon they had the movie, *She Wore A Yellow Ribbon*, which I'd heard on the radio had a lot of Indians, horses, and cavalry, and was otherwise spectacular, in Technicolor.

Passion to me was watching that 1870 Calvary Indian scout's horse galloping in such flight that nary a hoof appeared to touch the ground, as he outran arrow after blistering arrow, the brim of his cavalry hat pushing flat back against his head in the wind. Passion was the cavalry lieutenant, with the daring to tell the other lieutenant to remove his uniform blouse (worn over the shirt) so they could duke it out over a girl they both loved, the one with the yellow ribbon in her hair, so pretty they wrote her a song.

Nobody had televisions yet—they were hardly invented and nobody could afford them if they were, so if we had the fifteen cents it took to get in, we would go to the picture show on Saturday mornings and stay all day, until someone came and dragged us out.

I negotiated with Gourmet Mike, who was not yet fully awake.

"Gourmet Mike, if you drive me it would give you an excuse to maybe go see some *la-de-da* girl in Cazenovia before you go away to college."

"What!?" he rolled and grumbled.

I was tempting him with girls. I was counting on something better than movie popcorn to give me an edge. Scratching his head, he yawned, rolled over and sat up. He just happened to remember a girl he might be able to call in Cazenovia who hadn't left for college yet.

"Tell you what," he said, relenting. "I'll drop you off at the picture show. I'll go next door to the Lincklaen House hotel and use their telephone closet to call a girl I know up there. Then we can sit in their restaurant."

"Perfect," I said.

"I think I'll get an ice cream milkshake, with malt and an egg in it. Maybe I'll get a raisin Danish."

"Huh?" I grunted.

"We'll see," he said.

"Egg?" I asked.

"I'll wait with her there until your movie lets out," he said.

I backed away from Gourmet Mike's bed, stood with my mouth open, stupefied.

"An egg?"

"Huh?" Mike asked.

"Did you say egg?"

"Yes."

"Raw egg?"

"Of course."

"You crack a raw egg in with ice cream?"

"Maybe two."

"You put two slimy raw eggs in an ice cream milkshake, then you drink it?"

"Two tablespoons of malt, too."

The concept sent an axe to the pit of my stomach. I knew with anymore talk about raw eggs and a malt-whatever with ice cream, I might lose more than my ride to Cazenovia.

"Malted milkshake with an egg is a delicacy for the palate—it's healthful, too," Gourmet Mike admitted proudly, sitting up. "Go get in my car. Let's go."

"Agh!" I thought. There was no hope for him. But I was desperate for a ride to see the John Wayne movie. I backed out of his room, breathed some clean air in the hallway, ran out, and got in his car and waited.

The movie was everything the man on the radio said it would be. The movie music was great. I could sing the song by heart. *Round her neck, she wore a yellow ribbon* … I remembered every scene, especially when Captain Brittles talked to the Indian chief about them being too old for war, why they should drink whiskey and all be friends, that war was no good; the part when Captain Brittle's men gave him a pocket watch because they loved him, and he started to cry looking for his glasses to read what they had engraved on it; the part when the doctor and the wife of the commander had to operate on a man in a wagon to get a bullet out, on the trail, so he wouldn't die, and they slowed the wagons down so they didn't bounce around too much.

I memorized the whole John Wayne movie—which I should have, I guess, because Gourmet Mike forgot me there. Without realizing it, I sat through the same movie over and over for most of the day.

Then someone tapped me on the shoulder. I lifted my head. It was my dad.

"Ready to go home, son?" he asked.

I turned in my seat and stared up at him in a daze, wondering why he was there. I got up and walked out with him. My eyes glazed over while they adjusted to the daylight outside, now nearing sunset. I thought maybe I was dreaming. I walked cautiously as I squinted my eyes open just enough to see if I was still on the sidewalk.

"Where's Gourmet Mike?" I asked.

"Mike came home hours ago. When I got home, I asked him where you were or where Dick was. He said Dick was with your mother, and that's when he remembered he forgot you were with him, and he had left you in Cazenovia."

I stopped walking. I opened my eyes and looked up and stared at Dad.

He stopped walking and stared down at me.

"He forgot me?"

"Seems he did, son."

"He left me alone in Cazenovia."

"Yes."

"I'm a child! How could he forget me in Cazenovia?"

This forgetting me was getting old, I thought. When Dad opened the car door for me to climb in, I turned to him again and asked, "What is it with people forgetting me everywhere?"

Dad smiled and told me some of the greatest adventures in the world happened when we did something alone, and then we would know we had a great sense of accomplishment. He told me being alone wasn't a bad thing.

Now kids who grew up during the war had some not talked about superstitions that lasted for years, and the superstitions would get bigger as we got older. When we lived in Cortland, I'd get left at the shoe shine parlor sometimes when Dad would forget me and start walking down the sidewalk reading the morning newspaper, or there was the time he left me at Leonard's coffee shop until he remembered me when he got in his car to drive home. When Dick was little he was left behind so often and found by Mom's friends who would keep him until Mom or Dad came to get him, he learned how to shuffle cards and deal a double-down bridge game by the time he was five. Me—I'd usually just cry.

"Jerry, did John Wayne do anything alone in the movie?"

I told him yes, near the end of the movie, Captain Brittles (that was him) started to ride alone, to California, but he had his horse.

"Does Superman ever do anything alone, son?"

"Sure, all the time; nobody can keep up with him."

"You like watching farmer Parker call his cows."

"Yes."

"When you're not with him he calls his cows for milking all alone. He has no one to help him."

"I know."

"Your friend Mary, she has her own paper route, son. I know her dad drives her around, but it's her route; she does the work rolling the papers and throwing them and collecting the money."

Dad pulled the car over to the side of the road, brought it to a stop, and put it in park. He looked over at me.

"Son, how would you like to go on the best adventure any boy your age could ever possibly go on?"

"Sure."

He smiled, turned forward, put the car in drive, and drove back on the road.

"Tomorrow, Jerry me boy, you're going to have an

adventure of a lifetime."

"Me?"

"I'm going to show you that being alone is only a state of mind. When you need them, your friends will always be there for you."

I had no idea what it was going to be, and I didn't even ask, because I knew when dad said adventure—I trusted him more than almost anybody.

When we got back to the house, I looked around for Gourmet Mike, and saw him in the den where all the books were. He was packing to leave for college. I walked to where he was stacking his college books. I kicked him in the shin.

"That's for forgetting me in Cazenovia," I said.

I walked away.

He didn't say a word. He knew he had it coming for forgetting me. I went to the kitchen to make a peanut butter sandwich.

The next morning was Sunday and Dad woke me early. He told Mom that he and I would be spending the morning together, and we would not be going to church in Manlius with them. We drove, instead, to St. Mary's in Cortland, where I had been baptized and went to school and where I had my First Communion. We attended Mass. After Mass we went to Bucky's Diner. Dad flipped the quarter high into the air again, and Bucky called it and won, and clicked his heels and everyone cheered. I had a hot chocolate while waiting for breakfast and Dad put a nickel in the coin-operated phone—ding—and started talking to someone.

"What time does it take off," he asked. "What time will it land?"

Then he said, "thank you" and hung up the phone.

He winked at Bucky and told him I was going on a great adventure this morning. We had to be at the Thompkins airfield in thirty minutes, but we had plenty of time so I could finish my breakfast. I didn't have any idea what an airfield was and I didn't care. I was going to have an adventure.

When Dad drove into the airfield, I figured it out right away. There were four airplanes. Three small planes, and one silver plane was bigger. It said "Flagship" on its side. He said the bigger one was a DC-3, a passenger airplane. I knew there were Army airplanes in the war they called bombers, like the ones that flew low over our house in Cortland during the war, and I knew about fighter planes, but I had never seen a big airplane that just carried people. Dad walked me inside the building and gave the man at the counter some money for a ticket. We walked out to the DC-3, and he handed me the ticket.

I looked up at him.

"Son, this is your great big adventure—"

"Aren't you going with me?"

"—all alone, son."

"Huh?"

"You're going to get on this plane—you've never been in an airplane—and you're going to fly all alone to the Syracuse airport. When you land, someone will be there to meet you when you get off the plane and they will be anxious to hear all about your adventure."

"But Dad …"

"The airplane leaves in eighteen minutes, son. Have fun."

I looked him in the eye.

"Are you sure, Dad?"

"I promise, son. You're practically a decade old."

"What's that mean?"

"You're almost ten years old. You need a big adventure all alone."

I was more like seven or eight, but my dad was so right. Sometimes I felt like I almost had to run away or something, jump a steam freighter or do some adventure because I was getting tired of just watching other people do good stuff in the movies. It gets embarrassing when you sit in a classroom and think getting away from it all was standing up and walking over to use the pencil sharpener.

Dad put his hand out for me to shake, like a grownup, and then he told me to get on the plane and have a good adventure.

"Mind what they tell you," he said as I watched him walk away and get into his car, wave, and drive off.

I climbed the steps into the plane. When I got in, the aisle was tilted, so I had to walk uphill to get to my seat. I was the only one in there except the pilot and the American Airlines stewardess.

A stewardess was a lady in a uniform and a hat who made sure I was comfortable and had milk to drink, at least that is what she told me.

The pilot let me come into his cabin and look at all the instruments and feel the airplane steering wheel. The stewardess had me sit in the front seat and buckle a seatbelt, which I had never seen before, so she buckled it for me. I looked at the ticket in my hand. It said "$12" and "Syracuse Hancock Field." I didn't know where that was—and I didn't much care.

I'll never forget the loud roar of the propeller engine I could see out of my window when it started slowly spinning around, and then the giant puff of smoke belching out of it as the propeller turned so fast it became a blur. I could feel the plane starting to move. I watched us turning around almost in a full circle before we started moving forward, bumping up and down on the grass field, as it moved toward a long cement area. Then the plane started to move faster and faster, and the faster it went, my back pushed deeper and deeper into the seat back—faster and faster we went. I grabbed the seat arms looked out the window at things speeding by. Suddenly, my heart leaped into my throat. I saw the ground move from under us as the plane jumped up and I could feel myself getting lighter like I was on a ride at the county fair. We started to fly and the plane aisle wasn't tilted anymore. The floor was level, like in a house. We were in the air, and the trees and barns and buildings below us were getting smaller and smaller. The cars I could see below looked like ants on the ground. It was amazing.

Now I knew what it was really like to be a bird—or better yet, Superman. After a while, the stewardess told me we were getting ready to land in Syracuse. I could hardly wait to tell everybody about my plane ride adventure. It was like a flying carpet, seeing a cloud go by, and the houses and farms below got bigger and bigger as we came down. Imagine being taller than a tree. I could see the ground coming closer and closer, and then I could feel the plane land on the ground with a bump, and the propellers making a lot of noise until we came to a stop. The floor was tilted again. When the door opened, and I was told I could leave, I walked to it and stepped out.

There, right at the side of the field, was my dad, waving! Wow! He beat the airplane and was there—just like he promised—when I needed someone; my friends would always be there for me. What an adventure! I would never forget it for as long as I lived. In one weekend I got to see my favorite movie ever and memorize the song—"*Round her neck she wore a yellow ribbon—she wore it for her lover who was far, far away—far away—far away—she wore it for her lover who was far, far away*"—and I got to go on an adventure all alone. I would never be afraid of being alone or of any adventure ever again!

## CHAPTER FOUR
## CEMETERY SECRETS

The screen door slammed behind me.

"Dick?" I shouted.

No response.

"Dick!"

No response.

"Where's Dick, Mom?"

No response.

"Mom?"

I heard Mom's voice, muffled from her and dad's bedroom.

"I'm vacuuming!"

"Where's Dick, Mom?"

"Get the dust mop, dear. Dust mop your room—under your bed. Pick up and fold your clothes. Your dad called and he's bringing Aunt Kate for supper and to stay over. I want your room picked up."

"Where's Dick?"

"Get yourself a snack. There's peanut butter in the cereal cabinet, grapes in a bowl by the sink. Drink some juice."

"Do you know where Dick is?"

"Your father dropped Dick off at David Duba's house this morning. He'll pick him up when he comes home from the bakery."

Duba lived on the opposite end of the village from Shea's corner. His dad had a chicken barn with hundreds of chickens. They sold chickens and eggs. By now Dick and Duba were good friends, both with glasses. Dick's were thicker. If Dick had the higher IQ you couldn't tell; they both got into the same trouble. David had better grades in school, but Dick could probably tell you what was in an encyclopedia book before he looked. If Dick ever picked up a book it was rare, but when he did he would read it from cover to cover in one sitting and then give his teachers fits all year by knowing every lecture without ever opening the book again. He and Duba were thirteen, always together, and mostly talking about girls or how they were going to drag race when they got cars of their own. Dick tried to impress girls by saying he could drive Dad's Oldsmobile anytime he wanted, which he couldn't. Duba would do the same—tell girls he could get his dad's Lincoln anytime, which he couldn't, either. Sometimes Dad and Mr. Duba would take them out on back roads to let them practice driving. They both knew how to drive well. It seemed a lot of kids in the country, by twelve or thirteen, knew how to drive. Farm kids needed to know, and many had special driving permits and could drive on the road with tractors, implements, or farm trucks, hauling things or making deliveries. At nine, Barber would drive his dad's Packard around the farm while sitting on two pillows.

Mom came into the dining room while winding up the vacuum cleaner cord.

"Oh dear, I asked Dick to carry these boxes to the barn garage and put them on a shelf. I don't know what I'm going to do with that boy. I have a PTA meeting to go to and I'll be gone an hour or two."

"I'll take them out, Mom."

"Are you going to the Parkers?"

"Yes, ma'am."

The day turned into a sunny spring afternoon. After toting the boxes to the barn garage, I headed over to farmer Parker's to do what I loved to do—watch him call his cows in off the tall side hill pasture for their late afternoon milking.

"Caho bossies! Caho bossies! Caho bossies!" Farmer Parker yodeled in a strong, low voice, raising it when he said "bossies" like he was singing.

Farmer Parker wore his bib overalls everywhere, like Mr. Pitts and other farmers I've seen, but unlike their straw hats or John Deere baseball caps, he wore a train engineer hat. Farmer Parker didn't chew tobacco. Mike Shea, up at the store on Shea's corner said that sometimes people chewed tobacco to help stop the pains of toothaches. Farmer Parker had store-bought uppers, probably no tooth aches.

As soon as Buddy, his border collie, heard him sing out, the dog knew it was time to go to work. He'd jump up from a deep sleep and without so much as a stretch or a yawn, spring off the porch, cross the yard, over the road, up through the opened barbed-wire gate of the side pasture, straight up the steep hill to do what he did every afternoon—bring the cows down for milking.

"Caho bossies!" farmer Parker shouted. "Caho bossies! Caho bossies!"

Looking at the hilltop, we could see heads of cows bob up and down, up and down, from one side to the other for stride and balance, in a gentle motion, as they ambled down the hillside, one behind another. They were Holstein cows, which looked like they had big, black and white jigsaw puzzle pieces on their sides.

Buddy would run from one side of the cows around behind them to the other side, not making a sound, just keeping them moving, pointing them in the right direction, down their well-worn cow path, in no hurry.

"Why don't the cows run from Buddy, farmer Parker?" I asked.

"These are milk cows, son. They aren't beef cattle for stampeding. They're ladies and you can't hurry ladies."

The cows followed the single, dusty, worn cow path twice on most spring and summer days, winding gently down the hill. One behind the other they came, circling around the bushes and trees, down and out through the opened gate.

When the cows stepped onto the road, they were close enough to us to touch and farmer Parker would lower his voice and talk right to them, like he was saying, "Hello ladies, and did you have a good day, today?"

"Ca bosseee," he would say, "ca bosseee."

They walked down the sloping driveway around to the back of the barn and in through opened sliding doors, passing along either side of the green wagon parked in front of the door. The floor of the barn was concrete. There were whitewashed wooden milking stanchions lined up along both sides of the room, ten on each side. Watching, I learned how each cow seemed to know exactly where to go, once inside the barn. All twenty of them walked to their own spot where their milking stanchions were, carefully stepped up on the platform, over the gutter trough, and put their heads through the neck sections where their feed bowls were waiting for them. Farmer Parker would walk in front of each one of them, down a narrow pathway between the inside barn wall and the row of milk stanchions, close the stanchion and flip a bolt, holding it secure, so they couldn't pull their heads back out to leave the barn, until after they were milked.

He'd pour a full scoop of sweet feed in each bowl and move on to the next. Then, one by one, farmer Parker would bring a milking machine to milk them. After he moved the machine to another cow, he would "strip" the previous cow by hand, using a three-legged stool to sit on and a shiny bucket, making certain he got all of the milk. Leaving milk in a cow could be painful for a cow over time. A dusty radio with cobwebs sat high on a shelf, turned on, so his "ladies" could listen to music. Cows were smart, and because of them, we had milk to drink, butter, ice cream, and cheese.

On both sides of the room, just behind the cows, and a step down,
there was a long gutter trough built in the floor, about twelve inches wide and eight inches deep. It went behind the cows, the full length of the milking platform. If a cow had to do number one or number two, it would fall into the trough, behind them. Later, when the cows were let back out of the barn after milking, farmer Parker would shovel all that—they called it manure—into his green manure wagon and take it to the fields, as fertilizer.

As always, I thanked farmer Parker for letting me help bring the cows in, but this time I asked if I could ride with him on his manure wagon sometime.

"The spreader?" farmer Parker asked.

"Is that what you call it?"

"It's a spreader, son."

"Is that anything like when Huckleberry Finn tells his stretchers?"

"Same principle," he chuckled. "It all gets spread around pretty good, that's for sure. If you can be here early in the morning—and I mean early—I'll take you out on it."

"You bet I can," I said.

I waved and left for home.

As I walked toward home, I could see Gourmet Mike's

Chevy driving up the road. He was coming from college, in Syracuse, which was strange. He typically didn't come home, except sometimes on weekends if he needed money, or if he was going to play baseball at the stone quarry on Oran Delphi Road. Maybe this time his roommates couldn't stand smelling his cans and bottles and they threw him out. His Chevy slowed as it turned into our driveway. Walking alongside, I stuck my head in the passenger window.

"Hey. Did you come for some real food?

Mike smiled. "I forgot two books I need. I'm going right back."

There was a large carton on the front seat on the passenger side.

"What's in the box?" I asked.

He reached over, pulled the lid back, and showed me a fluffy white and gray rabbit with floppy ears.

"My professor asked me to take care of it so his daughter wouldn't find out."

"Find out?"

"He had to go to a conference in Albany for a week. He wants it taken care of while he's gone."

"You like college?" I asked.

"Bio-lab experiments are hard," Gourmet Mike said.

"What's a bio-lab?"

"We study living matter; living things."

Suddenly it dawned on me. I'd heard, when they said "experiment" in a biology lab, it meant curtains for an animal they were studying. I knew the older kids at our school studied dead frogs and things like that, because I had seen them on the school bus, in pickle jars—frogs, not kids.

Well, pickled frogs were one thing—at least they always seemed to have a smile on their faces, and at least they came already pickled in a jar. This was a live bunny rabbit that liked its neck scratched when I reached in through the car window. I had to find out what he meant when he said "take care of it so his daughter wouldn't find out about it."

I had to think—fast!

With the best detective questioning technique I could muster, I had to find out what experiments Mike was working on and exactly when the professor was coming back. That's how the Hardy Boys would have done it.

"What experiment are you doing?"

"Reproduction," Mike said.

"Huh?"

"My assignment is to study a male mammal and dissect a specimen. I have a choice of animals."

"Is this rabbit male?"

"Yeah."

Gourmet Mike jumped out of the car and ran into the house.

I scratched the bunny's neck and thought. First off, I didn't know what mammal meant, and second off, I didn't know what a specimen was, so I was totally in the dark, as usual. Nobody ever told me anything. But I did know what dissect meant.

When Mike came out of the house with his two books and got into the car, I asked him what male had to do with it, because I knew it either meant Mr. Johnson, our mailman, or something about being a boy.

"We're studying the male reproductive system."

"Huh?" I asked in a startled voice, confused about what he said. The car edged forward as he lifted his foot from the clutch.

I didn't know if I should run and tell Mom that Gourmet Mike had gone completely nuts now, or just go think about it. It was clear to me that Mike was becoming weirder, being away from home. I think this gourmet fever he had was bringing him to a point of murder. Maybe he had the capers. I needed one more clue. To stop him I needed to know when the professor was coming back.

"How long will you have the rabbit?"

"All week. His daughter can't find out about it."

I shook my head in pity for my brother gone nuts.

"I'll bring it here next Saturday when I come for the book Mom ordered for me, so you can see it and give it a carrot one last time, if you want, before the professor gets back on Sunday. Okay?"

"Yeah, okay," I said.

"After that it'll be too late."

Curtains! I thought. My jaw dropped open in

astonishment with how cold-blooded Gourmet Mike had become.

"Stand back!" he insisted and drove away.

I ran in the house to the book den and pulled the big dictionary down to look up the word "reproductive." Over a bookshelf, I could see Mom in the living room talking with Mrs. Westwood, the fifth-grade teacher.

"How do you spell 'reproductive?'" I shouted, interrupting their conversation with my sense of urgency. There were a few seconds of silence. "Tell me when you have a pencil," Mom shouted—never denying a youth an education of any kind."

"I have a pencil."

"R-E-P-R-O-D-U-C-T-I-V-E," Mom said.

Mom and Mrs. Westwood looked at each other, shrugged their shoulders, and went on drinking their tea and talking. I could hear one of them say, "Heaven only knows."

The dictionary was no help at all. It just said reproduction was stuff about making babies. No help at all. Gourmet Mike's brain was so far gone he obviously didn't know what he was talking about. A male couldn't have a baby, even I knew that.

I ran into Mom and Dad's room, picked up the telephone, and waited for the operator.

"Operator."

"Operator, I need to call Bobby Holbrook."

"Let me get him for you. What's the number?"

"I don't know."

"Oh dear, I would need a number."

"I don't know it."

"Are you an Antil?"

"Yes."

"Which one are you?"

"I'm Jerry."

"Hello, Jerry. I'm Myrtie. Nice to meet you."

"Hello, ma'am."

"Just call me Myrtie, okay?"

"Okay."

"Do you know what road they live on, dear? The Holbrooks?"

"Berry Road. It's like on the way to Tully, I think."

"That's out of my area …"

"Oh."

"But if you give me just a minute, I can call an operator friend of mine in that area and ask around."

"I can wait, thank you."

"I'll be right back, dear."

All I could think about was the floppy ears on the rabbit Gourmet Mike was going to dissect and murder. Myrtie came back on the line.

"Jerry, the Holbrook house doesn't seem to have a telephone. Would you say this is an emergency, hon?"

"Oh yes, for sure, it's life and death."

"My goodness."

"What do I do?"

"Well, let me read some names on Berry Road. Maybe you can recognize one of them and I could connect you so they can get a message to your friend. Wanna try?"

"That would be great."

"Let's try that."

"Thanks, Myrtie."

"How about Smith, do you know the Smiths?"

"No."

"Recognize the name Doxtator?"

"No."

"Do you know the name Paddock?

"Not sure."

"Kellish, how about Kellish?"

"I know a Tommy Kellish. He's in my grade."

"I'll ring them, then. With any luck it's his house and they live close to your Holbrook friend. Good luck, Jerry. I'll listen to see if you connect. If it's not his number, pick up again and we'll try something else."

"Thank you, Myrtie."

"You're welcome sweetheart. Don't be a stranger."

"Hello?"

"Tommy?"

"This is Tommy."

"This is Jerry."

"Oh, hi."

"Do you live near Bobby Holbrook?"

"Yeah, next house up."

"Tommy, can you find out if Holbrook could meet me, somewhere soon, about something important? If he can, would you call me back and tell me? He doesn't have a phone."

"I know," Tommy said.

Then I thought about it.

"No," I said, "better than that, if Holbrook tells you when he can meet me, could you call Barber and tell him, so he can meet with us, too? Then will you ask Barber to call me and tell me when and where to meet? That will all be easier."

"Sure, but it'll have to be later on. I have to drive the tractor over to a neighbor on the other side, who needs to use it tomorrow to pull tree stumps."

"That's okay. That will give me time to look through my Hardy Boys mystery book to see if there are any ideas in it that could help me."

"This sounds serious," Tommy said.

"It's my brother, Gourmet Mike. He's got gourmet fever. It's like he has capers again, I think."

"Poor guy."

"I know. Some kind of reproductive thing he thinks he needs for college. He's going to get it from a rabbit that will get murdered."

"Murder? That is serious," Tommy said.

Neither one of us had any idea what we were talking about.

It was amazing how much I could learn from someone when I used my Hardy Boys, boy detectives, questioning techniques.

Dad brought Dick and Aunt Kate home and walked into the house just as Mom called us to supper. Aunt Kate stayed during the week sometimes. Dick and I sat on one side of the table, Aunt Kate on the other side of the table, with her cane leaning on the arm of her chair. Mom was in the kitchen, getting bowls of food. Dad carried a platter in and sat down at his spot at the head of the table. Mom came in and sat at the other end.

Aunt Kate took forever saying grace, praying to all the saints in heaven who looked over everyone and asked the Lord to bless Dad for driving safely all the way from Cortland, and she asked the Lord to look over Dick. She was friends with the nuns in Cortland that used to teach Dick, so she knew about Dick.

Now we were trained to be gentlemen at the table and a gentleman never started eating until the hostess (this would be my mom at our house) lifted a piece of silverware. Once she lifted it, everyone was on their own. When Aunt Kate was done praying and said, "Amen," Mom blessed herself and lifted her salad fork.

"I saw Mike," I blurted. "He said he's studying reproductive thingies in a bio-something, so he's going to massacre a rabbit in his laboratory to get one—you know—a thingy!"

Mom's fingers fell limp, letting the salad fork fall out of her hand, dropping onto her plate with a clang.

Dad pursed his lips, holding back a grin. He knew enough to just sit back and keep quiet. He watched and waited for it to unfold.

Aunt Kate scooted around in her chair, thinking the clang of the fork meant there might have been hot food spilled.

Dick slowly turned his head sideways, leaned over, tilted it over me, and stared down, like he was looking at me through a microscope in a general science class.

"What in heaven's name are you talking about, Jerry?" Mom asked.

Dick pushed his glasses up over his forehead, resting them on the top of his head like the goggles of a World War I flying ace and continued to stare down at me. I locked eyes with him and stared back up, as if to say, so what if you're older, taller, and smarter, you don't scare me. Staring Dick down, I said to Mom, "Mike told me he needs a reproductive thingy, so he has to murder the rabbit he has before the professor gets back just so his daughter won't find out about it and try to stop him. He wants me to give the rabbit its last carrot, before he—you know."

Mom's eyes glazed over as she stared at Dad, kind of like she was wondering if maybe there was a mix-up of babies at the hospital, as if I wasn't really her child. Not knowing what to say, she closed her eyes and shook her head back and forth a few times, like maybe she could shake this nightmare out of her brain.

Even though I knew he probably couldn't see me without his glasses, Dick was still staring down at me.

"What!?" I yelled up at him.

"You're dumb as a stick, you know that?" Dick asked.

I wasn't going to argue with him, because I had had an exhausting day, and to be quite frank, I was confused with this whole mess. He did have a point.

Mom bristled, set her fork down.

"Richard, come over here, this instant."

Dick flopped his glasses back down, pushed his seat back, stood up, and walked to Mom, never taking his eyes off me, like he was waiting for something to crawl out of my ears.

Mom turned and leaned her face into his.

"What did I teach you about impertinence?"

"You told me to look it up," he answered.

"Apparently you haven't. I suggest you go to your room and look it up—and then have supper, alone, in the kitchen, after you have learned it. March!"

With two fingers, Mom delicately lifted her favorite salad fork again. Her salad fork was one of her few remaining remnants and memories of her past city life in Cortland, the afternoon teas, her bridge clubs, quiet socials—the city life she once enjoyed before we moved in front of a waterfall in the woods.

"Jerry," she said, "when you're older, we'll teach you about animal reproduction. But for now, I am certain you completely misunderstood your brother."

"Oh, I heard him right, all right, Mom," I said.

"Eat your vegetables, dear."

"But he's going to murder a rabbit, Mom," I pleaded.

"Sometimes science has to make sacrifices for medicine, so human lives can be saved," she said.

None of this made any sense to me. The phone rang, which was a good thing.

It was Barber.

"Meet us in the morning at the Delphi cemetery," he said.

"I don't know where that is," I said.

"Get a piece of paper so you can make a map."

I set the phone down, ran into the kitchen, and saw a big piece of butcher paper lying on the counter that once was wrapped around some liverwurst. I grabbed it and ran back to the phone in Mom and Dad's room.

"Ready," I said.

"You have to go through farmer Parker's place."

"Okay."

"Go out behind his barn, down into his back pasture, cross the creek, and go up his back hill to the top."

"Okay."

"Go straight across the big hay field up there, then down the northwest corner of the field."

"I climb down the other side of the hill?"

"Yes. That's where the cemetery is."

"Got it."

"Holbrook and me will be in the cemetery. Draw a good map so you don't get lost."

"I will."

"Northwest will be the farthest corner on the right.

"I got it. Northwest."

"Make it early," he added.

"I'll be there, I promise," I said.

"I have chores to do after I get back home," Barber said.

"I'm riding on farmer Parker's manure spreader in the morning, and I'm pretty sure that will be on top of that hayfield, behind the cemetery," I said.

I put the butcher paper on my bed, went back into the dining room, finished my supper, asked to be excused, pushed my chair in to the table, carried my plate to the kitchen, and headed to my room to set my alarm clock and finish drawing my map.

I stopped in Dick's room and asked him to tell me about the reproduction stuff. He gave me a look, trying to remember how old I was, and told me Mom would pound him if he did, so I should just go to bed.

It was still dark when the alarm clock rang. I sat up in bed, looked out my window to see farmer Parker's house lights already on across the way. I dressed quickly, folding the map down so it fit in my back pocket. In the kitchen I ate some shredded wheat in the dark. I hated the taste, but I liked reading the Indian stories on the divider cards in the box. Stories like what to do on the trail by your campfire, so you won't get bitten by rattlesnakes while you slept.

I left the house and walked through the gate over to farmer Parker's. The barn lights were on, so I went down to it. I could see my breath in the morning air. Inside the barn, Buddy was curled up on a workbench, asleep. The radio was playing music and early morning farm reports. Farmer Parker was busy milking. He lifted his head to say hello. Every time he "stripped" a cow, by hand, filling a shiny bucket with the last of her milk, he'd pour it through a cloth filter into big milk cans. The filter he poured it through was to catch flies or anything that might have gotten into the bucket by accident. When the cans were full, he'd stomp a lid down on the top of them and put them outside, on a rack, to wait for Mr. Vaas to come by in his truck and haul them to the dairy.

The lids were curved down at the sides, wider than the neck of the big milk can. This way they acted like an umbrella and would keep the rain out of the milk.

While he was busy milking, I walked through the opening of the two big sliding doors that led out to where the spreader was sitting, to take my first look at it, close up.

It was a green, wooden wagon with short sides, built like a long box, on four tall, metal wheels with long metal spokes. At the back of the wagon was a swirly looking, egg-beater-like wheel that had long, pitchfork prongs attached to it. I imagined the swirly wheel going around and around, the wire forks catching hold of the manure as it slid back on the chain belt I could see on the floor of the box. The chain belt probably moved when the wheels went around. Then the swirly wheels would spike the manure, pitch it out the back, and off the wagon onto the field he was fertilizing. Two large workhorses, Sarge and Sally, were already hitched up to the wagon, waiting. I rubbed their soft velvety noses, said good morning to them, one at a time. I could see their breath in the cold morning air. Farmer Parker had told me once that he was going to keep his horses as long as they were able to do the work, and then get himself a Ford tractor. He said Sarge and Sally could practically run the farm without him. I wasn't sure what happened next, so I decided to watch and learn, like my dad would tell me. I went back inside the barn where it was warmer, sliding the doors closed behind me.

Farmer Parker was hosing off milking equipment, putting

it away.

He asked if I wanted to help.

"You bet," I said.

"Go up the drive, cross the road, open the side hill gate wide. It's the same one as last night. Make sure to pull it all the way back, so the ladies don't step on the barbed wire and spook. I'll let them out when you're ready."

I ran outside, up the drive, crossed the road over to the fence gate, and did just what he said. I could hear the barn doors slide open, saw the bright yellow light from inside light up the dark ground behind the barn where the horses and the manure spreader were standing. All twenty cows, and the heifer following them, started coming out slowly, around the barn, around the spreader, up the drive toward me. Their heads were bouncing up and down, up and down, this way and that way, up and down.

They crossed over the road, right in front of me, and I talked to them. "Ca bosseees, ca bosseees, ca bosseees"—just like I'd heard farmer Parker say a million times.

They looked friendly enough. I could see them watching me as they went by, and I imagined they were talking to each other.

*I don't remember seeing you at the gate before, young man.*

*That's the Antil boy from across the way—my, how he's grown.*

They didn't stop, or even slow down. All they wanted was to stretch their legs, climb the hill, and graze in a nice sunny green pasture all day.

"Ca bosseees, ca bosseees," I said.

I just liked saying it.

"Is that all of them?" I shouted to farmer Parker.

"Lock her up," he answered.

I closed the wire gate, making sure I did it good. Buddy was standing there waiting for me, and together we walked back down to the barn with him wagging his tail. Farmer Parker already had the spreader backed all the way into the barn and was shoveling manure into it. He would shovel it into the wagon from the gutter trough on both sides for the length of the spreader. Then he would say, "Pull up, Sarge!" and the horses would start to move forward, until he shouted, "Whoa, Sarge!" and they would stop. He would shovel some more from both sides and repeat the process.

By the time he finished shoveling the manure into the wagon it was outside again, the manure steaming in the cold morning air. The gutters behind the milking stanchions inside were empty. He hung the shovel on two pegs on the wall and told me to jump up on the wagon and sit on the footrest. There was only one seat, in the middle of the front part of the wagon—where he would sit. The footrest below the front seat was the width of the wagon—like a bench—so I fit on it, hanging my legs off with room to spare. He closed the barn doors, climbed up into the driver's seat, untied the leather reins from a handle on the front of the wagon, and said, "Giddyap, Sarge, let's go!"

The leather, buckles, and chains of the halters, collars, and gear the horses wore creaked and jingled as they leaned forward to get the wheels rolling. They started walking on farmer Parker's command, pulling us around behind the barn, across the driveway toward the gate of the rear pasture. The cows by now were near the top of the side pasture and wouldn't need tending until milking time that night. Farmer Parker had me jump off and open the back gate so he could pull the wagon through.

Riding the wagon down the dirt wagon tracks in farmer Parker's back pasture was like being in a cowboy movie riding on a buckboard. The occasional snorting of the horses, the twirling of their ears with each step, the sounds of hooves, leather harnesses, and chains seemed to make the simple wagon come to life. We crossed the small creek over a small wooden bridge.

Clunk, clunk, clunk, clunk, clunk.

With snorts and heaves, Sarge and Sally pulled us up the tall, long back hill, higher and higher, until we were at the top. A level hay field lay in front of us. I looked around at the manure on the wagon; steam billowing off it in the brisk morning air. We were now on top of the highest hill in the Pompey Hollow area. Way down behind us in the distance I could see farmer Parker's house and barn. Across the road from it was my house, the waterfalls with the cliffs and woods on both sides.

When we got inside the gate the horses seemed to know where to go. They pulled the wagon across the hay field toward the place he wanted to start spreading manure. I could tell what part of the field had already been fertilized and what part hadn't. Each day, farmer Parker would start where he had left off the day before. Eventually all the field would be fertilized.

I remembered I had to ask him some directions.

I took the big folded piece of butcher paper out of my pocket, unfolded it until it covered my lap and then some. It was the map I'd drawn with a black crayon the night before when Barber told me where the Delphi cemetery was for our meeting. I spread it on my knees to get the creases out best I could. Then I raised it up proudly and asked farmer Parker to tell me where on the map I had to go to meet the boys, after we were done spreading. He pulled on the reins, told Sarge and Sally to turn. The wagon started to line up with the area he wanted to fertilize. When we got over the exact spot, he pulled back on the metal lever he was resting his left arm on. The chain belt on the floor of the wagon started to turn and make noise. The load inched its way, shifting backward slowly. The swirly, spiked wheels at the back of the wagon began to spin like spiked propellers and tossed the manure it caught in the forks way up in the air and all around the field behind us.

He pointed across the field. "See that sugar maple, over yonder, the big one?"

"The tall fat tree?" I asked.

"That's it, right next to that four-year-old elm?"

"Yes," I said. "I see it."

"Go between them, then down to the bottom of the hill. You will be in the cemetery, right where you want to be."

I was about to tell him thanks, when a gust of wind blew under and up from the ground and jerked the map out of my hands. It sailed way up into the air in big circles, like a kite out of control— like a tornado I saw in a library book at school. It flew away, high in the air and then behind us.

All of a sudden this map that held the directions to what would surely become a legendary first meeting at the Delphi cemetery—a map that only yesterday had been wrapped around liverwurst for Saturday's lunch sandwiches—became more valuable to me than the only map to the Lost Treasures of the Incas.

I jumped off the wagon and started around the side to go

get it.

"I wouldn't be doing that," farmer Parker said, but I couldn't hear him. I ran blindly out and behind the manure spreader, jumping up in the air time after time, trying to catch my treasure map, grabbed it with one hand and—

*Splat-split-plat-slap-splat-splat-split-plat-slap-splat-splat-split-plat-slap- splat-splat-split-plat-slap-splat—*

Pieces of smelly soggy manure, every size, shape, coloration, hit me all over my head and body like it was shooting out of a machine gun from a Saturday morning gangster movie.

Every inch of the front of my body, my face, my arms, and my head

was riddled with cow dung, and more was coming at me every second I stood there.

I couldn't move. My arms were stuck out like I was a frozen scarecrow. I was covered from head to toe with manure splotches—hot, wet, stinky, steamy cow manure splotches. Steam vapors rolled off my t-shirt. Farmer Parker had leaned on his side looking around at me and shaking his head, like he tried to warn me, but the wagon was still moving. It was almost empty now, and if no one is injured a farmer doesn't stop until a load is empty— or full, depending on the nature of the chore. Wagons were meant for loading or unloading. Nothing on a farm was about play. It was all about work. It was about getting things done and moving on to the next chore, while daylight and the weather held. My foolishness didn't stop the task at hand. I wasn't hurt, so the spreader kept rolling.

I wiped what gunk I could off my face with my map, out of my hair with my hands and the front of my t-shirt. By now the manure wagon was empty. Farmer Parker stopped, pushed the lever forward, tied the reins to it, jumped off, and handed me his bandanna kerchief to wipe my face.

"You need you a tub," he said. With his glove he brushed big globs off my t-shirt and jeans as best he could.

Without moving my lips or opening my mouth any more than I had to, I thanked him for the ride and walked across the field toward the maple and elm trees he pointed out, shaking a leg now and then like a cat with a wet paw. I was on my way to meet up with Holbrook and Barber for the first time ever in the Delphi

Cemetery. Farmer Parker watched me walk away.

I climbed through the fence and went down the hill. Holbrook, Barber, and Mary were waiting by the tombstones. I was surprised to see Mary. "Holbrook didn't have a ride," Mary said.

"He didn't?" I mumbled, not opening my mouth.

"Tommy Kellish telephoned and asked if my dad could drive him so I rode along, too," Mary said.

"Thanks," I said.

"So, is that okay that I came?"

I nodded yes.

Holbrook came around from the back side of a tree. Seeing me all splotched up his eyes bugged out and he yelled, "What happened to you?"

I wouldn't open my mouth any more than talking through my teeth.

"Stay away from me!" Holbrook spouted. "You look like an outhouse!"

He started laughing, doubling over and holding his sides.

"I know exactly what happened," Barber said. "He got himself caught at the wrong end—the working end of a 'honey wagon'—and it got the best of him."

I was trying not to talk until I could splash water on my face.

I heard people talking about honey wagons—now I knew for sure what it meant.

"I need a hose," I said through clenched teeth.

"Let's go into Delphi," Barber said. "We'll find a hose and a place we can talk there."

While walking into the hamlet, Holbrook was careful not to let any of the manure splotches rub off on him. He'd walk on the other side of the road or several feet in front of us, stepping backward so we could talk.

"Don't worry, it happened to me once. I learned my lesson," Barber said.

"What was the lesson?" I asked.

"Stay on the wagon until you're sure it's empty."

"Oh—right," I said.

Walking through the hamlet we saw Bases, the Mawson kid.

Everybody called him "Bases" because you'd never see him without a baseball glove on his hand. He even wore a glove while he ate. Bases sat tilted back in a porch chair waiting for a ride to a sandlot baseball game he was playing in. He had his spikes on, leaning his short legs up over the rail, his chair rocking in its balance. He was throwing his ball into his glove hand with noisy slaps, like he was either trying to keep busy before his ride came or break in his glove, except the glove was older than he was and everyone knew that no matter how busy you were, time had its own notion of standing still in Delphi. At first sight of the manure mess I was in, he did a double take, and his next throw missed his glove, and the ball flew over the porch railing, bounced in the grass. The chair legs slipped out from under him like stilts on ice. Rolling in laughter and holding his stomach and gasping for breath, he pointed at the garden hose by the porch, motioning approval to use it. He finally stopped laughing enough to sit up on the stoop and watch Barber hose me down. I took off my T-shirt, wrung it out and put it back on. My teeth were chattering. I was standing there shivering, but at least I didn't smell like the working end of a honey wagon any longer. Mary walked over to the sidewalk, picked up the baseball, walked back, and handed it to Bases. We all sat on the porch steps. I told them about Gourmet Mike and the rabbit, and what he was going to do to it. I told them we needed to save the rabbit so Mike wouldn't have to get arrested or go to an insane asylum or anything like that.

They all agreed, we couldn't let that happen. "You guys need a plan," Bases said.

"That's why we're meeting," Barber said.

"What would Dick Tracy or the Phantom or any of the 'Sunday funnies' detective guys do in a case like this?" Bases asked.

"The Hardy Boys would hide the rabbit and stall for time to think," I said.

Mary looked down at the floor of the porch in thought. "A rabbit needs food and water," she said.

"A rabbit just can't be hidden all that easy," Barber said.

"They could chew their way through a cardboard box," Holbrook said.

"Where can you hide it?" Bases asked.

I jumped up. "I've got it!"

"What?" Barber asked.

"Dick just built a tree house on the side hill in a big tree Gourmet Mike doesn't know about. No one will ever think of it."

Pointing at me with his baseball, Bases asked, "Where's the tree house?"

I looked up at him, gathered my thoughts.

"If someone didn't want to be seen, they should come down the ridge on top of farmer Parker's south pasture hill and follow the path from his corner fence down into our woods. They wouldn't miss it. It's not far from our house but so steep up the hill no one can see it from the house."

Dropping his glove and baseball on the porch Bases interrupted. "Hold on a second. I've got an idea—I'll be right back out." He ran into the house, letting the screen door slam.

Holbrook stood up quickly, pinching his T-shirt with his finger and thumb like he was holding a teacup. He pulled the cotton shirt away from his stomach.

"EWWWWW, I got some of it on me! Get it off! Get it off!"

Barber and Mary looked at him like, *aren't you the same guy who made fun of Jerry for the past half hour and wouldn't come close because he was covered with it?*

Bases burst out of the house, picked up his baseball and glove, letting the screen door slam again just a split second after his mom shouted at him not to slam the door.

"Okay," he said. "I've solved your problem, but you're all on your own. I've got a game to go to."

"What'd you solve?" I asked.

He pointed to a car turning onto Main Street.

"That's my ride coming."

We all got serious, leaned in and listened. We didn't say a word. We just listened.

"I just telephoned Paul Shaffer," Bases said. "He is in your brother Dick's grade, Jerry. He lives on your road down by Don Chubb's place."

"I know Paul," I answered.

"Paul raises prize rabbits to show at the state fair. I told him how to get to the tree house using the ridge. He said he'd go there now and leave a carrying cage in Dick's treehouse as soon as we hung up."

"So how do I get the rabbit?" I asked.

"When your brother, Gourmet Mike, comes back, you have to figure a way to get the rabbit from him. Take it to the tree house, put it in the cage, and then call Paul Shaffer to come get it."

"You'll have to figure a way to distract your brother," Mary said.

"No one will know where the rabbit went or what happened to it," Bases said. "His telephone is New Woodstock 37. But if you forget it, Myrtie, the operator, will know it."

This was perfect. We felt like we'd accomplished something, maybe saved a rabbit from being murdered. Mary told Holbrook her dad could take them home. She asked Bases if she could use the telephone. We split up. Barber started walking the mile to his house, down Oran Delphi Road. I started walking the mile toward mine, down Delphi Falls Road. Holbrook took his T-shirt off, hosed the spots off the front of it, while waiting for Mary's dad.

There was nothing better than best friends.

## CHAPTER FIVE
## BUNNY MAGNATE

When Gourmet Mike came home, I was hiding inside the barn garage, out of sight. I could see him drive toward the house and park and pull the car's emergency brake. My knees began to shake, but I stayed quiet. He got out of his car and walked into the house. I saw that he had nothing in his hands, so I ran, as fast as I could, to the car, grabbed the rabbit from the box on the front seat, closed the lid back down and bolted up the side hill into the woods. Just as promised, there was a rabbit carrying cage in Dick's tree house. Paul Shaffer must have found it easy. I left the rabbit in it and closed the door latch. Then I hurried back down the hill to the house and sat on the front porch, trying to catch my breath, waiting for all hell to break loose when Gourmet Mike comes out of the house to let me see the doomed rabbit the last time.

He finally came out, pulling the green sprig from a red radish he found in the icebox. He tossed the sprig to the ground, popped the whole radish in his mouth, chewing with his mouth open with crunching sounds. He motioned a "hey" to me and walked over to his car and started opening the passenger door to get the rabbit.

"Want to pet the bunny one last time?" he asked. "Give it a carrot?"

It was all I could do not to give Gourmet Mike a piece of my mind, but I relied on the Hardy Boys detective calm in the face of danger.

"I already gave him one," I lied with a blurt.

"Oh?"

With that Gourmet Mike pushed the car door closed, chewing his radish.

I remembered what Mary told me—I needed a diversion. I had to think fast, and I was shaking at the knees because Gourmet Mike was big, six-feet-six inches tall, and could pulverize me if he wanted to. I had to somehow keep him from looking in the box for the rabbit.

"Want an omelet?" I stuttered.

I didn't even know what an omelet was but I heard him onetime saying he cooked omelets. Probably murdered them, too. In another stroke of diversionary brilliance, I repeated, "I already gave the rabbit a carrot."

He swallowed the radish, savored its rank with a burp and smiled.

"Any eggs in the house? Let's go make some omelets."

I went in with him—in part to celebrate my victory of hiding the rabbit and in part because I was hungry. I didn't know what an omelet was, but I knew what eggs were and they weren't rabbit or some stinky cheese or frog, so I said okay. You have to keep an eye on gourmet guys—watch them real close. I was nervous the whole time we sat and I ate the omelet, which, except for the green pepper, wasn't all that bad. Mike said he had to make a telephone call, so I waited for him to do that and leave. After he was out the door, I picked up the telephone and asked Myrtie for New Woodstock 37 and told Paul Shaffer he could come on and get the rabbit.

I headed out the back door and up the side hill to Dick's tree house. He'd built it in the tree up off the ground, without a ladder attached or even climbing sticks nailed into the tree. You had to jump up and grab onto a board. Dick said that would make it harder for enemies to get into it. I think he just ran out of wood or nails or met a girl or had some other distraction. That happens to really smart people. The neat part about the tree house was that he'd built it in one of the few trees that leaned out over the side of the hill, about forty feet above the ground below. If you could get in it, you could look down at the house, the barn garage, driveway, and everything. I watched Gourmet Mike back his car around and drive out through the gate and down Cardner Road.

This time I really gave the rabbit a carrot and the two pieces of lettuce I had in my pocket and we waited for Paul Shaffer.

It wasn't long before I heard him coming over the ridge, down the hill and into the woods. He was blowing on his harmonica. He wasn't playing it loud enough to give him away—

just loud enough to pass the time, while walking through the woods. Different boys had different superstitions about the woods, ways of walking through it alone. I know—I was almost just getting used to the woods myself. My mom kept telling me there were no dinosaurs up there, but I sure kept finding a lot of fossils near the bottom of the falls. When he got outside the tree house, he put the harmonica in his pocket, jumped up, grabbed onto the board, and pulled himself in.

"Hey," I said.

"Hey," he said.

"Gourmet Mike is gone, but he always forgets books or something, so there's no telling if he'll turn around and come back," I said.

"I'll take it back up through the woods, then," Paul said, "instead of on Cardner Road."

"Can I come with you?"

"C'mon."

Paul climbed down from the tree house. I handed the carrying cage down to him, then climbed down myself. We started up the hill, through the woods toward farmer Parker's side hill pasture up to the ridge. When we would get to a barbed-wire fence I'd hold the cage, put my foot on the lowest wire and hold it down while I pulled up on the next wire above. This left a gap big enough for Paul to crawl through. Paul would climb through it. I'd hand him the cage over the fence and then he'd hold the wires for me. Kids in the country learned how to do these things for each other. A barbed-wire fence wouldn't slow us down. We knew a ripped shirt or a torn pantleg, caused by barbed wire were good for a certain lecture on the cost of clothes and on trespassing.

As we walked, Paul told me how he was getting his doe rabbits ready for the State Fair Livestock Competition in September. He had all spring and summer to get them to the right weight and coat. Easter was just a month or so away.

Paul loved his rabbits and had blue ribbons over the inside wall of his garage.

None of the talk about doe rabbits made any sense to me. I figured he liked making dough—as in money, not bread.

It was no time before we were walking along the top ridge,

above where all the cows were grazing. Looking down, I could see Doc Webb's place. Doc Webb was a dentist. Paul blew "Oh Susannah" on his harmonica while we walked. We passed the back of the Don Chubb's place and got to the ridge behind Paul's house. We climbed down from the ridge and walked into his back yard to the garage. Attached to the outside wall of the garage, about five feet off the ground, were three rabbit hutches with chicken wire on the sides and screen wire on the floors. One big cage had four beautiful, floppy-eared gray rabbits that looked alike. He called them his prize doe rabbits. Two other cages were smaller. One had a rabbit in it that looked just like the other four in the big cage. One cage was empty. When I pointed to the lone rabbit, Paul said it was his "buck" rabbit.

I wasn't sure what that meant—like was it for sale for a buck? "Buck" and "Doe"—I never knew he liked money so much. You couldn't tell it by listening to him play his harmonica, and he sure never told my brother Dick about it. Sometimes you just can't figure out older guys at all. Who would have ever thought my own brother, Gourmet Mike, could think of murdering something or be a gourmet for that matter—all the while going off to college, and right under everyone's noses, pretending he wanted to be a doctor?

I was a guest at his house, and Paul was doing me a big favor, so I wasn't going to be rude and ask him why the one rabbit, "Buck," was all alone and all the "doe" rabbits were in the other cage playing together and having all the fun.

"Want to see a picture with my ribbon in the paper from last year?" Paul asked.

"Sure."

He jumped on the porch and ran into the house to find it.

Just then my dad drove up and blew a quick honk on his horn. He rolled down his window.

"Hop in, son—I'll give you a ride home."

I jumped onto the porch, saw Mrs. Shaffer through the screen.

"Mrs. Shaffer, would you tell Paul that my Dad's here? I have to go."

"I will, honey. You run along and say hello to your mom for me."

"Yes, ma'am." I jumped off the porch and hopped in Dad's car. Just as I was about to close the door I yelled.

"Wait!"

I remembered we forgot to put the professor's rabbit Gourmet Mike wanted to murder in the cage. It was still in the carrying case on the ground where animals—foxes—might get to it. I ran over, reached in, and took the rabbit out of the carrying case. I looked at the empty cage next to "Buck," then at the cage where all the doe rabbits were playing. I decided their cage would be more fun for the professor's rabbit. He wasn't in trouble, like Buck, and needed to meet some new friends now that he's been saved. He had just lived through enough problems. I opened the cage, put him in with his four new friends, closed the door, and hooked the latch. I felt good when my rabbit looked up at me, almost like it was thanking me for saving its life.

"Bye, and behave," I said.

I ran back, jumped into Dad's car, and we drove off. "How'd you find me?" I asked.

"Myrtie," he said.

"How would a telephone operator know where I was?"

"Simple. I picked up the phone, asked her if she knew where my brood was, and she told me. She said Mike was probably on his way to see Nancy, his girlfriend, in Syracuse. Dick was probably with Duba in the school village, and you were most likely at Paul Shaffer's house."

"How would Myrtie know all that?"

"Did Mike come home?"

"Yes."

"Did he use the telephone?"

"Yes. He made omelets and then used the telephone."

"Did you call Paul Shaffer's telephone today?

"Yes."

"Well, there you go—and Dick probably talked to Duba this morning. Now hop out and see if there is any mail in the mailbox, son."

I was amazed at how smart my dad was—and now, at how much Myrtie knew about everyone. I remembered how she found a way to get a message to Holbrook's house for me. Myrtie could maybe help the Hardy Boys and my detective work, I thought.

I retrieved the mail, and Dad drove in the driveway and around back of the swings, where he always parked.

Inside the house, Dick, Duba, and their two friends Jimmy Conway and Jimmy Dwyer were playing Pitch, the high, low, Jack and game card game. It looked like Duba was winning. He had the most pennies in front of him.

"Dick or Jerry, one of you let me know who wants to get up early and help me sample Brewerton before the sun comes up," Dad said.

He walked down the hall toward his and Mom's bedroom.

Every once in a while, Dad would drive and meet a bakery truck in some town and hang a loaf of bread on everyone's door so people could see how good the bread was. Sometimes Dick or Gourmet Mike went with him. I never had yet.

"What's trump?" Dick asked.

"Hearts," Duba said.

"We're going to Suburban Park in Manlius when Mr. Duba picks us up," Dick said, "You go with Dad."

When Dad came back in, I told him I was going with him.

"Great," he said. "We'll stop on the way home for some fishing at DeRuyter Lake."

After supper Dad told me to get right to bed because three in the morning came early.

And it did.

"Psssssssst! Psssssssssssssssst!" Dad said in a low whisper.

"I'm up, I'm up," I said.

I had slept in my clothes, so I got up, put my sneakers on fast and went outside to Dad's car. He was putting fishing poles in the trunk.

"Hop in the back seat and get some sleep, son. I'll wake you when we get to Brewerton."

I asked him what we were going to do.

"Every now and then it's a good idea to advertise a product by letting families have a free sample of it."

"You give it away free, Dad?"

"That lets them try it to see if they like it."

"So, is that what advertising is?" I asked.

"Sometimes," he said. "Advertising is getting the word out about your product to a lot of people. The more people who know about it, the more product you will sell—even if only a small number of those people buy it. It's all in the numbers. Sometimes commercials on the radio let everyone know about it. Sometimes ads in the newspaper let them know. Sometimes it's giving away samples, like we're going to do today. Today we are going to hang a fresh warm loaf of bread on over a hundred doors in Brewerton right before people get up for breakfast; before they open the front door to get the morning paper off their porch or lawn. When they do, they'll see our bread. Maybe they'll try it for breakfast. If only twenty percent like the nice warm loaf of bread that could be twenty new bread customers. Maybe more. It's the numbers, son."

"How do we hang the loaf on the door, Dad?"

Dad slowed down, pulled off the road, came to a stop, and got out. Dad loved talking about business to anyone who was interested. He always said that every good question deserved a good answer. That's how we learn, he would say. He opened the trunk, pulled something out, and slammed it back down. He got in, reached over the seat and handed me a chipboard paper Indian headdress, which had colorful printed feathers all around it.

"With these," he said.

He pulled the car back onto the road and started driving. I crawled over the seat to the front, holding the Indian headdress. I tried it on. It went around my head, with cut-out chipboard feathers sticking up all around it. It looked almost real.

"Kids will like these," I told him.

The head bonnet had the name of the bakery on the front. It

stayed on your head by attaching the two holes in the end of it like a

lock.

"We'll put the bread in the middle of the head bonnet and the same ones that hold it on your head—will also fit right over a doorknob and hold a loaf of bread."

"How?" I asked.

Dad held his hand up like an Indian chief's sign of coming in peace.

"How?" I asked.

Dad held his hand up like an Indian chief's sign of coming in peace.

"How to you, too," Dad said, and we both laughed.

"We'll use three headdresses for every house so it will be stronger, hanging on the door. If they have more kids, each will get one that way. It's the numbers, son."

Dad was nice like that.

The bakery truck was waiting for us, and it followed us around the town. I would run up to every door and hang the headdresses with the loaf of bread on the doorknob. When I got back to the car, Dad would hand me another three headdresses and a loaf of bread, all ready to hang. If I could see any clue that the house had more than three kids living there, I would leave five or six headdresses around the bread.

When we were done, Dad turned the car around to head back home. Driving through town, near dawn, we could see kids already wearing the Indian headdresses.

"New customers?" I asked Dad, pointing to the kids.

"Their moms are happy new customers," Dad said.

My dad was smart. I had just learned how to advertise. We headed to DeRuyter Lake.

I was amazed by my dad. While we caught sunfish and perch, I kept asking him questions about advertising. He would always say the same thing, "It's the numbers, son. The more people you can tell about your product or service the more people will buy."

We packed the fishing gear up and headed for home. As we drove in through the gate, we could see Gourmet Mike's Chevy.

"What's he doing here?" I asked.

Dad didn't say anything. Mike was sitting on one of the swings. He looked upset. We found out my mom had called him and made him come home from college for an emergency family meeting. As we drove in Dick was walking out of the house carrying an encyclopedia book. Dad drove around behind the swings and parked.

"Now you've done it," Dick barked.

"Done what?" I asked.

"I don't know," he said.

"You're nuts," I said.

"Mom is on the phone with Mrs. Shaffer," Dick said.

"So?" I grunted.

"I think you've had it."

We went in the house to the kitchen. My heart was pounding because I probably was going to get stomped for stealing Gourmet Mike's rabbit. We waited for Mom to get off the phone. Mike sat up on the kitchen counter, grabbed grapes from a bowl, and waited. Mom came out of the bedroom, through the dining room into the kitchen with her hand to the side of her face, like people do when they have a toothache.

She stopped, caught Gourmet Mike's eye, reflected, turned around, and looked at me like maybe I should be in jail or reform school.

"Young man, just where did you get the rabbit you took over to the

Shaffer's house?"

I knew she knew.

"I couldn't let it get murdered, Mom."

Mom turned and looked at Mike again. The confession came easier than they both anticipated. Then Mom and Dad looked at each other for the punishment phase.

I didn't care, murder was wrong, they both knew it—even the president said that.

"Jerry, the rabbit you took from Mike was an Easter present for Mike's professor's daughter."

"What!?"

"Your brother was watching it for him while he was traveling so she wouldn't find out about it and spoil the surprise."

"Huh?"

"That bunny rabbit was meant to be an Easter surprise."

"I'm sorry. I'll go get it back," I said.

"Young man," Mom said, "it seems you put a buck rabbit

in with the Shaffer's breeder does, and now there is a slight problem."

My jaw dropped.

"What problem?"

I stared up at Mom; I looked over at Mike; I looked up at Dad. I looked around at Dick, who kept jerking his head toward the back door— motioning for me to take off as fast as I could and run away while I still had the chance.

Standing there, with the encyclopedia book open in his hand, Dick interrupted like he was Ben Franklin or someone.

"Rabbits have a gestation period of four weeks, can have litters of as many as eight to twelve rabbits when they birth," he read proudly and then stared at me, jerking his head again, like if I was ever going to run away from home, he'd cover the door for me, but now would be the perfect time.

He wasn't a buck rabbit," I declared confidently. "He never got in trouble of any kind."

Dad belched a short giggle, kind of smirked, but Mom twisted her eyebrows like a horsewhip and gave him a stern look, to be serious.

"Jerry, when a rabbit is a boy, they call it a buck, and when a rabbit is a girl, they call it a doe."

"Uh-uh. Nah—no way. That's deer," I insisted.

"*And* rabbits!" Dick barked, pointing to a section in the encyclopedia.

"Jerry," Mom asked, "do you have any idea, at all, of how babies are made?"

Dick raised his hand, started hopping up and down as though he was in school, wanting to be called on. Dad made a fist, and with his middle knuckle gently knocked on the top of Dick's head, a couple of times, as fair warning to shut his mouth, unless spoken to. Gourmet Mike just stared down at me.

"Yes, I said confidently. "People get married."

"Well, that bunny you stole just got married four times, and four times eight is thirty-two baby bunnies—or, times twelve, is forty-eight baby bunnies in four weeks," Dick blurted in one long breath.

"Is that true, Mom?" I asked.

"Yes, dear, I'm afraid so."

My shoulders slumped.

"What you need to know is that rabbits are livestock."

"Are they going to kill them, Mom?"

"Jerry, the Shaffers will likely sell them as livestock."

"Then somebody' else will kill them," Dick said.

"Son, if you want to save these bunnies from being sold, for meat or fur, you will have to think of some way to place them in homes where they can be pets."

"Want me to look up livestock?" Dick offered. Dad gave him another knuckle knock on top of his head.

"How long did he say?" I asked, looking up at my mom.

"Four weeks!" Dick said, slamming the encyclopedia closed with a pop.

Everyone stood there without saying a word, staring at me. Then Dick added, "Oh yeah, baby rabbits are called kittens."

Dad took the encyclopedia book away from him.

Mom leaned over with a stern look in her eye, to drive home her disappointment. "Young man, you owe your brother Mike an apology. Unless you can retrieve it, you owe his professor the cost of the rabbit that was to be a gift to his daughter. You owe Mrs. Shaffer for its care and feeding, and you owe a promise that you will take the litters off their hands, when they come, if you don't want them to become livestock. Do you understand me?"

My mind reeled and went blank.

Rabbits-bunnies-kittens! I was a wreck. My whole day flashed through my head. I got up at three in the morning. I put chipboard headdresses and loaves of bread on every door in Brewerton and caught four sunfish all before anyone here in the kitchen ever even woke up this morning. How could I have possibly gotten into so much trouble in that amount of time?

I closed my eyes, slapped the palm of my hand on my forehead—*splat!* Dick's idea of my running away was probably the only way out of this mess. I turned around in a daze, not even feeling the slap on my forehead, walked from the kitchen through the laundry room, out the back door, and up the steep side hill into the woods to run away. Maybe Dick was right.

Gourmet Mike got off the counter and followed me. I could see him out of the corner of my eye as I began climbing the hill.

"Wait up," he shouted.

He probably wanted to beat me up for losing his professor's rabbit, the Easter present for his daughter. I pretended I didn't see or hear him.

"Wait up," he shouted again.

I didn't have any idea where I was going, but somehow knowing he was following me made me a little braver. I went higher and deeper into the woods, up over the first falls, then over the second falls where I had never been before. I came to a clearing where there was a fence for a pasture. I got through the fence, trying to hold the wires from tearing my shirt. Then I turned around, looked Mike in the eye, and held the wires for him, admitting I knew he was with me. He didn't talk but crawled through.

We walked the field toward a tall, fat apple tree in the center. We were both startled to see two large Belgian workhorses standing under it. We stopped, sat down on the ground and watched the horses. They were twice the size of farmer Parker's Sarge and Sally. The leaves on the apple tree started to bend in the wind, which was gusting. The horse's manes blowing in the wind. The clouds started to darken and roll. The sky was clouding, moving, the wind started blowing the trees everywhere.

"This is the Pettacabbage place," Mike said. "The Pettacabbage family came here from Europe, where they lost their farm because of bombs during the war. They're really good farmers. Those are their Belgian workhorses. They're big, but they won't hurt us."

"Wouldn't matter," I grunted. "My life is over, anyway. Like a stupido I think I rescued one rabbit from you, and now thirty-two or more might get murdered because I'm such a lame brain."

Like a giant axe, the bolt of lightning shot straight down, through the clouds, ripping the top limb from the apple tree with one swipe. The horses bucked up and galloped off to a covered shed on the far end of the pasture.

Mike pushed me to the ground and plopped down next to me.

"Stay low on the ground!" he shouted. "Lightning strikes the tallest things in an area, and we'll be safe on the ground, until it blows over."

I peered up and watched the big top tree limb, still attached by a thin piece of bark, flapping and bouncing up and down on the ground in the wind. I began to trust Mike knew what to do. It felt just like we were in the movie newsreels of the war, waiting for the bombs to drop out of airplanes on us.

Lowering his head to the ground, Mike said, "When I was your age, I did things I thought were right but wound up to be dumb and embarrassing. Don't worry about it."

"You did?"

"A lot," Mike said.

"Like what?"

"I'll have to think. I'm sure I did some really stupid things. You did what you thought was right. You're still my brother, always will be my brother. Don't worry about it. Running away is never an answer."

Sometime just before the rain started, I got so tired from being up so early in the morning and from climbing the hill that, lying next to Mike now, I fell asleep.

When I woke, he was already sitting up. We were both drenched. The storm had passed, but it was late. The sky was getting dark. The ground was soaking wet. It must have rained a lot while we slept. We both knew that, to get home, we would have to climb back down the hill and past two seventy-foot waterfalls.

"Some storm. Feeling better?" Mike asked.

"Yeah."

"Let's go home, okay?"

"Okay."

We got up and started toward the fence we would have to crawl through, to go home. I held the wires for Mike, and then he held them for me. As we started down into the woods, above the second waterfall, Mike stopped and turned. His face was all serious, like we might be in danger. He warned me to be careful, as the ground was wet, real muddy, and very slippery.

We walked a little way further.

Then he stopped and turned around. Now I was getting scared!

"Okay, here's the deal," he said. "We have to climb down, right at the edge of both the upper second falls and the lower first falls. They have high, dangerous cliffs, tons of water flowing after a storm. I'm going to have to carry you on my back. But before I can do that, you need to know, I will need both my hands free, to grab onto trees and limbs, to keep us steady from falling and sliding down over the cliffs. It'll be up to you to hang on, stay on my back without any help from me. Can you do that?"

"Yes."

"Are you sure?"

"I'm sure."

I wasn't as afraid now, because I trusted Mike.

"Okay, then—get on my back, and don't let go until we're on the

ground by the back door of the house, okay?"

"Yes."

Mike bent down on a knee. I piggybacked on him, wrapping my arms around his neck, clenching my hands together. When he stood up, my legs just fit around him. I locked my feet in front of him. Mike leaned forward to keep his balance and stepped carefully, like Hawkeye from *The Last of the Mohicans.* He would grab hold of one small tree just ahead of him, secure it in his right hand like a ski pole, to keep his footing. Stepping carefully forward, he would reach out and take another small tree in his left hand. I held on with all my might and closed my eyes when we got too near the cliffs. Slowly, deliberately, we moved through the woods. The closer we got to the upper waterfall and its cliffs, the louder the water crashed, like thunder, rumbling the ground around us, the tighter I would hold on. If I opened my eyes, I could see down the cliff. I knew if we slipped, or fell, we could both die. I kept them closed as much as possible. I could sense, with each step, Mike carefully choosing which tree or branch he would grab, as he stepped forward to the next one he could trust. Just when we got to a point where the noise of the upper waterfall was behind us, I could see down the cliffs of the first falls. Down below it, the noise got louder again. This waterfall was bigger, even more dangerous. Mike carefully stepped over the corner of the lower waterfall's top edge, onto land, while he held onto a pine tree he could get his hand around.

I was too scared to cry, but I trusted Mike would do his best to save us. I tightened my grip.

This hill was much steeper. It led straight to the cliff.

In the distance, I could see Dick's tree house, so I knew we were going to be safe. Mike told me to hang on, tight, because, although we were safely away from the falls and the cliffs, we were coming to a grassy and steep, slippery hill. With no trees to grab now, his feet would slip and slide forward a bit. Then he would turn his body sideways, slide sideways a little, leaning down, grabbing whatever grass and weeds he could from the side of the hill, with his fingers for balance, until we reached the bottom.

"You can get down," he said.

I slid off his back. We just stared at each other. Mike looked at me.

"Dad taught me something, Jerry, and you should know it, too. Don't ever be afraid to do what you think is right. You did what you thought was right. We all do dumb things. Now you're in a pickle."

"I know."

"But you're smart."

"I am?"

"You're smart enough to figure this thing out, the jam you're in. You just don't think you are. Figure it out. Never be afraid to make mistakes along the way. It's the best way to learn."

He looked me straight in the eye.

"I'm sorry I took your rabbit," I said.

Mike extended his hand for me to shake.

"Well, now you can get it back to me so I can get it to the

professor, right?"

"I'll go get it now," I said.

"Get it tomorrow. It could rain again now."

"Okay."

"No harm, no foul. Deal?" Mike asked.

"Deal," I said, taking his hand and shaking it.

We both looked back at the churning water pouring over the roaring lower waterfall, turned, and went into the house. I never thought Mike was weird ever again.

In the house no one asked any questions. They saw we were safe and left us alone. Neither of us talked to anyone about what we had just gone through together—*we could never expect to describe it,* and no one would believe it, anyhow. We knew we had just experienced something that would bond two brothers together, forever.

Mom came up to us.

"Mike, take Jerry to Mary Crane's. He'll show you where to go.

The Cranes invited him to supper."

"They did?" I asked.

"Go put some dry clothes on and get ready to go," Mom said. "I'll pick you up at eight and bring you home."

Mike and I didn't talk all the way to Mary's house. We knew things were different between us now. When I got out of the car he said, "Good luck. You can do it."

For the first time I believed I could.

"I'm sorry I called you Gourmet Mike," I said.

"It's just a nickname, no worries."

"So you're not mad?"

"No way. You've got Bases, Mayor, now you've got Gourmet Mike."

He reached his arm out and shook my hand. Then he drove off.

Mary was sitting on her front-porch rocking chair. As I walked up she turned and puffed away a curl from in front of her eye.

"I heard about the rabbits," Mary started.

"You heard already?"

"And the mess you're in," she said.

"I'm in so much trouble."

"Don't worry, we can sell them for Easter."

"We can't sell thirty-two rabbits," I said.

"And why not?"

"We don't know thirty-two people who would buy them. If they don't buy them, I'll be stuck with them and still in the same trouble I'm in now."

"What are you going to do?"

"I'm thinking," I said.

Mary's mom leaned on the screen door.

"Jerry, your brother Dick is on the telephone, asking for you."

"He is?"

"You can get it in the kitchen."

"Hello?"

"You know that GASCO gas station in Manlius, the one Mom always goes to after church?" Dick asked.

"Yeah."

"Well, it caught fire and burned up."

"It did?"

"There must have been an explosion, too."

"Why are you telling me?"

"The sheriff has a reward for information to catch whoever started it."

"How much is the reward?" I asked.

"Fifty dollars," Dick said. "They would never give it to a kid, unless he was over eighteen."

"So, why are you telling me?"

"Figure how it started and who started it, and you could use the money to get out of trouble with the rabbits."

"There's no way I could—" I started.

Then Dick added one more sentence before he hung up—a sentence that only a Hardy Boys aficionado would have caught on his best day—and I caught it myself.

"What I can't figure out," Dick said. "is why Sonny's

sleeping cot was in the front room of the gas station, not in the back, where he normally sleeps."

Dick hung up, and I went back out on the porch to where Mary was.

"How much would it cost to get thirty-two or forty-eight Easter baskets?" I asked.

"Easter baskets!?" Mary asked.

"Like the Easter bunny brings, and fill them with candy?"

"You have bigger problems than candy," Mary said.

"An Easter bunny would do that, right, bring candy? How much would they cost?"

"Probably a lot," Mary said. "What are you thinking?"

"How much is a lot? And do you even know where we can get some baskets, enough candy to fill them, and still have room for a small bunny?"

"Mr. Moore has little baskets, over on Pompey Hollow Road, down by you. He sells apples in them, at his apple farm. I saw him unload a truck full of them. I'll go ask him how much fifty will cost. My dad will drive me. I can handle the candy," Mary added.

"How can you handle the candy for all that?" I asked.

Mary stood up and motioned for me to follow her. In her room, she got on her knees and pulled out the middle drawer of her bureau, like it was the vault at the Tully bank. It was filled—to the brim—with candy of every kind. Candy she had collected every Easter and Halloween, for years. Then she opened the bottom one, which was filled with jellybeans of every color!

"If you can get the money, I can get you Easter baskets," she said as she closed the drawers.

"But we don't know how much money," I said.

"I'll tell you how much you'll need, after I talk to Mr. Moore."

I was amazed.

"Tomorrow," Mary added.

Mom picked me up after supper.

When I got home, I went outside for a walk. I had to think.

I walked out to the front gate in the dark, then down Cardner Road to the bridge, just before the alfalfa field. I leaned on the bridge wall, stared at the water still rushing down as a result of the storm.

Suddenly, I had an idea. It was clear to me now, and it depended on only one thing. I stepped back, stood up straight and took a second to rethink the entire idea in my head again, so I wouldn't forget any of it. Then I walked quickly back up Cardner Road. This just had to work.

When I got in the house, I went to Mom and Dad's room. It was empty.

I closed both doors and picked up the telephone.

"Operator."

"Myrtie? This is Jerry."

"I know," she said. "Some storm, eh, hon?"

I told Myrtie the trouble I was in and what I had to do so that thirty- two or forty-eight bunnies wouldn't become livestock and get murdered. Occasionally, Myrtie would excuse herself to switch someone's call, or connect someone, but she listened to every word I had to say.

I told her about the reward money for the gas station fire and what the clues were telling me as a junior detective.

"I think the man who works at the gas station either started the fire by accident, with a cigarette or something, or he set it on purpose. Maybe he had a friend stay there for him, who was careless. I think he put his sleeping cot in the front room, because he knew he would get burned if he stayed in the back."

"Interesting," Myrtie said.

"But Dick says I'm too young to collect a reward. I need money to help save these bunnies."

Myrtie told me to let her think about it. She would call me when she had an idea or if she needed me to do something. I didn't ask her how she would know where I was because by now I was convinced she always knew. I hung up the phone and went to my room. No one said anything to me about anything. When someone was in trouble, everyone knew it was best to just leave him alone to work it out unless he asked for help.

The next morning Mr. Crane dropped Mary at the house and drove off. When she knocked on the door, I stepped out on the front steps.

"Say I can get the baskets, say you can get the money," she said. "How are you going to get thirty-two or forty-eight kids to want them first, and then how are we going to deliver them, if and when they do want them?"

"I'm going to advertise. It's all in the numbers, Mary."

"What do you know about advertising, Jerry?"

"Just let me worry about the advertising," I said.

"So, say we sell them, what do we do then?" Mary asked. "Who's going to deliver them?"

"You and me, Mary."

"Huh?"

"You're going to drive us around in the '38 Dodge pickup we have over in the alfalfa field."

"What!?"

"It's over in the alfalfa field, down next to the bridge."

"Are you insane?"

"We can deliver them all in that old pickup. You're driving us."

"I am? she asked. "I'm ten."

"Can you drive a stick?"

"Yes, my dad showed me."

"Can you back it up?"

"Yes."

"Drive it forward?"

"Yes."

"Whenever you want?"

"Yes."

"So there," I said.

"So there what?" Mary grunted.

"What are you afraid of?"

"I'm ten! That's what I'm afraid of."

"Well I'm only eight. You have to drive."

"That's all you are? You're only eight?"

"You're driving, Mary."

"How come we're in the same grade?"

"My dad said I'm going to be tall, like him—said I should be with older kids. Something like that."

"Okay, I'll drive," Mary said.

"We can't say a word to anyone, or we'll get clobbered or arrested or something," I said.

"What if it's hard for me to see over the steering wheel?" Mary asked.

"Then sit on a pillow," I told her.

"Well, we need to go to Mr. Moore's and get the baskets. Dad took me there before we came here. Mr. Moore told me he paid six cents apiece for them and would make us a fair deal. You don't have to pay him until later," she said. "I told him you and I would walk over."

"I wonder if there's any gas in the '38?"

"Why?"

"Let's go."

We walked to the front gate and down past the bridge and sitting in the alfalfa field was the old '38 pickup someone had left for Dad to use to haul rocks in and hadn't picked it up. I wiped off the windshield best I could, wondering if there was any gas in it and flipped the key to Mary.

"Huh?" she asked, startled.

I removed the cobwebs from the cab and steering wheel.

"You drive, I have to think," I said.

"You are nuts."

"Mary, there hasn't been a car or truck come by for two days, it'll be safe."

"You are nuts."

"It's only a mile, just down Pompey Hollow Road. You know the way already; you were there this morning and there's no traffic—so you drive."

She looked at me like I was crazy but got in and started it up. To drive it she had to sit on the very front of the seat, holding tight to the steering wheel to reach the foot pedals. Off we tumbled through mounds of grass in the alfalfa field and onto the road, Mary stretching her neck up to look through the middle of the steering wheel.

When we got near the Moore apple farm, Mary pulled off the road into an entrance of a pasture, stopped, and turned it off. She didn't want to take any chances getting caught driving. She didn't want to spook Mr. Moore into thinking he was aiding a couple of delinquents, regardless of how good our mission was. Where she parked we had to walk about two hundred and fifty feet to his house.

Mr. Moore saw us crossing his lawn. He opened the door and lifted a bulky burlap bag filled with something and tied with a string at the top. He pushed the screen door open.

"Hi, Jerry and Mary," he said.

"Hi Mr. Moore," I said.

"I know you didn't ask for this many but here are sixty one-quart baskets, just for good measure. They are a gift from me and the missus. You're doing a good thing, you two. God bless."

I took the bag—it wasn't heavy—and thanked him. He stepped back behind his screen door, and watched us walk away, back up Pompey Hollow Road.

Mary drove while I inspected the baskets.

"Look," I said. "Some of these have pink dye on the rims, some of them have blue dye on the rims. They'll be perfect for Easter."

I don't think Mary was listening to me. A truck was coming down Pompey Hollow Road toward us from the other direction. Mary mumbled through her teeth, "Please don't see me, please don't see me, please don't see me."

The man in the truck was Randy's dad, Mr. Vaas in his milk truck filled with milk cans. He was laughing, slapping the outside of the door of his truck with his hand, pointing at little Mary driving the '38. He whistled and waved as he drove past. Mr. Vaas was out delivering farmer's milk to the dairy.

"He won't tell," I said. "He's Randy's dad, the boy in the desk behind me in school."

"I know who Randy is—and I know his dad," Mary growled. "He drives our school bus."

Mary drove in our driveway and parked the '38 next to the barn garage.

She pushed out her lower lip and puffed the hair curl away from her eye.

"You'd better clean this up if we're going to use it. I hate spider webs and I see spider webs in this thing. And make sure it has gas."

I smiled at her and stepped out.

"And get rid of the spiders," Mary added.

I took the burlap sack into the barn garage and put it on a table. Mary used our telephone to call her dad to come get her.

At supper, Mom, Aunt Kate, Dick, and I were eating spaghetti with meatballs and sausage. Spaghetti was like a celebration at our table because everyone liked it. Mom mentioned that Dad would be there anytime, but we were not to wait. She asked me if I'd say grace—I think because she knew I was in the biggest trouble of anyone at the table and needed all the help I could get.

"Bless us, oh Lord, and these thy gifts for which we are about to receive, from thy bounty, through Christ, Our Lord. Amen," I said.

I was starved. This was my favorite supper. Well, maybe the lobster that Gourmet Mike brought home one time for Dad's birthday was better, but we only had that once.

We could hear the front door opening and the hall closet open and close. Dad passed through the dining room with a big smile on his face. He was loosening his tie and taking his business suit coat off, to put in his and Mom's room, next to the dining room. He came back out, rolling up his sleeves. He sat down at the head of the table, ready to eat. He looked at me.

"Jerry me boy," he started, "I want to personally congratulate you, and tell you how proud of you I am."

Everyone turned their heads.

I stopped sucking a strand of spaghetti and stared up at him, not certain if he was serious or joking.

"I'm not going to spoil it by revealing your resourcefulness or any of your plans, or secrets—" he started.

I'm getting clobbered I thought, not knowing what "resourcefulness" meant.

"—but here, son, here is your reward, for helping find the culprit who set fire to the gas station in Manlius."

"I did?" I whimpered.

"Everyone, Jerry, our junior detective here, came up with the clue the sheriff needed. A man, who moved the cot, was questioned and he confessed to accidentally dropping a lit cigarette, setting off the fire."

"He did?" I asked.

"Now, Jerry me boy, I know you have good plans for this money, so here it is—all of it. I'm not even going to ask how you intend to use it. I want you to know we all trust that you will do what's right."

With that, Dad pulled some bills from his shirt pocket, counted out ten five-dollar bills and put them in front of my plate near the middle of the table. I still had a strand of spaghetti hanging out of my mouth as I was bent over the plate. All eyes at the table followed the money from his hands, to where he counted and stacked it, one bill at a time, and right in front of me. We stared at that pile, more money than Dick or I had ever seen, in one place, at one time, before.

I bit off my spaghetti and looked at Mom, who was smiling at me. I looked around. Aunt Kate and Dad were smiling. I looked at Dick who had a confused look on his face. I knew he was trying to think of how I thought of the right clue with the information he gave me or how I told the police. I reached in front of my plate and took a five-dollar bill, handed it to Dick.

"Thanks for telling me about the cot. It gave me the exact clue I needed," I said.

Dick smiled big, took the bill, held it up to the light, like he'd seen someone do in the movies, to be sure it wasn't counterfeit.

"Glad I could help." He folded it into his pocket proudly.

Then he gave me a wink, like he would be there for his little brother if I ever needed him, picked up his fork, and stuck it into a meatball.

Tears came to my eyes for a second. It was just that miracles were happening, but better than that, all the family was rooting for me, and the rabbits. I was happy. That felt good.

I left the rest of the money in front of my plate all through supper. We celebrated my good fortune—without saying it. Everyone knew I might be able to save the rabbits from becoming livestock and getting murdered.

After supper, I walked over to where Dad was sitting and whispered into his ear, "Myrtie?"

"Myrtie!" he answered and smiled as I walked away.

I walked over to Mom and gave her two five-dollar bills.

"Mom, please don't ask me anything, but will you buy something nice for Myrtie? Something she will really like and really needs? Tell her it's from me?"

Mom looked me in the eye and smiled. "Yes, of course, dear."

The next day, around noon, I waited on the road to ask the mailman if there was such a thing as a postcard that already had a stamp on it. He told me there was. They cost three cents each. I had to get rid of maybe forty rabbits. So, I knew, according to Dad's advertising numbers, I needed to advertise to two hundred kids. I asked him how much two hundred of them would cost.

"Six dollars," he said.

I counted out six dollars.

"I'll leave them in the mailbox tomorrow," he said. "I have to get them from the post office when I get back from my route."

When they came, Dick and I sat down and wrote my name and address on the front of every one of them. That way, if anyone ever put any of them in the mail, they would come through the mail to me.

Perfect!

Now all I needed to do was tell two hundred kids about the rabbits and baskets before we could get forty to want them.

We needed the numbers!

## CHAPTER SIX
## IT'S THE NUMBERS

At school recess every day, for a week or more, my friends who'd met at the Delphi Cemetery—Mary, Barber, and Holbrook—and even the boy who sat behind me in class, Randy Vaas, volunteered to help me tell kids to meet us by the schoolyard fence for a secret meeting. During the course of one week nearly every kid came.

Kids would circle around as I made the announcement.

"Raise your hand if you think your parents would let you get a live Easter bunny as a pet and an Easter basket with candy in it."

"When?" came a voice.

"Easter Sunday," Mary said.

"How much?" a voice shouted.

"It's all free," I said.

"Free?"

"Think about it before you answer, because if your parents won't let you have a pet bunny, don't raise your hand."

Then, after my announcement and the kids' show of hands, Mary would make another announcement.

"Now, here's the secret oath," Mary said. "If your folks say yes and they send these cards back, do you promise to set your alarm clock for five o'clock on Easter morning and be by your front door, so the basket and bunny can be dropped off quick? Raise your hand if you promise."

In five days, ninety kids raised their hands. We gave each of them a postcard and told them their parents had to fill out their name and address and mail it back.

Barber would always be there, listening to the whole presentation, waiting for someone to ask what would we do if we ran out of bunnies on Easter—but if no one asked, he shouted it, like he was part of the crowd.

"What if you don't have enough bunnies?"

"Good question," Mary answered. "The bunnies will go to the first kids who send the postcards. But even if we run out of bunnies, the rest will still get a pretty Easter basket, with candy."

Everybody clapped.

Out of the ninety postcards we handed out, fifty-seven came back to me, each with the name of the kid and their address on it. All of them were either in Delphi; the village near Shea's corner and the school; Pompey; Apulia Station; Lafayette; or Tully. Mary and I got Barber and Holbrook to write down all the addresses by name of road and village, so we'd know where the kids lived.

Barber, Holbrook, Mary, Mayor, and Randy Vaas said they would all help on Easter morning.

Just after supper one night, Paul Shaffer called and asked me to come over. When I got there, he showed me four carton boxes in his garage. They were filled with baby bunnies.

"Forty-four," he said. "All healthy."

I never saw so many bunnies in all my life—some white, some white and gray, and some gray.

All I could do was— "Gulp!"

"Easter is Sunday," Paul said. "They'll all be weaned by Wednesday."

I didn't know what that meant, but I said, "Great, can we come get them at four o'clock Sunday morning?

"Huh?" Paul grunted.

"I'll give you a dollar now and a dollar on Sunday, if we can come at four in the morning."

Paul's eyes glazed over in a gleam as he smelled money, kind of like Gourmet Mike's eyes do when he gets a whiff of some stinky cheese. But he knew he had the advantage.

"Two dollars now, two more on Sunday," he said.

"Why that's highway robbery, Shaffer," I shouted. "All you have to do is set your alarm."

"Two dollars now, two more on Sunday," he said. "Or I sleep late on Sunday."

"Okay."

"Swear?" he asked, holding up three fingers like a scout.

"Swear!" I said, holding up three.

Neither one of us was a scout, but we figured that was as

good as anything.

"Two dollars," Paul said, holding his hand out.

"Deal," I said.

I counted out two dollars, handed them to him. I then got Gourmet Mike's rabbit, put it in a carton box and started walking home.

On Easter morning my alarm clock clanged so loud at three a.m. I jumped out of bed in the dark, knocked my desk lamp over while fumbling for it. I stuffed it under my pillow in one motion and found the off button, not wanting to wake the whole house. I got dressed in the dark and snuck down the hall while hooking my belt. Outside, Mary was already by the barn garage. Her dad had dropped her off after driving her around for her paper route. She was in her blue bloomer gym shorts, a yellow wool sweater, and sneakers. She had the '38 pickup backed into the barn garage and was loading the Easter baskets in the bed of the truck, placing them in neat rows. She then spooned jellybeans in the bottom of each with a feed scoop, to weigh them down so the wind wouldn't blow them around. Forty-four baskets would be filled with candy and delivered with bunnies. Thirteen would have extra candy but no bunny. Mary was good at math and she planned for enough candy.

I had my spiral writing pad with everyone's name and address broken out by town, village or hamlet. We were ready.

"Are you sure we won't get caught?" Mary asked, rubbing the sleep out of her eyes.

I was a morning person. I wasn't sleepy-eyed.

"It's Sunday, Mary—

"I know that!"

"It's Easter, Mary—"

"Huh?"

"It's three-thirty in the morning, Mary."

Mary was all business.

"Just stop," she blurted. "You're making me dizzy."

Then, in an irritated tone:

"You owe me nine dollars and eighty-five cents for the candy."

I dug in my pocket, pulled out crumpled bills. I handed her

ten dollars.

"Let's get in the truck and let's go," I said.

With the lights off, she started the '38 and drove slowly out of the barn garage and down the drive.

"You keep watch in the back to make sure the baskets aren't blowing around," Mary said.

We pulled onto Cardner Road, turned left up the hill. As we passed farmer Parker's house, his kitchen light went on, making Mary jump. She thought we might be seen or caught, but it was coincidence. Farmer Parker was just waking up.

"It's morning milking time," I said.

Mary seemed to get calmer the farther she drove. We passed Doc
Webb's place, then the Butlers' and Don Chubb's place. She slowed down and pulled into Paul Shaffer's driveway. She pushed the button and turned out the lights, then turned the key and shut the truck off. Paul came out of the garage in the dark, holding a flashlight, walked to my side of the '38.

"You got my money?"

I stepped out of the truck and gave him two dollars.

In the garage, with three flashlights, we were trying to figure whether it would be best to put the bunnies into the baskets here or keep them all in one carton and put them in the baskets when we delivered them.

The garage was dark and the night very still when out of nowhere it seemed, the glare of the moon flashed a quick, bright silvery reflection off the side of a big, long, midnight-black car that was driving up with its lights off.

"They caught us," Mary whispered.

"Who is it?" Paul stuttered, asking me.

"Maybe it's the president and we're all getting arrested," I said.

The mysterious car turned slowly into the driveway, grinding the stone pebbles as it crunched to a stop, just behind the '38 pickup.

We all froze.

It sure looked like the president of the United States was coming to arrest us. Certain it was we all almost had heart attacks. Mary backed away, stepping behind one of the bunny cages next to the garage to hide, in case she had to make a run for it and dash up the back ridge. Then we saw it was Dick's friend Duba getting out of his father's car. It was the big, long Lincoln. Duba's and Dick's best friends Conway and Dwyer got out as well. They told us they had come to drive us, for Dick. Dick was still home in bed but he had asked them to help get us out of the jam. They were all thirteen. No licenses between them, but thirteen and good drivers, and figured they could get away with sneaking the Lincoln out, if they were quick about it and had it back before daylight and before Duba's dad woke up. I knew some kids who were thirteen and had farm permits to drive on the road. I knew Dwyer and Conway probably had permits, maybe, but Duba didn't. Dick told me he didn't.

I was amazed. Knowing we were under ten, Dick's friends showed up to volunteer to drive us so we wouldn't get in trouble. Dick kept it a secret from me all this time, even stayed home so no one would get suspicious.

Older guys had come to help!

Just about that time, Barber drove up in his dad's Packard. Boy, was he ever happy to see Duba, Conway, and Dwyer there to do the driving—he beamed a grin in the headlights?

"It's a danged miracle," Barber whispered.

Barber knew that if his dad ever found out he'd taken the Packard off their property—he would become mincemeat. Worse than mincemeat if he drove it all over the countryside. Right after Barber got there, Randy Vaas's dad drove up in his milk truck. Randy got out, and the truck pulled away, on its way to the dairy.

This was getting good.

Randy was ten and wanted to be there for us, too. His dad was the one who saw Mary driving the '38.

"Where's Holbrook?" Randy asked.

"He's not here," I said.

"We would have gotten him," Randy said.

"I came straight from my paper route," Mary said. "I forgot about him."

As soon as Randy and Mary got the words out of their mouths, Duba jumped into Mr. Barber's Packard.

"I'll go get Holbrook—I'll only be ten minutes."

"Why are you in my dad's Packard?" Barber asked.

"I'll have to drive past our house. I don't want to get caught driving the Lincoln," Duba said.

Everyone knew he was right. He backed the Packard around slowly. He drove off, lights off until he was on down the road a way. Then the lights came on and the car lurched, squealing the tires.

"Oh, jeez," Barber said, watching his dad's Packard disappearing down the road, its engine revving.

We all knew the towns, villages, and hamlets that we had to deliver to only had one or two streets each, so we could do it safely. Nobody was out driving this early in the morning, anyway. It was about that time we were all surprised when my brother, Gourmet Mike, drove up. He said he was there to help us drive and he'd drive straight back to Syracuse after we were finished. This was too good to be true.

Soon the Packard pulled back in and Holbrook got out with Duba. Holbrook was barefoot, in jeans and a pajama top. Duba had to go into his house in the dark and up the stairs, find him in a room filled with brothers and no lights and wake him without waking up the whole house. Holbrook only had time to grab his jeans and his glasses.

We divided up the names from the postcards according to the villages they were in and divided the baskets by car. We counted the rabbits and put the right amount in each carton box. Mary carried the boxes out and put them in the right cars.

"Carry the rabbits and baskets separately or the candy could get peed on," Mary announced.

Gourmet Mike would drive Randy in his car to the school village. Duba would take Barber up to Pompey, circling around to Tully in the Lincoln. Dwyer and Holbrook took Apulia Station in the Packard. They would all meet up at Shea's store in the school village to switch cars and head home. Mary and I would take the hamlet of Delphi in the '38. It was just down the road.

We all had to get home after our deliveries, pretend we never left our houses, and go to church. With Gourmet Mike's and the older guys' help we would be done in no time. We agreed to meet at the Delphi cemetery, that afternoon at one o'clock, to talk about how it went.

Well, not exactly.

The kids agreed to meet, but when we asked Duba, Conway, and Dwyer if they wanted to meet with us, they told us not to even think about it. Helping us was one thing. Being seen with us—kids—in the daylight was another. Gourmet Mike had to go right back to Syracuse.

Kids understood these things.

"Be careful, you guys," Mary said.

"Mush, you huskies!" I said, just as Sergeant Preston of the Royal Mounties would tell his faithful sled dog, King, on the radio. "On, King!" he would shout.

"Wagons-ho!" Barber said, in a raspy loud whisper, as if we were in a John Wayne Saturday morning picture show.

"Don't get caught," Duba growled as he pulled his car door closed.

We backed the cars and the '38 around and out, headlights off as we all rolled away, in both directions, before pulling the lights on.

Mary, sweating bullets, but with more confidence knowing nobody had licenses, made it into the Delphi hamlet. When we stopped at each house, I would get out, run across the lawn to the house and deliver the basket and bunny, and she would slouch down in the seat so she couldn't be seen. One kid asked me who was driving the truck, and I told him the Easter bunny and that no one could see him! That seemed to work.

"Please don't see me—please don't see me—please don't see me."

Mary mumbled this every time a car or truck would come down the road and pass by.

We had everything delivered without a hitch—every kid was right by the door, like they promised, and everyone loved their bunnies.

We all accomplished our missions in no time and drove back home while it was still dark, as proud as Superman. Mary's dad was parked out by the front gate, leaning on the window, asleep in the car, as we passed. He knew she was helping deliver Easter candy and was waiting to give her a ride home. Mary drove past him, drove in the drive and parked the '38 by the barn, exactly where it was before.

"I'll see you later," she said.

"She stepped out of the '38 and started walking to meet her dad down by the road.

"Hold on, I'll drive you out," I said.

"Thanks," Mary said.

"First, give me a hand, will ya?" I asked.

"Whatcha need?"

I went into the back of the barn garage and rolled Dick's broken up popsicle cart out and to the back of the pickup. Mary grinned and helped me load it in. I drove her and the cart down the dirt driveway and we lifted it into Mr. Crane's trunk. He tied the lid down with a rope.

"Mr. Crane, if you can fix this, Mary can use it. It should be a good money-maker for her. It will hold a lot of popsicles and fudgesicles if you put dry ice in it. I think that's how it works."

Mary smiled and nudged her head down on my shoulder.

"Thanks, Jerry."

I got in the '38 and drove back to the barn garage, parked, sneaked into the house, and went back to bed.

I collapsed on the bed, but couldn't sleep right away, thinking of our great adventure.

Later in the morning, Mom called to wake us up for Easter Mass.

I opened my eyes and stared over my head, out through my window, thinking about the two-month-long nightmare I had just gone through. I thought about Gourmet Mike showing up out of the blue and helping.

At the church, St. Anne's in Manlius, I was sitting between Mom and Dad while Father Lynch was getting ready to serve Communion. When the collection basket came around, I pulled out the wad of money I had left over and counted how much it was—fifteen dollars. I unfolded and handed Mom ten dollars and asked her if she would buy a savings bond for Mary—and then I dropped the five-dollar bill in the basket.

I looked up at Mom and she smiled.

Dad gave me a wink and held his hand out for me to shake.

Everyone knew I'd come through for the rabbits for sure, with the help of all my family and the best friends any boy could ever have. What felt best was that they trusted me and my friends would do the right thing and didn't ask any questions.

In the back seat of the car on the way home from Mass, I leaned over and told Dick thanks for sending the older guys to help. I also let him know I'd given the popsicle cart to Mary's dad to try to fix—and told him I said it would be all right for Mary to use it and try to make some extra money with it. "She can use the extra money," I said.

"How about Holbrook?" Dick asked. "He needs money."

"Holbrook needs like a part-time job or something. He needs more money than from popsicle sales," I said.

"Who showed up?" Dick whispered.

I leaned over and whispered.

"Mike came from Syracuse. Duba came in his dad's Lincoln, scared the heck out of us. Dwyer and Conway were with him. They bailed us out big time. Really big time."

Dick beamed a smile, looked out the car window, happy our brother Gourmet Mike had shown up and that his school friends came through for me—for him. He had a look on his face as if it felt good knowing he and his friends who always seemed to be in trouble somehow were able to do something good for a change. He leaned over and whispered in my ear, "You kids see trouble again, SOS me."

"What do you mean?"

"You know SOS, don't ya?"

"Sure I do. It's dot, dot, dot—dash, dash, dash—dot, dot, dot—Save Our Ship."

"Right."

"Are you saying if we get in trouble, we can SOS you older guys to help us?"

Dick wrenched his lips in an agreeing smile, turned his head and looked out the car window again at farms as they passed by in great satisfaction. He was feeling good about himself and his friends.

I was beginning to realize just how smart he was. On that ride home from church on that Easter morning it dawned on me that my brother Dick figured out the scheme on how to help me with the rabbits long ago—by maybe getting Gourmet Mike there, by maybe leading me with hints and clues on how to earn the reward money for the burned down gas station, and by getting the other drivers—without ever talking or bragging about it.

Because of Dick's brains and Gourmet Mike's "buck" rabbit, it was going to be a happy Easter for everyone, *especially* for a lot of kids in Pompey, Shea's Corner, Apulia Station, Tully, Lafayette, Gooseville Corner, and in good old Delphi.

Later that day, at the cemetery, Mr. Crane dropped Holbrook and Mary off on time for our one o'clock meeting. Holbrook had on a clean T-shirt this time. Mary was in her new yellow Easter dress. Barber and Randy were already there, playing mumblety-peg with their pocket knives.

"You know, we should say thanks to Dick and his friends and your brother Mike," Mary said.

"I already told Dick thanks, after church," I said.

"Oh, good," Mary said.

"He said if we ever get in trouble, we can SOS him."

Hearing SOS gave us the chills.

We all knew, from sitting on the floor listening to telegraphed ship- to-shore shortwave radio signals during the war, that SOS was the most important signal you could ever hear in Morse Code. It meant there was big trouble. It meant a ship had been torpedoed or bombed and could be sinking. Every year during the war almost a thousand ships were sunk in the Atlantic Ocean alone.

"I'll write Gourmet Mike a letter at college and thank him," I said.

Everyone looked around at each other. Thoughts of an SOS suggested a possibility of more adventures. It was dawning on us for the first time. Our imaginations began to flutter in that afternoon's sun, reminiscent of the flickering of light and sound of the clacking movie projector in the darkened Saturday morning picture show. Imaginations that would let us wonder, each in our own way, just what other adventures we may have in store for us. What else could we solve together, especially with the help of the older guys? Who would have dreamed one little rabbit could have been such a big adventure?

It was then when Bases came walking up the drive into the cemetery. He guessed we were going to be here when he saw Mary's dad drive through the hamlet. He wanted to show off a new baseball he got for Easter. After passing it around, he stuffed it in the back of his worn-torn baseball glove and asked Mary to kindly latch it to a belt loop on the back of his jeans, to hang for safekeeping.

I thanked everyone for being there for the rabbits. We all felt good about making so many kids happy, especially today.

Barber said God would be proud of us this Easter.

Randy suggested we consider starting a club of best pals and said he'd be proud if we included him.

We stood in a circle, piled our hands together in the middle, and asked, "Pals for life?"

"What're we gonna call it?" Holbrook asked.

"We need an important-sounding club name," Mary said.

We all thought.

Barber felt inspired. He stood up straight and then stepped up on a tombstone. He raised his arm like a preacher.

"The Pompey Hollow Book Club!" he announced.

"Book Club?" Randy asked.

"Book Club!?" Bases asked.

"Will we have to read books?" Holbrook asked.

"Not a word if you don't want to," Barber said. "But carry a book if you leave the house on another mission. There ain't a mom in the county who will stop us from going to a book club meeting with a book in your hand, even on a school night."

Barber was eloquent.

"We might stop saying *ain't*, then," Mary suggested.

In full agreement, we spit in our hands and shook on it.

"Can girls be in the club?" Bases asked, while his eye caught Mary's new yellow Easter dress.

What next occurred began as a very loud, stone-cold silence.

Holbrook bolted back, thinking of how, if it weren't for Mary, he would have never had a ride to anyplace. Randy stepped back and thought of how Mary counted out all the rabbits and was always being there. Barber said, "Oh, jeez," remembering all the days Mary was there for us, at the playground fence talking to kids. I thought of Mary driving and finding the baskets and helping any way she could.

Silence reigned as if Bases was about to get drenched.

Slowly Mary's neck raised like a submarine periscope. She

leaned back from the circle of friends and in robotic motion she reached around behind Barber to Bases and dug her hand deep into his baseball glove hanging on his belt loop. She clenched the brand-new Easter baseball and lifted it out. She stuck the ball under her chin while stepping back from the group. Turning around, she gathered and lifted both sides of her yellow Easter dress with her hands and stuffed it like drapes into the waistbands of the blue bloomer gym shorts she had on underneath.

Looking Bases dead straight in the eye, with a bead you could only read about in an Edgar Allen Poe thriller, Mary took the baseball from under her chin, rubbed it with her thumb for grasp. She twirled her arm backward in three full windmill-like circles, kicked her left leg up over her head—and heaved Bases' brand-spanking-new Easter present over the tallest cemetery pine tree she could see (it looked like a knuckleball), barely missing a crow's nest. The baseball cleared three trees in the cemetery, in fact, with ease. In time, it hit the road down below with a thwack that sounded like a broken bat, landing farther than most of us, including Bases, could have rolled it down a paved hill. About that time a black feather from a frightened mother crow floated down, in circles, landing in the middle of the friends. Bases stuttered, stammered, searching his brain for the right words for an apology and most likely how he could explain to his mom—a girl—how he'd lost his new baseball or explaining it to the team counting on him to pitch with it in today's game without getting a considerable thumping. He cleared his throat and carefully crafted his new position.

"How about anyone who shows up can belong?"

Mary pulled her new yellow Easter dress from the sides of her gym bloomer shorts, straightened it like the little lady she was and brushed the loose hair from her face back up over the top of her head, tucking it in. Un-sneering her eyes, she turned and smiled as if nothing happened, and spit in her palm, again. We all leaned forward and shook again and spat—making it law.

Not only was the Pompey Hollow Book Club official and forever, it was coeducational.

Mary was made president.

## CHAPTER SEVEN
## IDLE SUMMER HANDS

"Holbrook and I figure if we spent the rest of the summer hopping tramp steamers maybe go to Casablanca or to Pago Pago or somewhere," I said, "we could sail part of the world."

"Casablanca is in Morocco," Dick said.

"I'm thinking Holbrook could make money working cargo holes so he can buy a water heater for his mom and maybe get a telephone for his sisters and I could explore the world with him, to keep him company and become a famous writer."

"That's nice, dear," Mom said. "Pass the potatoes to your brother."

"You'll need earrings," Dick said.

"Earrings?" I asked.

"Make sure they're gold," Dick said.

"Gold earrings?" I asked.

"Pure gold. Don't fall for any gold-plated crap."

"Don't say 'crap,' dear," Mom said.

"That way if you get throwed in the brig you'll need bail money.

You could melt the gold down, maybe with a candle. Aaargh!"

"Thrown," Mom said. "Don't say throwed."

"Can't they just bite on it and tell it's gold?" I asked.

"I guess," Dick said.

"I saw a pirate bite gold in Hong Kong, or maybe it was Bali or somewhere like that, at the picture show. I think it was Bob Hope. I wouldn't have to melt it down, I don't think."

Dad stepped in.

"Jerry, you and Holbrook have been camping out a lot."

"Sure. It's fun."

"Have you two met with any of your other friends this summer?"

"Not much."

"Don't you kids have a club like other kids?"

"The Pompey Hollow Book Club," I said.

Mom smiled.

"Aren't there regular meetings?" Dad asked.

"What are you reading?" Mom asked.

Dick gazed across at me. He knew the truth about our 'book' club and that it had nothing to do with books. He waited to hear what kind of explanation I had for the Pompey Hollow Book Club.

"Well, we met once so far at Barber's house. We helped him stack hay bales for his dad. Oh, and we made Mary president."

"That's nice dear," Mom said.

"Mrs. Barber fed us lunch with lemon meringue pie, and Mr. Barber gave us fifty cents each."

"Stacking hay. That doesn't sound like a club meeting," Dad said.

"It'll be easier for us to meet after school starts," I said. "Summer is busy on farms. Barber has a mess of chores and Mary, too. Besides her paper route, she's busy selling popsicles with the pedal cart in Delphi."

"Now we're getting to the bottom of it," Dad said.

"Bottom of what?" I asked.

"Sounds to me like you and your friend Holbrook need something to do this summer, like Barber and Mary have."

"We camp out, that's something to do," I said.

"Idle minds are a devil's workshop, aren't they, Mommy?" Dad grinned down at Mom.

"Huh?" I quizzed. "We're not idle, Dad."

"You camp out a lot, son."

"So? We're just bored sometimes, so we camp out."

"Camping's fun, son, but you'll both like having responsibilities, like your friends Barber and Mary. Rewarding responsibilities. I know your friend Randy rides with his dad nearly every morning, delivering milk cans to dairies, doesn't he?" Dad asked.

"Yes. I rode with them before."

"Your brother Dick washes dishes part-time at the Lincklaen House on weekends."

"That's because he's always in trouble," I said.

"Don't be fresh," Mom said.

"I just had an idea," Dad said.

"What?" I asked.

"What do you and Holbrook eat when you camp out in the woods?"

"We cook Spam and eggs in the old iron skillet Mom gave us."

"What else?"

"We cook hot dogs or cans of soup. Sometimes we have corned beef hash."

"Anything else?"

"We tried making toast, but it catches fire."

"Anything else?"

"If we have ears of corn, we throw them on the fire and shuck 'em after they cool off."

"Do you ever fry bacon?"

"Yes."

"Try frying the bread in the bacon grease, son, before you clean the skillet."

"That's a good idea," I said.

"That's a tasty way of toasting bread."

"Why are you telling me all this, Dad?"

"I'm just impressed is all, son—basic cooking skills, at your age."

"We cook pretty good when we camp. I can build a fire easy and we camp next to the spring on top of the cliff."

" What if I could show you both a type of cooking but instead of a frying pan and bacon and Spam and corn beef hash you'd cook with flour, sugar, butter, eggs, milk, and spices—in a cooking world you could both earn money from, right away?"

"Cooking?" I asked.

"And you could learn it in a day. It only needs practice after that."

"You really mean baking, Dad. I can tell."

"I would have said baking but thought maybe you'd think it's only for girls."

"No, I wouldn't."

"If you learn some of the basics at the bakery—and use

what you learn there to teach yourselves more. Son, as a baker you could earn a living anywhere in the world. In fact, if you learned to bake you could help around the kitchen here making desserts. We might even raise your allowance by a quarter a week—whatcha think, Mommy, think we could?"

Mom smiled approval. She heard the *learning* word, not the *allowance* word.

"Holbrook could get a summer job at any bakery," Dad said. "I'm thinking the Tully bakery, close to his house. He could earn money for that water heater or telephone he wants to get for his mother, whatever he needed. I know the Tully Bakery owner."

"He does need money, Dad."

"Why, if you could bake, son, you could earn your way around the world on a tramp steamer anytime they were ready to set sail."

"For real?"

"Every sailor or deck hand needs to eat, son."

"Everybody has to eat," Dick said.

"Get word to Holbrook. We'll pick him up in the morning and go to the bakery for a short course on baking," Dad said.

"I'll tell him."

"Tell him early and we'll have breakfast at Bucky's Diner."

"Okay."

Dad looked over at Dick.

"Dick, if you get the water softener instruction manual from your mother, I have a chore for you, too."

"Water softener?"

"Figure out how to keep it running and we'll raise your allowance, too. Another quarter a week. You have to learn how to change the filters and add the salt or chlorine regularly and keep it running."

Dick and I exchanged glances across the table. We knew Mom and Dad were generous, but neither of us remembered ever getting any regular allowance.

Dick was saving up to buy a car of his own and had twenty-six dollars from washing dishes.

"I can do that, easy," Dick said.

"You're good with motors," Dad said.

"Can I get a cash advance?"

Dad didn't answer.

"Jerry, I'm going to introduce you and your friend to a baker who could open a new world for you. You both have a flair for cooking."

The next morning Dad came into my room early, already in his work suit.

"Jerry me boy, rise and shine."

"I'm up, Dad."

"Let's go get your friend, we'll have a nice breakfast, and go meet a baker."

I got ready and met him outside.

Dad drove around the swings he parked behind in summers for shade and we headed off first to Holbrook's and then on to Cortland.

At the diner, Dad took a shiny quarter out of his pocket.

"Call it, Bucky!" he shouted, not taking his eyes off the flying quarter on its descent. Holbrook's eyes opened wide as he stared at the quarter in flight. With a grin he watched Dad slap the quarter down to the counter when it landed.

"Heads!" Bucky yelled.

Heads it was. Dad slid the quarter over the counter toward him. Bucky tipped his paper cap and placing both hands on the counter he lifted his legs up sideways almost above the counter and clicked his heels together.

"Bucky, the boys are about to become bakers. Jerry, so he can handle his new chore of making desserts for the family. His friend Holbrook here, so he can maybe get a part-time job to earn extra money."

He explained to Bucky how, since Holbrook and I grew up during the war, from about 1940 like so many kids today we never had the advantage they did when they were kids of licking the spoons in the kitchen and learning how to bake by watching or helping our moms, our grandparents, or others who baked every Saturday.

"How come it was different when you grew up, Dad?" I asked.

"We had sugar," Dad said. "We could watch our mom's bake."

"What did kids like us have?" Holbrook asked.

"Well, all throughout the war you didn't have sugar!" Bucky said. "For starters. No sugar, no baking."

"How come no sugar?" I asked.

"You grew up in war time, son, and with all the sugar being rationed, there was none left over for families to bake at home during the war—only a minimum amount. Now, with the war over, sugar is available again."

Bucky reached over the counter and shook Holbrook's hand hello.

"During the war sugar was needed to feed the fighting boys and the wounded in hospitals all over the world," he said. "Here at home we had to go without desserts most the time."

"Sugar rationing was important," Dad said. "We had to feed the troops who were fighting for us."

"But that's enough of that," Bucky started, "and to help you both out, I sure enough got some easy old recipes I dusted off after the war if you want them."

"Thank you," Holbrook and I said.

After breakfast, Dad took us to the "cake kitchen" part of the bakery in Homer, where they made the cookies, cakes, and sweets. Everything smelled good, like spices and raisins and sugar. People moving about were dressed in white with long aprons and paper baking caps. The cake kitchen was across the street from the bread bakery. Dad reached on top of a locker, grabbed two paper baking hats, and put one on Holbrook's head and one on mine.

We sat on stools at the small employee coffee counter, waiting.

A smiling baker came around from behind the mixing machines, walked over to us, sat down across the counter with a cup of coffee in his hand, and asked Dad, "What can I do ya for, Big Mike?"

"Me boy, Jerry, and his friend Holbrook here would like to learn about baking and making desserts. Maybe earn some extra money. I thought you might be able to give them some simple pointers, some basics."

The baker grabbed my hand and while shaking it he said, "Mighty glad to know ya, son. Jerry, is it?" He then shook Holbrook's hand. "Mighty glad to know ya, too, son. Holbrook?

You done came to the right man. I can out-bake and out-dessert any bake-off at any county fair. I'll be happy to teach them, Big Mike."

He poured himself another cup of coffee, filled a cup for Dad, and wedged a pencil up under the side of his white paper baking cap.

"How many we baking for, boys?" he asked.

"It should last 'bout a week—four, maybe five at the table each night," Dad answered for me. "For Holbrook here, there are a dozen or more in his house."

"More," Holbrook said.

"A baker's dozen, then," the baker quipped.

The baker man reached over by the phone that was on the counter, took the white pad sitting next to it, tore the top half of the sheets from the bottom half, and slid each pad to us. He took the pencil from his hat and a ball point pen from Dad's shirt pocket and handed them to us.

"Baking is simple, boys, if you always do it right," he said. "You might want to make notes. Rule one, baking is just like carpentry."

"It is?" I asked. "How's that?"

"If you don't measure correctly it won't hold together. Use the exact same measurement always, the right temperature always, and perfect baking time and rack cooling time, always. Never guess when baking. Follow the recipe."

"We can cook some," Holbrook said.

"Cooking and baking are different, son."

"How?" Holbrook asked.

"There may be a dozen different ways to cook a hamburger or make a soup—but there is only one way to bake. Remember that and you can bake anything. Rule two, you have to learn volume."

"What does volume mean?" Holbrook asked.

"Good question, son," the baker said. "Let's say you have two bowls of cake batter. Let's say that in each bowl was the very same amount of batter."

"Okay, two bowls, same amount in each," Holbrook said.

"Both bowls will make a two-layer cake. Both bowls will make a one-layer sheet cake."

"What's the difference?" I asked. "They're both cakes."

"Explain the volume thing," Holbrook said.

"Talking volume, son, a two-layer cake can go maybe six or eight ways—serve six or eight people—depending on how you cut it. But your bowl two, remember son, it's the same amount of batter—"

"I remember," Holbrook said.

"—if you made a one-layer sheet cake instead you can serve sixteen or eighteen."

"I get it," Holbrook said.

"You do?" I asked.

"It's easy," Holbrook said. "At our house I would go with sheet cake—same amount of cake going twice as far."

The baker let us scribble some notes and he continued.

"Just think volume with everything you bake, boys. If you put cookie dough on a baking sheet with a small teaspoon, you will get more cookies from your dough than you will if you put it on with a larger tablespoon. If you ever work for a bakery, Holbrook, they'll tell you exactly how much dough to put on the baking sheets. Smaller pieces of dough will mean more cookies."

It was making sense to Holbrook. He was good at math. The important thing we were learning was that baking wasn't just for girls, and it wasn't how much we baked but how we controlled the volume so we could have enough portions to serve everyone.

"Is it like having one or two scoops of ice cream?" I asked.

"Exactly, son. People like two scoops, but they're happy with one."

"It's making whatever you have go around so everyone can have some," Holbrook said.

"Big Mike, the boys are smart."

Dad smiled.

"It's good to run out, though, son," the baker man said. "You don't want desserts every night of the week. A dessert should be a surprise. If you're in a hurry, always remember egg custard. It's quick, easy, and I'll give you a recipe. You can bake it in the same baking dish you use for a sheet cake. Oh, and if you want to get fancy, add some pieces of raisin bread to your custard mix, and it will become raisin bread pudding by magic. Same time, same temperature."

The baker looked at Holbrook and asked, "How many in your family, son?"

"Eleven kids," Holbrook said.

"I thought I heard Mike right. Hold on, son."

With that, the baker winked at Dad, stood and walked back to where the ovens were. I looked up at Dad, who was smiling back at me. When the man came back, he handed Holbrook a rectangular glass baking dish, an oily metal baking pan, and a tin for making twelve cupcakes.

"The baking dish will fit in this pan, son. Put water in the pan when you make custard. Bake the custard resting the dish in the water. It won't scorch or burn."

He went behind the ovens again, came back and handed Holbrook two big cookie sheets, a measuring cup and two pie tins.

"For a mixing bowl and rolling pin, you're on your own, but your momma will have them. This will get you started."

Holbrook sat there amazed, looking up at the pile of baking stuff that was now his. He didn't know what to say. He thanked the man and promised he would become a good baker and maybe grow up to have a restaurant of his own someday.

"Boys, I just want to taste something you make sometime. Promise me I can have a sample?"

We both told him yes. I handed him back his pencil and Holbrook handed Dad his pen. Dad picked up the baking things the baker had given Holbrook, to take out to the car. He lined newspaper on the back seat and set the trays, pans, and baking dish carefully on top.

"I have a quick meeting at the bakery, so I'm dropping you both at the library."

"The library?" I asked.

"I want you to get a book, *African Queen*."

"*African Queen*?" I asked.

"You wanted to go around the world on a tramp steamer? You'll like the adventure. It's about Africa, the jungle, and a small steamboat. I'll come get you when I'm done or you both walk over to the bakery. Tell the librarian I'll bring any books you get back when you're finished reading them."

In the library Holbrook pulled out the encyclopedia's 'B'

volume and read about baking cakes and bread and pies and looked for cookbooks. I found the title *African Queen* in the card-index drawer. I memorized the Dewey decimal number for it on the index card. That told me what section and aisle the book was in, what shelf it was on. Like a code.

The book's beginning was slow so I cracked halfway into it. It's about two people on a scary river journey during World War I. It talks about a lot of jungle and all sorts of wild animals. This man, Charlie, owned a small cargo boat—the African Queen—and he delivered mail with it somewhere in Africa. The lady, Rose, had pretty eyes. After she told Charlie that Germans in the gunboat on the lake at the end of the river had murdered her brother, who was only a harmless Christian missionary, and that she wanted to go down the river and blow up the German ship, Rose then kissed Charlie really good. So then he said okay, and from then on he called her Rosie. A kiss can do that. I know. I saw it in the *She Wore a Yellow Ribbon* movie. Together they managed to steer the boat all through the winding, dangerous jungle waters, past deadly crocodiles, hippopotamuses, wild jungle birds, and monkeys, just so they could blow up an enemy gunboat—if only they could get to the lake.

Holbrook and I left the library, me with the *African Queen* book under my arm, him with two baking cookbooks.

On the way back to Holbrook's house, Dad stopped at the Tully bakery. He took Holbrook in and introduced him to the owner. The man invited Holbrook to come back and work part-time, whenever he could. He said he would teach him everything he needed to know.

When Dad and I got home I went to my room and laid down to read the part from the *African Queen* book where Charlie got out into the swampy water to pull the boat through the weeds and leaches crawled all over his body, sucking his blood. It got scary so I put the book down to think about the baking and what I would bake first. I fell asleep.

## CHAPTER EIGHT
## UNDER ATTACK

"Ahhhhh! The beasts! The beasts!"

Shouting, tossing, turning, rolling off my bed, flopping onto the floor—I started slapping my face, neck, and arms as I yelled.

"Pull them off me!"

"Cooooo!"

"Get them off me, Rosie!"

I woke up—startled from a scary dream—sat up, opened my eyes, looking around to see where I was. I wiped the back of my hand across my sweaty forehead, stretched my arms back and leaned on my hands to catch my breath and fully wake up.

I was dreaming I was on the African Queen with Charlie Allnut and Rose Sayer when the river got shallow, and Charlie and I had to get out over the side of the boat and down in the dark black water so we could pull the boat through the swampy reeds and the leaches attached to our skin with suckers that wouldn't pull off, and they hung on, sucking our blood.

I shivered thinking about it.

I stood up, went to the kitchen to get the egg basket off the top of the ice box and started walking to Mr. Pitts's farm to collect the eggs like I did every week. I needed some fresh air.

When I got back home with the basket full of eggs, I walked over to the front of the barn garage to see where talking noises were coming from.

The '38 pickup was backed into the end bay and both Duba and Dick were on the floor under it like surgeons—well, more like moonshine runners—trying to connect the brand new, what they called "glass pack," mufflers Dick bought with some of the money he had earned from washing dishes up at the Lincklaen House in Cazenovia on weekends when they had weddings.

"Glass pack" mufflers could get a guy a traffic ticket for making car tailpipes noisy in Syracuse. Some kids called them

*Hollywoods*—they made rumbling sounds when a jalopy (car) revved its engine while taking off or when the driver popped the clutch to gear it down. Neither Dick nor Duba had a license, so it didn't much matter.

Standing there with my basket filled with eggs, I announced my return.

Neither Dick nor Duba heard me or paid any attention.

"Small crescent?" Dick asked with his hand sticking out from under the car, looking for a little help.

I picked up the wrench and put it in his hand, stepped over and leaned out of the garage to see Dad driving up the driveway and around back of the swings to park.

Most times when he came home he'd just wave and walk into the house, but this time he stepped through the swings toward us.

I warned Dick he was coming our way—but he wasn't worried. Dick and Duba actually mastered the "cover up" and had a knack for being able to tell the truth in such a way they could wrap it around some smelly cheese-like fib and no one without proper training in law enforcement could tell. That was unless, of course, the county sheriff caught them both red-handed, dragging on back roads and brought them home to their moms and dads along with the truth from the law's point of view.

"What's going on?" Dad asked.

Dick stuck his head out from under the pickup.

"The muffler and tailpipe on this old '38 are filled with rust holes, so Duba and I are putting new ones on."

"Good," Dad said. "Holes in mufflers and tailpipes can be a noisy nuisance. Good job."

I looked at Dick like he was going straight to hell for lying, but then I thought about what he just told Dad. He did tell the truth—he just didn't embellish it with any important details that could get him a ticket for making a noise in Syracuse.

Dad took the egg basket from my hand and started walking to the house. He paused, turned back, scratched his head, stepped into the barn garage, this time closer to the '38 than he was before, and bent forward.

"Dick, I hate to be the bearer of bad news," Dad said.

Dick poked his head out from under the '38.

"What's that?" Dick asked.

"The pickup doesn't belong to us, son. It was loaned to me to haul some rocks. You've spent your money on something we don't own. Mr. Kehoe will be coming by to pick it up anytime now."

"He already came for it, Dad. Duba and I offered him twenty dollars for it and he took it. He bought a '48 already and said he couldn't afford the tires for it and this one, too. The '48 holds more in its bed. He took the twenty dollars and was happy. He gave us an extra key, too."

Dad looked pleased. Dick and Duba could now do something they always wanted to do—stay under the hood of a motor.

"Jerry, I have a meeting at our other bakery up north in Carthage. You flew to Syracuse that time, but you've never been to Carthage—farther north, almost to Canada. Want to ride with me to pick up a boat motor near there? If I want the motor, I have to pick it up before this weekend."

Seeing my basket of eggs in his hand reminded me of something.

"Dad, I saw six pheasants up by Mr. Pitts's fence—in the cornfield across the road from him. I went over and left some corn behind our fence so they might move into our woods and not stay out in the open where they could get seen and shot by hunters."

"Pheasants might be safer in the field than in the woods, son," Dad said. "They can run and fly to escape in an open field better than in the woods. Want to ride to Carthage with me?"

"What kind of boat motor?" Dick leaned out and asked.

"It's an Evinrude half-horse, I think. It's a small one, made before the war."

"Whose motor is it?" Dick asked.

"One of the bakery salesmen in Carthage told me his grandfather gave it to him, along with a wooden boat. He already had a bigger motor and offered it to me if I wanted it for you kids. He said I could have it and we could maybe get it tuned up. He says the motor runs. He'll keep the boat."

"Duba and I can tune it up for you, Dad," Dick said.

"It runs fairly good, son. I thought I'd take it by Brown's

Hardware in Cortland for a look. Jerry, do you want to go help me get it? We'll be back tonight. You and I'll take the motor to the hardware store Saturday."

He looked down at my bare feet.

"Get some shoes on. We'll go fishing. There's trout and salmon that far north, I hear."

All I could think was if a salmon ever got on our line, we would all have heart attacks. We wouldn't know what to do.

I said, "Sure," and ran into the house to get my sneakers. When I came out of my room, Dad was talking with Mom, who was sitting and meeting with Mrs. Cerio about an idea to get volunteer teachers to start night courses at the school for farmers and their wives who might like them. Some of the farmers and their dads went off to the war at seventeen and didn't have a chance to finish high school or go to college when they got back to the farm. Mom called me over to check my knapsack.

"I don't see a toothbrush," Mom said.

"We should be back before supper," Dad said.

I pulled my toothbrush out of my jean pocket and showed her. She took it from my hand and dropped it in the knapsack.

"Get a roll of film out of my purse for your camera," she said.

"Mom, I saw pheasants up by Mr. Pitts, across the road by the fence in the cornfield. I left corn behind our fence so they might stay in our woods and not get out in the open where they could get shot by hunters."

"Pheasants love corn. That was nice of you."

"Dad thinks they were safer in the field because they can run and fly easier there."

"Nature takes care of her own, Jerry. They may go in and eat your corn, but their instincts will have them return to the cornfield where they may be safer. That's the way nature is son. Have fun in Carthage with your dad. Take pictures."

Mom was good at knowing these things and putting a mind at ease— even though she was ready to let Gourmet Mike murder a rabbit just for science the time I thought he was going to murder it.

Then she went and ruined it all.

"Wild pheasant are game birds, just as the fish you catch

are game."

"Huh?"

"People hunt and fish game for food. You mustn't forget that, Jerry," Mom said.

Seemed animals could hardly win in the country.

Dad pulled around the swings, all the time looking in the direction of the barn garage at Dick and Duba under the '38.

"I hope they keep the noise down from that muffler in places where it would annoy people."

"You know what they're doing, Dad?" I asked, dumbfounded.

"I can read, son. The box he had the old muffler laying on said *glass packs*. I know what *glass packs* are. They're noise makers."

"If they're not legal, Dad, why do stores sell them?"

"The mufflers aren't illegal. The noise they make, in some cities, is."

Dad was like that. He would let us make our own decisions—as long as we were ready to accept the consequences.

We headed down Cardner Road.

"Where's the boat motor?"

"It's at a camp up on the Black River just beyond Watertown, closer to Canada," Dad said, turning right in the Delphi hamlet to head north.

All I could think of was the name of the river—Black River—and the African Queen. I'd never ridden with anyone in a boat with a motor before, so this would be an adventure.

"I thought we would get a little fishing in," Dad said.

"Is the river really black, Dad?"

"When we get there you can go ahead and take the boat and drive it up the river to the Carthage reservoir where I'll be waiting to meet you, and we'll put the motor in the trunk."

"Huh?" I grunted.

"He wants the boat in Carthage so he can haul it back to his camp filled with supplies. I told him you'd run it over to Carthage for him."

"Huh?"

Dad looked at me and smiled.

"What do you mean, *me*, Dad?"

"I want you to drive the boat into Carthage."

"Me?"

"You can do it, son."

"I can?"

"Just follow the river."

"You want me to drive a boat with a motor, a boat I don't row?"

"The river will do most of the work, son."

"What do you mean?"

"The Black River flows north; it'll float you there on its own eventually."

"Will I have oars?"

"Jerry me boy, pretend you're the captain of a tramp steamer headed off to Casablanca, or maybe even to Pago Pago."

Bloodsucking crawling leaches crossed my mind.

Driving north, we stopped at a bait house I'd never been in before and bought some worms—our favorite bait—a red and white plastic bobber and some lead sinkers for Dad's fishing box. Dad bought a flashlight with a lantern handle on it in case I needed it. Then he held up two tuna fish sandwiches wrapped in wax paper and asked if I wanted them in the boat, just in case.

I shook my head yes but my mind thought just in case of what? Why would I need a flashlight with a lantern handle on it or extra food?

"What if the motor conks out?" Dad asked, "If you have to wait for help to come and it gets dark, you'll need light and food."

He offered all that without my asking any questions. I actually felt better.

"What if it does?" I asked.

"Like I told you son, the Black River flows north," he said. "If the motor conks and you can't start it just let the boat float on its own or set the oars and row it into Carthage."

"I row good."

"When you get there, just remember to park it at the steel bridge. You can't miss it. It's just before you get to the reservoir."

"Okay. Steel bridge."

"There's a can of gas in the boat, and the motor should make it."

Dad slowed to turn off the highway onto a narrow dirt farm road. It went straight through a large, fifty-acre hayfield. Land this far up in northern New York didn't have huge hills that looked like mountains like where we lived at Delphi Falls, or even like the hills around Cortland.

On the back side of the field we were driving through were thick woods with tall trees with green velvety moss high on their trunks and sprawling, scruffy bushes everywhere. When we got through the hayfield, we entered the woods. The dirt road began to wind like a snake around trees in short, sharp curves, back and forth as though we were in a real jungle.

At the Delphi Falls, I was used to the woods being up high on the sides or the tops of cliffs and the steep hills by the creek. This was a ground-level woods like in the Tarzan jungle movies. This was just like Africa.

In the distance I could see a cabin with boarded-up windows. We drove up to it. It was wood-planked and painted a light shade of green. It was at the shore of the wide river. Two squirrels were running around on the moss-covered wood shake roof. Dad parked and told me to go check out the boat while he went into the cabin to find a broom. I looked through the car window at the river. It sure was black. I watched the water lumber slowly on by, and mysteriously, my brain began to register with the reality of it.

"Oh, my God."

This was the widest river I had ever seen and as dark black as coal. I cautiously got out of the car, stepped forward and had my first close look and how black it was. My heart sank. I could almost see the crocodiles and hippos attacking my boat, just like in *African Queen*.

This can't be good, I thought.

Dad brought an old broom from the cabin and handed it to me.

"Sweep the leaves out of the boat to get it ready, son."

As I swept, I noticed the boat bottom was dry, which was good.

"Why's the river so black, Dad?"

"Minerals in the soil is my guess, son, but it isn't black everywhere—only around Watertown and Carthage—maybe Pine

Camp. There are a lot of twists and turns between here and Carthage," he said. "You'll see it all."

I could hear birds, especially crows making loud cawing noises. Every sound seemed louder and more alive here on level ground than animal sounds did in the hills back at Delphi Falls, near my camp. Maybe the river here made the sounds echo, or maybe it was the thundering noise of the two waterfalls back at home that muffled or drowned out those animal sounds. I watched an eagle high in the sky, circling. I didn't dare ask Dad how deep the river was because I was afraid he'd tell me and give me a heart attack.

He handed me a one-dollar bill to keep in my pocket and we packed the boat with my supplies, the lantern flashlight, and a gas can. We walked out on the wooden dock with our fishing poles and cast lines for a while, but we had no luck—not even nibbles. I wondered how fish could even see in such black, dark water, or what they looked like.

"Jump in the boat and see if you can start it, Jerry me boy."
"Already?"

"Pull the choke out until she revs up, and then push the choke knob back in."

"Dad, are you sure … ?" I started.

"The throttle is on the handle, son. Turn the handle one way to go faster, turn it the other way to go slower. You'll get the hang of it."

"Will you wait here till I know for sure, Dad?"

"Just remember to turn it slowly, son."

"Okay."

"Watch out for floating logs."

"Logs? I will."

"And go around them."

I made certain to listen to my dad and to hear every word.

The motor started on the third pull of the cord. Dad grinned and threw the rope line into the boat and shoved me away from the dock.

"Don't go yet, Dad."

"Go out to the middle of the river and back here a few times."

"You'll wait?"

"Of course, I'll wait. Go back and forth to get the hang of it. If it conks, just set the oars and row it."

I did get the hang of it. It was easier than I thought—and it was fun turning the boat around in the water and watching it push a wake in front of it. I felt like a sea captain.

From the shore, Dad pointed toward Carthage, indicating it was time to leave and which way to go. He stood and saluted, a sharp salute, like I was now a sea captain. He waved goodbye, turned and walked toward his car and put the fishing gear in the trunk.

I remember watching him get in behind the wheel, the car door open and his foot still out on the ground. He watched me putter slowly on up the deep, black river for a few minutes until I was almost out of sight. I think he missed being a kid and adventures like the one I was about to go on.

He smiled and waved goodbye, lifted his leg in, backed around, and drove off, leaving me on my own.

I was alone on a strange river.

Other than my imagination scaring me at every animal sound and turn in the river, the ride down the river was a great adventure— maybe my best yet, and I wasn't even ten.

The more I saw the more I knew there was not a doubt in my mind—this was one of the best adventures of my entire life. It felt exactly like being deep in the jungles of Africa every second I was there. I watched that eagle drop like a bullet from the tallest branch of a towering tree to swoop up a squirrel too long at rest. The eagle missed, but the wind gust of its great wings caused the squirrel to roll two times while scurrying on the ground and into a hole for safety.

I ate a tuna sandwich with one hand, steering the boat with the other, without a worry in the world.

Cooooooooooooool!

The river ride eventually took me into a new to me northern city—one I'd never been in before. Boating into Carthage was an experience. It was my tramp steamer ride.

Soon I could see cars moving up high above the riverbank. I wondered if they could see me down here and if they knew I navigated downstream several miles, all alone, fearless.

On the right, up ahead, I could see the big old steel bridge and I could see Dad's car parked on it. He was waving from the railing. I thought of my airplane ride the time he was there to meet me when I landed.

I was above the reservoir dam, floating toward it. I couldn't see it, but I could hear it thundering and I was distracted by the noise. It sounded a lot like our lower waterfall behind our house, the Delphi Falls. The Black River was so calm the sound confused me at first.

Then I saw it. I realized what it was.

"Gulp."

I could see a calm, thin, flat-water line stretch across the whole river to where the dam spilled over. No ripples in it like the rest of the river.

"This can't be good," I mumbled.

I grabbed an oar and crawled to the front bow of the boat to try to steer it. Just beyond the dam's spillway I could see the treetops in the background peeking up behind the dam.

The calm line across the river was where the current of the river flow stopped and where it began to pool, about two hundred feet ahead. It was pooling and waiting to go over the dam. This was obviously the top of the reservoir-spill dam Dad told me about—and for sure the boat would go over it in heavy waters; go over and straight down, me and all, if I didn't get to the bridge and tie up.

This really can't be good, I thought.

Dad and his friend were down by the mooring under the bridge, waving to get my attention and shouting, "Cut the motor. Cut the motor!"

They threw a rope for me to catch. While reaching for it I accidently kicked the flashlight over the side and into the deep, dark river. It sank like an anchor, disappearing out of view just as I grabbed the rope.

"Hang on tight, son, while we pull you in."

My heart was pumping like the steam engine of the African Queen.

Dad and his friend pulled the boat in and began to tie it securely to the dock.

Dad's friend shook my hand and helped me out of the boat.

"Congratulations, young fella," he said.

"I made it," I said, happy to have my feet on the ground again.

"You just traveled several miles through wilderness and brought her in safe and sound."

"Wilderness?"

"Young man, did you see any bald eagles?"

"I did! One was flying in circles and then there was another one I watched one come down off a tree to catch a squirrel. He didn't get it."

"In that woods there are plenty of bears, bobcats, and wolves—all sorts. In daylight they mostly sleep."

"Bobcats?"

"You had you a real adventure, son."

The man detached the small motor from the boat while Dad finished tying the boat up under the bridge wall and out of the path of possible overnight rain. The man was going to come tomorrow with his bigger boat and pull this one, filled with supplies, back to his camp. I stood there staring down the deep black river, playing it all back in my mind.

I thanked the man for the ride and for trusting me with his boat. Dad set the boat motor in the trunk of the car and we drove a few blocks to the bakery.

I'd never been inside the Carthage bakery, only the Homer bakery. It was just as busy and as brightly lit. The bread oven seemed as big as the building. They were baking bread on the oven's turning wire conveyer racks and making doughnuts in another area. Everything smelled good. People everywhere were waving hi to me as we walked by, even though they didn't know me. One man stepped from behind a stainless-steel table, handed me two hot doughnuts and told me there was hot chocolate in the break room.

Dad pointed and said, "Take the doughnuts to the meeting room over there, son, so you won't bother the busy bakers. I'll come get you when we're ready to go."

The meeting room ceiling lights were already on. I had never seen a meeting room before, except maybe in a movie at the Saturday morning picture show. It looked important. There were big maps on two of the walls that looked like blow-ups of the New York State map in my geography book at school.

A long, shiny wooden conference table in the middle of the room had a glass on the top and eight leather chairs around it. I put my hot chocolate and one of the doughnuts down on a piece of newspaper and walked to the wall to look at the maps. The closer I examined them, the better I could see lines and circles carefully drawn on them. They looked like drawings of Tinker Toys. Lines and circles were everywhere. There was a circle around Binghamton, which was a city down below Cortland; a circle around Cortland; a circle around Utica, east of Syracuse; a circle around Syracuse; and a circle around Watertown and Carthage. Then there were smaller circles around all the smaller towns like Massena and Ogdensburg with lines connecting them to the bigger circles. Lots of lines and lots of circles.

I bit into my second doughnut, thinking about what it all meant, just as Dad came in and said we could head home.

"What are the maps for, Dad?

"It's where we meet and plan, son."

"Is this a secret room?"

"Well, secret from our competition. Those maps show all the bread routes for both of our bakeries—the one in Homer and for this bakery plant here in Carthage. The circles are the cities or towns where the grocery stores are that our route salesman deliver loaves of bread to in their bread trucks. The lines between the circles are the bigger bread trucks that deliver cartons of bread to the delivery trucks in the circles. Do you remember the truck that delivered bread to us in Brewerton so we could hang loaves on doors in the Indian head bonnets?"

"I remember."

Dad pointed to one of the lines that went from a circle around Homer to a circle around Brewerton and said, "That truck is this line, number thirty- one." Dad loved teaching things to people who listened. He got a desk lamp and held it up near each of the maps so I could take pictures in its light with my Baby Brownie camera.

I learned something new that day. Besides learning how to drive a boat, I saw how bread got from bakeries in Carthage and Homer to stores all over a lot of the state. I knew someday I was going to try it out—see how far I could go just by hopping bread trucks from town to town, connecting from truck to truck as I went. In the back of my head I had a feeling someday this knowledge could help my detective work kind of like Myrtie, the telephone operator helped.

## CHAPTER NINE
## SHERIFF HOOD

Dad took a quarter out of his pocket.

"Call it, Bucky!" he announced, not taking his eyes off the flying quarter on its descent. He slapped the coin down to the counter when it landed.

"Tails!" Bucky yelped.

It was heads.

Dad won the toss this time, but he slid the quarter over the counter toward Bucky and said, "Throw in a hot chocolate for Jerry me boy with my coffee, if you will, my good friend."

Bucky tipped his paper cap as a kindly thank you.

"It will be my pleasure, kind sir," and placing both palms on the counter, he lifted his legs up sideways almost above the counter and kicked his heels together.

Just as he landed his feet down and was about to speak, something caught his eye through the front window of the diner. "I wonder what's going on?" Bucky asked.

"Going on where?" Dad asked.

"Over there at the hardware store," Bucky said.

Dad and I turned on our stools and looked out the window. We could see the county sheriff's and a deputy's car parked in front of Brown's Hardware store across the street. People were standing around outside, talking.

Dad turned and looked up at the clock on the diner wall.

"It's too early. They aren't even open yet," Bucky said.

"Jerry me boy, let's walk over and see why the sheriff is there," Dad said. "Bucky, we'll be right back."

I ran to the car and grabbed my knapsack and pulled the Baby Brownie camera and two rolls of 127 film. Walking across the street, I loaded the camera. Dad told me no pictures unless someone said it was okay.

"Well hello Big Mike," the sheriff said. "Which one is this?"

"Sheriff Hood, meet Jerry," Dad said.

I put my hand out like Dad and Mom taught us.

"Hi, young man," the sheriff said while shaking my hand. "I'm Sheriff Todd Hood, and it's always nice to meet any son of Big Mike's."

"What happened?" I asked.

"Burglary, son" the sheriff said.

"Is that like robbery, Sheriff Hood?"

"Jerry, a robbery is when someone says, 'This is a stick up!' A burglary is when they sneak around like weasels in the night, and they break into places when no one is around."

My heart jumped into my throat. I was standing at the scene of a real crime. What would the Hardy Boys do? I asked myself. They would watch and listen, I told myself.

"Sheriff, can I take pictures?"

"Just be careful and don't touch anything," the sheriff said.

"Dad, can I?"

"Sure, go ahead."

I listened to everyone talking.

Someone had broken the lock on the door with a crowbar, but the crowbar wasn't anywhere to be found. It looked like maybe all they took were shotgun shells, but the owner wasn't sure until he could do inventory.

I stood by the door and got chills just looking at the same door where desperate criminals were standing in the dark during the middle of the night breaking into this place. It was like I was in a mystery movie. My Baby Brownie didn't have a flash, so I had to be smart and be sure there was some light on everything I took a picture of. I had to remember to stay calm so I wouldn't overlook a single clue.

I snapped a picture of a messy pile of 12-gauge shotgun shell boxes. On the floor was a folded, bent-up book of matches with the name Kelly's Truck Rest Stop—Groton, New York, on it. I didn't touch it. but I took a picture close enough so I could read the name in the lens.

I couldn't help noticing how neat everything was throughout the store except for where the burglars had apparently stolen things.

On a hunch, something I learned from reading Hardy Boys

mysteries, I walked around the entire store, step by step, remembering I was walking in the same footsteps as desperate criminals. If I saw something that looked like it was messed up or out of place, I snapped a picture of it with my Baby Brownie.

The hunting licenses pad was one of those things, because it was hanging two inches over the side of the countertop. I took a picture of it and of the ballpoint pen on the floor below it.

I took a picture of the shotgun rack, because there was a small .410- gauge shotgun lying on the counter in front of it. I saw a Daisy BB gun outside of its box on the floor. I took a picture of both the Daisy BB gun and the box.

I could hear the sheriff talking about dusting the place for fingerprints, but he suspected the burglars wore gloves, and that so far, from the looks of it, the only thing missing seemed to be shotgun shells. Someone else told the sheriff that the cash register didn't appear to be touched. The money was still in it and there was some more money in a cigar box under the counter. The store manager suggested that the burglars maybe thought opening the cash register might set off an alarm and they didn't see the cigar box.

"Some people are just getting their feet back on the ground after the war," the sheriff said. "They sure enough broke the law, but there's a chance they just needed shotgun shells to hunt for food."

"Go over to the diner, son," dad said. "Order something to eat."

"Okay."

"I'll be there shortly."

I said thanks to Sheriff Hood, went outside, looked both ways and ran across the road to Bucky's.

I had important detective work to do.

The second I was inside the diner, I said hi to Bucky and asked him if he could change a dollar bill for me.

"Is there trouble over there?" Bucky asked.

"They had burglars," I said. "They busted in."

I stuck fingers in my secret pocket and pulled out a dollar I kept for emergencies. I unfolded it and pressed it on the counter. Under his palm he slid three quarters, two dimes, and a nickel to me.

"Whatcha gonna eat, young man?"

"Is the phone a nickel or a dime?" I asked.

"Nickel."

"Want a hot chocolate?"

"Yes. Can I get an egg sandwich, too, please?"

"How do you like it?"

"Like you make it, with mayonnaise and bacon."

"Coming right up!"

I lifted the receiver, put it to my ear, reached up to the coin slot, and dropped a nickel in—*ding*—then dialed "O" and listened for the operator.

"Opporatorrrre, how may I assist you, paleeze," a sharp, loud voice said on the phone.

"Myrtie, is that you?"

"This is the opporatorrrre, how may I assist you?"

"Operator, can you get me New Woodstock 62 .It's near the Delphi Falls, please?"

"One moment, paleeze."

Her accent made me feel like I was in a movie. I hoped I had enough change for a long-distance call all the way to Barber's house.

"Sir, the Delphi Falls is in the New Woodstock exchange. One moment, paleeze."

While I waited, I wondered if this operator was going to talk to Myrtie in New Woodstock. In the reflection off the two tall, shiny coffee urns behind the counter, I could see my dad starting to leave Brown's Hardware and saying goodbye to Sheriff Hood. I heard static on the phone and then I heard Mrs. Barber.

"Hello?"

"Hold for aalooong disteeeance, paleeze," the operator said. "Deposit twenteeee cents, sir."

I dropped in two dimes—*ding-ding, ding-ding.*

Dad walked into the diner and looked at me on his way to the counter. I could see he was curious why I would be making a telephone call, but he had a pleased look in his eye knowing I figured out how to use a coin- operated telephone. Bucky poured him a fresh cup of coffee.

"Hello, Mrs. Barber, is Dale there?"

"Why Jerry, this is a long-distance telephone call, I could hear the coins drop. Where on earth are you, lad?"

"I'm in Cortland."

"Let me hurry and get Dale for ya, dear."

"Hello?" Barber asked.

"Hey, Barber, I'm in Cortland."

"Are you actually calling me long distance?"

"Yes."

"Oh, jeez! That's what Mom said. My first long-distance coin operated pay phone telephone call in history."

"We need a Pompey Hollow Book Club meeting right away," I said.

"What for?"

"Something's up, and we need to meet today, so I can tell everybody what I know. Can you call everybody?"

"Today?"

"Yes, today!"

"What time?"

I looked around at the diner clock on the wall and calculated how long Dad normally stayed in his office reading his mail on Saturdays and then the thirty-five-minute drive home from then if we didn't stop to fish.

"Say two hours from now," I said.

"Two hours, got it," Barber said.

"I'll get my dad to drop me off at the cemetery on the way home and I'll wait if I'm early," I said.

"Okay," Barber said.

"Tell everybody it's an emergency," I said.

"Okay."

I hung up so the call wouldn't cost more. I only had quarters left.

As always on Saturday, Dad went into the bakery office to read his mail.

"Son, your mother wants you to try on some shoes at Stillwell's. Go do that while I go up to the office."

I first walked down a block to the drugstore and gave the lady my two rolls of film for developing. She told me it would be Wednesday before they could be picked up. I wrote "Wednesday" on my jean pant leg so I wouldn't forget to ask Dad to pick the developed pictures up for me. I walked back toward the car. I saw Mr. Stillwell in the general store window and waved hi to him. I went into his store and tried on Buster Brown shoes. I told him about the burglary at Brown's Hardware. I told him they weren't sure if anything was missing and the money was still in the cash register. Mr. Stillwell told me his front door lock was broken just a month ago, and when he saw money still in the cash register, he didn't say anything—

I interrupted.

"Did they mess anything up?"

He walked over to a corner in his store where he had hunting boots.

"After they left, there were open boxes of boots everywhere over here, all small sizes."

"Hunting boots?" I asked.

"Hunting boots. But none missing," he said.

I tried on some shoes, took the pair Mr. Stillwell said fitted me best, waved goodbye and walked over to the bakery. Dad was standing outside, talking with his bakery partner, Mr. Durkee. He looked over at me.

"Did you find shoes?"

"In this box," I said.

"Let's go home, son," he said. "First I'll go pay Mr. Stillwell for the shoes. Get in the car."

When Dad started to get in the car he asked.

"Want to stop somewhere and do some fishing?"

I waited for him to close the door before asking, "Dad, instead of fishing today, can you take me to the Delphi cemetery right away and drop me off? The Pompey Hollow Book Club is having an important meeting."

Dad gave me a look, kind of like, "What books could be so important as to interrupt Saturday morning fishing?" But he didn't ask any questions.

"On our way, Jerry me boy. We're on our way. Next stop—the Delphi cemetery."

As we rode up Route 11, I looked at big barns on the right, some red and some mostly white and the farm pastures going by. Watching them I remembered how, during the war, men in white coveralls with POW sewn on their backs worked these same farms. POWs were WWII enemy *prisoners of war* American or allied soldiers had captured in Germany. Prisoners of war who hated Hitler and could be trusted were put to work on local farms that needed helpers. Most of the American farm boys were drafted into the army and were over in Germany fighting or on ships or in submarines or in bombers and fighter planes around the world, fighting Hitler and Mussolini and Japan. I remembered the POW prisoners never smiled or waved back when we drove by them during the war. I don't think they were allowed to look at us. The big barns reminded me of the hardware store. It was in a big white barn, so big they had tractors in it for sale. I couldn't help wondering if there was a formula, some numbers—like there was in advertising—that helped us with the bunnies or even like baking numbers, something that might fit it all together somehow and help us catch the crooks.

I could not hold it in any longer.

"We're going to catch those crooks, Dad," I said.

"Say that again, son."

"Dad, the Pompey Hollow Book Club— we're going to try to catch the crooks."

"The hardware store burglars? Your book club is going to—?"

"We read books, sure— I read most of *African Queen*, but we like to do good stuff like that better."

"I'm thinking your club is more about adventure than it is about books, son."

I didn't answer.

"Between you and me, son, that's what I been thinking all along."

"So, you aren't mad?"

Dad smiled like he always knew something was up, bigger than books, proud of our good-hearted nature and spirit of adventure for wanting to catch the burglars.

"Just like you always said, Dad, what kids should do during the war—help without having to be asked, especially if we saw someone being hurt."

He drove me to the cemetery, pulled into the entrance to let me out.

"Just don't worry your mother," he said.

I opened the door and got out of the car.

"I won't."

"Son, remember how Dick and Duba helped you with the rabbits?"

"You knew about that, him and Duba, Dad?"

"We knew, son."

"I remember, Dad."

"Think maybe they can help you again?"

I smiled and started walking up into the cemetery as he drove off. The Pompey Hollow Book Club felt a little more important to me somehow, with my Dad knowing the truth about us.

Mary, Barber, Randy Vaas, Mayor, and Holbrook were already there. Mary had been selling popsicles in the hamlet, so she took a break and parked her cart behind Bases's house. Barber and she walked to the cemetery together. Holbrook, Randy, and Mayor got a ride from Mr. Crane, but they would need a ride home unless they wanted to wait until Mary was finished selling popsicles.

I started to tell about the hardware store burglary and the pictures I took to see what they thought, and to ask them if the Pompey Hollow Book Club should send an SOS to Dick and Duba for help.

"Brown's Hardware was busted into last night," I said.

"What's a Brown's Hardware," Mayor asked.

"It's a hardware store in Cortland, down near my dad's bakery," I said.

"Who busted in?" Barber asked.

"Burglars, and something about it doesn't look right."

"What do you mean something doesn't look right about it?" Mary asked.

"Not sure. The sheriff thinks some poor guys did it, down and out from the war."

"Real bandits? Randy asked.

"I guess," I said.

"What did it look like?" Holbrook asked.

"I took pictures of everything I could but there are a lot of clues around, so I know I missed some."

"What kind of clues?" Mayor asked.

"From the clues I saw, I think kids did it, but I'm not even sure about that. It doesn't look like anything was taken."

"Why would someone break in and not take anything?" Mary asked.

"It's a mystery," Randy said.

Barber stammered in awe— "HOLY COBAKO!"

"What's wrong with you?" I asked.

"You actually met a real live sheriff?"

"Sheriff Todd Hood?"

"You met him?" Barber asked.

"Sure enough."

"Jeez."

"Met him and shook his hand. No big deal."

"Shut up, that is a big deal.," Barber said.

"Just foolin' ya— it was a big deal," I said.

"Who here wants to vote on our trying to solve the crime?" Mary asked.

We all spat.

"We're maybe going to need the older guys for this one," Barber said.

"Dick and Duba?" Mary asked.

"They're smart and can drive," I said.

"For sure," Mayor said.

We all spat.

"Who wants to get the older guys to help?" Holbrook asked.

"Jerry, was Dick telling the truth Easter Sunday when he said we could SOS him if we ever needed their help again?" Mary asked.

"Yes."

"Do you think he meant it?" Holbrook asked.

"He meant what he said. He liked helping us with the rabbits. He told me so."

"Good," Mary said.

"He said he liked your having the popsicle cart to make money with. He said all that. I promise."

"Who votes Jerry gives Dick an SOS to see if they'll help?" Mary asked.

We all spat.

The vote was cast and agreed to.

"How about we have regular meetings at school?" Mary asked.

"Will they be secret?" Barber asked.

"Why not?" Mary asked.

"We can meet Wednesdays at lunch," Holbrook said.

"First meeting everybody bring a book you've read and we'll trade them off so we don't look stupid if somebody gets suspicious or asks questions about our club," Mary said.

"I ain't reading a book," Holbrook said. "I do enough of that in school."

"Get one out of the school library and carry it," Randy said.

"Barber, you still call emergency meetings for here in the cemetery," Mary said.

Everyone agreed.

The meeting was over.

We walked into Delphi to stroll with Mary to watch her sell popsicles door to door from her cart. She treated us to one, half price, before Holbrook and I walked back to my house and Barber headed to his.

When we got home, Dick was in the barn garage with Duba, both under the hood of the '38.

At first, Holbrook and I stood at the doorway and watched. Stepping in closer, I cleared my throat and declared in a loud enough voice for them both to hear.

"Dick!"

"What?"

"Dot, dot, dot; dash, dash, dash; dot, dot, dot."

Dick raised his head out from under the hood and looked around at me and then over at Holbrook. He saw we were serious.

"What's up?" he asked.

"Brown's Hardware, you know it?"

"Cortland, what about it?"

"It was broken into last night and there are a lot of crazy clues," I said.

"Last night?" Dick asked.

"The crooks got away," I said.

Dick looked at Duba, then looked back at me.

"Let me get it right, is that the hardware store in the big barn at the bridge between Homer and Cortland?"

"Yes," I said, "on the left, right across from Bucky's."

"Okay," Dick said.

"Okay you'll help?"

"Me and Duba will take a look."

"Is this an official SOS you guys are taking, then?" Holbrook asked.

"Does it mean you'll help us?"

"No, not yet— I said we'll take a look. No promises, not until we know something," Dick said.

"We'll check it out, ask around," Duba said. "We'll let you know if and when it's a good SOS."

"When will that be?" I asked.

"You'll know when. I'll tell you," Dick said.

## CHAPTER TEN
## BACK TO SCHOOL

On the calendar tacked to the kitchen wall I looked at the crayoned "X" on Tuesday's square. Today was Saturday, the Labor Day weekend. School started on Tuesday.

Halfway through my peanut butter and jelly sandwich the telephone rang. I set the sandwich down, ran into Mom and Dad's room.

"Hello?"

"Jerry?"

It was Dick.

"Yeah."

"We're taking your SOS."

"For real?"

"Be in front of Shea's store Tuesday—during lunch hour!"

He hung up.

I didn't ask what he was thinking or what he and Duba came up with. All I knew was it might be another adventure for us. I had to get word to the Pompey Hollow Book Club to be in front of Shea's store on Tuesday. That was good enough for me. I set the phone down, thought for a minute and picked it up again.

"Operator."

"Myrtie, this is Jerry. I need Barber."

"A Saturday morning call so soon after you talked with Dick. Sounds important," Myrtie said.

"It is for sure."

"One minute, honey."

"Thanks, Myrtie."

"Let me know if you need my help again."

"I will, thanks."

"Hello?"

"Mrs. Barber, this is Jerry, is Dale there?"

"He's right here, honey."

"Hello?"

"Barber, better call Mary, set up a meeting?"

"What's up?"

"Dick and Duba took our SOS."

"For sure?"

"He just told me—we have to be at Shea's store."

"When?"

"Noon on Tuesday."

"Tuesday at noon? Shea's store?"

"All I know is Dick and Duba took our SOS, I don't know anything else."

"I'll call Mary. I'll set it up," Barber said.

"I'll call Kellish so he can tell Holbrook," I said. "You call Mary and the rest?"

"ROGER WILKO! OVER AND OUT!" Barber blurted and hung up.

I got chills knowing the Pompey Hollow Book Club was about to learn of our secret meeting set for our first day back at school.

Tuesday morning at school was antsy because we weren't sure what Dick and Duba had in mind—but we knew our first SOS call to the older guys was like no other call any of us had ever made before.

Besides the members of the Pompey Hollow Book Club—Dick, Duba and some of the older kids showed up in front of Shea's store. The agriculture and mechanic teacher, Mr. Ossant, happened to be walking by, biting into an apple. He paused and leaned on the maple tree to see what the commotion was all about. Student passersby, kids on lunch break gathered.

Crowds gathering in 1947, '48 and '49 could be entertainment, social, or they could be serious gatherings. It was natural for kids who lived through the war to flock to a crowd just to hear news—reminiscent of gathering to hear war reports. There were no televisions then and most kids growing up through the entire war only knowing about the war by watching Saturday movie newsreels at the movie house. We saw brave soldiers being sent all over the world to fight enemies and maybe die so kids could be safe and free. None of us could do anything all through that war except pray and help our parents, but there wasn't a man jack kid among us who didn't have romance and bravery running through our veins because of what we went through and what we witnessed.

Had we lived in Germany we would have been in the underground helping save German kids. We were always ready to volunteer. If we heard someone needed help, we drew to them like bees to honey. With party telephone lines in those days tying up the telephone, kids relied on gossip and listening in. No telling how many kids would show up by Tuesday, all said and done. About a dozen maybe, but we could count on more next time after word got out.

Dick and Duba waited on the top step in front of Shea's store. They already asked Mike Shea, the owner, if he would join us outside because maybe he could help us. Dick's thinking was that being that stores were being burglarized and Mike was a store owner, maybe he could give us some ideas.

Looking out at a couple dozen or so gathering around, Mike Shea said, "Well, since nobody can get into the store, I might just as well be out here getting some sun."

"Listen up," Duba barked.

We quieted down. Dick began.

"There was a burglary in Cortland—"

"Where?" came a voice.

"—at Brown's Hardware," Dick said. "It's that hardware store in the red barn on the left just before the bridge."

"I know that store," came a voice.

"And it looks fishy," Dick said.

"Real fishy," Duba said.

With only giving that little tidbit of information, and without a pause or a hesitation, Dick asked, "Who's in?"

No one had a clue what being "in" meant—didn't matter. Just the same as every Revolutionary War Minuteman would, the bunch of boys and girls all raised their hands, accepting the challenge. Mr. Ossant, the agriculture teacher, raised his hand because he always thought he was one of the kids. His shop was out behind the school, and he saw kids more than he ever saw any teachers.

The general feeling in the air was that any adventure to kick off the school year was welcomed. Dick started talking again.

"When Duba and I went to investigate the burglary, no one who worked in the hardware store thought anything was stolen," Dick said.

"Why would someone go and bust a door open and ransack a store in the middle of the night and not take anything?" Mary asked.

"Real fishy," Duba said.

"We need to investigate more and look at all the evidence," Dick said.

"I took two rolls of film of clues I thought I saw to the drugstore in Homer to be developed." I said.

"You have them back yet, the pictures?" Dick asked.

"They're ready tomorrow. I have another roll of film at the Tully drugstore— stuff I shot pictures of in Carthage."

"When—?" Dick started.

I interrupted, "Oh, I forgot! When I was in Homer with Dad, I saw Mr. Stillwell at the general store. He told me his place was broken into about a month ago. He told me he didn't see anything the crooks took, either."

"Fishy," Duba said.

"This is getting good," Holbrook said.

I got goose bumps.

"We need an investigator," Dick said.

"You mean a private eye?" Barber asked.

Dick looked out among the kids and caught the eye of Marty Bays, a red-headed boy in a grade ahead of me and the club members.

"Marty, how old are you?" Dick asked.

"Who wants to know?" Marty yelled back.

"How old are you?" Duba asked.

"Tell me why you need to know how old any of us are?"

"I heard you have a farm driving permit," Dick said.

"A permit for what?" Mary asked.

"For hauling milk to Apulia Station in his dad's truck," Dick said.

"I'm twelve," Marty said.

"You got a driving permit or not, Marty?"

"You betcha I do—and I'm also an official reporter for the school newspaper."

"What's that got to do with driving?" Duba asked.

"I'm trained to investigate, get the answers, and keep my eye on the prize."

"Can you get to Cortland is all I need to know," Dick said.

This mission required more than talent, it required means —Marty could drive, and he had his dad's truck every morning.

"Ain't supposed to but I sure enough could, I reckon," Marty said. "My early morning milk run to Apulia Station just may run a little longer than usual if I happen to mosey down to Cortland."

There were mumbles of laughter, most everybody knowing Marty's farm permit was restricted to farm errands. Farm kids like him could get a special driving permit at twelve. His permit let him drive the milk cans from their farm to dairy drop off at Apulia Station—which was just before Tully and on the way to Cortland and then to school. Duba turned to Dick.

"What if he gets caught?" Duba asked.

"Cortland's a whole county over," Dick said.

"So?"

"It's not like there'd be any state prisons involved in case he gets caught, in my thinking," Dick said. "He'd probably be taken home for a scolding after a sheriff bought him ice cream at a drugstore soda fountain and told him not to do it again."

"Yeah, it ain't like he doesn't have a driving permit."

Dick stepped up and addressed Marty. "Good," Dick said. "Marty, you go check out the hardware store people, and then the general store people."

"I'll do it," Marty said.

"Find out everything you can," Dick said.

"Tell 'em you're writing a newspaper story," Mary said.

"Sounds like there might be more than one or two burglaries—what if there's more?" Duba asked.

Dick wanted to stay concentrated on the task at hand.

"When can you go, Marty?" he asked.

"What say I do it Thursday?"

"Why Thursday?" Dick asked. "We need to know now."

"Well there ain't no pictures yet—not till Thursday. So if I go Thursday that-a-way I can go to the drugstore and pick up the pictures Jerry took—but I'll need some money to pay for them."

Dick leaned into Duba's ear.

"He's going to be good," he whispered.

Knowing Thursday was a school day and Marty would be gone the better part of the morning, kids volunteered to go with him. Dick and Duba decided to keep truancy to a minimum and told Marty to go alone but take a tablet and write a lot of notes.

"Yo," Marty said.

Dick reminded the agriculture teacher, Mr. Ossant, and the store owner, Mike Shea, that they didn't hear any of this meeting.

"Hear what?" Mike Shea asked with a grin.

"What meeting?" Mr. Ossant asked and walked away.

"Who can meet here Friday to hear Marty's report?" Dick asked.

Everyone raised their arms.

"Good luck, Marty," Mary said.

"Don't get caught," Duba said.

With that we broke up the first official Pompey Hollow Book Club SOS meeting. Most of us went in the store and got our candy or gum or whatever caught our eye from behind the glass that we had pennies or nickels for. Barber borrowed fifteen cents from someone for a pickled egg, and I borrowed a nickel of that from Barber for a Clark bar, causing Barber to have to negotiate a lower price for the pickled egg. All this high finance with me forgetting I had a dollar bill and eighty cents in loose change in my secret pocket left over from my boat ride on the Black River and my long-distance telephone call to Barber.

Mr. Ossant walked back to the school alone, so as not to be seen mingling with our group.

A passel of kids—more than forty this time—showed up at Shea's store for the Friday meeting, plus Mr. Shea and Mr. Ossant again.

Duba stepped up on the store steps next to Dick and turned to the kids.

"Listen up."

Dick lifted his T-shirt and pulled a spiral notebook he had tucked under his belt and a pencil from his back pocket. Not to spoil his reputation for never opening a notebook, he handed it down to Mary, Holbrook, Barber, and me, hoping one of us would take notes.

"Marty—whatcha got?" he barked.

We didn't recognize Marty standing in among us, dressed the way he was. His red hair was wet and slicked back, parted and combed like he was going to church. He even had his Sunday go-to-meeting coat and a bright red tie, trying to look like he was some hotshot newspaper reporter in a big city press conference ready just in case there were photographers lurking about Shea's corner on a school day. He had a clipboard in his hand and a pencil over his ear. Marty stepped confidently to the top step of Shea's store, turned to us, straightened his tie and barked like he was running for president and there was a crowd of thousands around him.

"I want to thank everybody for covering my back Thursday and special thanks to whoever managed to get me the 86 on the Social Studies pop quiz I wasn't there to take."

"I didn't hear that," Mr. Ossant shouted.

Not wanting our meeting to wake up the whole county, Dick barked, "Keep the voices down, you guys—and Marty, we can hear. Talk natural."

"Let's hear what he's got to say," Duba said.

Marty loosened his tie and lifted his clipboard to read his report. Someone had written on the back side of it in crayon, "The School Flame— only news that's fit to be tied!"

"Number one, sometime in the night between Friday evening and Saturday morning a week ago, the Brown Hardware store in Cortland was broken into."

"We already know that, Marty—" Dick started.

"Number two, although it was first believed that the perpetrators purloined several boxes of 12-gauge shotgun shells, this reporter has discovered that no shotgun shells were, in fact, taken."

"None?" I asked.

"Number three, this reporter interviewed the proprietor of the General Store establishment in Homer, one Mr. Stillwell, and discovered a similar break-in less than a month ago. The first thought, in this break-in also, was that nothing was taken—"

"Nothing?" Duba asked.

"—however, the General Store proprietor soon discovered a cash shortage of two hundred and seven dollars."

"From where?" I asked.

"From his cash register."

Dick interrupted, "What about the hardware store?"

Mary murmured approval of Dick's interruption. Keeping Marty focused was a good thing, as she didn't quite know where he was taking us with his report.

"Number four, with the new information in hand, this reporter took it upon myself to return back to the hardware store crime scene to further investigate—further. I discovered, upon my return, there was five-hundred and sixty-five dollars missing from their cash drawer, only found out at closing on Monday, them staying closed on Saturday because of the burglary and on Sunday for church-going like everyone else."

Dick interrupted.

"Wait a minute—wait a minute," Dick growled. "The hardware store people told us no money was taken."

"Correctamundo!" Marty snickered back. "So did the General Store owner at first—only to discover they were short two hundred and seven dollars from their till."

"The hardware store?" Barber asked.

"He said the General Store," Dick grunted. "Pay attention and just listen."

Dick stood back and let Marty continue.

"Number five, before I deducted any conclusions, I went to the drugstore in Homer and picked up the photographs taken at the scene of the crime by one Jerry Antil, to see if they could provide any further clues."

Mary leaned into Barber and whispered, "I wonder if we grab Marty and took his tie and coat off and messed up his hair, would he talk faster and get to the point?"

"Listen up," Duba barked.

Our very own Sherlock Holmes, Marty, boy reporter, pressed on.

"It's clear to me that photo evidence number one, number four, number six, and number seven indicate a kid was involved in the crime."

"How?" Dick asked.

Mary had a premonition and interrupted before Marty could answer.

"He said those things about the BB gun and stuff," Mary said.

"So?" Dick asked.

"So older crooks aren't interested in BB guns and .410 shotguns and size nine hunting boots," Mary said.

Marty pressed on.

"These pictures prove the kids involved were not burglars or robbers, or why else wouldn't they take these things and only just look at them like window shoppers and put them back down?"

"Maybe it's a whole family?" came a voice from the crowd.

"Photos two, five, eight, and eleven clearly indicate an adult was involved and most likely perpetrated the hardware store crime with a kid or kids."

"How so?" Dick asked.

"The picture is of the matchbook, which leads me to believe the adult is a smoker. The picture of the hunting licenses tells us any one of them could be over eighteen. The ransacked size twelve hunting boots and the messed-up boxes of twelve-gauge shells tells us it was an adult. The missing money tells me their modus operandi and that they have done this before and will probably do it again. If it was a kid alone, a kid would have looked at four-ten shells after looking at the four-ten shotgun and no one did, and as for stealing money, most kids have no use for money other than helping out our folks."

"That's a crock, Marty and you know it," Mary barked.

"What's a crock?" Dick asked.

"About a kid being there. I bet all that is a diversion."

"It was probably an adult and kid team," Duba said.

"The adult for money and the kid along for the ride, for fun?" Mary asked. "I don't see it."

"The kid along for a distraction, to mess up clues," Marty said.

Half of the kids clapped at Mary's and Marty's trying to make sense out of it. The other half clapped as if they were thinking Marty was starting to look better in his coat and tie.

Marty handed the photographs to Duba.

"I'll admit, country kids don't have a lot of places to spend money," Mary said. "Sorry I jumped at you."

"Farms being so self-sufficient," Marty said, "the thought of money to a country kid or the need for it rarely comes up, except maybe for comic books or bubble gum, but it's only pennies."

"He's right," Barber said. "Country kids don't steal. It's not in our nature."

Dick jumped up on the steps with Duba and Marty, grabbed the photographs from Duba and started thinking of questions he wanted to ask, as if he was inspired. He thumbed through each of the pictures and then slowed down, looking closely at the one of the opened cash drawers in the hardware store.

"Watch this," I told Holbrook and Barber.

"Watch what?" Holbrook asked.

"Dick's brain is clicking in. I've seen that look in his eyes before."

"Who's good at math?" Dick asked.

Dick was a genius at it, but this was no time to show off. Two kids raised their hands.

"What is two-hundred and forty-three minus thirty-six and six-hundred and fifty-one minus eighty-six? Dick asked.

"Are you saying AND like added up together? A voice shouted out.

"No," Dick said. "Sorry, each added separately."

"Two-hundred-seven and five-hundred-sixty-five," the voice shouted.

Dick made a mental note of who had shouted that math in case he needed to skip a math test, and maybe this person would take it for him. Then he nudged Duba like he was ready to come up with a plan.

"Watch this," I said. "I bet Dick and Duba know exactly what we have to do now."

Dick took a deep breath, looked around and waited for Duba's signal.

"Listen up," Duba barked.

Dick started to talk, and then paused like he had an inspiration. He bent up his knee and wrote something on a piece of paper resting on it. He handed the note to Mike Shea, asking him if he would go in and make an important telephone call for him. Mike read the note, nodded his approval and went in the store.

"Marty did good with his investigating," Dick said. "Jerry did good with his pictures of clues."

Holbrook punched my arm.

"But we aren't done yet. We're going to need volunteers, so listen up." "Listen up," Duba echoed.

"First, picture the cash drawer in every store register. It has slots in it for paper money, right?"

"Yes," came a voice.

"A slot for every kind of bill."

"What's your point?" Mary asked.

"If you leave a twenty-dollar bill, a ten-dollar bill, a five-dollar bill, and a one-dollar bill in a cash drawer—in their slots, it'll look like there is money in all the cash slots of the drawer, and if you were to look fast at the money drawer and saw those bills in the right slots you would think no money was taken until after the cash count at closing the next day when you came up short. That's how the general store was missing two-hundred and seven bucks, which took them a whole day to miss. There was a bill in every slot when Mr. Stillwell opened the cash drawer and looked—so he probably closed the cash drawer fast and figured the store wasn't money robbed."

Cheers went up.

"And if you leave a fifty and a twenty and a ten and a five and a one in their slots in the cash drawer—that's how Brown's Hardware looked in their cash drawer and didn't know they were missing five-hundred-sixty-five dollars for two whole days."

"Dang," I said.

"From the evidence Marty and Jerry brought us, it is clear that these break-ins and burglaries were only out for one thing—the cash drawers—and the mess they made on purpose was a decoy and with the bills in each slot of the cash drawers covering their crime, cash was the last thing the owners would think was missing until long after all the phony clues got cold and the crooks left town."

Duba whacked Marty on the back, congratulating him, and he stumbled off the top step.

Mike Shea came outside and whispered something in Dick's ear. Dick looked down in the direction of Holbrook, Mary, Barber, me, and Bases. Above the noise he asked, "What's your club called, again?"

"The Pompey Hollow Book Club," Barber said. Dick winced at our name but faced the crowd.

"With Marty's evidence, we think we've solved how the crooks took the money. Who here wants to volunteer in the Pompey Hollow Book Club and actually catch the crooks?"

"What's the Pompey Hollow Book Club?" a voice asked.

"It's a club, is all," Mary said. "We meet in the Delphi Cemetery."

"Do we have to read anything?" someone guffawed.

"Only the Sunday comics," Duba said, laughing.

Everyone gathered in front of Shea's store looked amazed at what they had learned so fast by watching how the older guys made deductions from the clues. Every hand went up and then came down, clapping approval.

Seeing hands in the air wanting to be in the club, Barber leaned into Mary. "You're the president, Mary. There's good money in it. Look at the hands here. What if the Pompey Hollow Book Club could draw a bigger crowd and charge dues?"

Mary gave him an elbow in the ribs.

"Everybody, Mike Shea just telephoned the hardware store about picture number five," Dick started. "That's this picture with the hunting license pad leaning off the counter. Just as I suspected, the pad of hunting licenses and carbon sheets behind them were each individually numbered and the license and carbon sheet with number 134 on it is missing from the book. We find hunting license number 134 and we find our crook."

The kids' roar sounded like someone had hit a home run.

"The problem now is that Mr. Brown at the hardware store knows this clue, too, and he's calling Sheriff Hood to tell him about the hunting license clue we discovered," Duba said.

"So, we have to work fast if we want to get to the crooks before the sheriff does. Still in?" Dick shouted.

Heads nodded yes.

Dick took his glasses off, rubbed them on his shirt and put them back on while asking Duba what time it was.

Duba knew Dick's brain was loaded for bear and ready for action and told Dick so the crowd could hear, "We've got twelve minutes before the school bell rings. Listen up, everyone."

Dick looked around, impressed that some girls showed up, probably wondering which of them he maybe wanted to kiss sometime or take to the amusement park in Manlius with him and Duba on a Sunday. We could see his mind thinking as he was stalling until something to say came to him. Then he campaigned with arm up in the air.

"Do we just find 'em, or do we catch 'em?" Dick asked.

"Let's catch 'em," Mary shouted.

Mr. Ossant stepped up on the steps, waving an arm in the air.

"Boys and girls, I'm with you all the way—you know that for sure, boy and how—but do ya think maybe you wanna think this through a bit? Burglary is a serious crime, and it could be desperate criminals we're dealing with. What say you give it some thought before you make a decision and maybe come back another day to discuss it?"

"Fair enough," Dick said.

He knew the deck was stacked in his favor. So he asked for a vote.

"Who wants to think about it?"

Both Mr. Ossant and Mike Shea raised their hands but lowered them when they saw no other arms were raised.

"Who here can find the farm-to-dairy milk hauler routing for all of Cortland County?" Dick asked.

"You mean home delivery or farm-to-dairy delivery?" Barber asked.

"Farm-to-dairy. Milk cans."

"I can, if Randy can help me," Barber said.

Randy's dad drove a milk can hauler truck every morning. He sat behind me in school. He helped us with the rabbits at Easter.

Then Dick said, "Okay, you guys meet up, get that information and we'll see you here Monday. Same time, same radio station. Get the names, addresses, telephone numbers, and everything, guys. Go."

Barber and Randy stepped up the steps into the store.

Dick went on, "Who here wants to try to see how many burglaries there have been in Cortland County?"

I raised my hand.

"Holbrook, Mary, Barber, and I can do that—the guys in our club. We can do it."

Holbrook slugged my arm. "What are you saying!? There's no way we can find all that out by Monday. What are you thinking?"

"Relax," I said, "I got an idea."

"It better be a good one," Holbrook said.

"It is. Just get you, Mary, Barber, maybe even Randy, Bases, and Mayor to the cemetery for a meeting tonight at midnight. Can you see to that? Barber can call them and help you get them there."

My thinking was the numbers. My theory was that the more kids we had involved in what I wanted to do tonight the less punishment would be handed down if we got caught.

Dick interrupted us. Duba told him he thought we were overpromised.

"Just calling the sheriff won't get you good information, Jerry," he warned.

"Why not?" Mayor asked.

"County clerks and sheriffs don't make a lot of crime things public until they're solved. Are you sure you can handle this?" Dick asked.

"We've got it handled," I said. "We'll find out how many. Who can drive us somewhere at three in the morning, if we need a ride?"

Although almost everyone was willing, Mr. Ossant and Mike Shea were the only ones of the crowd who had real driving licenses, not just farm permits. They declined.

"Hey Marty," I shouted.

"Yo!" he answered.

I nudged Holbrook to not let anyone hear him but go ask if Marty could be at the cemetery at midnight to meet with us, and if he could bring his dad's truck. I then reminded Barber to try to set up tonight's meeting.

Dick looked down at me, probably remembering the bunny episode. He shrugged his shoulders like we just might be able to pull it off.

"Duba and I'll check out the Kelly truck rest diner on the matchbook this weekend, without being seen," he said. "No talking about any of this, and we'll meet here Monday for your reports and a plan—noon."

Dick told Mike Shea and Mr. Ossant that it was important for them to make it on Monday, too. He said he didn't know why, but he just thought there might be a use for them. Mr. Ossant smiled, turned, and walked back toward the school.

With the few minutes before the school bell, everyone jammed into the store and grabbed whatever they could for a snack and threw money on the counter and hurried back to school before the bell rang.

Rule one in an SOS with the older guys, we were learning, was that everyone stayed out of trouble at least until the mission was accomplished. Everyone felt this was something big, but Mr. Ossant's warning made us realize the seriousness of what we might be getting ourselves in.

It made the adventure even bigger and better.

Just before midnight, I headed off in the dark through farmer Parker's driveway, out behind the barn, up the hill, and into the back pasture on my way to the meeting at the cemetery. I could see my way using the stars and three-quarter moon. Being in a tree-filled cemetery in the dark of night could be enough to unsettle a boy. While climbing down off the hill from the hayfield into the cemetery, I could see the headlights of Marty driving his dad's pickup and bouncing up the drive. Holbrook, Barber, Mary, Randy, and Mayor were riding with him. One was in the cab with Marty and four in the back end.

I had a lot on my mind, and was busting to tell what I'd learned in Carthage with my dad, which was only just starting to make sense to me.

They jumped out and gathered around in the dark.

"I saw secret maps at my dad's bakery in Carthage that may help us, but I'm not sure how, yet."

"So, what good are bakery maps to us?" Marty asked.

"I took pictures. I can show you pictures of the maps in the daylight. My dad held a desk lamp up near them so I could take pictures with my camera without a flash."

"What were the maps for?" Mary asked.

"What I remember was the circle and lines drawn on the map look to me like all the bakery trucks are connected somehow—all the way from Carthage down to Binghamton. My dad showed me. He told me if I studied the routing chart map, I could figure out how to hop a bread truck from town to town. If I had a couple of days to meet all the schedules, I could go to any other circle on the map, riding on bread trucks just by knowing their numbers and what their store routes were. Dad explained it all."

"It sounds like treasure maps with secret codes," Holbrook said.

"Yes. They're in a secret room, too, I think."

"What good do they do us?" Mayor asked.

"The maps show that the bakery in Homer and the one in Carthage are connected like Tinker Toys—lines and circles—to every town in the counties of Cortland, Onondaga, Thompson, Madison, and some others."

"So?" Marty asked.

"It means that a bakery truck driver goes to every grocery store in every one of them every day."

"Oh jeez! Holy cow!" Barber sparked.

"What?!" Mary asked.

"In one day the bread truck drivers could maybe ask all those grocery store owners who was robbed and then tell us who was broken into and who lost money," Barber said.

"Just what I was thinking," I said.

"What about stores that don't sell bread?" Holbrook asked.

"Yeah, like Brown's Hardware store?" Randy asked.

"Store people in small towns all belong to a thing they call a fraternity," Mary said. "Like the Rotary or something like that, and they all talk to each other every week. The grocers will know everything that's going on."

Marty grinned. "I got a feeling I know where this is going," he said. "Good thing I filled 'er up with gas and told my ole' man I was staying over at Antil's all night, because it sure sounds about like we're heading twenty-four miles down to Homer to talk to some bakery truck drivers."

"I told my mom I was staying at your place, Marty," Mayor said.

"So did I," Randy said.

"So did I," Bases said.

"I didn't tell mine," Mary said. "No one even knows I'm gone. I'll climb the tree to get in my room when I get home."

What a tangled web we were weaving just so we could catch the criminals before some adults caught them first or found out what we were up to and put a stop to our trying.

"Good," I said. "Everybody stays at our place and goes home in the

morning. My dad will take you all home. We'll drop Mary off at her house on our way back from the bakery in Homer."

"Let's head to the bakery," Marty said.

"We can't go until two-thirty in the morning," I said.

"Two-thirty?" Mary asked.

"No one is there until then—no drivers, anyway," I said.

We decided to sit around in the cemetery and tell jokes to kill the time. Marty was the only one with a wristwatch with hands that glowed in the dark. Mayor fell asleep first. Turns out we all fell asleep.

"Time to go," Mary said, poking each of us. "Get up and let's head to Homer. We'll be there just about three o'clock, as we planned."

"Anybody got any money?" Holbrook asked, rubbing his eyes.

"What for?" Mary asked.

"I'm hungry."

Everyone dug in their pockets, pulled out what they had and opened both palms in the middle of the group so a lit match could let us count the loot. On this early morning our total wealth was two jackknives, one with a broken blade, two rubber bands, a rabbit's foot key chain with no key, a burned-out radio tube, the beginnings of a marble-size ball of tin foil from gum wrappers, seventy-nine cents in change and two Indian Head pennies that were for saving and couldn't be spent.

It dawned on me I had my dollar and change in my secret pocket. I took it out and handed it to Holbrook.

"Good, we can all eat," Holbrook said.

"We'll go to Bucky's Diner after the bakery," I said.

Marty was a good driver and was used to driving in the dark, delivering milk cans to the dairy pickup at Apulia Station every morning before he went to school. It wasn't long before we were turning left in Tully and heading south on Route 11 to Homer and the bakery.

Too far to turn back now, I thought.

When we walked in the bakery loading dock, all the trucks were backed in and being loaded with cartons of warm bread. The gang followed me up the tall stairs along the wall into the bread truck driver's room, where a lot of men were standing around having coffee. I saw a man I recognized, Lindsey Pryor. I knew him from a time we picnicked at his house when his wife had a baby. I walked up to him.

"Aren't you Mike's boy?" Mr. Pryor asked. I told him I was and these were my friends. I asked him how his new baby was, the one we went up to Cincinnatus to see the morning his wife cooked us breakfast. He smiled and finally remembered. "Baby's fine. What on earth are you young folks doing up at this hour, this far from home? Are you in any kind of trouble?"

I reached into my back pocket and showed him pictures of the maps I'd taken with my camera in Carthage and asked him if the bread truck drivers in the circles on the map around Cortland could help us. We told him what we were trying to do, and that if we wanted to catch the crooks, we needed to see how many places in those circles had been broken into and what was missing. A lot of the bread truck drivers gathered around to listen.

"Jerry, if your folks knew you were out this late, there would be some mighty big trouble, let me tell you," Mr. Pryor said.

"No there wouldn't," I said.

"Are you telling us you don't think you'd all get tanned for coming this far from home, this late?" a bread salesman asked.

"My dad would just tell me to write a book about it," I said.

"Knowing his dad, I'm thinking he's right," Mr. Pryor said.

"And our plan is that nobody's going to find out," Marty said.

"Jerry, here's exactly what we are going to do for you and your friends. Our boys will find out all they can. Won't we, fellas?"

All the men agreed.

"I'll put the results in an envelope, seal it, and ask your dad to give it to you when he comes home at the end of the day, that is, if I see him today. It'll be Monday if I don't see him today. Will that be soon enough?"

"Perfect," Marty said.

We were amazed that we might be able to pull it off and deliver good answers to Dick and Duba by Monday, just as we promised.

"Now you all run along home, before you get me in trouble," Mr. Pryor laughed. "Jerry, your daddy would skin me, book or no book. Go on, now, git."

We were making so much progress we decided not to go to Bucky's Diner and to raid the ice box when we got home instead and save our pool of money for a Saturday morning picture show sometime. On the way we forgot to drop Mary at her house. When we got to my house at the falls, we walked in quietly, like mice, which was easy because the falls in the back yard made so much racket. We didn't turn any lights on and everyone sat around the table in the dark waiting for my signal before we took turns raiding the icebox. We knew by the light under a door my Dad was in the bathroom, shaving and getting ready for work. When he came out of the bathroom and walked through the dark toward the kitchen for some juice, I surprised him with a quiet, "Hey, Dad."

Knowing how much my dad liked adventures, I proceeded to tell him in the dark what we had been up to this morning and about meeting with Lindsey Pryor at the bakery.

Dad turned and stepped back, still in the dark, pulled his and Mom's bedroom door closed so we wouldn't wake her, flipped the dining room light switch on, and sat down at the head of the table.

"Well, I'll be," he said, beaming a smile. "Is this the

Pompey Hollow Book Club?"

"Most of us," Mary said.

"Read any interesting books lately, gang?" Dad chuckled, implying he knew about our club and supported us.

"Uh huh," I said. "Me and Holbrook are reading *African Queen*."

"I'm not reading *African Queen*," Holbrook said.

"I saw you reading on the bus," Mary said. "You're reading something."

"He's reading cookbooks, like baking cookbooks," I said.

"Shut up," Holbrook said.

"How's your job at Tully Bakery working out, son?" Dad asked.

"I really like it," Holbrook said.

"I read a lot of baking books and magazines, too," Dad said.

"Thank you for helping me get the job, Mr. Antil," Holbrook said.

"So, where were we?" Dad asked.

"We're going to catch the crooks who robbed Brown's Hardware," Holbrook said.

"We just came from the bakery, Dad. Don't blame Mr. Pryor. He was worried you'd be mad that we were up so late, and you'd blame him."

"You read the maps in Carthage, Jerry me boy. You read the maps and went to Homer just to come up with a plan?"

"Yes," I said.

"The bread truck drivers are going to ask all the grocers who else got robbed," Holbrook said.

"Did the Pompey Hollow Book Club figure this out just by looking at those maps in Carthage?"

"We're smart, Dad."

"Kids growing up in a war have to be smart, or the enemies can win, remember?" Barber asked.

"I do remember, son," Dad said.

"We made Mary president," Randy said. "She's smart and we all voted for her. If any of us see something where we think we can do good, like the hardware store burglary, our club just does what we think is right."

Mary spoke up.

"Kids from the war can sometimes see things grownups don't have time to see, Mr. Antil. We only want to help do good like we were taught. Doing something is better than doing nothing. The war taught us that."

"Sounds like you're on a mission, you have a team and have planned it out," Dad said.

"Barber is in charge of calling meetings," Mary said. "Jerry is in charge of getting the older guys to help us, if we need them."

"You mean, Dick, Duba and their buddies?" Dad asked.

"Yes," I said.

"Holbrook is in charge of getting other kids to help us, like Marty here. Marty drove us tonight," Mary said.

"You old enough, son?" Dad asked Marty.

"I have a farm permit," Marty said.

Dad knew a farm permit was only legal within a certain distance from the farm and only for farm hauling or moving farm equipment, but it was a permit for a young teenager to drive on the road and better than nothing. He looked around the table, recognizing Mary and each of the boys sitting with me. He smiled with pride and said, "You're smart—there's no getting around that one."

"We're all pretty smart, Mr. Antil," Randy said.

"Well, I do admire your spirit, kids, so I'm going to do you one better. Everybody pile in my car, sleep the best you can between here and our drive back to Homer, and we'll have a nice breakfast at Bucky's. Then I'll set you up with a table in the break room and as the salesmen come in from their routes, you can hear what they have for you."

"You mean the bread truck drivers?" I asked.

"We call them salesmen, son. They are bread salesmen. And Mary, I'm going to call your mom and dad at sunup and tell them where you are, that you're okay and not to worry."

Each of the guys witnessed the same dad I bragged about all the time, in action—and just as I always described him, he came through. Dad went back into the bathroom to tie his tie. We got up from the table and walked toward the door.

"Shotgun," Holbrook said.

We went outside, climbed in the car and waited for Dad to

come drive us to Homer. We were asleep before the car turned onto Cardner Road, heading back again to Homer.

At Bucky's Diner Dad flipped a quarter high into the air— "Call it Bucky!"— and we all ate breakfast and drank hot chocolate. At the bakery we collected the information we needed almost before the sun came up. Dad loaded us in his car and we headed home. Driving back we pulled up to Holbrook's and let Holbrook out. We stopped at the Crane's and let Mary out. Mr. Crane was sitting on the porch steps reading the newspaper. He had already delivered her papers because of Dad's call to him. He waved at Dad. We dropped Randy off at his house, Bases in the Delphi hamlet, and Barber at his farm. When we got home, Marty woke up and then nudged Mayor awake beside him.

"I'll drop you home," Marty said to Mayor.

Marty waved as they drove off. He knew Mayor lived on a back road and he had a good chance of not being seen driving in the daylight.

## CHAPTER ELEVEN
## THE PLAN

Dick and Duba played poker with friends at Conway's house on Saturday night, so they pretty much knew what was found out about the milk runs and routes. They came to the Monday meeting with some plans. Dick and Duba skipped out of a study hall to Shea's before the meeting to go over details.

Mr. Ossant drove up, pulled around the corner and parked on the other side of the street, not too close to Shea's store. He got out and took his place next to the maple tree, letting it shield him from cars passing by. The kids walking to Shea's during lunch hour gathered around out of curiosity, along with the older guys.

Duba and Dick got up on the top step, and Duba started the meeting with a growl.

"Listen up."

"Let's hear your reports," Dick said.

Randy spoke up first.

"There are twenty-three milk pickup routes within a thirty-mile circle of Cortland. We had an idea that if we need to contact every single farmer in most of three counties, a couple of us can go to three dairies and tape a message on every milk can the trucks pick up and return to the farmers so the farmers won't miss seeing a message we send."

"Good job," Duba said. "Good idea."

"My dad told me," Randy said.

"But wait, there's more," Barber said.

"Whatcha got?" Dick asked.

"We know the crook stole the hunting license number 134, right?" Barber asked.

"Right," Dick said. "So what's your idea, Barber?"

"Why don't we use the idea of messages on the milk cans to send every farmer that hunting license number so if anyone wants to hunt pheasant or deer on their posted land, they can ask to see the hunter's license before giving them permission?" Barber asked.

"And if it's number 134 they call Shea's store, tell Mike Shea the name and address the crook wrote on the license," Mary said.

"This could be one way we catch them," Holbrook said.

Most everyone applauded the brilliance of the "milk can route" discovery. Dick and Duba, even Mike Shea and Mr. Ossant looked impressed.

"Okay with you, Mike Shea, if the farmers call you if they find the number?"

"Fine by me," Mike Shea said.

"Somebody figure out how to write all the notes we'll need and then get them attached to the milk cans," Dick said.

"Who's got the next report? Duba asked.

Mary, Holbrook, Barber, and Randy each rolled out a portion of a big map Dad got them from the bakery. Mary and Holbrook got on the store's top step and Barber and Randy on the lower step. They held all four pieces of map up and together to make one large display. There was a big black circle drawn around the center of the map. Dick and Duba stepped out into the crowd to watch. I looked at my notes, lifted a yardstick I borrowed from Mike Shea as a pointer and began our report, pointing at the map they were holding up.

"In ten months there have been store break-ins and burglaries—" I pointed with my yardstick. "— here in Freeville, here in Dryden, over here in Munson's Corners, up here in Summerhill, here in Moravia, and over here in McGraw, and then the two we know about—down here in Homer and here in Cortland. All in all, the same MO."

"What's MO?" a voice in the crowd asked.

"It means modus operandi," Marty said. "It's Latin."

"Talk English," the voice said.

"Sorry," I said. "Twelve-hundred and ninety-seven dollars was stolen in all these burglaries and every store broken into was messed up."

"Just like the hardware store," Dick said.

"All little-kid stuff was messed up, boxes opened, left everywhere, but not missing," I said.

"They didn't take anything?" Duba asked.

"Were they robbed or not?" a voiced asked.

"They were robbed of cash," Dick said.

"Listen up!" Duba growled.

"Here's what we want you to pay attention to," I said.

I pointed at the big circle on the map.

"If we draw a circle connecting all the towns where someplace was broken into and money stolen, dead in the center of the circle—"

I pointed the ruler to Groton.

Duba and Dick shouted it together.

"GROTON!"

"Groton," I repeated.

"The exact town you took a picture of!" Dick said.

"What picture?" Duba asked.

"The matchbook cover—that truck rest on the matchbook," Marty said.

Dick and Duba jumped on the steps, clapping hands, applauding our efforts. We stepped down, smiling.

Mike Shea and Mr. Ossant seemed impressed.

"Let's go get them," Holbrook said.

"Just hold on. We've got to think this through," Dick said.

"What are you thinking?" Duba asked.

"We have to catch them in the act," Dick said. "We can't just rush 'em."

"I can't have any part of you kids facing danger like this, no sir," Mr. Ossant said.

"You're thinking something, Dick. Just what do you have in mind?" Mike Shea asked.

Dick pointed across Main Street.

"I was thinking about your old store, Mike," Dick said.

"This store?" Mike Shea asked.

"Not exactly. That old store of yours across the street."

"Our first store? It's boarded up."

"It's empty, right?" Dick asked.

"I store things in it, but it's pretty much empty," Mike Shea said.

"Good," Dick said.

"Whatcha thinking?" Mike Shea asked.

"Any objections, Mike, if we arrange the burglary of your old empty store across the street?" Dick asked.

"When?" Mike Shea asked.

"For this coming Saturday night?" Dick asked.

"Mind telling me what you have in mind, son?" Mike Shea asked.

"If we can bait these crooks to your old empty store—make them think it's got a lot of cash …" Dick started.

"Just maybe we can catch them red-handed," Mary said.

Mike Shea gave a belly laugh at the idea of it.

"You get me some volunteers," Mike Shea said, "and we can have that old place spiffed up sparkling—looking glamourous and stocked with useless inventory from storage. Why we'll have it looking prosperous by Thursday—cash register and all."

"Any volunteers?" Duba asked.

All the Pompey Hollow Book Club and eight other kids raised hands.

"You kids meet me here every day, on your lunch hour and we'll get the job done," Mike Shea said. "I'll see you all get enough to eat."

With the mention of food, the rest of the hands in the group went up. The promise of food guaranteed attendance would likely double, maybe triple, by the next day at noon.

Dick started to organize his thoughts and an attack plan.

"Jimmy Conway, what do you call that monster tractor at your

farm."

"That's a huge tractor," Barber said.

"It won't hardly even fit in their barn," Duba said.

"It's not that big, but it is big, I guess," Conway said.

"How big is it?" Mary asked.

"It's a Minneapolis Moline, near double the size of a regular tractor," Conway said. "My dad got it to drag four plows at once."

"Ooooooooooooooooh!" murmured through the gathering, most still accustomed to seeing teams of workhorses hauling and plow-pulling.

"Three times taller than a car," Duba said.

"Does it have a forklift in front?" Dick asked.

"Sure does. And it can lift twice its weight."

"Good," Dick said.

"What you got in mind?" Conway asked.

"Duba, Dwyer, and I will come by later to come up with a plan."

Then Dick turned to Mr. Ossant and Mr. Shea.

"Here's what's happening. Saturday morning, lunchtime, the Pompey Hollow Book Club, plus Duba, Conway, Dwyer, and me, will need a ride in our old '38 pickup to the truck rest in Groton."

"Why your '38?" Mike Shea asked.

"We need to lure out the crooks with bait. We need to look rag poor. Can either of you drive us to Groton Saturday and wait in the truck once we get there?"

We needed a driver with a real driver's license. Dick didn't want to get caught breaking the law while we were trying to catch criminals. It could be an embarrassment, a conflict of interest, so to speak.

"As much as we'd like to, kids, there is no way we can be involved with something like this," Mike Shea said. "You know we would if we could."

"I ain't touching this one with a ten-foot pole," Mr. Ossant said.

"My dad will drive us," Mary said.

"Perfect," Dick said.

"Everybody who's going, meet at Delphi cemetery, Saturday. Be there by ten in the morning."

Dick was understanding of Mr. Ossant's and Mike Shea's hesitance to contribute to our delinquency, so he made a plea in another direction.

"Can we at least get you both to get a poker game going?" Dick asked.

"What's on your mind?" Mike Shea asked.

"In the fire hall, Saturday about dark—a poker game—and keep it going until we're done?" Dick asked.

"I'm sure we could arrange a friendly poker game," Mr. Ossant said.

"And you could get Sheriff Todd Hood and maybe a

deputy or two to play with you?" Dick asked.

"There's no way Sheriff Hood will gamble for money," Randy said.

"Play for chips or corn nuts, whatever, just keep playing," Dick said.

"We can ask some folks," Mike Shea said, looking at Mr. Ossant.

"Boy and howdy! We surely can!" Mr. Ossant said.

"I'll make a few calls," Mike Shea said.

"Mike Shea, can we ask one more thing?" Dick asked.

"Name it, son," Mike Shea said.

"Can you put three hundred and fifty dollars in the register in the dummy store we set up across the street?" Dick asked.

"That's a whole lot of money, son."

"We'll need at least that much to guarantee we lure them."

"You'd better make dang sure you catch them," Mike Shea said.

"In very light pencil, can you write 'Stolen from Shea's store' on every bill somewhere?" Dick asked.

"You bet I can."

Dick broke up the meeting and asked the Pompey Hollow Book Club to wait a second.

"It's important you all look like ragamuffins Saturday," Dick said.

"Why?" Mary asked.

"You need to look poor as church mice," he said.

"That won't be hard," Holbrook said.

We told him we would. We had an idea of what the older guys were about to be up to. They'd never let us down in the past. We headed back to school before the bell rang.

## CHAPTER TWELVE
## IN THE SOUP

On Saturday morning cars crept into the Delphi cemetery, slowly driving up the dirt drive, one behind the other. It looked like a funeral. Conway drove in first and got out of his car and leaned on it waiting. Randy's dad dropped me and Randy off, backed out and left. Mr. Barber dropped Barber off, backed out and left. The last car was Mr. Crane driving in with Mary and Holbrook. Mr. Crane pulled under a tree limb, parked, and they all got out of the car. Dick and Duba were already there leaning on the '38. As we assembled to listen, Dick and Duba stepped over and asked the Pompey Hollow Book Club to line up along the dirt road into the cemetery. They walked around like they were drill sergeants inspecting us. Holbrook, Mary, me, Randy, and Barber lined up. They were generally impressed with our disheveled appearance. Our clothes torn and wrinkled. Dick spaced us along the dirt drive about five feet apart.

"Everyone get down and roll in the dirt."

"What?!" Mary growled.

"Get down and roll around," Dick repeated. "You need to look mussed."

We complied, getting an understanding of his reason. We even rubbed our faces with road dust. Then we stood up.

"Perfect!" Dick said. "Let's get started."

"Hold on!" Mary said.

"For what?" Dick barked.

"Now you guys do it. You, Duba, Conway, and Dwyer do it."

"Do what?" Dick asked.

"You guys get down and roll around. You have to look the same as us."

Our club wasn't old and all that well established, but we could tell this moment was the Pompey Hollow Book Club president's finest hour. The Delphi cemetery was our turf and our president actually made the older guys dance to her tune. She was a natural-born General Eisenhower. We were proud. They did it. They even offered a compliment.

"Good thinking," Conway said.

The rest was going to be easy.

Dick and Duba jumped in the cab of the '38 pickup with Mr. Crane driving. The rest of us climbed in the back and sat up proudly.

As we headed down the highway and country roads on our way to Groton, those of us in the back were getting dustier. We passed through the village and by the pretend store across from Shea's store. It appeared to be open and fully staffed. Kids were painting signs and milling about. Some were taping up "sales special" signs in the windows. A few of them saw us and waved as we drove by. Near the other end of the village by the fire hall, we could see several men carrying a poker table and placing it in the center of the fire station for the big game tonight. The shiny red fire engine was parked on the side of the building. We got to Tully and turned left and headed down Route 11 through Homer and Cortland and on over to Groton. When Mr. Crane saw the Groton village sign, he slowed to a crawl.

"I think it's up ahead two blocks," Dick said.

The '38 turned into the Kelly's Rest Stop parking area— the same one from the face of the matchbook. Dick, Duba, and Mr. Crane got out.

"Is it going to be safe going in there?" Mary asked.

"Don't let them see you talking," Dick said. "They maybe can read lips."

"From all appearances, it's a greasy spoon," Mr. Crane said.

The front window was filthy. Inside, there appeared to be a ceiling fan in the middle of the room slowly twirling around over a serving counter. Hanging from the center of the ceiling fan was a long, curling stream of sticky flypaper stretched down to just above the counter. From a distance it appeared to be dotted with dead flies caught on its glue.

"I hope everybody has had their tetanus shots," Holbrook said.

"Knock off the talking. Team— this is it," Dick said.

"Listen up," Duba said.

With his back to the restaurant, Dick whispered.

"I know it's a dump, but we have to pretend we're impressed, and we don't know any better. We have to pretend it's the best restaurant in town. If you make any faces like what a pigsty it is they'll see right through us and know we're phony.

"When we get inside, everybody make sure to listen good and follow our lead," Duba said.

We all piled out of the back of the '38 and walked in. Mr. Crane stayed outside with the truck. He lifted the hood and stuck his head under it like we were too poor to get it fixed at a gas station. When we stepped inside the restaurant there was a kid about Gourmet Mike's age with a push broom in his hand trying to look busy, but he wasn't very convincing. We lined up and sat down on the stools at the counter—the older guys, Dick, Duba, Dwyer and Conway on the left and the Pompey Hollow Book Club—Barber, Holbrook, Mary, Randy, and me on the right.

"Now you mind your manners, kiddos," Dick goaded in a made-up low voice as we each settled on a counter stool.

A man with a three-day bristly beard, a mustard and flour-splotched, dirty apron and a lit cigarette hanging from his mouth, walked up, blinking his right eye like a wiper blade trying to keep the rising smoke crawling up his cheek from hitting his eyeball. There was a pack of Lucky Strike cigarettes rolled up on the outside of his undershirt sleeve. He grabbed the percolator pot of coffee on his way over, picked up four coffee cups through their handles with his thumb and first finger, and walked them to the counter, settling them all down at once. He slid one to each of the older guys while he looked us over pretty good.

"How can I help 'ya?"

"We want four coffees and four cups of hot water," Dick said.

The man lifted his head back, flexing his eyebrows at Dick.

With Dick's thick glasses, he looked the oldest.

"I'll be figuring on what next after we get that," Dick added.

The cook lined up cups and started to pour the coffees, all while giving double takes to our crew, sizing each of us up. He had a look in his eye like should he let such vagabonds tie up his counter seats. He seemed a bit reluctant when he turned to get a pad to write down our order.

About that time was when Mary saw the front page of the daily newspaper lying on the counter in front of her and was inspired.

"Did you see all that money, Daddy?" she asked. Mary started to rattle on with a straight face. "Why I never seen so much money in all my life, Daddy. Did you see the money, Uncle Harry?" she asked.

Most of us choked on our saliva. Barber's face turned a dark shade of beet red. Dick and Duba leaned in and looked over at Mary. They were mighty proud of the girl's gumption and initiative, but not one of the older guys had any idea who was supposed to play "Daddy" and who was to play "Uncle Harry." Worse than that, they didn't know where Mary was going, talking about money. They sat there, trying to sort it out with stares, elbow jabs, glances, and eyebrow movements. They decided it'd probably be best to wait and see if Mary's blurt opened any other conversations of opportunity. It was now a waiting game.

It was the *Cortland Standard* newspaper on the counter with a picture of President Harry Truman, which inspired Mary to act presidential. We Pompey Hollow Book Club members sitting at the counter saw it and it was right then and there we knew we were proud she was our president. No question about it. This was her day, even if we didn't have a clue what money she was talking about.

Hearing about the mention of money, the sweeper man with the push broom moved closer in, getting a little more particular about the floor near Mary's stool, it seemed. Dick and Duba saw that and guessed what Mary was doing.

The cook put spoons on the counter by the cups of coffee in front of Dick, Duba, Dwyer, and Conway.

Duba broke the silence by reminding the cook.

"The young'uns each get a hot water," waving an arm toward us.

The cook stepped over and set cups of hot water down in front of each of us and turned to get the tea bags he thought we would want.

Dick and Duba went into action. Dick's decoy was first, as though he was at the Ritz hotel breakfast room in the downtown of a big city.

"Sir, us gentlemen will have us two bacon and egg sandwiches with mayo, but split up, half on each of four plates, if you'll be so kindly."

The cook paused a moment to visualize the math. He squinted his left eye a blink or two from the cigarette smoke rolling up that side of his nose and turned the other eye up in the direction of his brain for a second of thought.

"What about them?" he asked, nodding his head toward us kids.

That was Duba's cue. He could hold a straight face best. He rose to the occasion and went into action.

"Sir, is there a charge for the use of your ketchup?"

"Ain't no charge for ketchup."

"Then the little'uns will all have soup."

"We don't have no soup."

"We'll make do, sir, pardon me kindly," Dick said.

That being said, Duba stood up, grabbed the ketchup bottle from the counter, leaned down, took the cap off and handed it to Barber to hold, turned the bottle upside down, and began pounding the bottom of it with the palm of his hand, like a jack hammer, plunging ketchup splotches and spurts into every cup of hot water, one at a time, repeating to each kid in turn, "Stir it good, honey. Stir your soup."

The water in each cup slowly turned several lumpy shades of a murky red floating up like moss bark in a swamp pond with each splash from the ketchup bottle.

"Oh, they love their tomato soup," he added, looking up at the cook.

"Mmmm-mmm, good," Holbrook muttered under his breath, just like he heard on the radio commercial for soup.

Dick's Minneapolis Moline tractor friend, Jimmy Conway, who never hardly ever said anything, was so inspired by Duba's performance, he leaned in and offered.

"Stir it up good, kiddies. Blow on your spoon, case it's hot."

"We will, Uncle Harry," Mary said, with a smile.

At least now we knew who Uncle Harry was—it was Conway. We still weren't sure which of the older guys was Daddy.

Duba jumped in.

"Sir, can we trouble you for some soup crackers for each of the little ones?"

"Huh?" the cook grumbled.

"Crackers sort of top off a meal, don't ya think?" Duba asked.

"Oh boy, crackers! I'm starved," Barber announced, while handing the ketchup bottle cap back to Duba.

The cook was beside himself with all this dusty pomposity. He didn't know what to say, but he was certain he read about poor folk like us somewhere—*The Grapes of Wrath* maybe, even though he never opened a book in his life. He also didn't know what a soup cracker was. Ashes fell from his cigarette to the counter. He swept them off with one tidy swipe of his hand just as he slid a soup bowl filled with oyster crackers over to the middle of the four kids. This was about the same time the sweeper guy edged his broom over closer toward Mary.

"Just what money you talking about, little girl?" the sweeper asked. Mary looked up at him.

"Huh?" Mary asked.

"A bank? A store?" the sweeper asked.

Conway turned and leaned back on his stool, catching the sweeper's eye. "Pardon me, son," Conway, as Uncle Harry, whispered. His confidence in speaking up was building now that he had the privilege of being Uncle Harry. He considered the family appointment a responsibility, almost like he was now Mary's Godfather. He leaned toward the sweeper man, looking up and gaining his full attention with eyeball contact.

"Pardon me, son—" Uncle Harry started.

Sweeper man leaned toward him, as if he was on guard and ready to flinch.

"Betsy Lou here or none of the boys here for that matter ain't allowed to be talkin' to no strangers—if you catch my meaning."

"Huh?" was the best sweeper could do at the moment.

"The way the world is now," Uncle Harry continued. "Why you could be a German Nazi spy or maybe even a Red, one of them communist fellers or something."

"Why I ain't no such thing," the sweeper wailed.

He was almost indignant. He stood at attention with the broom like it was an M1 army issue rifle. He was offended at the mere suggestion of it all. His hand flipped some hair back from his face, almost resembling a salute.

"You got any identification, young man?" Uncle Harry asked.

"Huh?" the sweeper grunted.

"Show us you're a red-blooded American," Uncle Harry said.

Now the sweeper was totally bewildered. He looked for help from the cook, who was busy trying to blow off cigarette ashes he had dropped on top of the one piece of lemon meringue pie he had one slice of left to sell. The sweeper was beside himself. He scratched his head trying to gather whatever thoughts he had laying around. A fly flew from his forehead to the glue fly trap hanging down over the counter, got stuck in the glue and flap-buzzed its wings in vain.

All of us club members at the counter were so impressed with Conway. We picked up our spoons and started eating the disgusting watery soup concoction while listening to professionals in action.

Duba stepped in with added authority.

"You got any proof you're a American, son?" he ordered. "Driver's license? Social Security card?"

"Hunting license?" Dick asked.

"Most anything official will do, son," Uncle Harry added. "No offense meant."

"None took, sir."

The sweeper man fumbled for thought blindly stabbing through pockets with his hands looking for answers, until it finally dawned on him.

"I sure enough got me a hunting license," sweeper man said.

He reached deep in his overall pocket, pulled out a Roy Roger's imitation leather wallet, ran the zipper around three edges of it, opening it, and picked out and handed Uncle Harry a New York State hunting license. License number 134.

Uncle Harry held it out and showed it to Dick and Duba, so they could see the number on the hunting license, handed it back to the sweeper, and then outdid himself. "It sure is genuine. The man's American as apple pie, I reckon. Number 134."

Hearing the number 134, Barber spilled his hot "tomato" soup in Holbrook's lap.

"Sorry about any inconvenience, son," Uncle Harry said.

"We have to be careful these days," Dick added.

"So close after the war and all those commies around," Duba said.

"You're a good American," Uncle Harry said.

The sweeper gazed proudly at his hunting license and the new sense of power it gave him. He tucked it back into his wallet, zipped it up carefully, and slid it into his pocket.

Dick took a turn on his counter stool, slowly spinning around to face the sweeper. He took the stage.

"Betsy Lou here's talking about the trading post across from Shea's corner on Route 80 up there a way, past Tully. You may have heard of it," Dick said.

"Can't say I have," sweeper man said.

"You go north on Route 11 and hang right in Tully," Uncle Harry said.

"They have some fine bargains," Dick said. "They're only open on Fridays and Saturdays but little Betsy Lou it just ain't proper you talking about all that money. Ain't your business what people got."

"What money's that?" the sweeper asked.

"Oh, she's just talking."

"We don't get a lot of traveler folks in here, mister, I like to listen. What money is Betsy Lou here talking about? You kids want you more crackers?"

"See, they always have a lot of money in their cash register, it seems, until they get to bank it on Monday."

Conway turned and got in the conversation.

"Betsy Lou's aunt's cousin works there and was showing off the full cash drawer all braggadocios last week to Betsy Lou here, while we were on our way to picking apples at the Moore farm near the Cherry Valley. You know how them uppity people do at times?"

Sweeper man looked over at the cook.

"Their Betsy Lou here, saw the cash drawer, imagine that," sweeper man said.

"Time to go, kids," Dick said. "Drink up your soup, grab you some oyster crackers to balance your meal—we need to go find us some picking work while the sun's still out."

Mary cringed at the Betsy Lou moniker handed her, got off her stool, and pushed the front door open and walked out. Holbrook covered the wet spot on his jean pants with a paper napkin, promising Barber under his breath that he was going to kill him for spilling his soup.

The rest of the Pompey Hollow Book Club downed their tomato soups for the cause. The older guys got up and walked out, munching the last of their half-sandwiches. The check came to forty-seven cents.

Dick laid down a half dollar, swallowed his sandwich so as not to be rude talking with his mouth full, and said, "Keep the change, my good man. We'll be recommending your establishment to our friends."

On the drive back to the cemetery, we stopped at Shea's corner to check out the make-believe store. It looked real. The cash register they pulled up from the cellar was an antique, dusted off and piled with money. Each bill was faintly marked in pencil, "Stolen from Shea's store."

Dick and Duba asked Mike Shea if we could hide on the second floor of his store across the street and watch for the crooks. Mike Shea said he already thought of that and he would have sandwiches and soda pop up there.

"What's the plan?" he asked.

Dick pointed to the right of the store across the way. "Conway's Minneapolis Moline tractor will be parked around that side of the phony store with a canvas tarp over its front, so its size won't scare them away. When the crooks get here and break in, Duba will crawl around on the ground, get under their car and pull the spark plug wires out so it won't start."

"So they can't make a run for it," Mike Shea said. "What then?"

"He'll crawl back, climb up a wooden ladder resting on the tractor, pull off the tarp, push the ladder away, and ride on the front of it, like it was a giant bucking bronco, whooping and hollering. When the crooks come out and try to start their car, Conway will crank the giant tractor up, do a full U-turn with his forklift front, and go right in under their car from behind them and lift them, car and all, about eight feet up off the ground. Then he'll back it around with the crooks in it, head on down Main Street full- speed, Duba hooting and hollering and keeping them distracted, and they'll deliver them to the Poker party fire hall and Sheriff Todd Hood and his deputies."

It started off as planned.

The crooks sure enough showed up. Both of them—the cook and sweeper man. They parked in front, got out of their car. They carefully looked around to see if anyone was watching. The sweeper scooted around back of the store and then came back around, whispering that the coast was clear. They crowbarred the door open and broke in. It wasn't long before they came out with the loot and Jimmy had them and their car aloft, heading down Main Street, Duba hollering and shouting. The crooks tried to open the car doors to jump out. It was a good thing Minneapolis Moline Conway, as he would come to be known, loved milkshakes and studied just how they were made at the soda fountain in Manlius.

Each time Duba saw the car doors crack open so the crooks could escape, he would signal Conway to double clutch the Moline giant a few times and shake their innards proper. The tractor made backfiring blasts of fiery sparks like shotguns—so loud that the best the crooks could do in their dizziness was grab for things in the car they thought were door handles, rarely coming close. The backfiring belches woke up most of the village.

With the ruckus the monster Minneapolis Moline tractor made, and kids popping out of nowhere, from behind every house, all following behind the tractor going up Main Street—the fire hall door burst open wide just to see what on earth was causing all the commotion. Every light in the village was on now. The tractor turned into the firehouse drive like a giant dragon and came to a stop, the lifted car rocking. Duba jumped down off the tractor. The whole poker table group stood looking up at the giant tractor's head beams, with the car balanced high in its craw, staring down at them. Minneapolis Moline Conway pulled a lever and lowered the car like an elevator.

"Put your hands out the windows and stick 'em up!" Dick warned on one side and Duba on the other.

The crooks complied. The sweeper had a white handkerchief in his hand as a flag of truce.

Sheriff Hood and his deputies stepped to the sides of the vehicle; mouths open in surprise that we had pulled it off. They handcuffed both the men—the sweeper and the cook. They took the box of evidence and told Mike Shea he would have the money back Monday morning.

"That money don't prove nothin'!" the cook snapped.

"Sheriff Hood?" I said.

"Why, hello, Jerry," he said.

"Look in that one's wallet, Sheriff Hood."

Sheriff Hood took the sweeper's wallet and pulled the only thing in it, a hunting license.

"Take a look at his hunting license," Mary said.

"Number 134. Well what do you think of that?" Sheriff Hood asked.

"That should wrap it up," Dick said.

"There's a reward for this arrest," Sheriff Hood said. "Who gets it?"

Dick and Duba looked at the kids.

"You guys got any ideas how we divide it up?" Dick asked.

"What did Jerry do with that reward money from the gas station fire?" a voice asked.

"He used it all to save rabbits from being slaughtered last Easter," Mary said.

"All of it? You did?" Mayor asked.

"Every cent— well, I gave some to St. Anne's church," I said.

"How can we keep a reward in good conscience?" Holbrook asked.

"Holbrook is right, " Marty said. "It was a lot of small businesses that lost the money."

"How about we give it all to the fire department?" a voice in the back offered.

"Who said that?" Dick asked.

Bases raised his arm.

"Bases, you live in Delphi—are you meaning the Delphi Fire Department?"

"Well, how about this one and Delphi maybe split the reward money up?" Bases asked.

"Yeah, the fire departments," the crowd rumbled.

"Anybody think they got some reward money coming?" Dick asked.

'Shoot, no," came a voice. "We had more fun, more sandwiches, and more soda pop than any reward money can buy."

The crowd seemed in favor of the fire departments.

"All in favor of the reward money going to the fire department, raise your hand," Duba yelled.

Kids cheered.

It was settled.

We all pretty much left the fire hall feeling good. Most went home. The club members who went to Groton and the older guys, all except Minneapolis Moline Conway, went back to the Delphi cemetery, got into our rides home, and went our way, savoring another adventure.

The last we saw of Minneapolis Moline Conway that night was his daddy's monster tractor heading down Route 80 toward their farm. Its high beam headlamps looking like fire from a monster dragon. Cars would pull off the road and stop as it approached them. When we passed by Minneapolis Moline Conway —sitting in the back of the '38, we all waved and shouted up at him.

"Hi, Uncle Harry! Get a horse!"

## CHAPTER THIRTEEN
## THE THANKSGIVING CHICKEN COUP!

Mom was spooning creamed corn onto her plate, and she passed the bowl.

"We got a nice letter from your brother Mike today," she said. "Gourmet Mike wrote a letter?" I asked.

"That's not nice," dear."

"What's not nice?" I asked.

"Calling your brother that."

"He don't mind," I said.

"He doesn't mind."

"Oh, sorry. He doesn't mind."

"He says he's enjoying college and to say hello to everyone and he's looking forward to being home for Thanksgiving."

"You're not thinking of letting him cook, are you Mom?" I asked.

Mom ignored me.

"We got something else in the mail. A note for you."

"Me?"

"It is this very nice invitation from your piano teacher, Mrs. Cowling."

"What kind of invitation?"

"It's about the winter piano recital."

"I'm not going."

"I'm so proud to see she wants my boy among all the talented participants."

Mom held the invitation up.

"Look, everyone, Jerry's name is printed on the invitation, right here with all the other participants, see?"

As my mom pointed at the invitation, I lowered my face into my empty plate, for effect.

"Do I have to, Mom?" I pleaded.

"Of course, dear. Take some corn before it gets cold."

"I hate piano."

"Don't be childish. You do so well with it."

"But Mom …"

"You'll do fine. Start the sweet peas and pass the bowl to your father, dear."

It was my third year of piano with Mrs. Cowling. I played so badly that the only thing I remembered by heart were two stanzas of "Country Gardens," which happened to be identical to each other. For two years my piano recitals had been humiliating. I played the same thing. Holbrook said the only similarity between me and Mozart was that we both had an "r" in our names.

Dad threw me a life saver.

"We all remember Jerry's recitals."

He tried to keep a straight face.

"Why don't we let the boy find some instrument he might enjoy more?"

Mom threw a perplexed glare across the table at Dad.

"He really stinks, Mom. Put him out of his misery," Dick said.

Mom looked at Dick and at the same time raised her arm and pointed to the kitchen. It was a straight, arm-length pointing of her finger. Having to eat in the kitchen at home was like being sent to the principal's office in school. You might or might not get a lecture—but you sure would be the dishwasher that night.

"Go. Now! Eat in the kitchen. Jerry has tried his best."

"But he's no good," Dick said.

"March! I'll hear no more disparagement."

Mom wasn't whipped. She was weakening, but not without the final say.

"I'll call Mrs. Cowling Monday, and I'll tell her you won't be taking lessons this year."

"Really?" I breathed a sigh of relief.

"I'll also call Mr. Spinner, the band director, and see what can be done."

"Do I have to, Mom?"

"My children will experience music and the arts."

I knew enough to go look up *disparagement* in the dictionary after supper to see if there were any strings attached to her surrender.

"You and Dick will do the dishes tonight, tomorrow

night, and Sunday. Not another word."

There was a cost to my victory.

"And Jerry, if Mrs. Cowling insists you play in this recital, you will play," Mom added.

"If I'm not taking lessons anymore how could she insist?"

"From the looks of this pretty invitation Mrs. Cowling may already have the programs printed, and they would have your name in them."

Dad changed the subject.

"Mr. Contento at his bicycle repair shop in Cortland just happens to have an old reconditioned bike he asked me to take a look at."

"I know a Mr. Contento at Leonard's Coffee Shop, Dad," Dick said from the kitchen.

"Same gentleman, son. He has a bike shop at his home."

I stopped eating and paid attention to Dad's every word. I'd been hoping for a bike. One I could ride in the Memorial Day Parade with my friends.

"He gave me an excellent price for the bike if I would agree to take two guinea hens he'd won at the county fair off his hands. He said they needed the country. He has no place in Cortland for them."

"What's a guinea hen, Dad," Dick asked from the kitchen, "and will you put them at Mr. Pitts's farm with the chickens and geese?"

"No, son, these are real prize show birds, not farm animals. Sort of like peacocks. I'll bring them home tomorrow. I decided that since you're always reading veterinary books and maybe needed some extra money while you're saving up to buy a car, they could be your chore."

"No sweat," Dick said from the kitchen.

"I'll open a savings account in your name and make a weekly deposit for you toward new tires for your car, when you get it."

Although Dick and Duba had the '38, he still had his mind set on Lindsey Pryor's old Nash convertible he had promised to sell Dick for sixty-five dollars. Dick beamed at the thought of new tires.

"The bike will be for Jerry."

"For real? Mine?" I asked.

"I'll drop it here in the morning, between my visits to the bakery and some grocers in New Woodstock and Cazenovia."

"My own bike?"

"It's all yours, son."

"It's not even Christmas, Dad."

"Well, you need a ride to the Delphi cemetery from time to time, don't you, son?"

"Wow. Thanks Dad—Mom."

"Can't ride bicycles in the snow. It'll be an early Christmas present—from Santa. I'll stop at Brown's Hardware and get you a can of paint to paint your bike, if you want."

"Yellow," I said.

Mom and Dad looked at each other. There was a whisper from Dick in the kitchen, "What a nerd."

"I heard that, young man. No dessert for you," Mom admonished.

If anyone asked me why yellow, I wouldn't have told them my secret—that it was the color of the ribbon the girl wore in the John Wayne movie I saw four times in Cazenovia, *She Wore a Yellow Ribbon.* I liked the song, too.

That night I tossed and turned dreaming about my new bike and the Memorial Day parade—but also about whether or not there was a Santa. With my Dad saying the bike was a present from Santa and me knowing he got it at Mr. Contento's bike shop—I was confused.

In the morning I woke up to hearing the pecks and chirps. A bird was tapping its beak on my bedroom window. I rolled over and sat up and stared at it for a second. No bird could distract me this particular morning. I was in love.

Well, not girl love.

There was only one girl I was ever going to marry and that was Olivia Dandridge from *She Wore a Yellow Ribbon.* I didn't care how many lieutenants of the cavalry I would have to stand down to do it. I knew the other kind of love there was, too, like the love Captain Nathan Cutting Brittles had for God, his country, and the cavalry. He and I had a lot in common. When the time was right for me to ask for Miss Dandridge's hand, I would get someone like Captain Brittle's advice—maybe my dad's.

I was about to be in love with my new bike.

I got dressed and went to the kitchen. Sure enough, there was a small can of paint and a paintbrush on the counter. Dad left two handwritten notes.

The first note: *"Jerry, the only yellow they had was house paint. It will dry faster, son. Look in the barn garage."*

The second note: *"Dick Try to find the guinea hens. I let them loose and they ran away somewhere. Try to find and catch them. We may need a cage."*

The bicycle was beautiful—simply beautiful! Sleek, with big round tires, curved handlebars, and a shiny bell with a convenient thumb button.

T'ring—t'ring—t'ring—

It was all so perfect.

I loved my new bike!

First, I was going to paint it. After that, I would ride my brand- spanking, newly painted bike down to the Maxwell place on the corner, where I knew Mary was spending the day with pretty Linda Oats, and show it off to them both. Linda Oats was three grades ahead of me and Mary, old enough to be our aunt or something—but I'd been smitten with her freckly smile ever since the first day I saw her on the school bus when we first moved to Delphi Falls. She and Mary had known each other in Manlius or Syracuse or somewhere before they moved here after the war.

I didn't know why they called it the Maxwell place. I think it was because somebody famous named Maxwell used to live there during the Revolutionary War and had his name carved in a big stone on the corner when he built the cider mill.

Next to the house was the big old two-story apple cider mill barn, rotting and falling apart inside. Cider mills were barns, built right next to a creek or river. They had a tall, round paddle wheel, almost as tall as the barn, which went down deep into the creek. The movement of the water would turn the paddle wheel and the wheel would turn gears on the second floor, and those gears would turn a big stone wheel that would smash the apples. Apple juice ran down a drain pipe into a big, open wooden vat, about as tall as my chest, on the first floor. Most of the paddle wheel was rotted now. The barn was still standing there, barely.

The bike didn't take long to paint. I even painted it twice to make sure I did a good job. I moved the brush as smoothly as I could across the fenders, so the brush strokes hardly showed. It was a work of art.

When finished, I asked Mom to come outside and look at my bike.

"My goodness," she said. "It certainly is yellow!"

I beamed.

"Don't forget you have a dentist appointment today at Dr. Webb's."

"Huh?"

"Jerry, where are your shoes?"

"Do I have to go to the dentist, Mom?"

"I do wish you'd wear the watch you got for your birthday, Jerry." "But Mom—"

"I don't know what I'm going to do with you."

"It's Saturday, Mom."

"Go put something on your feet and be home before ten. Keep asking people for the time."

I went in the house and put on shoes while the paint dried. When it was dry to the touch, I walked around it a few times, just admiring it, still not believing I actually had a bike of my own. It was like a dream.

I carefully peddled down the gravel drive around puddles so I wouldn't splash and mess the new paint. On Cardner Road it was smooth sailing. I hardly had to pedal at all. I glided down the road like the wind was pushing me.

Farmer Parker's cows were in his north pasture that day, by Cardner Road. Most often, when I walked by them, they'd keep their heads down and noses on the ground as they grazed. For some reason this time they all lifted and turned their heads in unison and stared at me riding by. Maybe they hadn't seen a canary yellow bike before. I started to sing, *"Round her neck she wore a yellow ribbon—she wore a yellow ribbon all through the month of May—"*

Life was good.

Long before I got to the corner, I tried to imagine how best to show off my bike to Linda Oats and Mary. Should I casually ride by Linda's house, let her and Mary see me, then turn back? Should I slow down, just boldly turn into the driveway, and ride right up to the door? Should I stop, before I got to the house, get off, and push the bike onto Linda's front lawn, so she and Mary could admire its lines from the living room window?

It was too late. I had already arrived, so I slowed down, turned into her driveway, and came to a stop near the side door. I got off like I was getting off a horse and rested the bike on the kickstand.

What speed, what grace, I thought.

I stepped backward up to the side door while admiring my bike and knocked on the screen door behind me. Mrs. Oats came to the door.

"Hello Jerry," Mrs. Oats said.

"Hi, Mrs. Oats."

"If you're looking for the girls, Linda and Mary are in the mill barn."

"Thank you, Mrs. Oats."

"Be very careful out there and please don't go to the second floor," Mrs. Oats said.

"I won't"

"It isn't safe up there," Mrs. Oats said.

"I won't go up there."

"Everything is rotted."

"Do you like my bike, Mrs. Oats?" I asked proudly.

"Oh my," she said. "It certainly is yellow, isn't it?"

As I walked toward the old mill barn I thought about the two desperate burglars who had busted into all those stores, sneaking around at night, hiding in the dark, stealing all that money before we caught them. I had just finished reading a Hardy Boys mystery book, *The Secret of the Old Mill*, for the third time, where they found and caught the desperate money counterfeiters, but nearly got massacred while doing it. I really didn't want to go into the dark and dusty, damp old mill barn, so I didn't need a warning that it was dangerous. I had every intention of being careful in case there were crooks hiding or lurking or something.

The door was open, just a little. The wood was like a rotted board on hinges; the bottom of it scraped the ground when I pushed on it.

"Linda? Mary?" I shouted.

"We're up here," Mary shouted.

"Where are you?" I asked.

"Up here on the second floor," Linda shouted.

I could hear Linda's voice from the very place her mom, not more than two minutes ago, had warned me not to go. There were stairs going up one wall to the second floor. I looked toward the center of the barn, next to a huge wooden vat nearly as tall as I was and longer than a bathtub. It looked like it was filled with gloopy, disgusting, black, swamp-like water. From a distance, it looked as if something was moving around in it. There was a ladder leaning next to the huge vat, reaching up to a small square opening in the ceiling to the second floor. I decided to go up the stairs by the wall.

"Don't use the stairs by the wall," Mary shouted. "They're rotted."

I changed my mind and decided to go up the ladder, instead.

When I got next to the vat, it smelled dank and awful. It remindedme of rutabagas, which made me gag every time I had to eat them. The dark, grungy, stinky water in this huge vat smelled worse than a barrel of rotten rutabagas. I had to hold my breath, or gag. While I climbed the ladder, I couldn't help looking down in the vat. I could swear something alive was in it. Looking up was worse. I could see parts of the sky through the leaky mill-barn roof riddled with cracks and holes.

I finally climbed through the square opening, gasped a deep breath of fresher air than down by the vat and looked around. It was a nice, friendly old mill barn in a way, like it was a special barn with a story to tell, and kind of shaky at the same time, the way it was rotting so it was hoping someone told its story before it fell down.

"Be careful where you step. It's not safe," Mary said.

"Hi Jerry," Linda Oats said.

"Hi Linda."

"Mary was telling me about the Pompey Hollow Book Club and the stuff you do," Linda Oats said.

"She was?" I asked.

"You're all such heroes."

"I don't know about—"

"Is Mary your girlfriend?"

"Huh?"

"I think you heard me. Is Mary your girlfriend?"

"No."

First off, I thought, I didn't even know any guys in the Pompey Hollow Book Club who had girlfriends, and second, I didn't know if my mom would even let me have a girlfriend.

"But you like her, don't you?"

"What?!"

"Mary likes Jerry. *Na, na-na, na-naaaaa, na!*"

Mary's face turned a blushing beet red. "Stop it," she said.

Now boys, I could figure. We talked the same. We pretty much liked the same things. We even knew what each other's thoughts were, at times—like when we're tossing a ball or playing touch football. We could read minds, even Mary's, at our club meetings. I looked over at Mary for a second to wonder if she ever thought about liking me or was Linda Oats just talking. This sort of girl talk distracted me. It was all new and very strange to me. I never heard a girl just say something like this out loud or talk like this before, except maybe to Cary Grant in a movie at the Cazenovia picture show.

"You can kiss me, if you want," Linda said.

I honest to God rode my bike down here to show it off to Linda Oats and Mary. I came into this spooky old cider mill barn, against my better judgment, just to get them to come outside and look at my yellow bike. All of a sudden I'm on the second floor, where Mrs. Oats had said not to go, and I'm being tempted to kiss the very girl I'd been staring at on the bus ever since my first day of school when we moved here.

"I dare you to kiss me," Linda added.

Mary folded her arms in front of her, puffed a curl from her eye with a pout, tapping a toe and staring at me, confident I wouldn't do it. Her expression looked down at the floor with doubt but then back up at me as if she was hoping I wouldn't do it.

Linda wasn't embarrassed at all—she was smiling.

"Chicken?" Linda Oats asked.

"I'm no chicken," came out of me as easy as it would for any kid at the sound of that word, even though my knees began to wobble.

A boy my age could never let a dare go unchallenged, or I'd be branded for life. Even I knew that.

Mary's lips buckled a frown in disappointment.

Linda leaned forward, with a silly smile—her eyes closed, her lips puckered. She leaned forward a little more, and kind of held her cheek out. I considered whether to kiss her on the cheek, on the lips, or just climb down the ladder and go home. I bent over, my knees really wiggling now, and pressed my lips toward her face. Glancing over I could see Mary's lips snarled to almost a warning. As it turned out, none of any of this really mattered much, because just as my lips touched what I thought was Linda's face, somewhere, both floor boards I was standing on started to make squishing sounds, wobbling, just like my knees. Then they bent and creaked, and I began to lose my balance.

This can't be good, I thought.

And the floorboards creaked again.

I looked down at my Buster Brown school shoes sinking into the rain-soaked floorboards, while the boards turned to mush like sponges, under my feet, and then—

CA-RASH!

CA-RUNCH!

Down I fell, through the hole my weight had made in the floor. I caught my fingertips on a wood beam, which stopped my fall, for about the three seconds I was hanging there, eight feet above the open wooden vat below, still full of the dark, slimy-looking sludge water. My fingers couldn't hang on any longer—my eyes made a silent plea for help up into Mary's stone-cold eyes, which pretty much looked as though I had it coming, and down into the cider vat I went!

"AAAAAAAAAAAAAHHHHHHHHH!" I wailed.

*KAAAA-SPA-LOOSH!*

It was like falling out of a top bunk bed into a tub of mud, like when I fell out of bed in Cortland onto Dick, sleeping on the floor, before we moved to Delphi Falls—only colder, smellier, and wetter and deeper.

My whole body went underwater, like I was in a deep bathtub. I sat up to push my head above water for air.

"Are you okay?" Mary shouted, sounding almost as if she cared. I was not about to open my mouth.

I could see both girls' heads peeking down through the hole I'd made in the ceiling.

"I think he's dead," Linda Oats said.

"He's not dead, Linda, or he wouldn't be standing up and spitting out leaves," Mary said.

"Are you okay?" Mary whined, but in a tone as if it served me right.

I spit out an elm leaf and pulled one off my cheek and two from the top of my head. I looked out through the broken windowpanes on the back wall of the mill, where the tall elm tree was. Two pigeons were sitting on a window frame, waiting for me to move so they could take their morning bath. All that ran through my mind was, how did a boy answer Mary's question—are you okay?

So, I didn't.

I crawled out of the vat, my clothes covered with rust, mud, and goop. I stumbled outside, trying to wring the front of my T-shirt out. I pushed my bike home so I wouldn't get the new canary yellow paint smudged. My shoes made a squishy, sloshing sound all the way up Cardner Road.

Mom could see me coming in the driveway pushing my bike. She stepped out on the porch to see why I wasn't riding and pedaling the bike. When I was close enough for her to see the gloopy mess all over me, she quickly stepped inside and came out again, this time with clean underwear, jeans, T-shirt, and a bath towel.

"Not in the house!"

She held up the items.

"But, Mom," I started to plead.

She pushed them into my hands.

"To the falls!" was her final word. "Clean up and then get ready to go to the dentist."

I put the towel around my neck, the clothes under my arm, and pushed the bike around back, all the way to the waterfall, and put it on its kickstand.

I spent time under the falls, swimming around in the icy cold water, staring at my new yellow bike standing there, waiting for me like a trusted steed. My mind wandered a little about my cider mill episode, and I began to wonder if my lips actually touched Linda on her lips or just her cheek, right before I fell through the floor. It might have been my first kiss, and this was important information to have about a first kiss. I finally decided. Definitely her lips.

## CHAPTER FOURTEEN
## RUNNING AMUCK!

Dick came into my room and shook my shoulder. "Jerry. Wake up."

I didn't budge.

"Jerry. Get up."

I rolled over, barely opening the crack of one eye. I reached out, fumbling for my clock to see the time.

"Too early!" I grunted.

I squinted a grumble up at Dick. "What!?"

"The guinea hens are over at farmer Parker's place again," Dick said.

"What do you mean, again?" I moaned. "They've only been here a week."

"They're eating Mrs. Parker's garden seeds."

"So!? What day is it?"

This was the best I could do before I had some breakfast. Nobody liked the guinea hens ever since the minute they hopped out of Dad's trunk and scooted off. The feeling was mutual. Guinea hens had no use for people and were always roaming off the property, scratching up other people's vegetable gardens and eating the seeds just after they were planted. Our dog, Ginger, didn't even like the birds, and she liked everything.

Dick considered thumping me but stayed calm.

"So!?" Dick snarled. "So, Mom wants me to go over and run them off from farmer Parker's—to get them back over here. It's Saturday, get up."

"Good. Go run 'em off."

I rolled over, facing the wall, tucking my alarm clock under my pillow. In the home *chore* world, we pretty much stayed neutral when it came to someone else's chore problems. I was getting woken up because of the two stupid guinea hens Dad had taken for a special price on my bike. Everyone knew my chores were making desserts and walking to Mr. Pitts's farm and getting our eggs every week. Taking care of the guinea hens was Dick's responsibility. Everyone knew that, too. Watching out for them was his chore in return for new tires if he ever got the car he wanted to buy from Lindsey Pryor.

He shook my shoulder again.

"Jere, I got a job all day today and tomorrow, if I want it."

"What job?" I asked.

"Washing dishes, scrubbing pots and pans up at the Lincklaen House for two weddings."

"Washing dishes?"

"The pay's good. I need the money. I got to be there in half an hour."

"Half hour? Good. You've got time to go chase the guinea hens from farmer Parker's," I said.

"If you go chase them home; I'll give you a dollar," Dick said.

"No."

"Two bucks."

"Nope."

Dick grimaced, shook his head about loosely, as if it was a snow globe hoping for a fluttering of ideas.

"I'll give you the Daisy air rifle Conway gave me."

"Keep talking."

"The stock was broken off but I fixed it like new in wood shop. You can have it."

I rallied. It wasn't often one could get the advantage negotiating with Dick.

"The BB gun and two dollars," I countered.

"Why two bucks?"

"Me and some guys want to go to the picture show in Cazenovia."

"The picture show is only fifteen cents."

"There's a lot of us and we all like popcorn. Two dollars, the BB gun or it's no deal, go chase them yourself."

"Don't call it a BB gun," Dick said. "Call it an air rifle."

"Why not?"

"Mom hates guns. You can even use it on the guinea hens to scare them home. It won't hurt them."

"You sure it won't hurt them?"

"Aim at their butts. It won't hurt them. It will only scare them and chase them home."

"Two dollars."

"Let me see how much I got.

"And the BB gun is mine to keep?"

"Air rifle. Yes."

Dick jumped out of the room, went to his, came back with the BB gun, laid it on my bed next to me, and put three cartridges of pellets on my desk. I picked the gun up and looked at the newly varnished stock. It had two leather straps hanging from a ring on its side.

"This is nice," I said.

"Get up and get over there," Dick said.

"Where's the two dollars?"

Dick jumped out of the room again and back in as quick. "I only have ten bits," he said, meaning five quarters. "Buck and a quarter and this miniature deck of playing cards. It comes in its own case."

He held miniature cards out near my face. It was a deck of playing cards half the size of a normal card.

"Okay," I said, taking the cards from his hand. Dick then offered his fine print.

"The ten of clubs is missing. No one will know."

He flipped five quarters onto my bed and looked me in the eye for confirmation that we had a deal. When I sat up, he lit out of the room and out of the house.

I pulled jeans on, dropped the quarters into my left pocket, and picked up and shook the air rifle to see if the pellet chamber was full. It was. I rested it between my side and bent forearm, as John Wayne did in *Fort Apache*, and headed to the kitchen.

Mom was at the table, reading the front page of the newspaper, digging a spoon into half a grapefruit.

"I'm going to farmer Parker's to chase the guinea hens home."

"Good. Hurry, dear."

"I'm going to get some cereal first."

"No cereal."

"Huh?"

"Go get the birds, eat when you get back."

"But why—?"

"Mrs. Parker is beside herself. I don't know whatever possessed your father to bring those creatures home in the first place. They're not domesticated."

"What does domesticated mean, Mom?"

"They are such a bother. Go get them! Now!"

Mom had a look in her eye—probably from Myrtie's call telling her that Mrs. Parker was mentioning to folks on the party line about our guinea hens spoiling her garden.

Mom lifted her eyes from the newspaper, peered over her glasses, and said, "What are you doing with a gun? You know I don't like guns."

"It's not a gun, Mom. It's a Daisy air rifle. Farmers use them to scare pigeons and birds out of barns. Minneapolis Moline Conway gave this one to Dick. Everybody has one."

"I don't like them. Don't point it at anything."

"Can I go to the picture show with some kids?"

"Young man—move!"

"Can I?"

"You accepted a responsibility. Go do your job. We can talk and you can eat breakfast when you get back. Off with you! Go!"

Neighbors in the country liked to be good neighbors so they could mean their smiles and waves at each other when they passed on the road. Mom was not having a good morning. I left the house and told our dog Ginger to stay. Stepping on the yard at farmer Parker's, their border collie ran over to meet me. Buddy and I were old friends by now. We'd brought the cows down off the hill together a bunch of times. I bounced up on farmer Parker's back porch and knocked on the door. I couldn't see farmer Parker or the horses anywhere. The door opened and Mrs. Parker looked at me through the screen door. She was trying to remember which one I was.

"Hi, Mrs. Parker, I'm Jerry. I'm here to chase the hens over to our place."

"Oh, hello, Jerry."

"Hi."

"You gave me a start. I had to think. There are so many of you and your friends—forgive me."

"Sorry about the guinea hens, Mrs. Parker."

"It's just when I do my late summer and fall planting."

"Dick is supposed to take care of them."

"They get at my seeds and bulbs before they can root."

"I'll get them out of here, don't worry."

"Most ungraceful birds, in an odd sort of way. Such big bodies for those little legs. They can be such a nuisance at planting time."

I could smell bacon and syrup drifting through the screen door. It must have showed on my face.

"I'll get them out of here," I said.

"Thank you, Jerry. Would you like some breakfast? I have plenty."

"You bet I would. Thanks, Mrs. Parker. Let me get them across the road and I'll be back."

"I'll make some hot chocolate," she said.

I turned, jumped off the porch, and walked around the house to her garden patch on the north side.

Sure enough, the guinea hens were pecking away. They tried to look like peacocks, blue-silvery-gray with black heads, white face masks, and pintail crowns. They didn't try very hard. I was embarrassed just looking at them. They couldn't fan their tails like a peacock, didn't lay eggs like chickens, and were pretty much nothing but selfish troublemakers. They belonged in a zoo, not on a farm. I cocked the air rifle and walked out in the open for the showdown. I stood square between the garden in front of me and the barn at my back, so I could block their path. I planted my feet. I shouted best I could before my breakfast.

"Shoo!"

Both birds lifted their heads, looked at me as if they were telling me to go find my own garden, and went right back to pecking.

I looked about to be certain no one had witnessed that embarrassing moment.

This time I flapped my arms.

"Git! Go on, dumb birds, get out of here!"

They couldn't have cared less.

I was about to wish I hadn't taken the job when it came to me—BBs.

I lifted the air rifle, lodged it on my chest by my shoulder, remembering what I had learned from the shooting gallery at Suburban Park amusement park in Manlius. I took careful aim at one of the hen's butts and squeezed the trigger.

*Bop!*

The hen jumped straight up about four inches off the ground, almost into flight, telling me in no uncertain terms.

"Girgle, girgle, girgle, girgle."

It stood there frozen, staring at me.

I lurched forward, cocking my air rifle for another shot. The hen backed up two steps, turned around, and took off running, the other hen right on its tail. I ran tippy-toed across the edge of the garden, balancing so as not to tumble into the row of beets, went down through the dew-covered, sloping yard, chasing them with loud war whoops all the way across the road and through our gate. Once on our property they high-tailed it the full distance up the driveway to the green barn. They both ran like they had loaded diapers. I picked up pebbles and flung a handful to help them remember to stay near the barn where they belonged and to quit waking me up on Saturdays.

I walked back up to farmer Parker's, rested my air rifle in the kitchen corner, ate breakfast, and learned about Mrs. Parker's widowed sister, who was coming for Thanksgiving all the way from Erie, Pennsylvania. Mrs. Parker had an old wood stove with cream and lime-green enamel sides and chrome handles, a black top, and tin chimney. It went up the wall and bent into the top of the wall just under the ceiling. Next to the wood stove was an electric oven and range she was cooking on. She handed me a plate with three pancakes and four strips of bacon.

"Do you ever use the old wood stove?" I asked.

"If the electricity goes out a spell, we do."

"Neat."

"If it gets intolerably cold in the winter, Fay will put a fire in it to warm the place," she said.

"Is that what farmer Parker's name is—Fay?" I asked.

"Yes. It was his father's name."

Mrs. Parker took a small pot off the burner and poured hot chocolate into my cup.

"He likes when you come around, Jerry."

"I like coming, Mrs. Parker."

"He was so proud of your friends for solving that burglary in Cortland."

"That was fun and scary," I said.

"It made him wish he were young again. He enjoys watching you learn about the country and farming. You call him farmer Parker."

"Yes ma'am."

"He's told me he feels that's so respectful. He likes that. You boys and your friends are reared well. Parenting and schooling today must be wonderful," she added with a smile.

"Reared?" I asked.

Mrs. Parker sat up like a schoolteacher and said, "We can raise our corn and vegetables, but we must rear our children."

Mrs. Parker sipped her tea, smiling out the window at the dew on the lawn, probably remembering the days she would walk into Delphi and teach in the hamlet's two-room schoolhouse.

"Can I use your telephone, Mrs. Parker?"

"Of course. It's an old one. Do you know how?"

It wasn't like ours, where we just had to pick up the receiver and wait for Myrtie to come on. I lifted the earpiece off the hook, put it to my ear, turned the crank around two full turns, and waited to see if Myrtie came on.

"Operator," Myrtie said.

"Myrtie, this is Jerry. I'm over at farmer Parker's."

"Well hi, cutie, how can I help you?"

"Can you get me Randy Vaas, please?"

"Say good morning to Mrs. Parker for me, dear."

I turned and looked at Mrs. Parker.

"Myrtie told me to say hello to you for her, Mrs. Parker."

Mrs. Parker smiled.

"Hello?"

"Randy?"

"This is Randy."

"Barber told me he was staying over at your house last night to ride the milk truck this morning with your dad."

"He stayed over."

"Are they back yet?"

"They just got back."

"You guys want to go see *Annie Get Your Gun* at the picture show?"

"What picture show?"

"It started last night in Cazenovia."

"Sure."

"See who else can go. I got a buck and a quarter from Dick."

"Hold on a sec," Randy said.

I said to Mrs. Parker, "I like helping farmer Parker. He teaches me a lot.".

Randy came back on the phone. "My dad has to pick up feed and lime in Cazenovia. He said he'd take all the kids that could fit in the cab of the truck. I'll call around and call you back."

"Thanks."

"Is that the movie about Annie Oakley, the sharpshooter?"

"I think so."

"Barber and I'll call around and call you back."

We both hung up.

I thanked Mrs. Parker for the breakfast and apologized for the hens and told her I would see what I could do about keeping them where they belonged.

"Jerry, come any time. I always have enough."

I picked up my Daisy air rifle, went outside, scratched Buddy under the collar, and walked home.

I got to our barn garage and went in looking for a couple of nails and a hammer. I was going to find a place in my room to hang the rifle. When I picked the spot, I pounded both nails in the wall by my bed. After carefully resting the gun on them, the room took on a certain air. I stood back by the door and stared at my rifle on the wall next to my bed. The room seemed more grown-up for some reason. Little did I know this air rifle on my wall would be the beginning of some problems for me.

"Come eat some breakfast, Jerry," Mom said.

I decided not to test Mom's bad start to her day by telling her I'd already eaten across the road and had just pounded two nails into my bedroom wall. I went to the kitchen, pretending I was hungry.

"What was that pounding noise?" Mom said as I walked into the kitchen.

"Mr. Vaas is driving us to Cazenovia to see the *Annie Get Your Gun*
movie. Can you pick us up later?"

"Yes dear. Eat your grapefruit."

"You should go see Mrs. Parker sometime, Mom. She's a nice lady."

"I'm certain she is. But wasn't it Robert Frost who said good fences

make good neighbors?"

"If we had good fences, she wouldn't have our guinea hens in her garden, Mom."

Mom never answered me when she knew I had her stumped.

"Perhaps I'll invite her for tea one day."

"Mrs. Parker said we had good rears, Mom."

Mom lifted her eyes from the article about Eleanor Roosevelt and peered over her glasses at me.

By now Mom had learned not to overreact to what she and Dad called "Jerry-speak." She waited for my translation to come out. Her neck perked; she crinkled her nose.

"Excuse me?"

"Mrs. Parker said me and my friends were raised *good*."

Mom's eyes smiled.

"Raised *well*," she said.

"Mrs. Parker said me and all my friends were —well, she did."

"That's nice, dear."

The phone rang.

I jumped up from my grapefruit, went into Mom and Dad's room and picked it up.

"Hello?"

"Barber and I will be at your house in fifteen minutes with Holbrook, Mary, and Mayor," Randy said.

"Good," I said.

"We'll pick you up, and then we'll go into Delphi and get Bases, if he can go. Can you get us all a ride home?"

"Already have," I said.

I figured it best to tell Mom there were five to take home, spread out over half the county, *after* she came to pick us up rather than now, what with her morning disposition being so frail because of two guinea hens.

Mom completely forgot about the *pounding* question and was reaching for her purse.

"I have enough money from Dick, Mom. You can come get us anytime this afternoon."

The good thing about a Saturday morning picture show was that it only cost fifteen cents to get in. It started in the morning, sometimes with a Superman serial or cartoon. Then the newsreel and after the newsreel they'd show the first feature movie and then another if it was a double feature and repeat them and the cartoons all day. You could sit in the movie house the whole time for the fifteen cents. They even let people go in for free to find their kids to take home. Anytime Mom came for us after a few hours would be fine.

I felt for the five quarters in my left jean pocket, slid the case of miniature playing cards in my right pocket, took one last look at my Daisy air rifle on my bedroom wall, and headed toward the gate to wait for the truck to roll down over the hill next to farmer Parker's.

Nobody had a truck like Mr. Vaas's truck. I had ridden in it before with Randy when he did the early morning dairy run with his dad. A 1942 Dodge with a stake bed for carrying milk cans or feed sacks. It was originally made for the war as an army truck. The steering wheel could be unlatched and moved from the left side over to the right side. And the truck had pedals on both sides so it could be driven or steered from either side. Mr. Vaas thought they did that because different countries, where the war was, had different driving laws for which side of the road you could drive on. Someone else told me it was in case the driver on the left got tired or shot and killed and the soldier on the right could take over without stopping.

Mr. Vaas squeaked the truck's brakes to a stop and dropped us off in front of the movie house, next to the Lincklaen House, and drove away. We had a whole fourteen minutes to wait before it opened, so we gathered and sat by the curb.

People were really good about driving around us.

I told everyone about the guinea hens and how I got an air rifle from Dick for chasing them out of Mrs. Parker's garden.

Each of them, except Mary and Holbrook, already had a BB gun. I pulled the miniature deck of playing cards out of my pocket.

"He gave me this, too."

I held it up for everyone to see.

Holbrook reached deep into his pocket and pulled out a soft piece of fur about the size of his hand.

"Want to trade?" he asked.

"What's that?"

"Trade you this chipmunk for your cards."

I jumped up.

"Holbrook, did you murder a chipmunk?"

"No way."

"That thing is a chipmunk and it's dead!" I sparked.

"My dad backed the car over it."

"Where?" Mayor asked.

"On Berry Road, he backed over it with the DeSoto going to work in the dark. I found it squished when I walked to Tommy Kellish's."

Every nose on the curb wrinkled a stomach churning *ewww*.

"Mom wouldn't let me use her pancake spatula so I picked it up with a pair of Dad's pliers, hosed the guts off it best I could, and had to beg Mom to skin it for the pelt. Wanna trade it for the cards?"

I looked more closely at it."

"You can use it to polish your BB gun."

"And your mom just washed out the guts and all, just like that?"

"She skinned it. I had to promise to hang all the wash on the clothesline for three Saturdays in a row, if she skinned the chipmunk."

Barber spoke up.

"With eleven kids, six girls all ages, this could be a humiliating experience for a boy—people driving by, watching—him with a mouthful of clothespins hanging brassieres and panties."

Randy grinned.

"For a good trader, you're the one who got skinned, Holbrook," Randy said.

"Trade?" Holbrook repeated, holding the fur up to my face. The image of my air rifle on my wall flashed in my brain.

"Trade," I accepted.

The trade was done, and the movie house opened. We all emptied our pockets and handed our money over to Mary. She divided it equally, handed it back out—and had fifteen cents to spare. We went to the popcorn stand after paying for our tickets. The fifteen cents we had left over we put in the "iron lung bank" on the candy counter for the March of Dimes, for polio kids.

We loved the movie. All three times we sat through it. Annie was the best sharpshooter in the whole world. She hit every clay bird and glass ball they threw up in the air. She was better than the man, but they got married anyway and sang songs together. The music was fun. Mary asked me if she could borrow my Daisy air rifle to practice. I said sure. I asked everyone to keep their eyes open in the woods or fields for some turkey feathers I could hang from my gun on the leather strings.

# CHAPTER FIFTEEN
# IMAGE PROBLEMS

No one knew my secret—about the only other time I took aim at a bird with the BB gun and shot and killed it.

It was a sparrow. It didn't jump like the guinea hen. I watched its eyes turn blank. Both its feet grasped the twig it was resting on, and its body fell over, swinging dead in the breeze. I climbed the tree, crawled out on the branch, reached to the twig, and lifted the sparrow gently in my hand. Feeling the warmth of the lifeless body did something to me. I begged its forgiveness, buried it with a full-blown funeral—whistled taps and my mourning dove coos—and scratched the words *Poor Sparrow* with my knife on its tombstone.

Ever since that funeral, my BB gun had never been pointed, by me, at anything other than empty tin cans or bottles. Not even at guinea hens.

But now, just because of a chipmunk fur tacked on the wall—I got in trade for a miniature deck of playing cards—and my Daisy air rifle with two turkey feathers hanging from it at the ready just above the chipmunk pelt, I was branded a seasoned woodsman, like a Davey Crockett or a Daniel Boone, by most anyone who walked by my room and peered in. The Hardy Boys book I had leaning up against my window to block the porch light from shining through at night, with a *Moby Dick* book jacket to disguise it, didn't help my image.

I wanted to show a broader literary interest than the Hardy Boys, so I took the *Moby Dick* book jacket from a book in Dick's room. With both the gun and fur on the wall, the *Moby Dick* cover made me a whale hunter.

The Pompey Hollow Book Club kids were Saturday morning picture show junkies when we weren't fighting crime. We knew life as it should be, from growing up half our lives in a war, seeing the world in a way it shouldn't be. To us life was about right over wrong, good over evil, and trying to remember to make our beds in the morning.

Thanksgiving was a few weeks away. Relatives would be coming home, sometimes staying a week. There could be twenty or thirty family members, friends, and kids around tables celebrating Thanksgiving, having fun and eating a lot of food. There would be tons of leftovers all week.

"Big families have big responsibilities," Dad would always tell us when he handed out our special pre-Thanksgiving chores. Last year I had to help set the table, but with this Thanksgiving holiday coming, Dad had a different look in his eye, a look like maybe I had matured somehow over the summer and maybe I was ready for a whole new challenge and responsibility in the development of my life experiences. Maybe (it appeared to be on his mind) I could help the family get ready for Thanksgiving in a different way than I had before. This year at the helm of a chore befitting my new image.

I was walking through the dining room on my way to my room to oil my BB gun. Holding a cup of coffee, Dad stopped me.

"Jerry me boy," he said, "Mike's getting the pumpkins, apples, and cranberries for pies and sauces and seasoned bread from the bakery for the stuffing when he drives in from Lemoyne. Since he's the gourmet in the family, he'll be helping out in the kitchen."

I was afraid of that—Gourmet Mike in the kitchen.

"Dick's job is raking leaves and picking up the front and the back yards. Your mother is going to drive to Cortland Thanksgiving week and buy a fresh tom from the Rotary club, their annual fundraiser—"

I knew this was leading somewhere.

"But we'll need more than one turkey to feed everyone through to New Years. That's more than a month, son."

I stood there looking, not saying a peep.

"Son, think you and Holbrook can go up and help Mr. Pitts prepare four geese and ten chickens for cooking and gifting?"

I stood there.

"Okay, son?"

"Your mother and I want to give two of the geese and five of the chickens to the Holbrooks for their holidays. They have a large family, too. Fourteen or fifteen, isn't it?"

I nodded, but still didn't say a word.

"You two help Mr. Pitts anyway he needs help, chop wood to get a fire going for boiling water for pulling feathers, whatever else he needs help with, Mr. Pitts will tell you. Walk over this week and work it out with him, son."

With that said, Dad matter-of-factly picked up an axe resting on the kitchen counter—an axe that hung in the barn for chopping wood—and handed it to the one person he now thought was Daniel Boone. Me.

It was even worse than I imagined! I was smart enough to know that preparing the chickens and geese didn't exactly mean giving them a bath and brushing their combs.

I stared up at him with my mouth open, speechless.

"Close your mouth, son. You'll catch flies in it," he said.

I never once caught a fly in my mouth.

Mr. Pitts was a nice old man. He was a friend of mine who watched over our chickens and geese at his little farm in trade for his being able to eat chickens and sell eggs we didn't use. I walked over and picked up the eggs every week. Dad would drop off bags of feed and stack them on a shelf in his barn, high enough so animals couldn't get to them.

Now, under the wrong impression, my dad was expecting me, his only son with the daring to have nailed a chipmunk pelt and Daisy rifle with two turkey feathers on his bedroom wall, and Holbrook, my best friend, to go help Mr. Pitts flat-out murder ten chickens and four geese for the Thanksgiving and Christmas holidays.

I kept my mouth shut and thought.

People who lived on farms raised things to eat. I knew that. That didn't bother me. Hot dogs, hamburgers, and bacon were meat. Still, it was one thing to go to a grocery with Mom and put these things in her shopping basket, but it was a whole different kettle of fish to be standing there with an axe in my hand, thinking about the rooster at Mr. Pitts's farm with its *cock-a-doodle-doo*, knowing my job was to get it and nine of the others ready to be cooked.

I killed the sparrow and didn't sleep for days. I kept thinking. There was no way I was going to murder ten chickens and four geese. What harm did the chickens or geese do to me, anyway? The chickens cackled around, pecking at the ground, minding their own business, and they gave us eggs every day.

I stood there, mesmerized in thought.

The geese chased me, sure, which could be annoying, but they also chased away any fox that tried to get a chicken. My brother Dick chased me around the house, but there was no way I'd chop his head off.

Dad clicked his fingers three times in front of my face trying to get my attention.

"You okay, son?"

I snapped out of it.

"Sure, Dad."

It was final, I thought to myself—our animals living at Mr. Pitts's house were family, not livestock.

I wasn't going to do it; nobody could make me do it and I was pretty sure Holbrook wouldn't do it, either. Oh, he talked about being a woodsman and about deer tracking, but he'd rather be combing his hair and looking at girls. He couldn't even skin the squashed chipmunk.

I wouldn't dare say any of this out loud for Dad to hear. I knew if I told him I didn't want to do it he wouldn't make me. It would remind him of the Easter rabbit fiasco and he'd just get an older brother to do it. I couldn't let that happen, either.

I turned around, dragged the axe to my room and slid it under my mattress. I had to get a meeting with the Pompey Hollow Book Club and tell them what my dad wanted us to do. I went to Mom and Dad's room and picked up the phone.

"Operator."

"Myrtie, can you get me Tommy Kellish?"

"Jerry?"

"Yes."

"Are you getting ready for Santa, young man? It won't be long now."

"Yes ma'am."

"I love the comforter you gave me at Easter. I use it every day. It's cozy in the chilled air. Here you go, hon, you're connected."

"Hello?"

"Tommy, could you see if Holbrook is working at the Tully bakery today? I need to see him."

"I'll have to walk over there; my dad has the tractor."

"Your dad lets you drive the tractor?"

"If he's not using it, he does."

"Dang."

"I'll walk over now and call you back."

"Find out if he can meet at the cemetery. It's real important."

"Life or death important?"

"Yeah, this time it's my dad."

"What's up?"

"He wants Holbrook and me to murder a ton of chickens and geese."

"Uh-oh, that is serious."

"If I know Holbrook isn't working today, I'll call Barber to set up a meeting," I said.

"If he's home, want me just to go ahead and call Barber right off?"

Tommy asked.

He knew the cemetery was the book club's meeting place.

"Perfect idea. Thanks, Tommy."

About forty minutes later the phone rang. I grabbed it.

"Hello?"

"Early morning tomorrow, the cemetery," Barber said.

"How early?"

"Sunup. See you there."

We both hung up.

The next morning, I got up early, dressed in the dark and walked over through farmer Parker's place. I went down into his barn and said hello while he was milking. I stepped through the doors and said good morning to Sarge and Sally. I walked down back of his barn, over the creek, and up the steep wagon road to the top. I crossed the hayfield, feeling the breaking sun on my shoulder. I climbed down the other side between the maple and the elm into the cemetery.

Climbing down I made mourning dove *coos* with my hands, for some noise. Barber and Bases were playing barehanded catch, waiting. We sat on the ground and talked about the *Annie Get Your Gun* movie. It wasn't long before we heard the door of a new Ford open and close. Kids could tell the kind of car it was from the door slam. The car drove off.

We could hear the leaves rustling between the tall pine and maple trees up the hill into the cemetery. With a heavy morning fog, Holbrook and Mary were kicking the dried leaves around tombstones, deliberately stepping on dead branches and twigs, snapping them with their feet. Normally Holbrook and I could sneak through the woods like Indians, and not make a sound, but every kid knew, especially in a cemetery so soon after Halloween—not that we believed in ghosts or spirits or anything like that—we just never thought there *couldn't* be ghosts, either.

Mom read me a story of Ichabod Crane and a headless horseman, so I knew what I was talking. The book was written about Sleepy Hollow and that couldn't be all that far from Pompey Hollow, we figured. We suspected it was all true, so we made noise—lots of noise—walking in the cemetery in the fog.

Mary and Holbrook came into the open between trees. Holbrook had one candy bar in his hand. Mary had three. I figured her dad stopped at Hastings' store in Delphi and bought candy bars for each of us.

Mary handed one to Barber and one to Bases, kept one for herself. My guess was Holbrook ate his on the way up the hill through the cemetery and was carrying mine.

Holbrook took the wrapper off the candy bar, broke it in two, and held up both pieces. One was longer than the other, so he took a bite off the longer piece to even them up and held them up again to be sure they were even.

Good friends didn't look at something like this as cheating a friend—we'd just think it was funny.

Everyone savored the chocolate, like grownups with their morning coffee. Holbrook and Mary were still catching their breath.

"What's wrong?" Holbrook asked.

He knew my call to Tommy Kellish was a life or death call. He always wanted to get right down to business. What no one knew was it was life or death for some chickens and geese. Everyone stood in a circle.

"My dad gave me an axe and said for Holbrook and me to go up to Mr. Pitts's place and help him butcher chickens and geese for Thanksgiving and Christmas."

"Yeah, and—?" Barber asked.

"And two of the geese and five of the chickens are for Holbrook's to have for Thanksgiving and Christmas."

Holbrook looked at me.

"So what's the problem?"

"Holbrook, are you crazy!? There's no way we're going to murder any chickens or geese!"

"You have to dip them in boiling water right afterward to get the feathers off," Mary offered.

Holbrook could smell the gravy. He shrugged.

"I don't see a problem."

"Chopping their heads off would be easy," Bases said.

It was then Barber added a more educated, one might say more clinical, point of view.

"And then one of you will have to stick your hand in their *hiney*-holes and pull out all their guts and clean them."

"Huh?" Holbrook grunted.

Holbrook spun around in a complete, dizzying circle. His repartee sank to a low I could only attribute to our talking about chicken guts just at the time he swallowed his second half of the chocolate candy bar. He muffled a stutter.

"Now that could be a problem. What do you have in mind? What's the plan?"

Holbrook tried to sound in control, but his mind was failing him.

Our president scrunched her nose up, her imagination smelling the air a few times (for warm chicken guts) and flipped what was left of her candy bar up over her shoulder, loping it behind her.

I tried to gather my thoughts. They were nowhere to be found.

"How about the plan is that Jerry goes and tells Mr. Pitts what we're supposed to be up to—murder—but that we want to just go play in his barn all day instead, pretending to do it, while we think of something to tell his dad why we didn't do it? Jerry tells Mr. Pitts we aren't going to murder anything, and that's final," Mary said.

Bases and Barber said in unison, "Perfect!"

It sounded like a perfect stall. I rallied.

"I have an idea," I said.

"What?" Mary asked.

"Holbrook and I walk to Hastings' store and buy some chickens and geese that are ready to cook. No one will ever know," I said.

"You're all geniuses," Holbrook said, wadding up the candy bar wrapper and tossing it over his shoulder.

Mary felt the integrity of the adventure was a little cloudy, so she asked, "Who's in?"

Everyone spat.

"Where do you get the money to buy them?" Barber asked. "They've got to be expensive."

"We'll walk to the store now," I said. "I'll tell Mr. Hasting my dad wants to surprise the Holbrooks and their eleven kids, wants to order enough chickens and geese for the holidays, and that Holbrook and I can pick them up in two weeks."

"But how do you pay for them?" Barber asked.

"We'll ask him if he'll put them on Dad's store charge account."

"But that won't be telling the truth," Mary said.

That detail had never deterred us from executing a brilliant idea in the past.

"I know," I said, "but this is a life or death situation and it calls for a really big fib. 'Sides, Mom will understand and be on our side. She hates violence of any kind."

"Bull tacky!" Barber barked. "If your mom finds out you lied, we will all get our butts whupped but good."

"Oh, she'll kill us," I admitted, "but at least she'll understand—

"Dang straight she'll kill us," Barber interrupted.

"—besides, who here wants to stick your hand up *hiney* holes and pull guts out of a lot of dead chickens and geese?"

Not a hand went up. No one spat.

Bases leaned down, picked up the remnants of Mary's candy bar, flicked a stone chip and a dead pine needle off it, and popped it in his mouth.

"Good thinking, this is some really good thinking," Holbrook murmured, still holding his stomach. "If we're going to do it, let's get going."

We started the quarter mile walk toward Delphi, taking turns kicking a pebble down the road. This kicking a pebble sort of thing helped concentration if a person had a lot on their mind, and right then, we had a lot on our minds.

Here we were, about to have an adventure that was going to be bootstrapped by a fib. That alone could very well have landed us all in trouble. Every time one of us mentioned that we should maybe think some more about this before we did it, someone would say something like, "I wonder what chicken guts feel like when you pull them out?" Or someone else would add, "I wonder how hot guts smell?"— and we would kick the pebble a little farther than the last time so we could get there faster and get this over with. We were in a situation where we had convinced ourselves we were on the right side of a thin line between right and wrong.

The bell on the store's paint-chipped wooden door jingled. Mr. Hasting, without looking up to see who was walking in, said, "Be right with you, after I carry this bag out to the car for a customer."

When he came back in and closed the door, Holbrook and I explained to him what we needed for the holidays, as a surprise for my dad. Mr. Hasting scratched the two-day whisker growth on his cheek and said, "Yes, I can have ten chickens and four geese ready for you in two weeks. Want me to call your mom or dad to tell them when they're ready?"

Like a solemn High Mass church choir, everyone shouted together, "Oh, no!" Holbrook added, "And if they come in, please don't say anything!"

Knowing just about everyone believed a girl, our president took control. "Mr. Hasting, Jerry and Holbrook will come get them in two Tuesdays."

"We want to surprise my dad and mom, to show them how responsible we can be," I added.

Mr. Hasting smiled over at his wife, who was stacking acorn squash on a table, sizing us up out of the corner of her eye. Mr. Hasting mentioned to her that wasn't it nice helping families celebrate a joyous holiday season with such a wonderful gesture. He told us how proud he was of how grown up we were as he unwittingly became a conspirator to our scheme. He told us all to help ourselves to a free crème sickle. Mr. Hasting was now a part of our deception, unbeknownst to him.

Mrs. Hasting stared over at us as if she had an inkling we were up to something. She'd heard stories about Easter bunny rabbits and free candy. She'd seen Mary pedaling her popsicle cart around Delphi.

There was a simple rule all kids knew—the more kids we involved in our mischief, the more likely we'd get off with just a talking to if the law caught us—but for certain a whupping if we got caught by our parents. We knew this from experience, but we also knew we couldn't be distracted. The Pompey Hollow Book Club had chickens and geese to save.

That night something strange was in the brisk air outside. It turned colder than a block of ice in a washtub filled with Kool-Aid. I didn't like the shrill windy sounds that came with it. When it grew pitch dark, the winds kicked up into a new—and to me—mean personality.

The trees up the steep hill next to the house moaning and howling, drowning out the noise from the crashing waterfalls. It was enough to curdle your blood. I looked around the living room for something to crawl under in case I had to hide quickly. Even Ginger, our outdoor dog, had somehow snuck in and cowered next to Mom's footstool. Mom just sat under a lamp reading her book, as if nothing was happening.

This all started after dark, about the time I turned the living room radio on to listen to a murder mystery. While the radio was warming up, a low branch of a big tree on the side hill up by Dick's tree house started clawing down on the roof of the house over the laundry room, like it was raking leaves off the roof.

Dad was somewhere on bakery business. Tomorrow was only a half day at school, so Dick was staying the night at Duba's.

Mom was sitting in her easy chair, smiling, reading a book about the Von Trappe family in Germany and how they sang together.

I was lying on the living room floor, nearly scared to death from the noises outside and from the radio show.

I was listening to a chilling murder mystery program with shrieks and creaks of iron doors, shootings, stabbings, and black bats in the belfry looking for blood. Every time I heard a scream through the radio speaker, I would look around to see if anyone was in the room, sneaking up from behind. The wind outside, howling through the trees, didn't help. Every scream would give me a new layer of goose-bump chills. I'd spin my head back around, look at the glowing radio dial, and convince myself it was only my imagination.

One thing was certain. As soon as "Death at the Haunted Mansion" was over, I was hitting the sack. It was about to give me a heart attack. There is only so much a boy can take, surrounded by screams, high winds, and cold, dark woods at night.

Then it happened.

*Zzzzzzzap … pop!*

The whole inside of the house went black.

All the lights went out, and the radio went off. Everything electric that made noise, like the icebox, stopped. The house was pitch black, and as quiet as the city morgue in the radio program.

This can't be good! I thought.

My heart skipped a beat as I gulped.

"Mom!?"

"Looks like a fuse is blown," Mom said calmly.

It was easy for her to stay calm. She's a mother—mom's never get scared—and besides that she wasn't listening to my radio show, 'Death at the Haunted Mansion." I had no idea where she was now because I couldn't see in the dark.

"Can people come out of a radio, Mom?"

It was one of those questions you ask and, almost before you get it out of your mouth, you realized how dumb it was. I wasn't thinking clearly in the dark. I thought there had to be some coincidence in my listening to someone's bone-chilling scream through the radio—from a haunted mansion—and suddenly all our electricity going out, leaving the house dark,

right in the middle of the scream.

"Don't talk nonsense, dear," Mom said.

"But Mom—!"

"I'll see if we have some candles. We'll change the fuse, if I can find the fuse box, that is. I knew where it was in Cortland, but

I'm not so sure about this house," Mom said.

I was on my hands and knees, feeling my way along the living room wall toward the hall to the bathroom when Mom dropped the bomb.

"Jerry, we're going to have company all weekend with Mike's friends coming from college," Mom started.

"I know," I said, still crawling.

"So we'll need eggs."

"I know, Mom."

"Walk to Mr. Pitts's and get a basket of eggs, dear."

"I will. I'll put the basket by my bed and do it when I get home from school tomorrow."

"Now, dear."

"Huh?"

"Tonight, Jerry."

"What? When? I always get the eggs on Saturday, Mom. Can't I do it tomorrow after school?"

"Right now, dear, while it's on my mind. Stay where you are. I'll bring you the basket."

"Are you serious?"

"Of course, I'm serious. Why would you ask such a question?"

"This is crazy!"

"Don't be impudent."

"Mom, I can't even see you, much less the basket. It's even darker outside. How am I going to find Mr. Pitts's house?"

I could hear the wind picking up, through the dark and trees outside, inviting me outside and into the human sacrifice.

"The moon will light the road," Mom said. "I'll wait up for you to get home."

She nearly stumbled over me while I was trying to stand up in the dark. I grabbed the basket she was holding, just to keep from falling over again.

"Off you go."

I knew if I tried to talk my way out of this, Mom would give me the "*You're the oldest boy here, so you're the man of the house tonight and the eggs are your responsibility*" talk.

This talk could sometimes go on for days. I took the basket, which wasn't my regular egg basket—it was my Aunt

Kate's sewing basket with a broken handle and a big hole in its upper left side scratched through by Mittens, the cat, sharpening her claws. Mom emptied it every time she needed more eggs than usual, because it held more than my egg basket.

I had fun going to see Mr. Pitts and playing in his barn—in the daylight. It was a small barn. It didn't have electricity. It had a stable for his horse, Nellie, and one for his cow, Bessie. It reminded me of Christmas.

Whenever Mr. Pitts was in the barn at night a flickering kerosene lantern hung on a post between the stables, and another hung on the post by the side door that led out to the chicken coop. The barn had a glow, with the golden straw on the floor and hanging from the loft above, and the bright golden yellow and orange "harvest" corn in the wooden manger bin with the chicken wire sides, set in the middle. Mr. Pitts called it *cow corn* because before bringing it to the barn the stalks were stacked and tied standing in the field at harvest time for the sun and air to dry it on the stalk. Then the ears got chopped into two and three-inch cobs by hand. Bessie ate the cobs all through the winter when snow covered a small green pasture behind the barn. Against the wall there was a horse-drawn carriage buckboard. It had a leather bridle and harness neatly lying in the back of it, behind the bench seat. He would hitch Nellie up to pull it to Hastings' store in Delphi, or other places he needed to go. The chicken coop was next to the barn.

One time I asked Mr. Pitts why he didn't have electricity or a car.

"Well, long as I got matches, a good tooth to strike 'em on, (he'd always grin a toothless grin) a walkin' lantern will do me fine," he'd say. "Ol' Nellie here has some good years left in her. More than me, prolly. Why would I want to learn me to drive one of them jalopy cars for, anyhow? I seen 'em in the big-un"—he meant World War I— "and had no use for 'em back then, neither."

"Were you in World War II, Mr. Pitts?" I asked.

"The big-un son, World War I. Well, it weren't a big war like the war we just had. You and your pals saw a bigger one, that's for sure. Anyway, give me a horse ever' time."

Then he would spit his "tabackee" with a *patooooie* sound, wiping his chin with the back of his hand.

Everything Mr. Pitts ever said to me made perfectly good sense—and as it would turn out, especially on this particularly scary, windy, cold, and dark evening. I felt my wayalong the front hall wall in the dark to our front door and my possible demise.

I mumbled, "If we at least had a kerosene lantern like Mr. Pitts, I could see. If we had a horse and buggy like his, I would be safer getting there. Horses can see in the dark."

"Don't dally, young man. No stalling."

"I'm going."

"Here, put this sweater on."

Without so much as a spark of light to guide her throw, Mom hurled a wool sweater at the very last sound she heard—my voice. It must have sailed through the darkness like a warning storm cloud as it landed squarely in my face.

"Say hello to Mr. Pitts, dear. Don't keep him up late talking. Mr. Pitts has been sick, and your dad's been taking him to a hospital for checkups in Rochester. But don't mention it. Tomorrow's a school day for you. Go to bed as soon as you get home."

With an aim like that, who would argue with her?

It wasn't a full moon like it was in "Death at the Haunted Mansion," on the radio. It was a quarter moon, but I could see the parts of the road and driveway that would reflect its light. The trees next to the house and the woods on the cliffs and hills all down the road were pitch black and daring me with every step I took. Their branches creaked and moaned, the leaves making all sorts of flutters, shudders and groans, like something wild was running through them. I didn't know these woods yet.

"This can't be good," I mumbled.

I walked as fast as I could down the driveway, avoiding tripping in puddle holes. I could have walked faster, but I wasn't totally convinced I wouldn't be turning on a dime between strides and heading on back to the house. I made it to the end of the driveway and to Cardner Road. This part wasn't too bad, because for the first time I could see a glimmer of light way down at the corner. There was a house and the old mill barn on the left (where pretty Linda Oats lived) and one on the right where the Burlingame sisters lived. Both houses had lights on. All I had to do all the way to the corner was stare at the lights and keep telling myself I was almost there.

Just as I reached the corner with lights in bedroom windows looking down at me like owls, I had thoughts of turning around and going home. The wind howled through the broken windows of the old cider mill barn next to Linda's house. A window shutter clacked back and forth, slapping the outside wall like an angry iron skillet. I had to turn right to go up the hill.

Looking up the hill, I remembered how steep it was, even only halfway up to where Mr. Pitts lived. It gave me more chills. Somehow it looked steeper in the dark. I stood shivering, near freezing, staring up the hill, wondering if Mom would believe me if I told her there were no eggs, if I just turned around and went back home. Not only were there dark, noisy trees on both sides of this hill, all the way up, they were so big they blocked out any chance of moonlight for the entire hill. It was like a black cave that went up. It was getting serious.

I started to walk up.

I managed to get up to Mr. Pitts' without having a heart attack. It was so dark I could barely see his house. Against my better judgment, I stepped in on the drive and walked slowly, approaching his front door in the pitch of night. There were no lantern lights on in the barn or in the house. I could hear geese honking in the barn, warning me to leave—warning me to go back where I came from, and I wouldn't get hurt. I hoped he was home, because I hated the thought of going into the chicken coop in the dark alone to find eggs, especially with no light, from under chickens who didn't want people taking their eggs in the middle of the night, and with a mad rooster and mean geese who wanted to protect the chickens.

None of this was looking good.

It was a small, unpainted, sun-bleached two-and-a-half-room gray house.

I stepped up on the wooden porch and knocked on the window of the front door.

Nothing.

I pressed my face to the glass, trying to see through what appeared to be a doily lace curtain behind it.

It was dark inside.

I knocked again.

Nothing.

Then I saw a match-spark ablaze, and a small glow of light got bigger and started to move a shadow on the wall inside. I could tell Mr. Pitts had lit a match, and then a lantern. There was a warm golden look in the room. My heart started beating again. He held the lantern high ahead of him, making his shadow bouncing on the floor and wall behind him look like a monster. I could see his face coming closer to the door. He was wearing a long flannel nightshirt and a sleeping cap flopped over his ear, like the father wore in the storybook about the *night before Christmas and all through the house*. His shadow moved from wall to wall as he walked to the door. It was like a haunted house filled with ghosts. I knew they were his shadows, though, so that was fine.

He pulled the lacy door curtain aside delicately with stubby callused fingers and peered out through the glass at me—then opened the door.

"I wondered if Missus would be wantin' eggs for the weekend—I been 'spectin' ya, son."

"Yes, sir," I said. "It's just that there's no car at home for a ride, so I had to walk, and Mom has company coming."

He handed me his lantern, stepped back inside and lit another for himself. He pulled boots on, came out, and led me to the chicken coop.

"Walking is good fer ya, son."

I didn't answer.

"Ya oughta get a horse," he chuckled.

He opened the coop door and stepped in. The coop was half the size of my bedroom. One wall about my height was stacked with thirty square wooden apple crates on their side, floor to ceiling, with straw in each for a nest. There was a mother hen nesting in every one of them, murmuring cantankerous late-night cackles under their breaths, wondering why the early wakeup.

Mr. Pitts put his hand under every chicken, one at a time,

and never stopped talking to me. It was almost like we were sitting in a barbershop and catching up.

“If you *coop* chickens, son, this is how you collect your eggs. You’re
the boss. Just reach under them quick-like. If you *free range* them—”

“What’s free range mean, Mr. Pitts?”

“Means ain’t no coop. S’when you let them free all day and all night, spread the seed for them to peck and scratch at. No feeder. It’s more natural for them. I don’t have the space—too close to the road.”

“Oh.”

“Free range you have to learn where they scatter the eggs, but they will lay the same place every time. You have to beat critters to the eggs free range, or the critters will eat them. Early morning is the best time to find the eggs when you free range.”

He took one, sometimes two, eggs from the nests of sleepy chickens that never moved and handed them around his back to me to put in the basket.

One egg he handed around was as heavy as a rock. He turned to catch my eyes, giggled as I looked at the make-believe egg, and took it back. He held it up to his lantern for me to get a good look at it.

“This here one is made from *alabaster*. A new chick thinks it’s a real egg, and while trying to hatch it, it puts her in a way and she starts laying her own.”

He put it back under the chicken.

“If you free range, always remember they sleep high at night—fence posts, trees, rooftops, on about anything high enough up to sleep safe and lay low at daylight.”

“Do you like chicken, Mr. Pitts?”

“I eat ham, bacon, and chops. I eat butter, eggs, and cheese. I eat apples and carrots. I’m partial to Nettie’s tomatoes. I don’t ask nuthin’ more from a chicken than their eggs, and I swallow more tabackee than I care to.”

“Mr. Pitts, my dad wants me and my friend Holbrook—”

“I know Holbrook, son.”

“My dad was us to come help you murder chickens and geese, but we don’t want to hurt any of them.”

I waited for Mr. Pitts to say something. He didn't.

"You think my friends could come here and mess around in the barn and just pretend we did it with the chickens?"

Mr. Pitts stood with his back to me, not talking.

"We can get chickens and geese from the store instead. Can we come and play in the barn but no killing, Mr. Pitts? Please?"

Mr. Pitts turned slowly, lifted the lantern. He could tell my eyes looked serious and I wasn't just trying to get out of a chore.

"I'll have to think on that one, son."

"Please, Mr. Pitts."

"Your pap is 'spectin' me to do it."

"We'll get them at Hasting's, Mr. Pitts."

"I'll have to think on that one, son. Give me a day. Lemme think on it."

"Okay."

He turned away from me.

I didn't know why, but I had a feeling Mr. Pitts knew Dad had asked me to help him butcher the chickens and geese. I also had a feeling he was telling me all about chickens because he knew the chickens, geese, and ducks would maybe come to our house someday and he wanted me to know how to watch after them. Maybe he was getting too sick to watch them. I wasn't sure.

"You like the woods yet, son?"

"I like the woods a lot."

"Your daddy tells me you like it more than when you first come."

"Not like tonight, though. It's best if I can get up there in the daylight and build a campfire before it gets dark. Me and Holbrook sleep out. I do alone sometimes. I don't like the big cold winds, though. It's scary with the cold winds."

"Nights like this is for critters," he said.

I didn't need to hear that.

In no time the basket was over the top full and we backed out of the coop. Mr. Pitts saw to it the door and the gate were closed and latched tight.

"That ought to do ya through the weekend," he said. "On that other thing, come see me after school tomorrow, son."

He took the lantern from me and turned away.

Then he added, "We've had a fox or two lately. Sneaky critters they are. Show 'em who's boss."

I knew foxes liked to get at chickens—and knowing there were maybe foxes somewhere around was not something I wanted to hear, especially tonight—I still had to walk all the way home.

"Thanks, Mr. Pitts. Good night."

Just as I put my foot on the dark road in front of his house, I heard his door close. I looked around and saw he had blown out the lanterns and had probably gone back to bed.

I started on my way back home down the very steep hill. The basket was bulky, so I swung it at my side by its wobbly handle to keep balance as I walked.

Something seemed different from when I came. The wind had stopped, and there were no strange or spooky noises in the woods—on either side of the road.

It got still.

It got way too still all of a sudden—an eerie quiet.

Then, from behind me—

*Ka-chop!*

I stopped and froze in my tracks. My heart pumped like a Model A. Something was following me. Was it a fox's paws jumping into the middle of the road? Was it a wild-eyed screaming owl stretching open its claws for a new kill and dropping a snake from its beak on the road in favor of the eggs it saw in my basket?

I started to walk faster.

*Ka-chop!*

My walk became the fast walk people do in a manner they think disguises fear, like someone is following them in a mystery movie. Its general purpose is to get away without appearing like you're running. Down one of the darkest and steepest hills in the area I went, at a speed that was not smart.

*Ka-chop! Ka-chop!*

That was enough for me—no time to be smart now—every boy for himself!

I began running so fast down the hill I nearly stumbled at

the bottom just trying to slow down. Turning left, at full speed, in order to go back up Cardner Road, I could feel my feet sliding inside my P.F. Flyers like they were three sizes too big.

*Ka-chop! Ka-chop! Ka-chop!*

Louder and closer!

*God—I promise to clean my room every week—God, I promise to do anything my mom says—Oh, God—please don't let it catch me.*

Running faster than even Superman without leaving the ground didn't seem fast enough. I could hear my loud heavy breathing and feel my heart pounding all the way through my ears. The thought occurred to me to drop the basket, but for some reason I held it tighter, swinging it even more quickly. My sneakers slapped echoes on the pavement. But it was still behind me.

*Ka-chop! Ka-chop! Ka-chop!*

Then it stopped.

There were no more noises. It happened that fast.

Nothing was chasing me anymore.

But I didn't dare slow down.

"Thank you, God," I panted.

Still running full-out, I figured I was either safe from it now or it was ahead of me, waiting to ambush me, and nothing much else mattered.

I ran the length of the dirt driveway and leaped up the front steps, ran inside and dropped the basket on the dining room table, which had a candle glowing on it. I could hear Mom on the telephone talking to Dad, asking him where the fuse box was.

I personally had had more than any one boy could stand in one night. I went to my room, took my sneaks off, got under the blanket with my clothes and socks on, and covered my head. I figured if I even lived through the night it would be a miracle. Whatever was out there chasing me, now knew where I lived.

What else could possibly happen?

Mom woke me in the morning. I decided to keep last night to myself. I got ready for school quickly. By not telling anyone about it, it might go away like a bad dream. I didn't know what had been chasing me. All I knew, it was fast, and it must have been huge.

The school bus stopped. When I got on, Mr. Skelton

looked at me as if he knew something wasn't right about me, but he couldn't put his finger on it, like I was a little green.

If he only knew what I had been through, he would have understood.

I sat in the very first seat, right behind the door of the bus because it was empty. I grabbed the rail in front of me with both hands, to steady my nerves. The bus started down Cardner Road.

"What on earth?" Mr. Skelton asked.

He hardly ever talked while he drove.

"Wonder what that is?" Mr. Skelton asked.

I looked out the front window to see what he was looking at.

"Looks like broken chicken eggs," he said. "Why, they're everywhere. My goodness! Did you ever? Well I never."

I rubbed my eyes and looked again. Broken eggs— a row of them, in a straight line right straight up the middle of the road. It was my eggs, I thought to myself. It was eggs making the noises, the eggs slipping through the hole in the basket and nothing was chasing me last night.

I rested my head down on the rail in front of my seat and buried my forehead on the backs of my hands. How could I be in school and be so lame- brained at the same time? I couldn't believe I could be such a dunce.

"I wonder how they got there?" I asked Mr. Skelton, using a Hardy Boy diversionary technique.

I hoped Mr. Skelton would just drop the subject and not open up a whole conversation about it. Sometimes conversations led to the truth, and I wasn't ready for that.

Later that day, when the school bus dropped me and Dick off, Dick walked in the driveway toward the house and I started walking down the road to go talk with Mr. Pitts about Thanksgiving, like he had asked. Looking down the road, I could see his buggy turning on the corner and heading up Cardner Road, riding full trot. I stopped walking on the side of the road and waited for his wagon.

"Whoa!"

Nellie came to a stop, bouncing her head up and down a few times, enjoying the run in the brisk air. Holding the leather reins in his left hand, Mr. Pitts reached down to the floorboard, lifted a woven wicker basket filled with eggs, and handed it out to me.

"Ole Nellie just followed your trail of eggs," Mr. Pitts guffawed.

I could tell in his smirk he knew the trouble I might be in. I took the basket and stepped back from the buggy.

"Thank you, Mr. Pitts."

"Hold on, son," he said. He leaned down and picked up a burlap bag with a bailing twine bow tying it closed. He handed it out to me.

"I'll do it."

"You will?"

"I'm thinking this Sunday is good to bring your friends by."

"For real, Mr. Pitts? We don't have to murder the chickens and geese?"

"I'm too old to get in too much trouble. Merry Christmas, son."

He didn't say another word. He winked a smile at me and told his horse, Nellie, "Giddyap!" then turned the wagon into our alfalfa field so he could pull around and head back down Cardner Road.

"Thanks, Mr. Pitts."

He waved his arm first and then turning around in the wagon seat he tilted the visor of his wool cap like a gentlemanly salute, smiled, and shouted, "It's Charlie, son. Call me Charlie. Merry Christmas."

He clicked a *ktch, ktch* with his mouth, slapped the reins down gently on Nellie's behind, and off she trotted.

When I got into the house and put the new basket of eggs in the kitchen, Mom asked, "Does Mr. Pitts need more chicken feed?"

She was assuming the lack of eggs last night was a nutritional thing.

"Maybe," I said.

I went to my room and looked at the burlap bag. It had a tag made from the back of a piece of an old wall calendar he had cut out. On it he had written "To Gerry, from Charlie."

I knew he'd spelled my name wrong from the Christmas card my folks sent out once where the printer spelled my name wrong on it. It wasn't Thanksgiving yet, much less Christmas, but I decided to open the burlap bag. I was amazed. Charlie gave me his hunting knife and holster, two long turkey feathers, and a World War I water canteen with cook pot attached. There was a lantern in the bag, a bottle of kerosene, and a box of stick matches. These great gifts that once belonged to Charlie put me in the Christmas spirit right away. I sat at my desk, wrote him a thank you letter, walked out, and put it in the mailbox.

## CHAPTER SIXTEEN
## A PEEK AT DEATH

Late Friday night I was restless, but I didn't know why. I couldn't sleep. I didn't want to read, and I didn't feel like listening to the radio.

I got up off my bed, grabbed my knapsack and the bedroll from my closet shelf, and snuck down the hall in the dark and out the front door. There was no wind. The air wasn't cold. I decided to go up to my camp on top of the cliff across the creek. I walked out to the swings and sat in one of them, thinking. Should I walk down through the alfalfa field and up to my camp the back way and keep dry, or should I cross the creek here and climb the cliff, the shortcut way up by the big white rock? Or should I just go back to bed?

I remembered the lantern and canteen Charlie gave me. I ran inside and got them. Outside I lit it and made my decision.

The icy cold creek water on my legs reminded me I hadn't filled my canteen at the house. I stopped in the middle of the creek, took it out of my knapsack, unscrewed its cap, bent down, and dunked it under the water in the brook until I could hear the air bubbles as it was filled with creek water. I screwed the top back on, slid it into my knapsack, and put it on my back for the climb up the cliff.

At my camp I laid out my bedroll and hung the knapsack and lantern on a tree limb. I walked around gathering branches, twigs, and leaves, and started a fire. I stacked some larger logs off to the side, to keep it stoked all night. After the kindling started to burn, I blew out the lantern. Sitting by the fire and watching the warm glow of my camp was one of my favorite things to do now that I was getting used to the woods.

I leaned back on my bedroll, covered up, and looked up at the stars through the trees.

I fell asleep.

I woke at dawn and sat up, stirred what was left of the fire with a stick, listened to the birds, and watched a chipmunk running around the base of a tree and keeping a careful eye on me. I drank some water from the canteen.

I put my hands together to blow a mourning dove call.

"Whoo—eee—who—who—who—"

"Whoo—eee—who—who—who—"

It wasn't long before a dove landed close to me and walked about, looking for where the sound had come from, listening for another call.

"Whoo—eee—who—who—who—"

"Whoo—eee—who—who—who—"

I hadn't brought eggs to cook. I had my can of Spam, but I didn't want to open it and waste half of it. I decided I'd just drink my water now and go for a walk along the top of the cliff by the upper waterfall. I'd hike around looking for animals and eat when I went back down to the house. While I walked, I finished off my canteen of icy cold creek water.

Back at camp, I scooped handfuls of dirt over the fire, smothering it out before I headed home. I packed up and started back to the house the way I'd come up last night, down the cliff hillside. I got down as far as the white rock and rested on it a minute. I wasn't feeling good all of a sudden. Something wasn't right. Sweat beaded on my forehead, and I never sweated like that. I slid further down the cliff, to the edge of the creek, and stood up straight, holding my stomach. All of a sudden, something slammed me, and I had a sharp cramp that felt like I'd been punched in the stomach. I bent over and braced my hands on my knees a few seconds before I could straighten up again.

When I looked at the stream, I noticed dead fish floating by in some white bubbly foam. My first thought was that they'd been killed by animals, maybe muskrats. I had never seen anything like that before. I started to wade across; and in the middle, two more dead fish floated by, and then six more, all floating downstream in the foam. I crossed quickly, threw my knapsack on the bank, and crawled up, looking back over my shoulder at the water.

From the top of the bank, I watched hundreds of dead fish floating downstream in the foam. I doubled over with another sharp stomach cramp.

"Ayiiieee!"

This time, I ran into the house as fast as I could.

"Mom, Dad, come quick, you have to see this!"

Dad was gone to work, but Mom walked out from the kitchen. Mike ran out of his room.

"Hurry!" I shouted.

I opened the back door and led them to the side of the creek.

"Oh, my Lord!" Mom said.

"Something's killing them!" Mike yelled. "Some chemical."

There were dead fish floating down the creek everywhere you looked. Then I had another stabbing stomach cramp, and bent forward almost to my knees, nearly knocking the wind out of me. This time I was holding my stomach.

"Ayiiieee!"

"What's wrong, Jerry?" Mom asked.

"Jerry, did you drink from the creek?" Mike asked.

Still bent over, I told him, "Last night I filled the canteen from the creek and drank it this morning instead of cooking breakfast."

"Mike," Mom said, "Get in the car this minute and drive Jerry to Dr. Morrow in Cazenovia."

"Okay," Mike said.

"Drive carefully, but hurry. I'll call him right now and tell him you are on your way and why you're coming."

Then she said, "Jerry's been poisoned—hurry!"

Mike and I didn't say anything the whole trip to the doctor. I could see his worried eyes. I kept thinking about the dead fish.

When we got to Dr. Morrow's house, Mike stopped short and parked by the side nearest the door to his office and jumped out. Doctor Morrow was waiting by the door and took me right into his examining room, telling us that after Mom called him, he called the sheriff, who told him that a new employee at the dairy in New Woodstock had accidentally spilled the cleaning chemicals and ammonia they used to clean their dairy equipment into the creek. He asked me how much I drank, and if it was from last night's water or this morning. He said last night's water would have been very dangerous. He said that last night's water would have had more chemicals and ammonia in it, and I'd need to try to get it out of my system. When I told him it was from last night, but I only drank it this morning, he broke three eggs into a glass and made me drink them down, raw.

"This will help you throw up," he said.

He handed me the glass with the raw eggs in it.

"Throwing up will help get the poison out."

I threw up right away. I threw up two times, in fact. His phone rang, and someone told him the ammonia in the stream was killing all the fish. He told the caller they should quickly warn the farmers along the creek for at least twenty miles, tell them to keep their livestock away from the stream, and families, too. He told Mike that I would be very sick, but I should be okay since I drank it this morning and it hadn't had a chance to work through my whole system yet.

"Keep an eye on him and make him rest twenty-four hours. Most of the fish probably died closer to the dairy, which was a mile or so above the lower falls."

Mike drove me home, and Mom made me lie on the couch.

I kept throwing up in a pot all day and early into the night. I wondered if I was going to die, like the fish.

Dad sat up tall in the chair near the couch all night, making sure I was okay.

I woke up while it was still dark and ate some cereal. I felt good. Dad had already gone to work.

Later that morning, Dick and I were on the ground by the barn garage tossing acorns in the air and talking about the dairy and the trouble they were in for killing all the fish. Dick was lying on his back, one foot on the ground with his knee bent, the other leg resting across that knee. He was throwing acorns into the air and watching where they landed, studying their trajectory, he would say.

Dad's car pulled through the gate, up the drive, and around behind the swings. He took packages from the back seat and started to the house.

"How you feeling Jerry me boy?" he shouted.

"I'm good," I said.

"Who wants to go fishing, and then to Carthage and stay all night?" Dad's other bakery was in Carthage, where I took the boat ride on the Black River through that woods.

Dad didn't wait for an answer. With him, this we knew as his warning shout, like a ship that shoots a cannonball over your bow to get your attention. Dad wanted to give us the *lure* of fishing, and then a proper amount of time for us to think about it. His strategy was to let us get the thinking out of the way, so there won't be wasted time talking on the subject. True adventures were best done on impulse, with little thought and planning, he would say. Those are the most fun and appreciated—because everything would be a surprise.

"I can't go, I have to work," Dick said.

I looked forward to any adventure with my dad and ran into the house to pack my knapsack. I went to tell Mom I was going. She was in the book den, talking to Dad. Mom had been reading about colleges for Gourmet Mike's Masters after he graduated from college. I didn't understand his having to go to two colleges.

She called me over.

"Let me feel your forehead. How are you feeling, Jerry?"

"I'm good. It's all out of me."

"Are you sure?"

"I ate a lot of cereal this morning."

She felt my forehead while she asked me to open my knapsack, so she could see what I had packed.

"Where's the toothbrush and comb?" she asked. "And put a pair of underwear in there and put on socks. Where's your Baby Brownie camera? Don't forget film—I have some in my purse. Take a roll."

Mom was good at packing.

She told me to have fun in Carthage.

Dad and I walked to the car. Dick was still lying on the ground, throwing acorns in the air, but he managed a wave goodbye.

"We'll go to Sandy Pond first, to catch some sunfish for our supper, maybe a bass or two," Dad said.

I knew we would get to ride in a wooden rowboat at Sandy Pond, and he'd always let me row. We traded off like that. I would row, while he sat and untangled the lines of four fishing poles so we could actually fish.

What was great about Dad was he wouldn't just say something like,
"We're going fishing," he would say, "We're going to catch our supper!"

What could be more fun than knowing we were going to accomplish something?

"Thanks for sitting up with me last night, Dad," I said. Dad looked over at me.

"You're welcome, Jerry me boy. Things happen in life. You weren't hurt, that's the important thing. We just have to say our blessings—get past it and move on—be strong. What say we get past your swallowing half the creek and getting sick by catching some fish for our supper?"

Dad had his work suit on, so I knew that meant we might stop at a few grocery stores along the way. He would always see if the bread was fresh and straight on the shelves and when we got to Carthage, he might have to go into the bakery to meet someone. In the meantime, though, Dad knew how much I loved rowing, so he started to sing at the top of his voice.

*Row—row—row your boat*
*Gently down the stream*
*Merrily—merrily—merrily—merrily*
*Life is but a dream.*

I sang along with him a few times, just to get in the mood of having another adventure.

*Row—row—row your boat*
*Gently down the stream*
*Merrily—merrily—merrily—merrily*
*Life is but a dream.*

When we got to Sandy Pond, he pulled the car around behind the fishing lodge and restaurant and asked me if I wanted a soda pop.

"No thanks."

I told him I would meet him by the boats.

"Pick out a good one, Jerry me boy," he said.

A good boat was pretty simple to pick out. One with no water in it, which meant it didn't leak, one with two oars in it that were in good shape and one with a rope and anchor. Whenever I picked the boat, I always pretended I was the new captain getting aboard. I would introduce myself.

"Hello, boat—Hello, oar—Hello, other oar—Hello, anchor—Hello, anchor rope. Hello, little dragonfly, looking for some food."

It was fun. Of course, if Dick was with me, I wouldn't go through this ritual—at least not out loud, anyway.

Dad bought coffee, sandwiches, and nightcrawler worms in the lodge, came out tucking his tie between two buttons of his shirt to protect it from getting worm guts on it. I had the boat turned around. He handed me things to put in the back where he would sit—four fishing poles, a tackle box, and the bag of sandwiches.

"Put the sandwiches in front, by you," he said.

One time someone asked him why he always had four, sometimes six fishing poles.

"I have kids, they have friends," he said. "With kids and their friends, you need a lot of fishing poles."

Now most people would think that was very thoughtful and generous of my dad to be prepared like that, but there was a smarter reason. Kids drop things, and he needed more poles than the kids with him just to replace the ones we dropped in the lake by accident. Catching fish with my dad was never interrupted by a lost fishing pole or two. It was a matter of efficiency. I rowed us out to a place Dad said was far enough. He dropped anchor and tied the rope to the oar hinge once it hit bottom. I liked knowing we were connected to the bottom of the lake. It was like having our world of adventures get bigger somehow.

Dad put a bobber on the lines. A bobber was either a ball of cork or a red and white plastic ball, which floated on top of the water, attached to the fishing line. When a fish nibbled on the worm, the bobber would bounce down under. That was when you'd pull on the line a bit to 'hook' the fish and reel it in. Dad was good at knowing when to reel in. Sometimes he would tell me when I had a bite and when to yank the pole and reel it in.

While we waited for nibbles, Dad talked about Charlie Pitts and how sick he was.

"The doctors are trying to do everything they can, but he could use our prayers, son."

I said an "Our Father" and a "Hail Mary" to myself while Dad talked, and I promised myself to say a rosary for Charlie when we got home.

Between the two of us, we caught fourteen sunfish, some perch, and one bigmouth bass, and kept them all for our supper.

"How are we going to cook them, Dad?"

"The owner of the Imperial Hotel, in Carthage, is a friend of mine. He'll cook them for us in the hotel kitchen and eat with us."

Every time Dad had to stay overnight on business in Carthage, he stayed at the Imperial Hotel.

Now you would think, by the name, that the Imperial Hotel was a royal palace or something, but it wasn't. It was dark when we got to the street it was on, so it wasn't easy to see it clearly.

The streetlamps were lit, so that helped. It was a wood-planked four- story hotel, like a big old haunted mansion. It looked gray in the dark and had a lot of windows. It was built on a corner, where two streets came to a V, and the front of the hotel came to a V, too.

In the dark it had four spooky-looking floors, with sitting porches along two of the floors. One side of the porch, by the front door at the V, had eight wooden rocking chairs. Across the street was a train terminal, with about ten sets of train tracks set side by side. Four trains of box cars were parked, waiting for something or someone. I couldn't see any engines, just the box cars.

Two old men were sitting on the side porch, rocking away. One was lighting a pipe, and the other was pointing at something across the street and telling the other man a story.

When we got to the hotel's front desk, a man took our fish and gave Dad a hotel room key.

"Usual, Big Mike?"

"The usual," Dad answered. "Mr. Franks, meet me boy, Jerry. Jerry, meet Mr. Franks, the owner of this fine establishment."

"Chief cook and bottle washer is more like it," Mr. Franks said.

He shook my hand, and then Dad and I went up the stairs in the front of the lobby.

I learned that "the usual" meant room number six, on the second floor, with a small porch. Dad told me he liked that room because if the hotel ever caught on fire, he could shimmy from the side porch of the room down the tall white column to the sidewalk below.

"How would *I* get down?" I asked.

"On my back, of course," he answered without a second's hesitation. Sometimes I could ask some really dumb questions.

Inside number six were two rooms—one was a big room with his bed on a rug, and a sink on the wall. The other was a smaller room, with just an old iron bed on a hardwood floor. It was perfect—a first—my own hotel room. Dad and I had to share the sink in Dad's room and everyone on the floor shared the bathroom out in the hall. I had a window at both ends of my room. One window on the one side of my room overlooking the railroad station, the other window overlooking the other street. I put the knapsack on my bed, and we went downstairs to the hotel restaurant.

Well, it was more like a bar, but it had tables. In the corner stood a tall cooler, which looked exactly like an aluminum soda pop bottle with a glass door. It was filled with soda pop and beer bottles. The top of the cooler came to a point and had a big bottle cap top.

Dad and I pulled up barstools, and Mr. Franks brought out a big platter filled with our fish he had scaled, cleaned, and pan fried. He gave us plates, forks, knives, and napkins. He stood on the other side of the bar with his plate. The fish was so good. There was a stack of sliced bread, and Dad told me if I accidentally swallowed a fish bone, I should eat a big piece of bread, fast. Swallowing the bread would get the bone down my throat safely, he would say.

Knowing we'd caught our supper that very day at Sandy Pond was almost as much fun as camping out up by the white rock at Delphi Falls.

After supper, Dad told me to thank Mr. Franks for cooking

our fish and to get to bed. He said we would get up early and head for home. I told Mr. Franks the fish were great, and thanked him for cooking them, and for the orange soda pop. He told me we could bring fish any old time, and it would be his personal honor and pleasure to get to share them with us. Dad had nice friends, everywhere.

Dad gave me a key to room number six and I left him and Mr. Franks sitting at the bar. It was fun walking through the lobby and then up the long, tall carpeted stairs to the second floor. I was a little scared going into the dark room but when I found the light switch it was better. I left the key on the table next to my dad's bed, and I went into the other room where I was going to sleep. The bed had a light shining on it through the window from a streetlamp. I saw that the bed had small steel rollers on each leg, so I pushed it a foot or two out of the light and crawled in.

Sometime that night I woke up, trying to remember where I was, and I could hear Dad snoring loudly in the other room. I lay in my bed awhile with my eyes half open, staring out the window at the streetlamp and all the moths circling around it to get warm. I remember thinking what a great adventure I had been on today. And then I fell asleep again.

*KAAA-BLAMMMM! KUNK! KUNK! KUNK!*

I thought I was having a heart attack. In the dark my whole body flinched. My arms and legs sprung out and grabbed the sides of the mattress. I opened my eyes, looking in the dark at the ceiling, to see the ceiling lamp had moved somehow. It actually moved from where it was. I thought maybe someone had crashed a truck, or a train, into the hotel. Dad was snoring, so I knew he was still in his room.

*KAAA-BLAMMMM! KUNK! KUNK! KUNK!*

This time I knew the ceiling lamp moved. I could see it.

This can't be good, I thought.

There was not a question in my mind. We were definitely being attacked by monsters from Mars who were landing on the roof of the hotel. I'd heard on radio where it happened in New Jersey once.

*KAAA-BLAMMMM! KUNK! KUNK! KUNK!*

Now the ceiling lamp looked like it had turned around cockeyed just so the space creatures could crawl through it. I was doomed for sure. I was going to die. *I'm going to die*, I thought. *Please, God, don't let me die.*

I could feel the sweat on my face and hands.

Dad was still snoring, so it must have been the people from Mars were afraid of snoring noises. I knew Mom sometimes slept on the couch because of Dad's snoring.

I waited for the final attack—for the ceiling to come crashing in—for the final breath of life. That's all I remember.

In the morning, I first thought about not opening my eyes, in case I was surrounded by Martians. I could hear Dad brushing his teeth and gargling at the sink. I heard his door open and shut, and I could hear the key locking it. With my eyes closed, I grabbed both sides of the mattress for safety, opened my eyes, and looked up at the ceiling—then at one wall—then another wall—then the floor. The only thing that had moved during the night was my bed. It had rolled, clear across the floor—with me in it—almost to the other side of the room, and completely around in a circle. I got dressed in nine seconds flat, unlocked and darted out the door and down the stairs two steps at a time. Dad was just starting up the stairs, with a cup of hot chocolate.

"Oh, good, son, you're up," he said as I loped down the steps.

"Go sit on the porch and drink this while I make some calls, and then we'll head home and have a nice breakfast in Watertown, on the way."

It amazed me how loud snoring could save a man's life! I certainly hoped that when I got older, I could snore as loudly as my dad, to keep the aliens from attacking my room in the future.

I took my hot chocolate out to the side porch where the rocking chairs were. The same old man, with his pipe, was in the same rocker he was in last night, and his friend was in the one beside him.

I sat next to him.

"Morning, son."

"Morning, sir."

"Sleep well, son?"

*KAAA-BLAMMMM! KUNK! KUNK! KUNK!*

"Wha-wha-wha-what was?" I stuttered, my arm jerking my hot chocolate cup, nearly spilling it.

"Son—it's a train yard over there, and that was a train—see? Look, there's one moving, right now."

*KAAA-BLAMMMM! KUNK! KUNK! KUNK!*

"So *that's* what I heard all night?"

The old man stopped rocking and looked at me.

"Son, I'm only going to say this once, because no one is around to listen."

He leaned toward me.

"A train yard has trains in it, see?—and they're supposed to move around and connect with each other—and yes, when they have a lot of cars attached, they make banging noises."

He smiled at me with a sparkle in his eyes while he started lighting his pipe again. I could see empty rocking chairs on both sides of us rocking back and forth, back and forth, because of the last train's connection—*ka-blammm!*

The old man watched my eyes looking at the chairs rocking and he leaned toward me again, like he was going to tell me a big secret.

"Ghosts," he whispered.

He leaned back in his chair, puffed on his pipe, began to rock, and with a twinkling in his eyes, he winked.

We drove through downtown and were heading out of Carthage on Route 11 to Watertown to have breakfast before we headed home. We were listening to the radio—Arthur Godfrey was talking about Lipton's soup. I was thinking of my getting to sleep in my own room and the rocking chairs at the hotel and the sounds of the train box cars.

While he was driving, Dad kept looking over at me, with something on his mind (I could tell), and then he would look back at the road. He reached for the radio knob, turned it off.

"Son, Charlie Pitts died this morning."

I looked over at my dad.

"I know he was your friend, so I thought you should know. Sheriff Hood called me at the bakery."

He stopped talking and looked over at me.

I stared up at him, stunned in disbelief. I let what he said sink in and turned my head straight forward again when it finally hit me. I stared down at the floor of the car. Tears flowed on their own from my eyes. My cheeks grimaced as my lips tightened.

"They found his cow loose on the road."

"Bessie," I whimpered.

"They walked it back to his place and found him on the ground at the gate to his field."

Dad looked at me.

"We'll drive straight home, okay, son?"

I couldn't stop the tears. My mouth hurt now. I couldn't see through my eyes.

"He had a heart attack. Just keeled over."

Dad touched my hand with a folded handkerchief. I took it. I looked up.

"Did it hurt?

"I don't think so, son. God took him quick."

My voice cracked and wobbled.

"Charlie was my friend, Dad."

"I know, son. I know."

I just looked down at the floor.

"Sheriff Hood said there were some things in a burlap sack in his house. Charlie had written your name on it, so he's holding it for you."

"He did?" I asked.

"Charlie thought the world of you. He thought of you as a son. He lost his own boy in the first world war. You reminded him of his son."

"I did?" I couldn't stop crying.

"They're boxing up the chickens, geese, and ducks and taking them to our place and putting the feed in the small barn. You want to take care of them?"

"Charlie told me how."

"Should we build a coop for them?" Dad asked.

"No." But I didn't want to talk for a while, so I didn't say any more. Neither did Dad.

He didn't say any more until I was ready.

I thought of Charlie and his old barn that always made me think of Christmas because it had bright golden straw everywhere that glowed like a Christmas card. He had one cow, one horse, and not much else. I remember the barn's inside brighter at night if he hung a kerosene lantern on a post when he had to milk his cow or do some work.

Then the thought came to me—Charlie knew he was going to die. That's why he kept saying, "Merry Christmas."

When we got to Tully and turned onto Route 80 toward home, I spoke for the first time since Watertown, "We can free-range them, Dad. I know how."

As we drove through the gate at Delphi Falls, Mom and Dick were throwing chicken feed around by the small barn, and the chickens were getting used to the place. The geese ran right at the car and chased us up the driveway and around behind the swings.

I wanted to be alone, so I went to my room and pushed the door closed. On my bed was a burlap bag with bailing twine around the top. It had a scissor-cut out of the back of a calendar page attached to it, like the last one, where Charlie had written "Gerry."

I opened the bag and found another lantern from his house. In a paper sack was a bottle of kerosene, four wicks, and two large boxes of safety kitchen matches. In a small box was a framed picture of Charlie in his soldier uniform in 1891. I put everything on my desk. That night I kept my promise, kneeled down by my bed and said a rosary for Charlie.

Every morning after that, I would get up earlier than anyone else and go gather the eggs from all the spots where the hens would nest to lay their eggs. It took me a few days to find them all. Once I had, getting eggs in the morning was easy. I would always tell all the chickens, geese, and ducks, "Charlie says hello."

## CHAPTER SEVENTEEN
## A NEW PLAN

All my friends were in the cemetery for Charlie's funeral, but everyone was so sad nobody spoke. Mary sang with some of the church choir. From then on, I was so busy at home before and after school learning about the care of farm birds, I didn't have much contact with my friends, but they understood. About the time I was beginning to get comfortable with taking care of the chickens, ducks, and geese, I went into Mom and Dad's room, picked up the phone, and asked Myrtie to get me Barber.

"Isn't it sad about Charlie?" Myrtie asked.

"Real sad," I said.

"He was such a nice man."

"He was my friend," I said.

"Your mom told me, Jerry. I'm so sorry."

"I walked to his place every week for eggs. I miss him."

"He didn't have a phone, but I would see him and his horse and buggy at the church up on the hill sometimes," Myrtie said.

"Yes, ma'am," I said.

"Here's Barber, hon. Say hi to your mom."

"Hello?"

"Barber, I need to set up a meeting—the sooner the better."

"Why? What's up?"

"Charlie Pitts died."

"Jerry, are you looney-tunes? I was at his funeral. I stood next to you."

"We need a new plan," I said.

"You sound like a train wreck," Barber said.

"I am a train wreck. No way am I going to get away with not slaughtering the chickens and geese now," I said.

"You mean the chicken and geese plan we already had?"

"Yeah, it won't work. No Charlie, no Charlie's barn means no plan," I said.

"It's too late for the weekend," Barber said.

"Tomorrow?" I asked.

"How about we all meet at lunch tomorrow at school?"

"That'll work. Thanks."

"I'll set it up. First one to the cafeteria, save a table," Barber added, and we hung up.

We all wound up in the cafeteria line together, so we talked while we slid our trays.

"Thanks for everybody coming to Charlie's funeral," I said.

"Mary, you sang that hymn real good," Randy said.

"Charlie would have liked it," Barber said.

"From now on the Pompey Hollow Book Club will meet at Charlie's gravestone in the cemetery," Mary said.

"So where are the chickens, ducks, and geese now?" Holbrook asked.

"They're at my house," I said.

"All the chickens and geese?" Holbrook asked.

"All of them. Ducks, too."

"Do you have a coop?" Barber asked, picking up his daily bowl of tomato soup and small bowl of Jell-O.

"Nah, they're free ranged now, all over the place," I said.

"You don't have them in a coop?" Holbrook asked.

"No," I said.

"Free range?" Barber asked. "Ain't no way your dad won't find out you didn't slaughter some for the Thanksgiving table."

"Your goose is cooked," Holbrook said.

"I'm a goner when he catches me lying," I said.

"He's sure enough going to catch you," Randy said. "He can see all of them every time he comes home. I bet the geese chase his car."

"That is going to make it tougher," Holbrook said.

"I'm sunk. I might as well run away," I said.

"Why are you giving up so easy for?" Mary asked.

"We lied to Mr. Hasting," I said.

"Don't forget you charged chickens and geese to your dad's account at Hasting's store," Holbrook said. "Hasting is sure to call your mom or dad."

"We only have to hide them," Mary said.

"Hide what?" Randy asked.

"Jerry's chickens, ducks, and geese. We have to hide them," Mary said.

"Are you nuts?" Mayor asked.

"I think Mary's got a screw loose," Bases said.

"We just have to catch them all and hide them somewhere until after Thanksgiving," Mary said. "That's all we have to do."

"Where do we hide them?" I asked.

"In your barn garage," Mary said.

"It doesn't have any doors," I said.

"Your barn garage doesn't have a door?" Mary asked.

"Not the big barn, but the small one, the stable barn attached to it does," I said.

"So, it's settled. That's where we hide them," Mary said.

"We just have to catch them?" I asked.

"Right!" said Bases, Randy Vaas, Barber, Holbrook, and now Mayor, who had joined us in line.

"It's not going to be easy," Barber said.

Sliding our trays, we all mostly got chili and beans, chocolate pudding, and chocolate milk. End of meeting.

For nearly two weeks Holbrook, Bases, Barber, Randy, Mayor, Mary, and I sat at the same table in the cafeteria, planning how we were going to get thirty chickens into the barn without anyone seeing us doing it or knowing anything about it after we'd done it. We decided that a Monday night was the right time to do it.

"We'll wait up on the cliff at the white rock, across the creek from my house," I said.

"How long do we wait?" Mary asked.

"Until after dark, for when the time is right, when all the lights in the house go off and everyone goes to bed and falls asleep," I said.

I taught them what Charlie taught me about chickens. I knew free range chickens without a coop roosted on fences or higher on tree branches at night when they slept. We decided it would be best to catch them while they were dozing and just carry them one at a time into the barn.

"Once they're in there, you'll have to go in every day, Jerry, and see they have plenty of chicken feed and water," Mary said.

Barber thought Mary was sounding like a mother hen.

"Yes, dear," he said with a giggle.

Just as soon as he said it, he said, "Oh geez,"—realizing full well he had crossed the line with our president.

Mary reached in front of Bases, picked up Barber's dessert bowl of Jell- O, and dumped it into his bowl of tomato soup. He got the message.

"The geese are going to be another problem," Holbrook said.

"They're mean," Randy said.

"They sleep on the ground at night, but they're too mean to catch by hand," I said.

"You have ducks, don't you?" Mary asked.

"The ducks will pretty much follow us anywhere," I said.

"The only thing we haven't thought of is how everyone is going to get to Jerry's house without being seen that Monday night and how we'll get home after," Randy said.

Bases must have been dozing or engrossed in protecting his chili bowl from Mary because he repeated exactly what Randy had just said.

My brother Dick walked past our lunch table.

"Dick!" I shouted, to get his attention.

He paused, gave me a look like didn't I know it wasn't cool for older kids in school to even pretend they know much less talk to younger kids.

"What?" he growled as if this better be good.

"Dick, this isn't an SOS or anything like that, but we're doing something secret next Monday night and everyone here needs a ride to our alfalfa field after dark for a couple of hours and then a ride back home," I said.

"So?" Dick gruffed.

"So, can you get that done?"

"Why? What's up?"

"I'll tell you later. Not here."

"Two shakes," Dick said. He walked away and over to the lunch table where Duba, Minneapolis Moline Conway, and Dwyer were sitting with some girls. Dick leaned down to their table and talked with them. Each of them, in turn, raised their head up and stared over at us, one at a time, and then lowered it back into conversation. Dick stood up, turned, and walked over to our table.

"We can arrange it," he said, "but you'll have to rake leaves."

I knew this was Dick's chore for Thanksgiving, to rake the leaves, so I said, "No problem, I'll rake our leaves."

"No way," Dick said.

"What!?" I asked.

"You'll *all* rake leaves," Dick said.

"Huh?" Holbrook asked.

"The leaves in Duba's yard, the leaves in Conway's yard, and the ones in Dwyer's yard—all this Saturday—so we can go to Suburban Park before they close it for the winter," Dick said.

We looked at each other.

"And you'll bring us there?" Randy asked.

"Yes."

"And you'll wait as long as it takes and take us all home?" Mary asked.

"Yes."

"Deal," Holbrook said.

"Hold on," Barber said.

"What now?" Dick asked.

"Jerry, we don't want your dad to get suspicious since Mr. Pitts died," Barber said.

"He'll ask me about it for sure," I said.

"The Dubas have a chicken barn," Barber said. "Dick, you have to tell your dad you heard Duba is going to help Jerry and Holbrook butcher the chickens and geese."

Dick didn't have a problem with that. Actually, he thought it was pretty clever. He said okay and walked away.

Dick and his friends were fourteen and still didn't have driver's licenses, but their word was their bond. If they said they'd do something, they would do it.

On Monday night I pretended I went to bed early. I closed my bedroom door and crawled out my window in the dark moonless night and made my way along the edge of the hill leading up to the woods until I was at the gate. I ran down to the alfalfa field. Duba's dad's long Lincoln was there, already in the middle of the field, with Dick and Duba in the front seat. I wasn't sure who was in the back seat.

As I walked down into the alfalfa field, Minneapolis Moline Conway drove in with his dad's '48 Dodge. Dwyer with him. It drove up next to the Lincoln, stopped and turned its lights off. Car doors opened all at once. Randy, Mary, Holbrook, Barber, Mayor, and Bases stepped out.

"How long's this going to take?" Duba asked.

"I don't know," I said. "Maybe an hour. I don't know."

"Take off," Dick said. "We'll be here when you get back."

We all ran to the edge of the hill behind the alfalfa field and climbed up the back hill. We moved through the dark like a pack of wolves. We were on a mission that could not be denied. We made it up the hill pulling each other along when we had to. We made it to the top and then over to just above the white rock on the cliff by my house to rest and plan.

Looking down from the top of the cliff we could see the white rock halfway down and the creek below. We could see the barn garage and stable barn and the house. One at a time we climbed down the cliff. We made it down to the rock, some sat on it and others gathered around to form a strategy.

"How far do the birds go from your barn?" Barber asked.

"Maybe twenty feet. I don't know, maybe thirty feet. Front, sides, and back," I told him.

"Not daytime, I'm talking when they roost at night?"

"Oh. Well a lot of them will roost up on the suspension wires inside the barn garage."

"If they're already in the barn garage, why do we have to catch them?" Mary asked.

"I told you the big barn garage has no doors," I said. "It's open in front."

"Oh, that's right," Mary said.

"We have to put them in the small stable barn next to it," I said.

"We'll need catchers and runners, then, or we'll waste a lot of time," Mary said.

"Explain," Holbrook said.

Mary stood up in front of the white rock, turned to us

and lectured.

"We need to start with the chickens. Once we start grabbing them, they may get smart and scatter. Half of us need to be catching and handing them off to a runner, who will hold two at a time and run them into the small barn."

"I gotta pee," Bases said.

"Well, turn around and do it!" Mary barked. "Don't interrupt."

"I agree with Mary," Randy said. "We pair up into teams— catchers and runners on each team."

"Let's break the place into coordinates," Barber said.

"What's that mean?" Mayor asked.

"Team one takes the left of the barn and the back," Barber said.

"Team two the inside of the barn. Team three the right side and front."

"You runners be sure to keep count," Mary said.

"Chickens first, then the geese and ducks," Barber said.

"We need thirty-one catches," Mary said.

"Thirty," I said. "We have thirty chickens."

"Thirty-one," Mary said. "You have thirty chickens and one rooster. Thirty-one!"

"I wouldn't tick her off," whispered Mayor.

He remembered the cemetery "baseball" incident and the Jell-O flop. How right he was.

After the last light in the house went off, to be safe we waited thirty minutes for my mom and dad to fall asleep. As we passed the time, we teamed up, broke off in pairs, and planned our individual attack strategies. I volunteered to make the sacrifice.

"After we get all the chickens, I volunteer to let the geese chase me into the small barn," I said.

"Geese bite," Holbrook said.

"The ducks will follow them," I said.

Holbrook volunteered to close the door quickly behind me after they were all in.

The time was right. We wished each other good luck and slowly began making our way down the cliff to the bottom edge by the creek.

"Oh, geez," Barber whispered.

"What now?" Holbrook asked.

"My ma will shoot me for getting my school shoes wet," Barber said.

No one much cared.

Mary stepped in the creek first, Randy followed, and then everyone else ceremoniously stepped in and waded across the icy cold creek, knowing that the sacrifice of getting a "talking to" for wet shoes was far outweighed by the importance of our mission of stopping fourteen murders.

Mary was the runner on her team inside the barn. In the dark she snagged the back of her dress on a nail poking out of a worktable and ripped it considerably. Making the best of the situation, she reached her hands around behind her and tore the dress all the way down through the bottom hem. Lifting it up from both sides and around front like an apron, this let her hold three or four chickens safely in it instead of one in each hand.

Humility had its own reward.

Aside from the black and blue marks I had on my butt and legs from goose bites, and the scratched knee and elbow from falling off a tree branch from holding two chickens that were flapping their wings like crazy, I was okay. Holbrook tore the knee out of his jeans while doing a racing, diving tackle on one of the hens. The hen won. The rooster threatened the lives of both Randy and Mayor until Randy had the foresight to throw a burlap bag over its head, momentarily blinding it. Soon after that, a goose pecked Randy squarely in the behind, taking him a few inches off the ground, as a goose will do, sending him sliding headfirst in chicken and goose poop on the grassy side of the green barn. Holbrook's glasses fell off in the dark when the rooster broke free from the burlap bag long enough to look him straight in the eye, caw once, scare the hell out of him and then jump over him, flying into the barn on its own steam. Barber accidentally stepped on Holbrook's glasses while sliding, tripping over Randy, and falling in goose poop himself. His heel pushed a lens out of the eyeglasses, but they weren't mangled all that bad. Holbrook could still see out of one side if he held his head at a proper angle. After the geese chased me into the barn, forcing me to land in a wheelbarrow, tipping it over, we made the count, closed and padlocked the door with a wooden peg, and hid behind the barn garage, trying to catch our breaths, looking to see if any blood was coming through our clothing and trying to calm down. Bases found a cloth chicken feed sack in the small barn, pulled it from his belt, and handed it to Mary. She could wrap it around her torn dress with a string to restore her ladylike modesty. Everything went pretty much as planned.

We spent half an hour in the dark behind the barn garage, like chimpanzees, picking feathers off ourselves, our teammates, out of our hair, wondering if the smell would ever come out of our clothes.

"I smell so bad, Ma will never notice my wet school shoes," Barber mused.

"Will you all come to my house the Monday after Thanksgiving and we'll sled our hill?" Mayor asked.

"What for?" Mary asked.

He thought the Pompey Hollow Book Club was inspiring.

"Can I join your club?"

"I thought you already did," Mary said.

"You showed up, you're a member," Holbrook said.

"Maybe we'll come—if there is snow," everyone affirmed, still flicking feather and chicken poop specks from their clothing. Randy had a stick and was scraping goose and chicken poop from his pant legs. We were all too busy to explain that joining didn't involve much more than just showing up.

The plan for hiding the chickens and geese worked perfectly. Side by side, no one downwind from each other, we walked the drive onto Cardner Road and down to the alfalfa field—as c*hampions.* The two cars saw us, lights went on—loaded up with our troops and started to drive off. Just down the road about fifty feet, Duba's long black Lincoln jerked to a sudden stop, screeching its tires, rocking the front of the car up and down while the driver door blew open. Duba jumped out of the car choking and coughing and wheezing from the stink—squeezing his nose and hopping like he had a hot foot and screamed,

"OPEN THE GOL-DANGED WINDOWS!"

Randy must have been in his car.

The windows rolled down. He let it air out a few seconds

and got back in and drove away.

I walked home, climbed in through my bedroom window, took all my clothes off and dropped them out my window to air out on the ground outside.

By late that Monday night before Thanksgiving, there wasn't a chicken, duck or goose to be seen or heard anywhere, thanks to the Pompey Hollow Book Club.

Mr. Hasting had the store-bought fowl right on time as he promised. Holbrook and I walked from the store to the house with them in three big sacks. We put all but two of the geese and five of the chickens in the icebox for when Mom and Dad got home, which would be any time. Holbrook used our telephone to call Tommy Kellish to walk over and ask his dad to come get him. Then we went up the side hill and climbed into Dick's tree house to hide out. We thought it best to stay out of sight in case there were questions. We hated questions, especially when we were guilty. I personally never knew what to say. I would just stand there with my mouth hanging open.

Holbrook would stand there and point at me.

## CHAPTER EIGHTEEN
## HAPPY THANKSGIVING

On Thanksgiving Day, the house was filled with people of all ages, which was exciting because we always knew Christmas and Santa were not far behind. There were aunts and uncles and cousins and Mom's friends in from Cortland for the day to look at the falls and have a Thanksgiving meal. I had completely forgotten about geese and chickens and was enjoying my second piece of pumpkin pie when Dad called for me to come to the kitchen.

*Gulp!* My knees buckled.

To me, my dad always looked extremely tall when I thought I was in trouble. Whenever I was guilty, I always thought I was in trouble. He was standing there in an apron, serving food to people as they came in for second helpings while Mom poured coffee all around. He stopped serving and turned.

"Jerry, this was a very nice Thanksgiving for everyone, and we owe a lot of it to you and Holbrook for the effort you both went through in getting us chickens and geese. Thank you, son."

"You're welcome, Dad," I stuttered.

"Be sure to thank Holbrook for us, too, son."

"I will. For sure."

Then he looked me straight in the eye, smiled a little. I remember it was a friendly smile, not a mean smile when he leaned down, took my hand, and put seven price tags in my palm—five chicken price tags and two goose price tags.

"Your prices seem reasonable, son—do I owe you for these, or do I owe someone else?"

My life passed before my eyes. Caught! I was caught! Holbrook had left the stupid price tags on the chickens and geese from Mr. Hasting. I knew I would get caught.

I fessed up.

"We got them from Mr. Hasting."

"I already know, son—the store name is on the price tags."

"It is?"

"And now you're going to work for Mr. Hasting every Saturday after we come back from the bakery until you earn enough and they're paid for, aren't you?"

"Yes, sir," I replied.

"And Mr. Holbrook is seeing to it that Holbrook bakes four iced two-layer cakes for Mr. Hasting to sell, to make up for their chickens and geese."

"Mr. Holbrook knows, too?"

"He knows."

I was so worried I was going to get killed and so bothered by my conscience for lying, I thanked Dad and promised him I would never let him down ever again.

"You didn't let me down, son."

"I didn't?"

"I'm proud you took a stand for something. I suspect the Pompey Hollow Book Club did what they thought was right. You all protected what you thought was important to you."

"So, you're not—?"

"Next time, trust me, son. I would understand. Now, go let them all out of the barn so they can get some air."

"You knew they were in there, Dad?"

"Happy Thanksgiving, Jerry me boy."

"Happy Thanksgiving, Dad."

## CHAPTER NINETEEN
## CHRISTMAS

Waiting for kids to take their homeroom seats and the classroom to quiet down, Mrs. Bredesen walked over to my desk and handed me a hall pass.

"Am I in trouble, Mrs. Bredesen?"

"You're not in trouble."

"What's this hall pass for?" I asked.

"You're to go see Mr. Spinner, the band director, during recess."

It meant Mom got me out of piano, but who knows what else she got me into.

"Good morning, class," Mrs. Bredesen started. "It's that time of year again. Who's looking forward to celebrating the Christmas holiday with family or friends?"

Every hand in the classroom went up.

"Now class, what is it I want you all to try and remember? It's always

better—"

Every kid chorused.

"It's always better to give than to receive."

"Very good, class."

That was the starting gun. This little Christmas talk was about all it took for every kid in the room to start thinking of Christmas, Santa, and receiving. None of us gave a whit if we got eighty-nine-cent flying ace pilot goggles with the imitation lamb wool ear straps, a box of Lincoln Logs, a tube of Tinker Toys, some modeling clay, a book, or a record. Christmas and the rustling of wrapping paper were on their way and in our dreams every night and from here on out. This was the best time of the year, for any kid. The season's diversions helped us get through five years of a world at war.

"Now class, the boys and girls who are seniors this year are doing something very special for the families of the boys and girls who graduated before them and were wounded or lost their lives in the war—the men and women who fought or helped around the world throughout the war. Show of hands if you knew someone who was killed, lost or wounded during the war. It could be a family member, a friend's family member, even someone you knew or just heard about."

Every hand in the room went up.

"Class, as their legacy, the senior class wants to have a bronze plaque engraved for display in the front hall wall of the school. A plaque honoring past students killed, wounded, or missing during the war. Now plaques are expensive and so to pay for it, the senior class is going to have a roller-skating party at the roller rink in Cortland the Thursday before our Christmas break. Who would like to help?"

Every hand went up. There were probably only two kids in the whole room who knew how to roller skate.

"Now class, the grade that encourages the most children to attend the roller-skating party and raises the most money might get their picture in the newspaper. Let me have your ideas," she said.

One at a time, each idea volunteer stood up with a good idea on how we could get the most kids from our room to go. The ideas ranged from giving roller skating lessons during recess to the kids who wanted to go to the skating party, to guaranteeing anyone who went to the skating party an A in either geography or arithmetic, their choice.

When it was my turn, I summoned all the creativity I could muster that early in the morning by thinking about things my dad taught me while riding with him in his car. I stood up.

"It's a numbers game," I began.

"What's that mean?" a voice asked.

"He means we need to get the word out," Mary said, thinking of the bunnies.

"We have to get some really important-looking roller skating party *identification* cards printed," I said.

"Like the Buster Brown Shoe Club membership card I have?" Randy asked.

"Just like that," I said. "But our card is advertising the skating party, and then everyone will want one to carry in their wallets and they'll show it off to their friends like they were important or valuable. You know, advertising."

It made sense to all the Pompey Hollow Book Club and some of the other kids. Bases dozed off, plopping his head down on his desk with a thump. I must have said the card idea with such conviction that some of the others thought I knew what I was talking about—which of course I didn't.

"Congratulations, Jerry," Mrs. Bredesen said.

"For what?" I asked.

"You are the official chairman of our grade's roller-skating party attendance promotion to benefit the Senior class War Memorial plaque fund raising."

"I am?"

"Good luck. You may select anyone in the class to help you."

"Here we go again," Holbrook said.

Of course, I would pick the Pompey Hollow Book Club—Barber, Mary, Holbrook, Randy, Mayor, and Bases, if he wakes up. I was thinking maybe Judy Finch, and Mary Margaret Cox, too, if the teacher insisted that I use a lot of kids. These two knew all the girls. I'd think of more if I had to.

By way of notes posted on Mrs. Bredesen's bulletin board, the whole class was invited to Mary Margaret's house for a holiday party. Her mother was a teacher. When invitations were posted on the classroom bulletin board our mothers mostly made us go. After Mary Margaret's party there was a party that same week at Mary's to learn how to square dance to the new square dance record she got for her birthday.

When the recess bell rang, Mrs. Bredesen turned to me.

"Jerry, you may be excused to go to the band room."

I stood and left the room.

Now Mr. Spinner, the band director, was a nice enough man. He always had a smile on his face. His clothes smelled of cigarette tobacco and his fingers and nails were brownish yellow from smoking. He enjoyed making jokes, like the time in a band recital when he introduced a piece the band was going to play as "*Locked in a Stable with the Sheep*"—when it was supposed to be called "*Rocked in a Cradle of the Deep.*" Kids didn't always get his jokes, but he would squint his eyes in a grin, prune his lips in a quirky smile, raise his baton and turn around to conduct his band.

The band room was across the hall from the gymnasium and next to the furnace room in the basement. It had windows running the length of the side wall that looked out at empty school buses and one smaller one in the center of the back wall. A glare reflected off Mr. Spinner's eyeglasses at most angles, making him look like a friend of Little Orphan Annie or Daddy Warbucks in the Sunday comics, where they just had white circles for eyes. The band room was filled with five rows of bent-wood chairs in a half circle around a conductor's podium in the front center.

"Hello, young man," Mr. Spinner said, with a big smile. "Come in and take a seat."

"Hello, Mr. Spinner."

"Your mother called."

"I know."

"We'll get right down to business and have you on your way in no

time."

We sat down on chairs facing each other.

"Jerry, I want you to tell me all your interests."

"What do you mean?"

"If I know your interests, I will try to select an instrument to your liking and aptitude."

I assumed if Mr. Spinner thought I had a musical "aptitude," he never saw me play piano.

"I like to camp in the woods, ride my bike."

"Please continue."

"I like going to Barber's or Mayor's and stacking hay bales. I like playing king of the mountain in their barns. I like to help farmer Parker call in the cows. I want a horse. I like the Pompey Hollow Book Club. I like to play Pitch with Holbrook and swim. Swimming's fun—"

Mr. Spinner hid a yawn with the back of his hand.

"Music, do you like music, Jerry?"

"I like listening to music on the radio or at the picture show. I like *'She Wore a Yellow Ribbon,'* and sometimes I sing in the car with my dad."

Mr. Spinner squinted his eyes into a smile, pruned his lips up in an approving grin, and nodded his head gently. He reached to his side and opened an instrument carrying case that was resting on the chair beside him and lifted two parts of a black clarinet from it. He carefully assembled them and asked, "Jerry, how about the woody, somewhat dulcet tone of the clarinet?"

I shrugged my left shoulder.

"Hokay."

He wasn't happy with my answer.

He pulled the clarinet apart, returned it to its case, thought for a moment and opened another case—this time lifting a trumpet from it like he was lifting a gold crown. He wriggled his eyebrows as if he were about to share a lewd secret and asked, "How about the brassier sharpness of the heralded trumpet—?"

I yawned.

"Maybe a French horn? Or a mellow trombone?" Mr. Spinner asked.

Again, although this time with a shrug from my right shoulder.

"Hokay."

Mr. Spinner, still not convinced, wouldn't give up. He wrinkled his eyebrows, returned the trumpet to its case, placed his fist on his cheek, and tweaked his sideburn with his forefinger, thinking. With his other hand, he pointed to the drums in the back of the room.

"How about the simple beat of a drum?"

"Hokie-dokie."

The only musical talent I was aware I had was that I could make a dove call blowing through my hands that attracted doves and sing some show tunes from movies at the Saturday picture show. To me, playing a musical instrument would be like me removing my own appendix. Mr. Spinner's instruments were all just pianos in different shapes and sizes.

"Young man, you're supposed to help me here."

"How?"

"Certainly, there is a preference in your mind's eye that might stir your imagination. Certainly, you have a sense of or feeling toward a particular sound—a spirit, perhaps—of an instrument. The passion you feel might fit your personality and a desire to express yourself through music."

I considered a short nap, while sitting up.

"Jerry, hasn't there ever been that single moment in your life—that one moment when you expressed yourself with a simple gesture that showed your true feelings? You wanted to rejoice and relive it again and again, study it in your mind? You wanted to share it with the world? Certainly, there must be one moment in time."

Mr. Spinner bent his head, peering at me over his glasses, in hope.

"Think Jerry, think! What was that one point of expression that comes to your mind again and again?"

"One?"

"One. That first one thing that comes to your mind."

"When I kissed Linda Oats?"

There was silence.

Mr. Spinner's head dipped. It slumped in defeat, flopped down to his chest, bouncing loosely. Then he lifted his head and glared at me over the tops of his glasses for the longest time. The glare of his glasses sent a flickering of the sun onto my heart like a rifle scope.

Suddenly, magically, his eyes popped white like flashbulbs. He pruned his lips to that smile again, thrust his right arm straight up, jumped off his chair, and stood tall as if he wanted to touch the ceiling light in joy.

"The tuba!" he shouted.

It was as if he had discovered electricity.

He sat back down with a thunk, smiling and waving both of his hands in the air like he was conducting a full orchestra.

"A tuba wants exuberance, Jerry—a tuba needs caring. It needs to be held, and above all else, a tuba needs a great pucker to warm its cold curves, its corners and elegant bold crevices with the breath of warm life that will become a beautiful sound. A tuba needs to be kissed, Jerry! The tuba, it is!"

I was looking to see if the band room door was locked and did the math in my head on how long it would take me to get out or through the open window on the back wall.

Mr. Spinner jumped straight up again. This time his feet left the floor, like he'd won a car raffle. He hurried to the back of the room through the maze of bentwood chairs, his arms conducting full orchestra, tipping one music stand and letting it fall over in his excitement. As it tipped over it took another two with it. At the back of the room he reached around the big sousaphone stand, pulled out the tuba's mouthpiece and carried it delicately back, as though he had retrieved the Holy Grail. He picked up the music stands as he passed them, backing into a chair and knocking it over in the process.

"Jerry, put your lips together—pucker and blow—like this— BblbBblbBblbBblbBblbBblbBbBblbBblb."

I tried.

"Pfffffft?"

"Like this, Jerry—BblbBblbBblbBblbBblbBblbBblbBblbBbl."

"BBBbbbppppfffttt?"

"BblbBblbBblbBblbBBblbBblbBblb, Jerry."

He pressed the cold metal mouthpiece into my palm. It was big enough to be used as a funnel in the kitchen.

"Jerry, take this mouthpiece home and practice."

"Huh?"

"Do your BbbBbb lip exercises and blowing techniques—"

"But—"

"You will begin your tuba lessons tomorrow."

"I will?"

"Be relentless, young man—purse your pucker—and—welcome to the band!"

I couldn't see through the white glare of his glasses, but it sounded like his discovery might have brought a tear to his eye. He had saved another country bumpkin youth from the monotony of a corn row.

I put the mouthpiece in my pocket, tried to hide it with my shirt tail, and went back to my classroom.

The word spread through school like wildfire.

"Jerry got stuck with the tuba."

When I got home, I handed the tuba mouthpiece to Mom. She lifted it to her nose, smelled it.

"I'll boil it."

At supper I announced my busy Christmas calendar and what would otherwise be a demanding whirlwind social season ahead.

"Mrs. Bredesen made me official chairman, Mom."

"That's nice dear, pass the potatoes to your brother,"

Mom said.

"I'm in charge of the senior class Christmas roller skating party War Memorial money raiser for our grade."

"That sounds worthwhile, son. Tell us about it," Dad said.

"The grade that gets the most kids to go to the senior's roller-skating party, and collects the most money, will maybe get their picture in the newspaper."

"Big deal," Dick said.

"We're going to advertise, Dad. Of course, we'll win easy— piece of cake. I'm thinking we'll make the front-page headlines."

I could almost hear the crowd cheering. Mom set her salad fork down.

"Don't be fresh, dear."

"Huh?"

"Speak like a gentleman, not like a big shot. Nobody likes a big shot."

Dad passed a platter of pork chops and looked down the table at Mom with a smile.

"Remember our evenings at the roller rink, Mommy?"

Mom smiled back.

"I loved the beautiful organ music—and, my, but you were so graceful on skates." She blushed.

"We certainly could cut a rug, couldn't we?" Dad asked.

"When's the roller-skating party, son?" Mom asked.

"What's the money going to be used for again?" Dad asked.

Delighted their walk down memory lane was over, I said, "It's Thursday before Christmas break. The seniors are raising money with a roller-skating party so they can pay for a bronze plaque for anybody who ever went to the school who were drafted and killed, wounded or lost during the war."

"Worthy cause," Dad said, bowing his head.

"Most worthy cause," Mom said.

"Such thoughtful children. A wonderful Christmas gift for all the families of those who served, whether they were drafted or volunteered. What a delightful community spirit that school inspires."

"We're going to thumb-tack a notice on the bulletin

board in our classroom. You know, Dad, we're going to advertise?" Dad smiled at my reference to advertising. "This is an important event, son."

"We know."

"Maybe you should do more than advertise."

"Huh?"

"Maybe you should sell tickets in advance, so you'll know how many people are going and how much money you make even before the skating party."

"What do you mean?"

"And you might come up with some way to get store owners to lend a hand, as well."

"But we don't have any tickets, Dad. I think kids just pay when they get off the school bus at the rink."

"Let's think about it," Dad said, passing the corn.

"Dad, I had this one idea of getting something important-looking printed. You know, like the Buster Brown Shoe club membership card. Some advertising we could pass out and show everybody."

"I like that, Jerry me boy, good idea!"

"I was thinking something that could fit in a kid's wallet or pocket."

"Or in a purse," Mom said.

"Son, if you'll write down all the information a printer will need, I'll give it some thought and have something nice printed for your grade to use."

"How much will that cost, Dad? We don't have a lot of—"

"Your mother and I will donate the printing so your class can do a good job getting kids to go to the roller-skating party, won't we dear?"

Mom added, "Don't be a braggart, son. Be a gentleman."

"Gee, thanks, Dad. Thanks, Mom."

I got up from the table, ran to my room, got all the papers with the information about the roller-skating party, and handed it to Dad.

It was nearly three weeks before Christmas vacation. I was immersed in the Christmas spirit, woke early, and was sitting on the edge of my bed looking out my window and thinking of the upcoming holiday. All I could see between our house and farmer Parker's across the way was a brown lawn, wet mud, and patches of crusty, half-melted snow piles. Every kid on earth was hoping for fresh white snow soon, a lot of snow. Me included.

This Christmas was going to be spectacular, snow or no snow, if I had anything to do with it, I convinced myself. Every week all summer, I mowed Doc Webb's lawn, for a dollar-fifty each time. He'd always throw in a bag of maple sugar candy.

I had Christmas shopping to do, and a dollar-fifty a week added up to a lot more money than I'd seen in one place since the Pompey Hollow Book Club's Easter bunny kidnapping caper's reward money. I never counted what I had, but it stacked neatly on my closet shelf. I only took money from the pile once, to buy a tire patch kit for my yellow bike, as I recall. Oh, then there was the time I bought two rolls of red, white, and blue striped crepe paper. I decorated the spokes on my bike with it so I could ride with the Pompey Hollow Book Club in the Memorial Day parade in front of Shea's store and the school.

I remember asking Mom one time if there was a Santa. She told me straight out, Santa only came for people who believed in him, so that was good enough for me. I still had money left and I was going to be the best Santa's helper ever. He could bring the good stuff, and I'd just pitch in, a little, and get presents for my friends, brothers, and aunts, and for Mom and Dad. I had a special present for Aunt Kate.

## CHAPTER TWENTY
## SO MANY TO THINK ABOUT

Every Saturday morning I rode to Homer with Dad, and as he did every Saturday morning, Dad took a shiny quarter out of his pocket, flipped it way up in the air so it blurred it spun so fast, high enough to nearly touch the ceiling.

"Call it, Bucky!" he shouted, not taking his eyes off the flying quarter.

"Heads!"

"Tails," Dad reported, after slapping the quarter the second it landed on the counter and looking at it.

Bucky put both hands on the counter and jumped his legs up sideways, clicking his heels together in the air.

Dad slid the quarter over anyway.

"How about an egg and olive sandwich for Jerry me boy, here—so he has the strength to carry the mail this morning?"

Bucky clicked his fingers.

"Gotcha!"

He pointed at me with a wink.

My errand for Dad on Saturdays was getting the post office box key from the hook on his office wall, walking across the street, and fetching all the bakery mail back to him. While he opened and read it, I had time to walk to the general store three doors up the street. This store had all kinds of things to buy and a pretty Christmas tree already decorated for gazing through the window to inside, by the front door. On my first "planning trip" for Christmas, I mostly walked around the store, looking and thinking about everyone I had to buy for. I considered it more of a reconnaissance mission. I needed a plan. I decided I would go home and make a list of names, and what I wanted to get each. I picked up a roll of wrapping paper. It was on sale and had a likeable Santa all over it, with drawings of store- wrapped presents and candy canes. I bought it and a roll of crinkled paper and a gold ribbon to go along with it.

Driving back to Delphi Falls, I asked, "Dad, for Christmas, if I want to tell Aunt Kate I know she's my grandma, will I get in trouble?"

"Jerry, that would be a generous, thoughtful, and wonderful gift. You would never get in trouble for something like that."

"If she's our grandma, why do we call her Aunt Kate?"

"Do you think you can understand it if I explain, son?"

"I'll understand."

"Aunt Kate is your mother's real mother. When your mother was four, her husband left them."

"You mean, he like ran away?"

"Yes, son."

"He was bad, Dad."

"Aunt Kate didn't want your mother to grow up without a father—so her sister and her husband adopted your mother. They loved your Mom just like she was their own. With her sister then becoming the adopted legal 'mother'—your grandmother went by 'Aunt Kate' from then on."

"Can I tell her I know, Dad—that she's my grandmother not the bad stuff?"

"You can share it with her. It would please her no end, but it would be her secret to share with others, can you understand that?"

"Yes, sir."

"You're a good boy, Jerry me boy!"

Dad looked down in my shopping bag, which was set between us on the front seat.

"What else do you have in mind, son?"

"What do you mean?"

He pointed at my shopping bag.

"Anything I can help you with? I can keep Christmas secrets, and I have personally met Santa Clause three times—well, two times, I'm sure of. I can't be positive about the third time."

He didn't say anything more about the wrapping paper and ribbon between us. I could tell he knew I was up to something very large.

We turned in Tully to drive toward home.

"I want to help Holbrook have a good Christmas, Dad."

"That's nice, Jerry. You're a good friend."

"Do you think Santa will go to his house?"

"I guarantee it, son."

"You can do that?"

"I can personally guarantee it."

I knew I could trust my dad, but I knew I needed tighter security on my Christmas secrets. I wanted to get to my desk, make a secret Christmas shopping list, and plan my shopping. I had to think and be organized.

In the matter of security and privacy, my room lacked one important element—a doorknob. My privacy was at the mercy of anyone just pushing my door open or closed. It was always ajar. I think it was a wartime thing. During the war, people couldn't buy metal knobs and locks because of iron and steel shortages. They needed all the steel to build warships and airplane fighters and bombers. It was just before the war when Dad and Mom decided to remodel the old country dance hall into the house it was now. We couldn't move from Cortland until after the war was over. It just took longer for the war to be over than anyone thought it would.

Thinking security, I had an inspiration.

I ran out to the barn, found the hammer, a nail, and a small scrap of wood, maybe three inches in length. Back in my room, I turned the radio on and the volume up, as loud as it could go, blasting the always arguing "Bickering Bickersons" radio show. I needed noise to camouflage my nail- pounding.

In this radio show, Mr. Bickerson was yelling at his wife, Mrs. Bickerson.

My hammer pounded the nail while the Bickersons bickered on the radio.

*"Blanche, you've never appreciated me. You've never appreciated anything I do," Mr. Bickerson shouted.*

*"Why should I?" Mrs. Bickerson shouted back. "You said 'I do' and you haven't done anything to appreciate since."*

*"How can you say that, Blanche? Blanche, how about that time I came home from a whole day's fishing at the pier for our supper and you made me get the fish out of the house and take them to the garage? Blanche, I worked all day that day trying to catch those five trout and three smelt."*

*Blanche yelled back, "They all smelt. That's why I wanted them in the garage."*

I had put the nail in the middle of the board, and pounded it into the door jam, right next to my door. The small stick of wood would now spin like the propeller on the DC-3 I flew on from Ithaca to Syracuse.

It was perfect. One turn and the piece of wood would hold the door closed. Another turn and it would let the door push open. My secret Christmas shopping list would now be safe. I sat at my desk and started writing names of friends, names of kids at home, names of kids away at college, and names of kids married and away, too.

For the Pompey Hollow Book Club guys I wrote Barber, Mary, and Holbrook on the list. I added Randy, Bases, and Mayor.

For family, I wrote Dick, Gourmet Mike, my uncles and aunt Dorothy, Mary, some cousins, Mom, Dad, and Aunt Kate.

"Yikes."

It was a lot of names. I hoped I had enough money.

I started my list again, with Dad and Mom, and moved backward. Dad was my favorite person, besides Mom, so I wanted to get him something special. At the general store in Homer I had seen some Sock-Mocs I thought he would like. They were half socks and half moccasins. The great thing about them was that they were only $2.14. The Sock-Moc—perfect for strolling about the house, in quiet comfort, with style and flair—just a hint of adventure. Dad would love them.

Mom was next. With Mom, I had to be careful. Anything I gave her

would make her cry. Anything any of her kids gave her would make her cry. The trick was to find something that would just make her cry, not want to hold me on her lap for half an hour, hugging me and telling me what a good boy I was. I had lost whole pieces of dessert to my brothers during a hug like that. One time, Dick told Mom that I had told him how much I loved her, and that I'd said she was the best mom on earth—while all along, he was staring at my piece of lemon meringue pie. That hug cost me my pie and the last piece of meatloaf on my plate (although Dick denied it). It was simple. Mom would get a handkerchief. That way, when she opened the package and started crying, she could keep her hands busy wiping her eyes, and not hugging me. It was settled. Handkerchiefs it was, for both Mom and our grandma, Aunt Kate. Aunt Kate would also get my other special surprise.

My brother, Gourmet Mike, was easy. Weren't no secret he was a
gourmet. I still wasn't certain what a gourmet was, but I figured it meant he cooked and ate things nobody liked, without a dare—like snails, frogs, and really bad-smelling cheeses. I knew exactly what I was going to get him— some Limburger cheese. Mike Shea sold it at his store. It was so stinky you could smell it from the barbershop next door. Holbrook dared me to smell it up close once, and I nearly passed out. It smelled worse than rutabagas. Limburger cheese—perfect for Mike.

Dick was next. Dick was sometimes getting beaten up, mostly for flirting with other guys' girlfriends. I remember walking home from St. Mary's School in the first grade, back in Cortland, and seeing Dick lying on the sidewalk with a boy sitting on top of him, threatening to punch him for even talking to his girlfriend. Dick was lying there, denying everything, all the while never once loosening the grip he had on the books he was carrying home for the boy's girlfriend. I'd get Dick a box of Band-Aids.

The next few weeks would be busy catching rides with Mom or Dad, scouring stores to do my shopping. On a lunch break at school, Holbrook and I walked down to Mike Shea's store. With my nose pressed to the window of the butcher counter cabinet, I asked Mike Shea how much Limburger cheese he thought a dollar twenty would buy.

"Son, are you looking for cheese in a jar or a freshly cut wedge?" I looked up over the counter and caught his eye.

"Would a gourmet like it in a jar better or a cut wedge better?"

"Oh, definitely a fresh-cut wedge, a gourmet would know," he answered, without hesitation, appreciating I knew enough to ask. I wondered if Mike Shea could sense an air of importance about me, what with my new responsibilities as the official chairman of our grade to help the senior class's Christmas roller-skating party. I think it showed in my face.

I bought a very nice size wedge of fresh Limburger cheese

that Mike Shea wrapped carefully in the double sheets of butcher paper he tore from a big roll and wrapped with string.

"Want me to keep it refrigerated for you, until you come and get it after school?" he asked.

Holbrook and I looked at each other like—what was he talking about? Why would we walk all the way back here after school just to get cheese I could easily put in my desk? Besides, I would be busy with my numerous important roller-skating party official chairman responsibilities for our grade.

"No thanks," I said.

"You sure?" Mike Shea asked.

"I'll take it with me. But thank you."

On the way out of the store, a stack of handkerchiefs on a shelf caught my eye.

"Mike Shea, are those girl's handkerchiefs or boy's handkerchiefs?"

"The girl's ones are on the left, the boy's handkerchiefs are on the other aisle," he said.

This was too easy.

I bought two girl's handkerchiefs and now I had four of the presents done. I saw a box of Band-Aids behind the counter, but I figured Dick might see them back at school or on the bus, so I decided to get them and Dad's Sock-Mocs in Homer when I went there with Dad onSaturday.

Holbrook agreed with a compliment.

"Superior thinking."

After school, I locked myself in my room and wrapped Gourmet Mike's gourmet cheese, tied a bow around it nicely, tight like a shoelace. Mike Shea had given me two boxes—one for each of the handkerchiefs, so they were easier to wrap. I tied bows on them. There was only one safe hiding place near Christmas, next to the wall by the piano in the living room. People could put presents and packages there for Santa to leave under the tree, along with the ones he brought. The rule was nobody could look at or touch these presents, so I knew they would be safe there. That night I knelt and prayed that Santa would not forget my best friend Holbrook and his family.

It only took another Saturday to find my aunt's, uncle's, and cousin's presents. I bought five-dollar savings stamps for each of the Pompey Hollow Book Club members (they cost $2.50 each) and got them each a Christmas card to put it in. I would hand them the cards the last day of school before Christmas break. I had everything else wrapped and put over by the piano with the other presents.

I got home from school the next day and went to my room. On my bed was a big box with a cardboard lid. I lifted the lid slowly to look inside and slammed the lid closed quickly in disbelief.

I needed to catch my breath.

Maybe I saw it wrong. Maybe someone delivered someone else's printing. I lifted the lid up slowly and peered in. The box was filled with skating party tickets—not advertising fliers, not advertising cards, but expensive-looking, oyster patterned, embossed and engraved skating party tickets, and one rubber stamp for imprinting "THANK YOU!" and an ink pad for the stamp.

I dropped the box to the floor and began desperately counting the tickets.

There were three hundred of them.

Both my hands raised and slapped on my cheeks.

"Oh my God! THREE HUNDRED TICKETS!"

There were only twenty-eight kids in my grade. There weren't three hundred kids in the whole school old enough to even go to the roller-skating party. Forget the school, there weren't three hundred townspeople in all of the school village and Delphi combined who could go. I think Dad had a ticket printed for every kid on the planet.

I was about to have a heart attack.

I put one of the tickets in my left jean pocket. I put the "THANK YOU!" rubber stamp in my other pocket and slid the box under my bed, kicking it with my foot to the wall, to hide the rest of the tickets that were about to be the death of me. I needed time to think.

I went out to the kitchen where Mom told me Mike was home from college for the weekend.

"Jerry, Mike is going to drive you to the party," Mom said.

"What party?"

"The party at Mary Margaret's. Her party is tonight."

I had completely forgotten the party.

"Go put a clean shirt on," she said. "I'll pick you up at ten-thirty."

The Pompey Hollow Book Club members plus a lot of other kids in our grade were there already. Holbrook, Mary, Barber, Bases, Randy, Mayor, plus Mary Margaret, Smith, Kellish, Lowe, Finch, Sexton, Paddock, and Fish were there and others still coming.

Most everyone was talking about Christmas.

I motioned for Barber, Mary, and Holbrook to step outside for a second. On the way out, I caught the eyes of Randy, Mayor, and Bases and motioned to come join us. Once outside I turned and pulled the printed ticket out of my left pocket, and the "THANK YOU!" rubber stamp from my right pocket. I held them both up and got it over with.

"I thought my dad and mom were going to get advertising fliers printed for the roller-skating party. Just like the Buster Brown Shoe Club cards."

"That's what you told us," Mary said. "Just like Buster Brown cards."

"That's what I asked for."

"We know," Holbrook said.

"I asked for a card for every kid in OUR grade," my voice cracked and whimpered, on the verge of either tears or a possible nervous breakdown.

"Good idea. Did he get fliers printed?" Holbrook asked.

"Are they nice?" Mary asked.

"Why are you so green?" Barber asked.

"That thing in your hand doesn't look like a flier," Holbrook offered.

"They got roller skating party TICKETS printed."

"Tickets!?" Mary asked.

"Roller skating party tickets, which we have to sell."

I held up the sample ticket again.

"They threw in this 'THANK YOU!' rubber stamp and an ink pad."

I held it up again as well.

Everyone stared at the ticket in my hand and tried to make sense out of my confusion. Mary thought the ticket was pretty and liked the oyster shell background.

"Kids will like these," Holbrook said.

"Everyone will want one," Randy said.

"But there's a slight problem," I added. "Dad got three hundred of them printed."

"You mean thirty, right?" Mary asked. "You said three hundred."

"He actually printed three hundred tickets, just like this one."

"Oh—Jeez," Barber said.

"He must have misunderstood me. We only need twenty-eight advertising fliers for our grade. Now I have three hundred expensive oyster shell tickets hidden under my bed and a stamp ink pad. My Dad went nuts with his numbers! I'm a failure as the official chairman."

"Uh-oh," came from most of the kids.

"You can't just throw them away," Barber said.

"You're going to have to tell your dad about the mistake," Randy said.

"You mean tell my dad I gave him bad information and he wasted money printing stuff?"

"You have to tell him, or we're stuck with these and we're sunk," Holbrook said.

"Anyone got any better ideas?" I asked.

Randy threw us another anchor.

"How do we get rid of the three hundred roller skating party tickets when there aren't three hundred kids in the whole school?" he asked.

"Are we even allowed to have tickets to sell?" Mary asked.

"I think we're sunk," Mayor said.

Mary Margaret happened to be listening at the screen door. Her mother was a schoolteacher, so Mary Margaret looked at our problem through a different set of eyes.

"Why don't you give the tickets to my mom to give to the school principal to hand out to all the grades for them to sell in their own grade?"

It was a thought. Mary stepped up.

"Why don't we sell all the tickets ourselves?"

"Huh?" I gulped.

"There's no rule says we can't," Mary said.

"Then we will be sure to win and maybe get our picture in the paper," Bases said.

The kids paused to reflect on the concept.

"No rule says we can't," Mary said.

"Is there a rule says we can?" Mayor asked.

"Wouldn't our printing tickets be like counterfeiting?" Holbrook asked.

Mary Margaret stepped outside, closed the screen door behind her, and added some brilliance of her own.

"Mary's right. The rule is the grade that gets the most to attend the roller-skating party wins, isn't it?" Mary Margaret asked.

"That was the rule," Holbrook said.

"The rules never said anything about the kids we get to go have to be from the same grade—or even from our grade for that matter," Mary Margaret said.

"That's right, nobody ever said anything like that," Mary said.

"Why not each one of us take twenty tickets and we go ask everyone we know in school who wants one and we sell them that way and give all the money to the seniors?" Mary Margaret asked. "We can use the tickets as proof that it was our grade that got them to go."

That was such a brilliant idea I wanted to give Mary Margaret a big kiss, but her mom was sitting by the window, peering out. Her mom made me pound the chalkboard erasers one time during recess just for running in the halls. One kiss and she'd probably make me paint her house.

Holbrook said, "Jerry, call your mom and ask her if she can bring the tickets when she comes to pick you up so we can divide them here."

Mom arrived with the tickets and went inside for tea with Mrs. Cox.

The Pompey Hollow Book Club and Mary Margaret each got twenty tickets. I got nineteen. That was all we needed because that was the number of kids at school— a hundred and seventy-six— who could go if they wanted to.

Mary said, "At school Monday morning, tell anyone who wants a ticket to pay before the roller-skating party or they can't get on the bus—and write down everyone's name."

This was genius. Here we were all worried about how to sell the tickets and she told us to trust everyone to pay—that everyone wanted to go, and nobody would cheat us. A brilliant idea.

And just about the time we were all realizing what a great idea that was, the Pompey Hollow Book Club's very own president, Mary, came up with still another idea.

"When you give each kid their ticket, instead of writing their name on the sheet of paper, have them sign their name for it on a pad. Remember the rabbits, Jerry? This will be our written proof we were the ones to get them to go to the roller-skating party."

It was because of these ideas I nominated both Mary Margaret and Mary to be president of our grade. Holbrook and I voted for them both, using two separate ballot boxes so we wouldn't get caught.

We met in the school cafeteria for lunch on Monday. Not only had we sold all one hundred and seventy-six tickets, we had rubber-stamped the remaining one-hundred-twenty-four tickets with "THANK YOU" and had given half of them to Mike Shea at his store near the school and half to Mr. Hasting at his Delphi store to give to people who dropped donation money in a jar for the bronze plaque. When we gave our completed lists of names to Mrs. Bredesen and explained what we had done, she told the class to sit and behave while she left the classroom to go speak with the principal to see if we had broken any rules.

She came back into the room with a big smile on her face.

Our teacher congratulated the class for thinking "out of the box" and announced that the school Christmas roller-skating party this year would raise more money than ever before. It would be a very nice Senior Class War Memorial plaque remembering those we had lost.

Even Mom and Dad were proud of us.

"How did you all sell so many so quickly?" Dad asked.

"Well, we each had twenty—well me, nineteen—and we walked into every classroom and announced, 'I only have twenty tickets left for the roller-skating party. Who would like them?' I guess everyone thought there were only twenty tickets left, and they didn't want to miss out. We sold them in minutes."

Dad and Mom smiled at each other.

"Your class is to be congratulated," Mom said.

"It was the other kids' ideas," I said.

Mom was most proud of her gentleman.

## CHAPTER TWENTY-ONE
## A BIG OOPS!

"Yikes!" I shouted, sitting up in bed, just waking up. "I forgot all about Santa."

I put my feet on the floor and looked out through my window, seeing it had snowed all night, and what ran through my mind was that Christmas was coming, Santa was coming, and I hadn't thought of a present for Santa. I'd thought about everyone else but not Santa.

I pulled my clothes on, bundled up, and ran out to the barn. I was trying to slide the small barn door open without letting the pile of fresh-fallen snow that had drifted onto the door nearly up to my waist tip over inside on the barn floor. I knew it would have been smarter to shovel the snow away before trying to open the door, but it would have been smarter than that not to have left the shovel in the barn, where it wasn't needed anyway, in the first place.

Sometimes being smart could be tricky in the country, and sometimes, like then, it could save you a lot of work you weren't particularly in the mood for—like shoveling snow.

It was also smart to buckle your galoshes (boots) so you wouldn't trip over them. It was way too late for me to think of that, because as soon as the door slid open, I raised one leg way up in the air to step into the barn over the snowdrift. The buckle of that boot in the air got caught somehow on the buckle of the boot still on the ground, and I began tripping forward, hopping on my left foot at least halfway through the room, ultimately losing my balance just in time to fall headfirst into an empty bucket Dick used for carrying chemicals to the water softener.

CLANG!

The noise of my head clanging into the empty bucket scared Ginger, our outdoor dog with her nubby tail. She ran out of the barn through the pile of snow yipping, while my whole right boot came off, pulling my shoe with a knot in the lace and sock off with it.

This was not a good start to a Christmas holiday, and by now I had forgotten why I had gone to the barn in the first place. I knew it wouldn't be long and I would remember, but before I could do anything, anyway, I had to take the knot out of my shoelace, put my sock, shoe, and boot back on, and this time, buckle my boots.

It was moments like these that gave me a better understanding of why Mom would always say, "Don't forget to buckle your galoshes, dear."

Oh, yeah—I remembered. Santa!

I had gone to the barn to look for something I could leave reindeers' harvest cow corn in, for when Santa Claus came. The harvest cow corn I would get from farmer Parker's barn this afternoon when I went there to help him call in the cows.

I knew carrots were popular with deer, but I thought corn might last longer, and maybe the crunching sounds on the night before Christmas would wake me up so I could at least see the reindeer. Santa always brought our Christmas tree and decorated it in the night, so I knew that task alone would take him a little more time than he'd take at houses that already had a Christmas tree. His reindeer would have more time to rest and eat some refreshing cow corn. I even asked Charlie Pitts, before he died, if Santa's reindeer would like cow corn, and he said, "Oh ya, you betcha they do."

You couldn't get proof any better than that, so I knew I was doing the right thing. Ole Charlie would have let me have as much corn as I wanted from his cow corn crib. He was a nice man, a friend, who always reminded me of Christmas, and I missed him, a lot. I considered him a best friend of mine, ever since he didn't laugh at me, or tell anyone about the time I dropped the eggs on the road.

Behind an empty nail keg in the small barn, I found a garbage can lid with its handle smashed flat down that somebody must have driven over with the car. It was perfect! I would turn it upside down, fill it with cow corn, and leave it on the floor by our fireplace. For sure, Santa would see it when he came down the chimney, and he would know it was my present for the reindeer. I'd write a note for him. I also planned to leave an empty, rolled-up, paper potato sack, just in case Santa decided to take the harvest cow corn with him and feed the reindeer throughout the evening. This was some superior thinking and bound to get me on good terms with Santa Claus. He was the one person all kids wanted to be on good terms with. I could even imagine him coming down the hallway, to my room, and telling me a personal thank you for being so considerate, that is, if he had the time. Santa Claus was a very busy person.

Aunt Kate had come to stay with us until after New Year's. Gourmet Mike had driven in from Lemoyne until after Christmas when his college started again.

It was a very cold evening, icy cold, on Wednesday before Christmas when Gourmet Mike stacked wood by the wall in the living room and built a nice warm fire in the fireplace before he sat down at the table to join us.

For some reason, while sitting at the table, Mom seemed to be getting uneasy, edgy. It wasn't like her. She kept making strange contorted faces. It was as if she had something heavy on her mind, or she had forgotten something really important and was trying hard to remember what it was. We were busy eating and not making a lot of noise, so none of us paid all that much attention to her. She would lean out of her seat over to the left, turn her head around to one side, stick her nose up, and kind of smell the air. Then she'd lean out the other way, turn her head to the other side, stick her nose up, and sniff again.

"What's wrong Mom?" Dick asked.

"It's very warm in here," Mom said.

"The fire's going good, Mom," Gourmet Mike said.

Befuddled, she looked forward in thought. She set her salad fork down, pushed her plate away and declared in no uncertain terms.

"What is that horrible stench?"

The only problem was that neither Dick nor I quite understood what the word "stench" meant or even implied. Gourmet Mike knew it from his experience as a gourmet, but we weren't to know that. An afflicted gourmet would understand stench, I was later to find out.

Mom pushed her chair back.

"Children," she demanded, "everybody line up, over here,

right now."

There was always trouble, regardless of our ages, when Mom referred to us as "children." What has she caught us doing now? was the first thing that would normally run through our heads, and what is a *stench* was the second. We stood, hoping for a clue. With such a pained expression on her face, we weren't about to argue.

We all got in line. One by one we walked up to Mom, and she sniffed the air around us, and then asked the next one to step forward and get sniffed. After we were properly sniffed, Mom told us to sit back down, and in one final act of desperation, she repeated in words we would understand, "What on earth is that horrible smell?"

"So that's what *stench* means," Dick said. He proclaimed it like he'd discovered pasteurization.

We all began to sniff the air.

Boys in the late 1940s had simple senses of smell. We could smell food being cooked—cabbage, the farthest away—various and assorted farm fragrances—and, of course, dirty socks.

We could smell Christmas trees. Not much else.

"Smells like Jerry's room," Dick said.

Aunt Kate cracked him on the knuckles with a wooden serving spoon.

Mom pushed her chair back further. Like she was on a mission, she stood up and started sniffing the air—first, in a full circle around the dining room table, then in a short loop through the kitchen and then out into the living room.

We followed her. Not too close.

She made short, snorting, sniffing sounds with her wrinkled-up nose, using a wriggling upper lip as antennae. We could hear her from across the room as she made her way along the wall, around the corner, into the living room, moving closer and closer to the piano, and over to the floor by the wall, which was piled with Christmas presents. Her snorting vibrated the piano strings of the upright. At one point she stopped abruptly and knelt down on one knee.

"Call Ginger in," she demanded.

Now, truth be known, calling Ginger in was probably the simplest chore there would ever be at our house. Ginger was our half-beagle, half-cocker spaniel. Although we only kept her outside, all she ever wanted to be was an inside dog, so she never left the door. Ginger spent her entire life leaning on a door, wanting to be let in.

Mike opened the door just enough to wake her from a nap without tipping her over and called her name, as a matter of courtesy. Ginger went nuts with joy and popped in at the tiniest opening of the door, like a kangaroo that didn't have to be asked twice. She never calmed down until she had jumped exactly three times for each and every person she saw, and then she ran, at full speed, two times, throughout the entire house. Every time she turned a corner, her paws on the carpet sounded like she was sliding into third. She was just making certain nothing had changed, or that she hadn't missed anyone.

Mom called Ginger over, held her by the collar, pointed her at the pile to get her focused and slowly led her snout to one Christmas package at a time. At one point in the process Ginger yipped, almost like something had bitten her. She tugged backward against the collar causing her normally tight furry skin to wrinkle up over her eyes like a bloodhound trying to back away from a pile of clues at any cost. Mom let go of her collar and with her thumbs and first fingers, she lifted the suspicious package up from the pile.

Ginger ran to the door, begging to be let out.

Something began to ooze from the package.

"Someone bring me a dish," Mom demanded. "Hurry!"

Dick ran one over to her, chewing on my ear of corn that was on it, and handed the plate to her. She put the plate under the package, now leaking a gummy, gooey slime.

She turned and gave me a stern look.

"Jerome, suppose you take this out to the garbage barrel, bring the plate back, and meet your mother in the kitchen. Mike and Dick, supper is being delayed, both of you go into Dick's room and close the door."

This couldn't be good.

When I got to the kitchen, all I could think of was there was trouble in the air for me, or in this case, a stench.

First off, she knew the Christmas package was mine, because the tag on the present said, "To Gourmet Mike, from

Jerry."

Second, when she called me Jerome, I was very likely to get beaned or lectured.

Third, anytime Mom called herself "Your Mother," rumor was she wanted no witnesses, just in case she accidentally drew blood, or murdered somebody.

"Jerry, I want the absolute truth."

Now this offended me. I almost always told Mom the truth, except for the time I kissed Linda Oats in the cider mill. I told her I'd tripped on a step and fallen into the cider tub, trying to help someone reach for a broom to sweep up the place. Or the time I told her I had eaten the disgusting rutabagas she'd served for dinner, which smelled like swamp water, when I really only hid them on a ledge under the supper table until after everybody went to bed, and then I got them from their hiding place, took them up into the woods next to the house, and properly stomped on them with my heel, eliminating even the slightest possibility they could ever go to seed and grow again.

"Jerome, do you have any other food wrapped and over there as presents for anyone?"

"No, ma'am," I said.

"Just what was in that package, child?"

"Limburger cheese, for Mike, because he's a gourmet."

Mom smiled. It was the kind of smile when I thought she was going to give me a hug. Thank God, she didn't. This whole thing already cost me my corn, maybe even my supper.

"I will give you fifty cents, dear. When you go back to the store, you can buy Limburger cheese in a jar that will be just as nice for your brother. It's such a thoughtful gift, Jerry."

"You're not mad Mom?" I asked.

"I'm not mad, son."

I felt better.

"By the way, son, where did you get the package of Limburger?"

"At Mike Shea's store, near the school," I replied.

"Didn't anyone at the store tell you cheese should be refrigerated?"

"Mike Shea said that word, Mom."

"What word, Jerry?"

"That 'frigertate' word, like you said, but Holbrook and me didn't know what he meant."

"You mean Mr. Shea offered to—" Mom started.

"He likes when we call him Mike, Mom."

"Are you telling me he offered to refrigerate the cheese for you?"

"I didn't have any more money, Mom, in case it—that *frigertate* thing— would cost me, so we didn't pay any mind to it."

Mom stepped back and stared at me with eyes glazed over, the way she did when she thought I had a fever or some rare disease. Then she walked over to the ice box, pointed to it like a teacher pointing to a chalkboard.

"Jerry, this is a *refrigerator*."

"Huh?"

"It keeps food cold and fresh."

"Well, I'll be," I said.

"Surely you —" Mom started.

"I sure thought that was an *icebox*, Mom."

I reminded my mom, once again, that when we moved to the wilderness, well, a woods in the country, there were some things I just stopped learning altogether.

"Mom, I swear—in Cortland, we called that thing an icebox and nobody ever bothered telling me someone had gone and changed its name to refrigerator."

Mom stood there with her mouth open and didn't argue with me, because she knew I had her stumped.

"Well I'll be," I said.

"Go to bed, dear, and tell the boys to put their pajamas on and go to bed, too."

## CHAPTER TWENTY-TWO
## SKATING PARTY

I had never been to a roller-skating party. It was more fun than a hayride—well, it got to be after I learned how to balance on roller skates, and I stopped falling down and crashing into railings and poles and walls. Mayor's T-shirt was blotched with orange drink because his hand holding his paper cup smashed against the wall. Holbrook's right lens fell out of his glasses.

He shrieked like a girl.

"Nobody skate!"

It had no effect in the middle of a skating party with the organ player with her eyes closed, smiling and playing "Somewhere Over the Rainbow" and everybody holding someone's hand just so they could keep from falling down.

Once most of us got past the part where our knees would wobble in and out and our arms made big circles backward like windmills while we tried not losing our total balance, it started to be fun. It wasn't long before everybody could skate—or at least thought they could, and holding hands was better, with much less hand cramping.

After I skated late into the night and finally took the skates off to go outside and look for a school bus, I bounced when I walked, as if the skates were still on. I almost had to learn how to walk again, taking steps and not sliding my feet. I'd heard of Navy sailors having sea legs when they first got off their ships—I guess this would have been called skate legs. I got on the closest bus, which was dark inside, stepped in, walked tenderly to the back where it was even darker, and sat down next to Mary, whose reflection I could see in the bus window.

Well, now. Not only was Mary a really good roller-skater, and we skated together this evening a bunch, while sitting on the bus she couldn't have been prettier with her hair combed back in a ponytail and a yellow ribbon she must have put on while sitting there. It reminded me of the "yellow ribbon," Olivia Dandridge wore in my favorite all-time movie, and it caused me great pause to be looking at Mary in a way I hadn't ever looked at her before. After all, she was the president of our club, the Pompey Hollow Book Club, and I had a deep and great respect for the office of what might possibly be, to my and the boys' very limited understanding of government and politics, the very first girl president in these United States of America.

At her parties we'd square dance, but like ladies and gents in the movies, we didn't play Post Office or spin-the-bottle like some of the older kids. The thought never entered my head. As the bus started backing around, right next to Bucky's Diner, to get on Route 11 and head north out of Cortland, I looked all over the bus every time we passed under a streetlamp that washed the inside with light as we drove by. The inexperienced, part-time, substitute night bus driver ground the gears like a coffee grinder. The bus jerked on up the highway. There was a full moon.

I told Mary how much fun the skating party was.

Tightening the yellow ribbon on her ponytail, she couldn't have agreed more.

On reflection, I wish she hadn't agreed.

You see, I could see Mary's reflection from time to time in the bus window. I could see the yellow ribbon; the same yellow ribbon Olivia Dandridge wore in my favorite movie—or have I said that already? I remembered how awkward my first kiss in the old mill was. Even Tom Sawyer had a better first kiss than I did. I remembered Mary's frown of disappointment. I thought, and I'm practically eleven—well, I would be in a couple or three years or so, anyway.

While sitting next to Mary, I slowly raised and stretched my arms up and out with a loud, obvious, cartoon-like noisy yawn, just as if to send a signaled message—like *it sure is getting late and maybe I'll just take a short nap on the way back to school and not be kissing any girls*—and that was about the time I rested my right arm conveniently on the seat back, right behind Mary's neck and ponytail tied with the yellow ribbon. What a coincidence, I thought. Perfect.

A lot of kids on the bus who never had a beer in their lives were singing, "Ninety-nine bottles of beer on the wall, ninety-nine bottles of beer

—if one of the bottles happens to fall, ninety-eight bottles of beer on the wall—Ninety-eight bottles of beer on the wall, ninety-eight bottles of beer—if one of the bottles happens to fall, ninety-seven bottles of beer on the wall—"

The situation I found myself in caused me to have to gather some much-needed thought. Faced with a yellow ribbon and a pretty smile, I needed a strategy with Mary here—president or not.

I reflected on the time Dick tried to explain boy and girl courting to me. He said courting, in a city like Cortland, was different than courting in the country, around Delphi Falls. He said city courting was a long, drawn-out series of visits to a girl's home, and then perhaps a supper or two with her parents at the table and then maybe a picture show and popcorn with a chaperone sitting a row behind them. If it was going well after all that, the boy and girl could maybe hold hands or sit in the parlor or on the porch swing and talk, with the parents in the next room.

"Dang," I said.

"Country courting was different," Dick and Duba both insisted.

"How's it different?" I asked.

"Kids in the country live miles away from each other—" Duba started.

"It's like the wilderness," I said.

"—and they have to court different than the city," Duba said.

"Why?" I asked.

"It comes down from the pilgrims," Duba said.

"Huh?" I grunted.

"Every minute counts in the country," Duba said. "No taxis, no trolleys, no city buses in the country."

"And Indians," Dick said. "Don't forget country folk never knew when they would be attacked."

"How do you court in the country?" I pleaded.

"You kiss."

"Huh!?"

"In the country, courting is pretty much kissing, simple as that."

They were emphatic.

"Yep—lots of kissing," Duba reinforced.

After remembering that whole Dick and Duba lecture about courting in the country, I was inspired. At "eighty-five bottles of beer on the wall," I saw the reflection of the yellow ribbon once again when we passed a lonely streetlamp as the bus drove out of Homer. I closed my eyes, didn't even think about it, leaned in like a B-17 bomber over Berlin, did a good ole' tuba purse-pucker with my lips even Mr. Spinner would have been proud of. I planted a kiss on my president, Mary, the likes of which she was not likely soon to forget—a kiss that might could be the envy in Hollywood—and held the kiss easy through "seventy-four bottles of beer on the wall."

Still kissing at "fifty-nine bottles of beer on the wall," I was considering forgetting about Olivia Dandridge and maybe painting my bike green.

It wasn't until fifty-six bottles, with what had to be an all-time record kiss for school bus number 23, when I opened my eyes in my bliss just to see if Mary maybe needed some oxygen and to possibly oblige her with a breathing spell. Doing so, my eyes looked up from our kiss at our reflection in the window from a barn's spotlight at Preble Crossing. In the bus window glass, Mary's eyes appeared to be wide open and staring straight up at the ceiling. Her lips were all puckered up and waiting. It even appeared she had fresh lipstick on them. I never knew Mary to wear lipstick. The thought of how her lips could be puckered if I was kissing them crossed my mind.

"Forty-three bottles of beer on the wall" and now I was curious. I looked again—this time with my brain—

Oh my God!

I was kissing her chin! Holy Cobako! I thought.

I had planted a kiss on Mary's chin, just outside of Bucky's Diner in Cortland, with my best pursed-lip pucker, and stayed planted on her chin like a blithering idiot, absolutely convinced I was the next Errol Flynn all the way until the bus slowed down and jerked at the stoplight in Tully to turn right toward the school village. The jar of the turn jostled us loose, lips and chin.

I actually considered jumping off the bus and walking the

ten miles home.

Mary didn't say a word and didn't laugh. Her thumb and finger wiggled her chin from side to side, trying to get the blood circulating again. She did rest her dreamy eyes on me like she understood I was under a lot of stress what with being official chairman and all and the skating party ticket sales and everything that went with that. Presidents understood those things. When the bus stopped at the school, I started to stand up to run away.

"Hold on a minute," Mary said and she leaned over, took my cheeks in both her hands to control the aim, pulled my face toward hers, and gave me a good-night kiss that made me forget about Linda Oats. It was the best good-night kiss ever in history, I was certain. Mary smiled, pulled the ribbon from her ponytail, and handed it to me to keep.

I went home, crawled into bed with all my clothes and shoes on, and pulled the blanket up over my head. Smelling the perfume on the ribbon, now wrapped around my finger, I decided kissing was definitely very good, very hazardous but very good, but from now on I was more likely to hold hands or just have supper, and court like the people in Cortland court. Courting in the country could give a boy a heart attack.

## CHAPTER TWENTY-THREE
## O' HOLY NIGHT!

On Christmas Eve my aunts and uncles, Gourmet Mike, and Mom and Dad were in the living room around the fire. Aunt Mary and Aunt Dorothy played Christmas music on the phonograph while Mike played the piano. Everyone was having a good time, singing Christmas carols. I sat near Aunt Kate and listened as she read to our cousins *The Night Before Christmas*, which was one of my favorite poems. I knew it by heart, but it was nice hearing someone read it, so I could imagine it. After a while, the little kids had to go to bed.

Little kids at our house at Christmas time were everyone in school or younger. Aunt Kate walked me to the bathroom to brush my teeth. Then she tucked me in and gave me a kiss goodnight. That was when I gave her my special Christmas surprise. I touched her cheek and whispered, "Merry Christmas, Grammy. I love you, and I'm happy you're my grandmother."

Her cheek trembled. I knew a family secret. I could see a warm smile sparkle up in her eyes as the glare of the porch light reflected on a teardrop through her glasses. I could see it was a happy tear.

"Merry Christmas, my wonderful grandson, Merry Christmas. Thank you. Thank you."

She stood up, took her cane and shuffled down the hall, wiping her eyes with a hanky.

The adults sang while the kids were in bed, so Santa could come. But if Santa came during the night, everyone always promised to wake us up early, to see what he brought.

Sometime past midnight and half-asleep I could hear a noise outside my window. It seemed to shake the house.

There was a—

THUMP! THUMP! THUMP!

Then a jingle, jingle, jingle.

THUMP! THUMP! THUMP!

Then a jingle, jingle, jingle.

I sprung up, ran down the hall in the dark and looked for the trash can lid I'd left for Santa's deer.

"Hey look!" I said to myself in my loudest whisper. "The cow corn is gone—the cow corn is gone!"

All of a sudden, the front door swung open and hit the wall behind it loudly, almost giving me a heart attack. Gourmet Mike jumped in and yelled in a loud whisper, "Quick, Jerry! Santa's still on the roof!"

He knelt so I could get on his shoulders. Outside we went in the dark to see Santa and the reindeer. He carried me to the flagpole, this side of the swings, for a good view of the roof, and turned around to face the house.

"Oh darn," Mike said as we turned full circle, "the reindeer finished the corn you left, Jerry, and they must have taken off."

He pointed to the left end of the roof. The trash can lid I had filled was up there sure enough, but empty now and nestled in some snow on the roof. There were two long deep ridges in the snow on the roof. Gourmet Mike told me they were sleigh tracks.

It was amazing! We came within seconds of seeing Santa and his reindeer. We stared at the roof for a while, and Mike took me into the house and back to my room.

"Try to sleep, Jerry. Mom will be waking you soon. Merry Christmas." It was almost impossible to get back to sleep, but I managed.

It was early Christmas morning, still dark, when Mom came into my room, woke me, and left. The hallway was aglow from the Christmas tree decoration's reflections, and from the decorations Santa had left in the living room. Every year it was such a big surprise to see the tree for the first time, early Christmas morning. The anticipation of it made it seem to get bigger, with more lights, more beautiful shiny balls and icicles than the year before. I still remember the candle lights that bubbled up magically. The presents were under and around the tree. Aunt Kate, Mom, Dad, Gourmet Mike, and Dick were already in the living room, waiting.

Mom, Aunt Kate. and Dad were beaming smiles at me. It

was still a secret, but I think Aunt Kate told them how happy she was that I knew she was my grandmother.

Aunt Mary sat on the floor by the tree handing out presents. Everyone watched while the person opened it and told who it was from. Dad loved the Sock-Mocs and put them on right away. They fit perfectly and looked comfortable. He gave me a neck hug, thanked me, and whispered in my ear, "Jerry me boy, your bike was pretty much your Christmas present this year."

"I know, Dad. I love my bike," I said.

"But here's a special Christmas present for you, son, directly from Santa."

"From Santa, Dad, for real?" I asked.

"Santa arranged it personally, Jerry. I met him twice, ya know."

"Twice that you know of, Dad," I said. "I remember."

"Son, the owner of the Tully Bakery delivered a new hot water heater to Mr. and Mrs. Holbrook late last night and had it hooked up for them—it's big enough for the entire family. What is it? Seventeen in all?"

"For real, Dad? You mean now they can have hot water in the house?"

"Your friend Bobby had it nearly half paid for, son, working part-time in the Tully bakery after school or on weekends. Half his pay stub from now on goes to paying it off—but they can pour hot tub baths starting this Christmas morning. I know he's your best friend and thought you'd like to know, young man. Merry Christmas, son."

I couldn't believe my ears.

Mom opened her handkerchief box, picked up the lace hanky and started to tear up. To save myself a half hour and my hot chocolate, I hurried over to her, gave her a kiss on the cheek.

"Merry Christmas, Mom."

"It's lovely, dear—thank you, so much."

Then Mom took my arm and pulled me close and whispered in my ear.

"Jerry, your bike is your present from your dad and me, dear—"

"I know Mom."

"But here's your aunt's Christmas present for you."

"What do you mean, Mom?"

"Dr. Porterfield from Syracuse University was your aunt's professor in college. He and several war veteran gentlemen, including some pilots who flew B-17s in the war, contacted some railroad union officials they knew from the service and were able to get your friend Bobby's father, Mr. Holbrook, a full journeyman status with the railroad union. The Holbrook's eleven children are from a combination of two families. They are such good people. God bless them. Now Mr. Holbrook will make more money, steady money, working full-time and qualify for their retirement pension, too. I know Bobby is your best friend, Jerry. It's a present to him and you from us—Merry Christmas."

I stood there trying to take it all in. I was in awe. I thought that maybe now Holbrook could get a telephone.

Aunt Kate loved her handkerchief. She pulled me closer than she ever had and gave me a hug and whispered in my ear. It was almost as if it was in her young, motherly voice, her voice as it would have been back in 1906, when she was the mother of a four-year-old girl. "You're one wonderful leprechaun, my grandson. You're a special young man."

Then she patted me on the cheek with a happy smile.

Gourmet Mike cheered when he opened his Limburger cheese. He gave me a wink. He asked Mom if she had any crackers in the house. I couldn't believe he was going to eat the same stuff that made Ginger want to be an outdoor dog. I guess gourmets will eat anything. His present to me was showing me where Santa was on the roof last night. With that, I knew I could still believe one more time.

Dick opened his Band-Aid box and scratched his head.

"Don't you get it?" I asked.

"No," Dick said.

"It's for when you get beat up."

He stared at me, like he might want to get up and slug me, but the more he thought about it, the more sense bandages made. Dick was smart. He leaned over and whispered, "We need to talk."

"What's up?"

"Duba and I did something."

"Uh-oh, what'd you do?"

"We don't want you getting sore at us."

"What'd you do?!"

"I finally have enough money to buy the Nash convertible from Lindsey Pryor," Dick started.

"So?"

"Duba's got enough to get the roadster he wants."

"So, what's that got to—"

"We heard about the new hot water heater and the railroad union thing for the Holbrooks …"

"That's all good, right?" I asked.

"So Duba and I decided to give the '38 to Holbrook, so his mom could drive him to the Tully Bakery after school whenever he needed to go, so he wouldn't have to walk anymore."

I began to tear up.

"You sore?" Dick asked.

"Why would I be sore?"

"Well, we were going to give it to you for Christmas."

"Holbrook is my best friend ever. He needs rides to work."

"So, in a way it is for you—a Christmas present for your best friend."

Not only were the SOSs Dick and his friends had come through with huge for the Pompey Hollow Book Club, but this was the biggest gift he and Duba could ever think of doing. He told me they put the '38 in Holbrook's drive after midnight last night with a note tied to the steering wheel with its two keys.

My aunts loved the records I gave them, one of "Oh Come All Ye Faithful" with Bing Crosby, and one of "Rudolph the Red-Nosed Reindeer" with Gene Autry.

We sat around the tree for the longest time, opening presents, singing songs, and drinking hot chocolate. Then we had to go back to bed and sleep late so all of Santa's helpers could get some rest. It was hard trying to fall asleep again, but I did.

It was a very nice Christmas—the best Christmas ever. I kept the secret about hearing the reindeer always in my memories. I kept the secrets about each of Santa's special visits to Holbrook always in my heart.

On the Monday after Christmas, Mom dropped me at Mayor's farm to sled. Along with Mary, Holbrook, and Barber,

Randy and Bases showed up. It had snowed all weekend, so it was a perfect Christmas, with tons piled up for sledding all day and into the evening.

After Mayor carried the snow sled from the barn, Holbrook pulled me inside the barn to talk in secret. He gave me a neck hug and said nobody ever had a better friend ever in the history of the world. He told me he cried when he saw it all happen—the water heater, the '38—for his mom, the union for his dad, hot water finally for the family, and for him. Then he added, "But if you ever tell anyone I cried, I'll beat the crap out of you."

"Our secret," I promised.

"Ever tell anybody I hugged you, I'll pound you to a pulp."

We took turns pulling the sled up the hill a million times. After dusk, we'd follow boot tracks in the snow up the sledding hill in the moonlight, so we wouldn't slide down the steep hill where the bull was, hoping we were in a safe snow groove, sledding back down the hill.

The side porch light flicked on and off, on and off, on and off, and then back on.

"That's my mom, calling us in," Mayor said.

"My ears are frozen. All I can hear is a dog barking," I said.

The porch light flicked off and on again. This time we all saw it. We let the sled slide down the steep hill on its own and walked down the hill. It flew past the bull and under the barbed wire fence and into their snowy driveway.

"I'll put the sled in the barn," Mayor said.

Farm kids had to pick up toys and sleds to keep tractors and farm equipment from rolling over them.

Holbrook walked ahead of Mayor, slid the barn door open for him and waited outside.

Inside the farmhouse, Mayor's mom told us to close the door behind us.

"Everyone stand on the mat by the door and take your boots and shoes off," she said.

She took our coats, scarves, hats, and mittens and threw them in a box by the door.

"My goodness," she said, "you're all soaked right through and your boots are filled with snow."

Sergeant Preston of the Royal Mounties and King had been through worse than this during every radio episode we ever heard.

Not only could we take the cold, we were beginning to thaw from being inside a warm house.

When I could open my eyes fully, I saw Mayor's brother's Christmas present on top of their small kitchen table. It was a genuine red and silver American Flyer train set—train track, and all—even complete with a "choo-choo" whistle, electric transformer and everything. Wow! It had an engine with an engineer painted on the window steering the train—a coal tender behind that—a flat car behind that—a passenger car behind that, with real looking people painted in the windows reading their newspapers or just looking out the window at us. There was a caboose behind all those. A caboose just like the ones we wave at every time we see a train go by.

It was the first time I'd ever seen a model train set that wasn't in a department store Christmas window decoration.

We knelt on the floor around the kitchen table of this cozy small farmhouse, our cold cheeks resting sideways on the blue and white checker oil cloth covering the table. We watched the train go around and around on the track.

Mayor's mom, Mrs. Pidgeon, made grilled cheese sandwiches, cut in half for each of us to share, and gave us some tomato soup. She put the plates and soup cups on chairs between us, so we could eat and enjoy the train at the same time.

"Careful you don't spill," she told us.

We'd slurp hot tomato soup and eat our grilled cheese sandwiches in the warm, lingering glow of a wonderful 1949 Christmas passing through our lives. Resting our cheeks on the warmth of the oilcloth on a small kitchen table on Penoyer Road, each imagining the conductor waving at us as the train engine steamed by, or passengers busy reading their newspapers, looking up at us from the Pullman car flying past, or whoever was sleeping in the caboose waking up just to wave.

"I put harvest cow corn out for Santa's reindeer, and they ate it all," I said.

"Reindeer love cow corn," Barber said, beading his eye for better focus on the smoke puffs coming out of the train engine's smokestack racing around the table.

Clickety-clackety, clickety-clackety—

"Remember the ketchup soup in Groton, and Uncle Harry?" Mary snickered, warming her hands with her cup of soup.

Mary and I glanced at each other and smiled, remembering our kiss on the skating bus. Kneeling next to her with our cheeks on the warm oilcloth, staring at the train racing by, I happened to look up at the lone light bulb wire hanging from the ceiling over the small kitchen table. There was a little sprig of Mistletoe scotch taped to the lamp pull chain. I tapped Mary's shoulder, pointed up to it, and friendly pecked her happy smile quickly, this time right on the lips. Her grin and her never telling anyone about the school bus kiss were my Christmas present.

"How about when we hid the chickens and geese?" Randy reminisced.

"Boy did we ever stink!" Mayor said.

"Santa left me a new baseball," Bases said.

"I got new shoes," Barber said.

Clickety-clackety, clickety-clackety—

"I wonder where it's going," Mary whispered.

"The train?" I asked.

Holbrook had contentment in his eyes we hadn't seen in some time. "Anywhere we want it to," he said with a smile. "Anywhere we want."

*Whoooo! Whoooooo! Whooooooooooo!*

Watching the train puff its smoke and every eye glued to a promise of a dream come true in every puff, I thought out loud. Then I said to myself, "I have to remember to tell Charlie thanks when we go to the cemetery for our next meeting. He was so right about reindeer liking harvest cow corn at Christmastime."

## EPILOGUE
## SOME OF 1951 AND MOST OF 1952

It was March in 1951 and spring was coming soon, but not today.

Dick and I stepped off the school bus to a midday blanket of powdery white snow covering like confectionary sugar a refrozen layer of that morning's melted crust that lingered from the thaw earlier in the week. We started walking the long driveway to the house when we first saw the car. We didn't recognize it; it didn't belong to anyone we knew and it began driving from the house down the long snowy drive toward us. The snow crunched under its tires and we could tell by the stature of the person's silhouette we could make out that it was our dad in the back seat, as a passenger. A stranger was driving and what appeared to be a hospital nurse with a white nurse's cap and navy-blue cape snapped around her neck was sitting on the passenger side of the front seat. We stopped walking as the car approached so we could say hi to our dad, but the car didn't stop. We bent down to look in through the closed car windows as best we could in the glare of the sun. Dad was waving at us, but the driver didn't slow down enough for eye contact or a courtesy wave. All the windows were closed tight, and the car kept moving. It didn't slow, it didn't stop the entire distance to the front gate. We turned to watch as the car drove off.

Maybe he didn't open a window because there was snow on the ground and it was cold. Maybe he wasn't feeling well. He'd been coughing a lot lately. Maybe they were going to the doctor to get him some penicillin.

We could see Dad turn around in the back seat and wave at us a gentle, sad wave. His eyes squinted from the tears we saw glistening in the light. Dad was weeping and neither of us knew why or where he was going. We stood and watched him out of love and respect, just in case he was still watching us, until the car turned down Cardner Road. It picked up speed and drove out of sight. I started to cry. Our dad looked so sad staring back at us. He had never left us without saying goodbye like this before—that's just not how he was and neither of us had any idea why now. Why didn't he stop to talk? We ran as fast as we could into the house to find Mom standing in the book den, staring out the front window in tears.

"Where's Dad going, Mom?" Dick asked.

"Why wouldn't he talk to us?" I asked.

"Why was he crying?" Dick asked.

I was eleven and I never felt quite as alone as I did at that moment. Never. Without taking her eyes from the long driveway Mom told us to get out of our school clothes and meet her at the table. She made hot chocolate for when we got home so we could sit and talk. After we changed, Mom had us come into the kitchen and get our cups and take them to the table. Now seeing us with her she was smiling a little. I think it was because we were home and she wasn't alone anymore. Mom had not been separated from Dad since the day they met and fell in love in 1919. If he ever traveled on business, he would write her a three- or four-page letter every day he was gone.

She sat at the end of the table.

"Boys, I have something to tell you. I need you to be strong and to be my men of the house. We will get through this together," she started.

The phone started ringing. We let it ring.

"Your father and I chose not to tell you about what I am going to share until we were sure. We didn't want to worry you unnecessarily."

"What's wrong, Mom?" I asked.

"Tell us what, Mom?" Dick asked.

"Your father has tuberculosis, and it's a very bad disease."

"TB," Dick said.

"Yes, TB. When he passed you on the driveway, the hospital nurses were driving him to the TB sanitarium, where he will have to stay until he gets better."

"Is that why he was coughing so much, Mom?" I asked.

"Yes, dear. Tuberculosis attacks the lungs and it affects people's breathing."

I started to tear up.

"Is that why he wouldn't talk to us or say goodbye?" I asked.

"Oh no, son, and I don't want either of you to think that. Please don't think that for a minute. It's just that they don't know a lot about tuberculosis. They think it may be highly contagious in the early stages, like polio, but they're not sure. Once the people from the sanitarium came today and told your father they confirmed he had TB, he couldn't and wouldn't risk exposing you to it. That's why he could only wave to you. He loves you both so very much—he would never not want to say goodbye to his children. Your dad even asked the driver to wait until he saw the school bus come so he could at least wave goodbye."

Our minds could get around this a little better, but the air was still tense. Dick and I couldn't conceive not ever being with our dad again.

"Can we go see him?" Dick asked.

Mom looked down at her hands to gather her thoughts.

"I'm so sorry, boys, but you can't—not until he's better—not until they know it's safe for you to see him and for them to confirm that he isn't contagious. Just pray for your father every day. Pray that he will be safe and come back to us healthy and strong."

"How long will Dad be gone?" I asked.

Mom looked at each of us.

"It could be a year—it could be—"

Knowing the statistics, that TB was the number one killer in America, Mom wept. She was a strong woman, but her face dropped into her hands in a despair we had never seen before. Dick jumped up and ran in to her and Dad's bedroom and came back with a handkerchief.

"Thank you, dear," she mumbled.

Mom looked at the tablecloth as she wiped her eyes, avoiding eye contact that would start her tears all over. We stood, pushed our chairs in, and walked around by Mom. We each put a hand on her shoulder as we walked by and went to our rooms. I lay on my bed and stared at the ceiling. I kept thinking of Dad looking around in the rear window of the car, a tear in his eye as he waved. I turned over and buried my face in the pillow so no one could hear me cry.

The next morning was Friday. When the school bus came, we weren't out at the gate. Mr. Skelton honked the horn a few times, and then drove off. None of us got out of bed until later in the morning. Mom didn't say a word about our missing school. She felt that this was a time for us all to be together and wanted us close to her in case any of us had any questions. The house was quiet all day. Dick was sitting on the floor looking in the encyclopedia to learn about tuberculosis. When it was time to get ready for supper, we went into the kitchen and fed ourselves. Most of the afternoon and even now, Mom was on the phone talking to our aunts and cousins about Dad going to the sanitarium and about the TB. Dick made a salad for Mom and warmed up two meatballs he found in the refrigerator and put them on a plate, in case she was hungry. Neither of us said a word to each other all day. We walked around in a trance and looked out windows and teared up when we'd see a picture of Dad on the piano or the one of him on the wall in the hallway.

After dark we went to bed again. I knelt by my bed and said prayers so my dad would get better, not be in pain, and be home for my birthday or for Christmas or anytime. Just so he came home.

The next morning, Saturday, Mom woke us up smiling. She had made breakfast and asked us to come as she had it on the table. It was like she was a new person. She told us that God would answer our prayers. She got us out of bed and told us now was the time for us all to be strong and that our dad had been through worse than this in his life. With the Lord's help and our prayers, he would get through this, too.

"What was worse than this, Mom?" I asked.

Mom looked around at each of us and told us something we had never heard before. She asked us never to bring it up unless our dad did first.

"It was a difficult time for your father when his daddy fell off their barn roof in Minnesota. He died when your dad was just a boy like you. Your father was the youngest of seven and so hurt by losing his father like that he could never bring himself to talk about it or think about it."

"Is Dad going to die, Mom?" I asked.

"All your dad would want now is for you to do the best

you can, in everything you do, and to go on with your lives just as he taught you. If you do that for him, it will give him the strength he needs to get well again."

We promised we would. I asked her if we could write him.

"It would be better to tell me things for him. I'm allowed to visit him, and I would relay the things you want him to know and any other news from us. That way, we can talk longer during my visits, and I could keep his spirits up. I could keep his mind busy with all the things we want to tell him. It's important we make sure he keeps positive and wants to get better and come back home."

We understood this.

I told Mom I was going camping.

"In the snow?" Dick asked.

I got up from the table, went to my room to get dressed, and grabbed my knapsack and Charlie's lantern.

I felt like a grownup and not a kid anymore. I couldn't explain it. I was only eleven, but it was just not the same as before, somehow. I grabbed my knapsack and bedroll and headed out to the barn. Our two horses were standing close to each other, getting warm, soaking in the morning sun, but not moving or eating their broken bales of hay lying on the ground before them. Horses could sleep standing up, so I wasn't sure if they were asleep. I slid the stable barn door open and went in, stuffed my knapsack with as much hay as I could stuff in it, and then got Jack's saddle down off the rack. I brought it to the opened doorway and put it on the floor. I went back to get the saddle blanket. I paused and walked back to the door and looked out at Jack. Jack was a tall gray gelding who loved a ride and a climb up our hills. His winter coat was still thick and feathery, even though it was March. He lifted his head up and looked at me like he was waiting for me to make up my mind as to whether we were going with a saddle today or going bareback. It made no difference to him.

"Bareback," I said. I put the saddle on the rack and threw the saddle blanket over the stall door where it belonged. I adjusted the straps on my knapsack, hooking the lantern to them, put it on my back and stepped out of the stable, sliding the door closed. I put Jack's bridle on and led him away from Major's side. Major was Dick's horse. I needed enough space to jump on Jack's back with the help of a cinder block.

We rode the driveway and down Cardner Road, across the small bridge at the creek and into the snow-covered alfalfa field. Jack raised his head high, his nostrils flaring puffs of morning air. He shook his head as though he were waking himself up. Jack knew we were going to climb the steep hill to go to my campsite next to a spring behind the cliff. He liked to go camping with me. He was a smart horse and knew his footing wouldn't be as sure on snow-covered ground. We got to the back edge of the field. From there it was a steep, near straight up climb. I decided to grab a tight grip of his mane, hold on and ride him up to see if I could stay on while he climbed the hill. Jack's thick coat helped my legs get traction, and the bare, leafless trees let me see ahead. I squeezed with my legs and held a bunch of his mane in my fist. Jack's nostrils snorted steam every time his legs sprung forward like claw hammers, pulling us higher, while his hind legs pushed like springs, kicking snow until we reached our trail at the top that was more level to our campsite. Steam pounded from his nostrils like a coal train engine. We got to the site and I slid off his back, dropping the reins to the ground.

I took off my knapsack and looked about in the snow near my fire hole for where I wanted to sleep. The shallow hole was covered in snow. I dragged my knapsack around a square patch of ground to brush the snow away. Once clear, I packed the remaining snow solid to the ground with my feet. I gathered armfuls of dry leaves and made a mattress. I hung my knapsack on a tree branch and gathered logs, building the fire bigger than usual so there was more heat glowing off for both Jack and me. When it was going strong I gathered and stacked enough wood to take us through the night.

I mounted Jack again and told him we were going for a ride. When I was on his back, I realized that, for the first time, I'd mounted him with no help of any kind—no cinder block, no hand up.

We headed deeper into the woods by the upper waterfalls, which were frozen over. A small amount of water was trickling over the falls, dripping down the massive icicles that were melting slowly in the morning sun. I rode through the woods to the back fence on our property line and turned left to go north as far as we could. It was a longer ride than I had planned—a ride I had never done on horseback. When we came out of the woods into a clearing, we were across from where Charlie's old place was before they burned it down. I rode Jack to the edge of the field that faced across the road to Charlie's property and we stopped. We stood there. Jack snorted puffs of steam. I remembered my friend Charlie. I thought about the good times he and I'd had together. How he let me play in his barn. How nice he was to us all the time. I remembered how he got sick and how Dad would come back from work to drive him to a hospital in Rochester, so he wouldn't be alone for treatments before he died. I remembered when he died. I wondered if Charlie had tuberculosis.

A tear blurred my vision—thinking of Charlie and wondering what I would ever do if my dad died. I pursed my lips, wishing both he and Dad could be here right now so we could all go ice fishing at Pleasant Lake.

A breeze kicked up. Jack turned and followed our tracks back to the camp. I took his bridle off and hung it with the knapsack. I stacked more firewood. I had my heavy coat, my corduroys, two blankets, a pile of dried leaves for a mattress, so with the fire, I had all I needed. I unbuckled the knapsack and pulled out a quarter bale of hay I had stuffed in it. I didn't pack any food for me. Jack leaned his head down, smelled the hay, then lifted his head and turned toward me to thank me. He started munching on it. His back leg sprung as he relaxed. Horses can lock their knee joints. They will balance on three legs, resting one in case they must move suddenly in the night. The horse's natural predator is the wolf. Their defense is speed. They always keep one leg unlocked so they can move quickly.

I didn't need the lantern. I sat on a log by the fire and made some mourning dove calls for a while, trying to warm my hands.

"Whoo—eee—who—who—who—"

"Whoo—eee—who—who—who—"

I watched a squirrel carry an acorn up the side of a tree and wondered where he had them all buried for the winter.

As darkness came, I unrolled my blankets and, lying back, I

watched the stars over the creek side of the cliff, and I listened to Jack munching on his hay.

I looked at the North Star beyond a silhouette of a single dead leaf hanging from a branch surrounded by a full moon above, the leaf twisting in the wind. I wondered what my dad was doing.

I wondered if he was coughing a lot.

I wondered if he was losing any more weight. I wondered if we would ever go fishing again.

Watching the stars that night I made the decision I wasn't going to talk about this with anyone at school other than Holbrook, Barber, or Mary, Randy, or Bases. I trusted my friends. Mary and I never kissed again after that Christmas. We still smiled at each other, but she had a new boyfriend and we would see each other whenever the club met, which had been a while. My friends wouldn't mention my dad unless I told them I wanted to talk about it. We knew each other like that. That was why we were such good friends. We were like brothers and sisters. Holbrook loved my dad, too.

I fell asleep that night knowing the rest of school that year and the next wouldn't be the same. School would never be the same again.

On Monday I was walking down the school hall pulling my jacket off. I noticed a girl I had never seen before. She was walking in my direction, looking like she was lost. She was tall and slender and had curly brunette hair. She had a plaid pleated skirt on and a green sweater over a white starched blouse. She had a pretty sparkling smile, and I could see a smile in her eyes. I told her my name and asked for hers. She told me she was Judy Sessions, new here from Baltimore, Maryland, and she was staying until next November while her parents were doing something—traveling or something, I don't remember.

She was staying with her uncle, Ted Dwyer, who lived around the corner from Minneapolis Moline Conway.

I asked her if she had a locker.

"Not yet," she said.

"Use mine," I offered.

"Really? Thank you," she said.

"I never put a lock on it, if that's okay."

"I don't need locks," she said as she placed two books on the top shelf and hung her green sweater on one of the hooks, closing the door.

"Thanks for sharing, Jerry—and it's nice to meet you," she said. She smiled, turned, and walked away.

That same day, when I got home, a letter from my brother Mike was lying on my bed. In it he wrote that every week he was going to send me a new word to look up in the dictionary to learn and use in a sentence. His first word to me was "pedantic." I didn't know what it was, so I got the dictionary and looked it up. His second was "copious." His third was "prevaricate." This was fun. Every week his letters and new words would take my mind off worrying about Dad, a little, and I got to learn a new word.

On Saturday I saddled Jack and rode down past Doc Webb's place to the end of the road and up the back hill to the big corner. Just across the road was Ted Dwyer's place, where Judy was living until she had to go back to Baltimore.

I rode across the road at Gooseville Corners and onto their snowy front yard, dismounted, and knocked on the door. Judy came out.

"Want to go for a ride?"

"Hold on while I put something warm on. Want to come in?"

"Nah, I'll wait out here."

When she came out, I mounted Jack, took my foot out of the left stirrup, and offered a hand so Judy could use it to climb up. Now she was just behind the saddle with her arms around me, holding on. I knew Judy was older and in the eleventh grade, but it didn't matter to me, I liked her. Right now, we were on my horse riding back down the hill to my house for some hot chocolate. We passed the Reynolds' place, the Shaffers', Don Chubb's place, the Butlers', and then the doc's. Doc waved and shouted for me to check out his new syrup cabin when I had a chance. I waved back that I would as we rode on past.

Mom was at home when we got there. She said hello to Judy, and they talked about Baltimore while I warmed up some milk. I had put Jack in the barn garage, still saddled, with some hay so he would be okay for a little while.

We drank hot chocolate and Judy and Mom talked.

Later I walked Judy out back to see the waterfalls, even though they were frozen over. We walked to the barn garage and I brought Jack out so I could take Judy home. Before we mounted, Jack moved his head around and nuzzled Judy like he liked her and wanted to say hello. Judy put one hand under his chin and with the other patted his nose and then the side of his neck. They became fast friends.

On the way to the Dwyers', Judy rested her head on my back. I could hear her humming a song I couldn't make out, but I liked hearing her voice. We didn't talk the whole ride back. She held me tight and kept her head on my shoulder.

When we got to her house Judy slid over to where she could reach her foot into the stirrup I had taken my foot out of. She held onto the back of the saddle and swung around slowly. I turned to help her and she paused, looked me in the eyes, and kissed me. She kissed me a wonderful long warm kiss. Then her head moved back, and she looked in my eyes.

"I had fun, Jerry. Thank you for thinking of me."

She lowered herself to the ground, rubbed Jack's velvety nose goodbye, and ran into the house, waving at me just before she closed the door.

If it weren't for my dad being at the TB sanitarium, this growing up could be a good thing, I thought.

When I got home and unsaddled Jack, my world was shaken again. Mom was packing a suitcase. She told me that the sanitarium had called while I was out riding, and Dad might need surgery. They wanted to remove a part of his lung. She had to go stay near him for a couple of days while he went through tests and they talked it over with the doctors.

Mom kept packing and told me to tell Dick to please be mature and behave while she was gone, and that she would be back in a few days.

After she drove out, I walked behind the swings and opened the door of Dad's Oldsmobile, which hadn't been used since he'd gone. I sat in the driver's seat. I thought of him sitting there. I grabbed the steering wheel like it was him driving and could smell him in the car. I thought about wanting him to meet Judy.

I went inside and heated up a tuna and noodle casserole for Dick and me for when he got home.

I told Dick about Dad and the operation he might have to have—taking some of his lung out.

Dick said he didn't think someone could live without both lungs.

I bolted around in a blind rage, running toward him, and pushed him in a slam against the wall so hard his head bounced off it.

"You take that back!" I screamed. "You take that back!"

Dick stared at my fists, my jaw clenched, tears in my eyes. I just gave him a cold stare. He apologized.

We went to our rooms to calm down. I fell asleep without eating.

Judy and I went riding as often as we could and liked each other. I didn't know what love was so we didn't talk about that—I just knew that when we were together, we were happy, and when we weren't together, we couldn't wait to be together again.

One time when Mom visited Dad, he told her how to get me a job if I wanted one. I said yes—Dick, too, if he wanted a summer job away from the Lincklaen House. She told us at supper. Dick was all for it, so Mom said she would take us to the place on Saturday, introduce us to the owner, and see if it worked out. She said Dad wanted it to be a surprise, so she would tell us about the summer job when we got there. It would be for the whole summer, from Memorial Day to Labor Day.

On Friday night I went to a school dance with Judy. We danced every slow dance. We square danced when they played one that sounded easier than most. We would pair up with Mary and her boyfriend.

I told Judy that in the morning I would be looking at a summer job my dad had arranged. I knew nothing about it yet, as he wanted it to be a surprise. Judy told me she was praying for my dad every day to get better. She was nice like that.

The next morning Mom drove Dick and me to a place called Snook's Pond near Manlius. It was part of a spring-fed lake that was used as a swimming hole in the summer. It had a building with men's lockers and changing areas on one side of the pond and another with ladies' lockers on the other side. At the end of the pond was a concrete walkway with chairs on all three sides and a diving board. Just at the entrance to Snook's Pond, after the parking area, were two small square huts that had big wood-flap shutters that, when lifted and held up with wooden poles, showed the counters on the front three sides. One shack was where people paid to get in and rent lockers. The other was a snack bar. You could get hot dogs, popcorn, and soda pop—all you wanted, in that one.

Mom introduced us to Mr. Snook, who walked us around the property and gave us the tour. He told us that if we wanted the jobs, it meant running the snack bar and three times a day going around the grounds, picking up empty bottles and papers and raking up cigarette butts. He said both of us could work—but it was seven days a week from Memorial Day, when they opened for summer, to Labor Day, when they closed for the winter.

"Do you want to think about it, boys?" Mr. Snook asked.

"What does it pay?" Dick asked.

"Nothing, son, it doesn't pay," Mr. Snook said, "but it'd be your business for the summer, and you'd run the snack bar as your own and you keep any profits you make. How does that sound?"

"We'll take it," Dick said.

On the way home Dick asked Mom to ask Dad if he could make a list of what we should buy to stock it, where to buy it, and how to pay for it and what we should charge for things like hot dogs and popcorn and pop.

Working at Snook's Pond, the summer flew by. We got to wear swim trunks all summer, take turns selling hotdogs and soda pop or swimming whenever we wanted. We got to drive the orange Allis Chalmers tractor and wagon from our shop to the storage room down the driveway to get cases of soda pop for the snack bar.

On the day after Labor Day, summer vacation was over. I walked around the place doing a final pickup, knowing that I would probably never see it again, and I would miss it. I thanked the place for helping us pass the time so we didn't mope around worrying about our dad and missing him.

When the car pulled up to the house for the last time after the pond closed for the year, I ran to the barn, saddled Jack and trotted down to the Reynolds' hill and up to Judy's. As soon as she opened the door, I took her by the hand. I didn't say a word, and I led her out to Jack. I started to mount.

"Hold on a second, mister," she said.

She took my face in her hands and gave me a kiss.

"I missed you this summer."

"I missed you," I said.

"Did you have fun at the pond, selling your hot dogs?"

We rode for a couple of hours around the Conway and Dwyer farms. We never stopped talking. I was telling her about the crazy people we saw at Snook's Pond and how to make twenty hot dogs at once so they were always hot and fresh. She told me about the books she read and that she was getting sad because she would have to leave soon. I didn't want to talk about that so we just rode. She held me close.

School started the next day.

Mom had arranged for me to go visit Gourmet Mike at Lemoyne. It was his senior year. I had grown almost ten inches since Dad went into the sanitarium. I shot up to six feet, three inches.

Mike had invited me to come up for a weekend and stay at his fraternity house. I packed a bag. Mom drove me to Syracuse and dropped me off. The next week was Thanksgiving, so he told Mom he would drive me home.

The weekend was fun and went by quickly.

As soon as we got home and walked in the door, Mom asked us to join Dick at the table, as she had some news.

"Your father and I thought it best not to worry you, so we kept it from you that he had his surgery last Friday."

"Is he okay, Mom?" I asked.

"I'm happy to tell you that your father is doing fine, and with prayers, he could be home by Christmas if he heals well and has no complications."

I remember looking at Mom to see if her eyes were

comfortable with what she was telling us or if they were nervous eyes and maybe hiding some bad news. She was smiling. I believed her.

"The doctors make him cough several times a day to keep his lungs clear. It is very painful for him to cough—but he knows he has to, so he does his very best."

"Does he still have two lungs?" Dick asked.

"Yes, they only had to take the top portion of one of his lungs—so he still has two lungs."

We were so happy and now couldn't wait to see our dad again, after a year. There was a holiday dance at the school that night. Mom drove me and stopped to pick up Judy. She and I danced all night. This might be the last time we get to dance, we thought, since she might have to move back to Baltimore any day.

We got busy during Thanksgiving with family. Then I started to get letters from Judy. She had moved back to Baltimore. Her parents had come during the school break and got her with no warning and gave her no time to say goodbye. She wrote me a letter that I held all night. We wrote back and forth for months. Judy always signed her letters, Love and Prayers, Judy. I missed her. But I missed my dad, too.

It was the morning of Christmas Eve, but the house didn't feel like Christmas as it always had years before. There was a lot of snow on the ground. We hoped for snow at Christmastime, and it was still snowing heavily, and the house seemed cold now, still and quiet.

I got out of bed and went to the kitchen in my pajama bottoms and T-shirt. Dick was there.

"I'm making your favorite," Mom said.

I knew it was poached eggs. Mom knew I loved poached eggs. I would put one on a slice of buttered toast and eat it like an open-faced sandwich.

Mom asked if we could help fold the clothes right after breakfast so we could get ready for Christmas. She told us Uncle Don and Aunt Mary were coming today from Harrisburg with our four cousins, Tommy, Timmy, Teddy, and Terry. Aunt Dorothy and Uncle Norman were coming in from Washington with their daughter, Karen. Gourmet Mike would be here.

Mom made no mention of Dad. We were afraid to bring it up so early.

We didn't want to make her cry. If Dad wasn't here, we thought, this would be the first Christmas without him. We felt the same—there wouldn't be a Christmas without Dad.

We moped around the kitchen, eating, talking, and folding our clothes as Mom piled them on the counter. It was almost two o'clock and I was still barefoot and in my pajama bottoms and T-shirt. Dick was looking at the pile of presents lying by the piano. Mike had come and was sitting on the piano bench playing "Volga Boatman," most of which he had memorized.

I went in my room and fell asleep.

The next thing I knew, Mom was pulling on my toe. "Jerry, get up, get up. Your dad is coming home!"

"What!?"

"Your father's coming home!"

I sat up and rubbed my eyes. It was dark outside. Mom had a big smile on her face. I wasn't sure if I was dreaming or really awake.

"Mike Shea just called and told me that the man who is driving your father home stopped at the store and went in to buy a newspaper. Mike Shea went out to the car and said hello to him. He said he looks good, but he thought it would be nice to call us and let us know they were on their way—the man and your dad!"

I stood up. I could hear Dorothy and Norm laughing and talking with Dick and Mike in the living room. I brushed by Mom and went to the bathroom.

When I came out I looked from the hall through my bedroom window. Mary and Don were driving in with their lights on and had a big Christmas tree tied on their car roof. I didn't think we were going to have a tree this year. I started walking down the hall to get dressed when the telephone in Dad and Mom's room rang. I rushed in and picked it up.

"Hello?"

"Hello, is Jerry there?"

"This is Jerry."

"Jerry, this is Doctor Webb."

"Oh, hi, Doctor Webb."

"Merry Christmas, young fella. I thought you would like to know that your daddy just drove past my place on his way home. I thought you would like to know, what it being Christmas and all."

"How did you know he was coming?" I asked.

"Us old fogies have our own SOS system, too, don't ya know," he laughed. "We invented it. Have a BULLY GOOD Merry Christmas, son! Mike Shea called me with the news."

I dropped the phone receiver on the floor and ran out through the dining room past Dorothy and Norm to the front door and pushed it open.

Mom shouted for me to put something on but I was already out the door and off the porch. I jumped off the front step barefoot and started walking quickly through the snow toward the gate, not taking my eyes off the top of the road up by farmer Parker's hill, looking for headlights from the car Dad would be in. I knew the car Dad was in would be coming over that hill any minute now.

Mary opened the window of her car as I scurried past and shouted, "Jerry, you will catch your death, go put something on."

I kept walking as fast as I could, keeping my eye on the top of the hill.

Finally, almost to the gate, I saw the lights and a car come slowly over the hill, inching down around the curve. The road was not plowed and slick so they were taking their time. I hopped out on Cardner Road. The car turned into the driveway and paused a moment. The back window opened down halfway, and a hand came out for a shake.

It was my dad.

IT WAS MY DAD!

As the car moved forward, I grabbed his hand and squeezed it, walking alongside.

"Jerry?" he asked.

"Yes," I started to cry. I'd grown ten inches since he saw me last and I wasn't sure he could recognize me. It frightened me to think my dad might not remember me.

"Remember us fishing at Little York Lake, Dad? Remember I rowed us out in the boat at Sandy Pond, Dad? Remember when you beat my airplane to Syracuse, Dad?

Remember teaching me how to make desserts, Dad? Can you remember me, Dad?"

When we got to the house the family was outside on the porch waving and cheering. Just then Dad squeezed my hand and I heard him say, "You caught croppies, Jerry me boy, we cooked at the Imperial House, remember, son?"

"Room number six, Dad."

"Room number six," he answered. He remembered me.

The car stopped and Dad got out slowly. He was still tender and healing from his lung operation. When he stood straight, he looked at me and how tall I was. He ran his hand back and forth over my brush cut.

"You sure have grown, Jerry me boy—you sure have grown." I stared in his eyes.

"I'm still the same, Dad—just like you're still the same."

He shook my hand, put his arm around my shoulder, and we walked into the house with everyone cheering, laughing, crying, and all happy again.

Mom barked at me.

"Go take a warm shower so you don't get frostbite."

"No! I'm not leaving my dad!" I barked back.

"Well, at least go put some pants and shoes on."

I did do that, got a sweater, and came out and sat on the chair next to the couch where Dad was resting, smiling, watching everyone all talking at once.

Don, Norm, and Gourmet Mike were putting up the Christmas tree and Mary, Dorothy, and Mom were bringing out boxes filled with decorations and lights.

Dad asked Dorothy for writing paper and a pen or pencil. He wanted to write a friend in the TB sanitarium and wish him a Merry Christmas.

I thought back, remembering the night I laid on that same couch, when I was poisoned from drinking the creek water. I remembered Dad sitting where I was sitting now—sitting tall, watching over me all night long, his silhouette crested by moon glow.

I sat up taller in the chair.

When I woke it was still dark outside. The house was quiet, and all the lights were out except for the tree. The Christmas tree was a spectacular glow of lights and colors and shiny, sparkling decorations. The presents were stacked underneath. Dad was still lying on the couch with a blanket over him. He had the pen in his limp hand and paper on his lap—but he was asleep.

I got up and took the pen and paper off him and put them on my chair arm.

His eyes opened and he smiled.

"Can I have some water, son?"

I got him a glass of water from the kitchen.

"Want a fire, Dad? I know how to build a good one."

"That would be nice, son."

I moved his writing papers to the seat of my chair and built a big fire with the largest logs. While I built the fire, I could recall the time I left the tin lid filled with ears of harvest cow corn by the fireplace, for Santa.

I stacked some wood, enough that would take us through most of the night. I wasn't sure what time it was, but I knew everyone would be getting up soon to celebrate Christmas.

I walked back to the chair. Dad was asleep again. I took the water glass from his hand and set it on the floor beside him. I picked up his writing paper and his pen and sat down in the chair.

I didn't read Dad's entire letter, but I did read one paragraph.

*"I'm sleeping on the sofa, the first night home, just to be in the thick of things for Christmas in the morning. My boy Jerry, is roughing it on a less comfortable chair right beside me while he and I catch up. He doesn't seem to mind. Watching him there makes me recall the many nights he would sleep in a bed roll over the falls here at Delphi Falls. The horses would come around grazing or just snooping far into the night.*

*Jerry didn't mind horses, woodchucks, squirrels, rabbits, foxes, deer, some bears, and a load of wild birds that roamed the upper falls some of the time."*

I stopped reading.

I remember looking up at the glowing tree.

I remember looking over at the burning fireplace. I remember watching my dad sleeping.

I remember feeling a tear roll down my cheek.

"There is a Santa Claus," I said. "He came tonight."